John Otto was born in Auckland, New Zealand. After working as a motor engineer, he finally left the profession to study landscape design and eventually started his own landscape design and construction company.

His great passion in life is science and astronomy and writing science fiction novels. He is married with two sons and divides his time between an alpine village in New Zealand's South Island, and the city of Melbourne, Australia.

As a child he pondered the universe - and still does.

By the same author

Footprints In The Dust
ISBN 978-1-84386-198-0

John Otto

BROKEN PLANET

Vanguard Press

VANGUARD PAPERBACK

© Copyright 2007
John Otto

The right of John Otto to be identified as author of
this work has been asserted by him in accordance with the
Copyright, Designs and Patents Act 1988.

A CIP catalogue record for this title is
available from the British Library.

ISBN 978 1 84386 347 2

*Vanguard Press is an imprint of
Pegasus Elliot MacKenzie Publishers Ltd.*

www.pegasuspublishers.com

First Published in 2007

**Vanguard Press
Sheraton House Castle Park
Cambridge England**

Printed & Bound in Great Britain

<u>ACKNOWLEDGEMENTS</u>

I am indebted to my son, Dr Justin Otto, for his input to
the manuscript. His suggestions were an invaluable
contribution to the final draft of this book.

I would also like to thank my wife, Judith and son Paul for
their valuable comments. My brother Geoffrey and his
wife Anne for their keen interest. To Nellie and John,
thank you for leaving Holland and settling in New Zealand
and for your support.

And, thank you to all those many readers
who demanded a sequel.

Chapter One

Planet Earth was still resolutely orbiting the sun in the outskirts of the Sagittarius spiral arm, halfway from the galactic centre, just as it had done for four and a half billion years. In the Northern Hemisphere it should have been a vibrant autumn, in the Southern Hemisphere an awakening spring.

Revolving on its axis, turning from west to east, should have resulted in day and night. But now there was only cold, eternal darkness. A world without seasons. A world without life. A broken planet.

*

Alone in starship *Argo's* viewing blister, David White gazed through the observation port's clear, flexiglass curving from floor to ceiling, which allowed him an uninterrupted view of the barren lunar landscape below.

Sitting in his personalised contoured chair he contemplated the magnificent peaks of the Leibnitz Mountains, the highest on the Moon. As they slid from view, icy fingers of sadness reached for him, reminding him that he was just one of a thousand chosen souls exiled to the Moon. That he was one of the luckiest humans alive was of little comfort. They could never return to Earth. Destruction of the planet had been complete. The Drogs had taken his world away, but they couldn't steal his memories.

*

Early in humankind's history, space faring beings crossed an unimaginable distance across the vastness of space and visited Earth. Human DNA was harvested and they produced another human race with accelerated evolution many light years from Earth.

Less than a score years ago the enhanced humans returned to their spiritual home and, keeping their genesis secret, formed the Vision Foundation which became the wealthiest and most successful scientific company on the planet; covertly accelerating Earth's technology so that she could protect herself against an old enemy. Years earlier than expected, the Drogs, an interstellar, highly technological civilization entered the solar system and altered the orbits of four asteroids and targeted them at Earth. Repelling three of the asteroids, the Foundation engaged the Drogs in a fierce cosmic battle. When the enemy fleet retreated, a final attempt by the Foundation failed to divert the fourth and largest asteroid – a planet killer.

*

In Warstill's quarters, the lighting was restrained, the temperature cool – conditions that were perfect for Drogs. Their home planet's star had been a little cooler than Earth's. And with its thinner atmosphere, and its fusion-furnace producing a lower intensity of radiation than Sol, there was insufficient energy to power violent storms as Earth had encountered.

The Drog commander was in a foul mood. His inflammatory bowel problem was playing up again. He was overdue to swallow a measure of genetically engineered bacteria. They would, he was told, make a home in his gut and deliver therapeutic proteins just where they were needed. 'How long,' he muttered, 'does it take to engineer the blasted things?' Sitting at his quarter's workstation, he'd been doing a routine systems check, hoping to find some minor fault so he could claim a victim to release his frustration upon, but every system was within normal operating parameters.

Restlessly, he rose from his chair and lumbered over to a full-length mirror fastened to a wall close to his sleeping cot. Flicking his crimson cape from his broad shoulders, he straightened his beige tunic that reached to his knees. His belly rumbled uncomfortably and he dealt with it by loosening his belt. Releasing a large belch, he felt marginally more comfortable. But his reflection pleased him – it always did. He was the most impressive looking Drog on board. He had no doubt. Reaching for his ever-present comb in a pouch by his side, he attended to his splendid mane of frost-white hair that spilled down to his shoulders.

Fully satisfied with his reflected image, he turned and strode to his quarter's single porthole and threw a switch to darken the room. Hands clasped tightly behind his heavily muscled back and hunching forward he gazed out at the jewelled darkness. A grunt of satisfaction escaped his low-slung mouth. He knew that ultimately the mighty Drogs would be in total control of a large area of the habitable zone of the galaxy. It was not an unattainable goal. Only the Foundation stood in their way. One day they would meet up with the Foundation cruisers again and it would be on his terms. Even so, a vague uneasiness enveloped him.

His heavy brow puckered in a frown. In their last encounter, the Foundation had destroyed two Drog cruisers and twelve fighter craft with minimal loss to themselves. A tendril of worry nagged in a corner of his mind. Foundation humans were unpredictable, which made them such a difficult adversary. Begrudgingly he admired them, but deep within him he nursed a fervent hatred for the grotesquely, ugly creatures.

His belly gave out a long rolling rumble and it was answered with an impressive drawn out belch. Flicking the lighting back on, he turned away from the porthole and returned to his workstation. His chair sighed in protest as he settled his bulk down. Calling up the channel link to his aide, he organised a meeting with his three battle strategists on the bridge.

The Drog cruiser's acceleration was constant and equal to their home planet's gravity, which was slightly, less than Earth's. Warstill's heavy footfalls echoed off the passageway's metal walls, even though the floor was thickly carpeted. He was hoping that one of the strategists would be late for the meeting so he could vent his frustration upon him. Coming to a halt at the bridge entrance, he waited impatiently for the circular door to iris open, then stomping through, he brushed past the assembled strategists to his workstation. Sinking down in his chair he swivelled it to face his team. His intimidating bulk dominated the bridge.

Warstill gazed up with deep-set eyes under heavy lids at the three strategists and looked them over, one after the other. Only Vabor met his gaze. The other two nervously studied the carpet.

Clasping his blunt digits together, Warstill leaned forward in his chair. 'I have sent my report of our success and failure of our encounter with the enemy to our grand commander.' His voice was a low rumble. 'Over the years we wait for his reply you will have ample time to reflect on your incompetence. What have you got to say for yourselves?'

Vabor's olfactory senses picked up the scent of his comrades' fear. He steeled himself before answering and decided to play to his commander's vanity. 'Well, sir, under your command it was far from a shattering failure, and your suspicion that the Foundation might have a presence on Earth was correct. You had no choice but to destroy the planet.'

'True, Vabor,' the commander replied, his tone turning reasonable. 'We are not a cruel race. We would have preferred to spare Earth and only enslave the humans. And it's true that you say that I had no choice. The Foundation is solely responsible for the destruction of the planet.'

'At least now, sir, humans will present no danger to our ultimate goal, which they might well have done in the far future. It is we that let you down, and the three of us must learn from those mistakes so that we can secure our great nation's ultimate goal.'

The two timid strategists visibly relaxed. Vabor's agile mind had skilfully calmed their commander. They lifted their eyes from the carpet in relief.

'Well I'm pleased to hear of your resolve to do better in the future,' Warstill acknowledged as he leant back in his chair. 'Our retreat from the battle was a tactical one. The odds will be in our favour when next we meet with the Foundation. But let me warn you. Never take the enemy lightly no matter what the odds are.' He dismissed them with a wave.

*

David White had been unable to sleep, and his personal computer, Basil, sensed it and suggested *Argo's* viewing area might help calm his tangled thoughts. It was eerily quiet in the chamber – a fortress of solitude. Below, Crater Tycho and its bright ray system spread out before him – the massive terraced walls and central elevations reaching for him from a rough and pitted floor. This desolate but strangely beautiful world would be home for one thousand refugees evacuated by *Orion*, one of three Foundation starships.

Argo and *Vela* were in closed lunar orbit and would remain there while their battle scars were repaired. *Orion* occupied the only lunar starship-landing pad at the Foundation's base, situated in Mare Australe in the southeast, which extended well into the Moon's far side. Because of this and with most of the base underground, it had remained undetected by Earth's astronomers.

The colonists, including David's father, were settling in to life in their underground warrens. David and his mother would be joining him just as soon as a moon bus arrived to take them to the base.

As Crater Tycho disappeared below the horizon, David leaned forward, taking in a great walled plain, peppered with tiny craters spread out before him. Glancing to his right when the chamber's door whispered open, he found himself, as always, catching his breath as a willowy long-legged young woman entered. Her deep red jumpsuit contrasted her night-dark eyes, and her lustrously blue-black hair was cropped short, accentuating her fine facial bone structure.

'I couldn't sleep,' she said. 'I figured the lunar landscape might help calm me down.' Folding herself gracefully into the chair next to David's, she swivelled it so that they faced each other. Leaning forward, she brushed his cheek with soft fingers. 'Have you told your mother of your decision yet?'

'Not yet, Amber. I think it's best to wait until we meet up with my father at Moonbase.'

She nodded her understanding and studied him without speaking.

'Nothing's going to change my decision,' he continued with quiet intensity. 'I just hope my parents are of like mind.'

Her dark eyes returned his gaze. Her hair shimmered in the soft moonlight. 'Well if you do change your mind I will understand.'

His mind rebelled at the thought of living on the Moon without her. Leaning forward, his gaze unwavering, he clasped her hands. 'My decision is made,' he said. 'There is absolutely no way I'm going to change it.'

'Then I'm glad.' Her voice was low and charged with emotion. To lighten the mood, she suggested they spread-eagle themselves on the ceiling to floor viewing blister. 'The flexiglass is tough and will easily support our weight,' she explained. 'It will feel like we're gliding with wings over the lunar surface.'

He chuckled. 'Now why didn't I think of that?'

As she rose, she pressed the music channel on the chair's control panel. Making their way to the curving flexiglass, Johann Strauss's *The Blue Danube*, broke the silence.

'How appropriate,' Amber said reverently. 'I remember seeing that classic old movie *2001 Space Odyssey*. The great visionary, Arthur C Clarke wrote the book and assisted with the production. The film had the same background music.'

Pressing himself against the diamond coated, scratch-resistant glass, David felt his stomach lurch, his pulse race. A tide of nausea and vertigo threatened to overwhelm him. He felt he was falling, and the age-old fear of avoiding just that was imprinted on his brain as a safety mechanism. Shutting his eyes and clamping down on his feeling for long seconds, the nausea passed. Opening his eyes once more, he was relieved to see the world had stopped spinning. The ethereal moonscape stretched out before him in pristine clarity. Sunlight washed in a great white sweep across the lunar mountains, casting dark shadows at their base as they flattened out to a vast plain sprinkled with craterlets. Amber was right. He was an eagle, soaring in an unnatural black sky, gazing down at unfamiliar terrain, far from home. Feeling light-headed, he realised he'd been holding his breath too long, and let it out in a long sigh, and noted that the designer glass didn't fog up.

He felt an urge to soar down to the ancient surface and touch it. Soon, he told himself. Soon you will be able to. Amber chuckled and he turned to her, eyebrows arched.

'It's the music,' she managed to get out between her laughter. 'My computer, Beth is responsible. She composed it

16

and is very proud of it. I told her it was a beautiful composition and as a consequence she never misses an opportunity to play it to me. Her sensors have obviously told her where I am and she's just cut into the music channel.' David chuckled. 'Our computers are developing quite an attitude and personality.'

Shortly they would return to their cabins and prepare to be transported to Moonbase; but for a short while longer they returned their attention back to the world of shadows and sharp contrast below.

*

Jarrod Dryden awoke with a start. He'd been dreaming that once again he was adrift in his escape pod that had separated from his Interceptor after a hit from enemy fire. Still wrapped in the shreds of his dream, anger welled up from deep within him.

His thoughts went back to the time it was revealed that he was one of three special humans born on Earth. Learning that his parents were genetically engineered voyagers from the stars, but with human DNA was a shock. And later, when shown the gestation tanks where he and his twin sister Amber had been conceived and born, he'd become angry. But the anger was tempered by his mother's explanation. An egg of hers was carefully selected as was his father's seed and they were developed in artificial wombs – tanks. That he could think of his mother and father as his natural parents, despite the unusual circumstances, was a relief.

And in the artificial womb, he'd received a heightened immune system, along with implantation of biological microchips, that had combined with his brain in early foetal development while the cells were still multiplying. A few short months ago prior to the invasion by the Drogs, his enhancements were awoken. One of those skills was fighter pilot capability. Two Foundation accident victims were both Interceptor pilots, and as a result, Jarrod as second reserve, accepted his powerful destiny and took command of his own fighter-craft – a sleek pencil-thin Interceptor. His implanted knowledge gave him the confidence of a fully-fledged fighter pilot.

The two traffic accident victims were responsible for the discovery of alien technology being traced back to the Foundation. Prior to autopsies, scans revealed microchips deep within their brains. As British exchange students, the Dryden twins first heard of the alien technology while watching television at David White's parent's guest house in New Zealand where they were billeted.

With the imminent arrival of the Drog fleet, many countries transcended national rivalries, the pressing danger finally registering and uniting humanity to a degree never seen before. The Foundation's offer to defend the planet was accepted, as Earth's defences alone were no match against the interstellar, highly technological Drogs.

Earth had all her eggs in one basket. That she had no extra-planetary colonies was foolish. She had no insurance, even though it was known that throughout the entire life of the planet there had been many species' extinctions. Indeed if there hadn't been then mankind would not have evolved. Perhaps the dinosaurs would still be ruling the planet. But now only a thousand regular humans remained. Colonists on a barren new world. A world antagonistic to mankind. A world where the Foundation had created on a miniscule scale conditions vital for survival.

After sleeping seven hours Jarrod should have felt refreshed, but he was exhausted by the intensity of his dreams. His personal computer, Bud, sensing his mood played soft music. Jarrod recognized his favourite baroque composer Vivaldi's composition, *The Four Seasons*. But even the great master couldn't lift him out of his sombre mood. Sadness for Earth was imbedded deep. Human's finite tenure on the planet had ended and he would have to come to terms with it. His father, Wade, the commander of *Argo* had promised him that the Foundation's fleet of three starships would hunt down and not rest until the Drog armada was destroyed. The prospect of revenge gave him a sudden fierce joy. Work had begun in the ship's service hangar on restoring the Foundation's full compliment of Interceptors, and already his cockpit – the escape pod, was cradled in lacy patterns of metal alloy as it was being attached to its new Interceptor body.

*

In her dream, Lisa Harrison was reunited with her foster parents, the Grants. They were sitting in the starship's dining area and she felt joy that they hadn't perished along with the rest of mankind. Then she awoke and the reality stabbed her. Tears spilled down her cheeks at losing them, and poor, broken Earth shrouded in eternal darkness. Her eyes fell shut beneath thick lashes, as she tried to return to the comfort of her dream.

So much had happened over the last few months, and she thought she'd come to terms with it. Her mysterious past had been revealed. Seventeen years ago two Foundation operatives in New Zealand perished in a house fire. Foul play was suspected but never proven. No trace of their baby was found in the burnt out ruins, but a baby girl was found a few days later, abandoned outside a church in Auckland City. A subsequent DNA test by police forensics proved the baby's DNA didn't match the victims. But unknown to the police, the Vision Foundation knew that the victims' daughter wasn't actually their biological child.

The Foundation was unable to access police files in New Zealand to ascertain the link, if any, between the infant's DNA and the Foundation, but hoped in time to track her down as her brilliance surfaced. They hadn't considered the possibility that she would be hiding that brilliance for almost her entire life.

She'd always felt insecure and never wanted to stand out amongst her peers. Because of this she deliberately answered a proportion of questions in exams and tests incorrectly, so that she appeared average. It wasn't until she met Jarrod and Amber that she allowed her brilliance to surface and re-awakened the interest of the Vision Foundation.

After living almost her entire seventeen years in New Zealand, she learnt that she had been conceived and born in London in an artificial gestation tank at the Vision Foundation, just as the Dryden twins had. A genetically designed human, born with the correct number of chromosomes and genes, which

19

shaped her primary life pattern. A superior, upgraded human with alien technology implanted in her brain. And now her enhancements had been activated and she was learning to handle them, one by one.

*

David had his nose pressed hard against one of the transporter room's view ports, gazing at the lunar mountains in the distance, which were lit up like islands in a dark ocean. A spot of light twenty degrees above the ancient world's horizon drew his attention. As he watched, it swelled and intensified. 'Is that our moon bus?' he asked an *Argo* crewmember close by.

The crewmember peered over David's shoulder. 'Yes,' he confirmed. 'That's the space to surface personnel ferry that's going to take you to your new home.'

David didn't correct the crewmember that he had no intention of living at Moonbase permanently.

'And if you scan to your right,' the crewmember added, 'you will be able to see the base just coming into view above the horizon.'

David gazed down but couldn't recognize anything that looked like an artificial structure. Moving aside, he let Amber try.

Her keen eyes focused downward. 'Yes,' she said excitedly. 'I can see a huddle of domes. Five in fact.'

For a moment David had forgotten about her enhanced eyesight, just as the crewmember had forgotten David was a regular human with inferior vision. He would have to be patient and wait until they boarded the ferry, and it took them closer to the surface.

The upward trajectory of the personnel ferry was programmed in, and its even acceleration had taken it close enough for Amber to make out its dumpy egg-shaped hull. With no atmosphere to deal with, it was unnecessary for the craft to be streamlined. A warning electronic gong blared out, accompanied by a flashing red light. It was time to take their allocated seats and wait for the ferry to dock.

20

Five minutes later, the craft, dwarfed by *Argo* had drawn close. Matching orbital velocity with the starship the docking procedure began, and twelve minutes later *Argo* announced completion with a muffled thud that vibrated faintly through the transporter chamber, as the ferry locked securely to the huge spacecraft's mooring latches. Checks were carried out for possible leaks at the docking collar seal. With none detected, further safety checks were done and duly completed. Air pressure inside the two craft was equalized, and a blinking green light and a single electronic chime declared all safety procedures completed.

The Foundation crewmembers rose to their feet. Dr Mary White, David, Lisa and the twins followed suit. The transporter hatch irised open with a soft hiss and they were ushered into the ferry by one of its crewmembers. Mary White was shown to her chair and sat facing David and Amber. She was a handsome vibrant woman, just turned forty. Traces of grey barely showed in her close-cropped ash blonde hair, and the navy jumpsuit she wore accented her blue eyes that were wide with anticipation at reuniting with her husband, Gerald once more.

A ferry crewmember checked that all his passengers were safely buckled into their belt restraints before returning to his seat beside the pilot. The craft's entrance door whispered shut.

Mary White felt a faint vibration as the mooring latches' preloaded springs released and gently pushed the ferry from *Argo*. Twenty seconds later the ferry's thrusters were activated, accelerating the separation still further. When the thruster jets abruptly shut off, the craft gave the illusion of pausing in the blackness of space before turning and accelerating on a downward trajectory. Mary consciously fought to relax, but she couldn't deny the tight feeling of excitement of soon being reunited with Gerald.

Weeks ago, at the request of the British government, Mary and her son David had journeyed to London. At a hastily convened meeting, the British Prime Minister and other important officials questioned them about their relationship with Jarrod, Amber and Lisa. As a result of the support she and David gave the Vision Foundation at that meeting, the company invited them to join the asteroid diversion mission – a far safer option than remaining on Earth.

Back in New Zealand Gerald had reconciled himself to the fact that it was unlikely he would ever see his family again. But he'd comforted himself, that away from Earth, they at least, were in a far safer place than the rest of humankind. Then he'd been surprised by a last minute invitation from the Vision Foundation to join one thousand of Earth's finest young minds in an exodus to Moon.

Mary gazed over to David who wore an electric-blue jumpsuit. In the dim light, the pupils of his blue eyes were huge – an echo of hers. He smiled back. Words were unnecessary.

With *Argo* out of sight there was no perception of speed. The ferry seemed to be poised in the darkness of space with a carpet of unmoving stars as a backdrop. But that soon changed as once more the ferry slowly turned on its axis. From her tiny view port Mary looked down at the ancient, scarred surface, taking in its barren beauty. But it was a world hostile to life. And it was now mankind's only home in the cosmos, made possible by the Foundation's high technology and generosity. Fingers of reflected moonlight filled the cabin with an uncanny light. No one had spoken since the ferry had accelerated away from *Argo*. Their thoughts were abruptly interrupted by an announcement by the pilot that the ferry would be landing at Moonbase in five minutes.

Moonbase and *Orion* further distant were now clearly visible to David as he gazed down at the cluster of grey domes in the cratered plain. He could even make out the scorched ferry-landing pad streaked with radial blast marks from landing exhausts. And protruding from the buildings he recognized a number of solar receptors, antennae and what must be other sensory devices.

'The base is much smaller than I imagined,' he said directing his statement to Amber. 'How could they possibly accommodate another thousand colonists?'

'That's because most of the base is underground for shelter from solar radiation,' she answered, and then added in her characteristic eloquent way, 'the lunar surface is incompatible with life.'

David nodded. 'Of course. I should have realised that.' As he continued to gaze down he could see tractors and huge dump trucks churning up the regolith around the base. And now as they drew closer, David became alarmed. It seemed the ferry was accelerating and must surely smash into the Moon, but it was an illusion. A moment later he was pushed back into his chair as the ferry's thruster jets fired in braking mode. His head pressed hard against the seat's neck rest. For long seconds he'd held his breath, trying with difficulty to hide his fear, especially from Amber.

'Oh thank goodness we've landed.' Relief flashed across Amber's face as she turned to David. 'I thought we were going to crash! Didn't you?' She laughed in nervous relief.

'No. At no time did I think we'd crash,' he said seriously.

'Liar,' she said good-naturedly.

'Well maybe I was starting to get a little concerned,' he conceded. He held her stare.

Mary White chuckled. 'He's teasing you, Amber.'

'Okay. I admit it. I confess I was a little concerned.' A crooked little smile spread across his face.

As soon as the hatch of the ferry opened, they were assailed by a smell akin to wood smoke. It was the scent of the Moon and every surface in the transit tunnel was coated in the fine, grey dust that clung to everything it touched, including the confusion of cables, pipes and air ducts which snaked across the walls. As they made their way through the tunnel their footsteps echoed off the fused glassy, rock walls.

It was just unbelievable the events that had overtaken them in a few short months, Amber mused. Amongst all the sadness, a feeling of excitement fought for her attention. Drawing close to the end of the tunnel, the base's circular door irised open. Gerald White, slimmer than she remembered him, was waiting to greet them. He wore a navy jumpsuit like his wife's and had a broad grin on his face. Out of the corner of her eye she saw Mary White stride out and overtake their group, eager to be reunited with her husband once more.

Gerald embraced his wife. 'Welcome to Moonbase,' he said

grandly. 'Welcome to our new home!'

Amber's stomach lurched. Perhaps David's parents had already decided to remain on Moonbase? Perhaps David will too? She turned to David with a worried frown.

He caught her concern. 'Don't worry,' he said, anticipating her question. 'I'm sure after discussion, my parents will decide to journey on with us. It probably hasn't crossed my father's mind that's all,' he said reassuringly. 'And even if they do remain on the Moon it won't influence my decision.' He grinned. 'Looks like you're stuck with me.'

Amber smiled, but inwardly she was by no means reassured. If his parents did decide to remain on the Moon, David may not be able to break the strong bond. And, she determined she would not try to influence him in any way. It was his decision, and his alone.

David moved ahead of the group to meet his father. They shook hands warmly and patted each other heartily on the back. And then it was time for Jarrod and Amber to greet Gerald White.

Gerald ushered them into the base, looking at each one of them keenly for their reaction.

Amber found herself catching her breath as they advanced into the heart of the complex. 'It's huge!' She gazed up at the fused glassy ceiling high above and then dropped her eyes and took in the incredible complex. Moonbase was a town. There were a number of small restaurants, a bar, and even a small park with a water feature that fountained high above them in the weak gravity before drifting lazily back once more over rocks, and strange grassy shrubs that dotted a dark, reflective pool of water. She wondered if the shrubs were real.

Gerald smiled at their reaction.

But something was missing. Amber looked directly at Gerald. 'I don't see any children playing?'

'The only children on the base are those that were among the thousand souls rescued from Earth by the Foundation's starship *Orion*. At the moment they are undergoing orientation and psychological counselling. And no children, I've been told, have been born at Moonbase. I suspect the mortality rate is very

24

low amongst the Foundation personnel so it hasn't been necessary.'

There was only a faint scent of wood smoke in the air compared to the transit tunnel. Soft, soothing music played over the sound system, adding to the sense of unreality. But it wasn't a dream or a movie set she assured herself. Just a strange reality.

They followed Gerald as he showed them through the base. The complex was too large for them to see everything on one tour and some areas were off limits. There were grassed areas and even a few tall spindly trees dotted from place to place. Foundation personnel bustled around. Some nodded politely but did not attempt to engage in conversation.

Amber was shown to the room that she was to share with Lisa. It was small but functional with a wall screen showing in real time, work being carried out on the surface by tractors and machinery.

'If you want to change the channel,' Gerald explained, 'you just – '

Amber cut in politely. 'Yes we are familiar with its operation. It's identical to *Argo's*.'

'Right. And the computer in the corner you will be familiar with as I'm told it's linked directly to your personal computer on *Argo*.'

Amber and Lisa glanced at each other and burst out laughing.

Gerald gave them a puzzled look.

'We're sorry,' Amber giggled. 'It's just that our computer, Beth…' She saw Gerald arch a questioning eyebrow. 'Yes, she has a name and she has a unique personality as well. It seems wherever Lisa and I go, Beth will be close by.'

Gerald smiled. 'Well you will be aware then that you can contact anyone through your…err…through Beth. I'll leave you both to freshen up. Two doors down there's a bathroom.'

When Gerald left to show the others their quarters, the girls inspected their room more closely. The fused glassy regolith walls were bleak, the floor the same except it was polished smooth but was softened by a turquoise rug between the two beds. And the bedspreads were a bright red.

25

Amber looked sceptical. 'I'm not too sure the colour scheme works, are you?'

'Well if we were back on Earth before its destruction and in the tropics, the bright colours would be fine,' Lisa reasoned. 'But I suppose it does take away the cold look of grey walls and floor. Anyway it doesn't really matter. It's only temporary. Our real home will be on *Argo*.'

Amber smiled inwardly. There had never been any doubt that her friend Lisa would be journeying on to the stars. Like herself, Lisa was a Foundation genetically designed human, and Amber remembered Lisa saying she'd fantasized about voyaging to the stars all her life.

A day passed quickly as they further explored the base. Now they were suited up and climbing a short metal ladder into a transit vehicle for a surface tour of the area around the base. Even though the vehicle was pressurized they had the added safety of wearing a pressure suit in case of loss of air. Their helmet visors were open, but could be closed quickly in an emergency.

Gerald followed his wife, son and his three friends into the vehicle and then made his way over to the driver's seat.

Gerald laughed at their puzzled expressions. 'I'm not kidding. I'm the operator. No need to worry,' he said reassuringly. 'I've driven it once before and satisfied the Foundation that I'm competent. Trust me. It's real easy to drive. Just watch.'

Gerald pressed a yellow button on the dash. The vehicle's hatch whispered shut. Then he flipped a blue switch. 'The air in the airlock is now pumping back into the base,' Gerald explained. 'Nothing so precious can be wasted. Our vehicle, though, remains pressurized.' He waited a few minutes for a green flashing light above the hatch to signal that the air and all sound with it had drained away from the airlock. When it did, the egress hatch slowly opened. At that moment there were no machines working in their forward vision, so there was nothing to interrupt their view of the stark lunar beauty. Gerald gave them a moment to soak it in. Expressions of awe and sadness rippled across their faces. The mountains on the horizon were awash with light and seemed unnaturally close. Cradled above, Earth was a glinting, crystal globe in the velvety darkness, no longer a blue and white world. The dust and ash in its atmosphere reflected back into space all the light received from the sun. And beneath that shroud of brightness their broken planet was dark, blacker than any night. No sunlight could penetrate. An eternal night without stars. Once familiar continents were now no more than great slabs of granite floating on currents of magma. Earth was reforming itself.

All of them at that moment were lost in the memory of how Earth once was. They knew they would have to let go of the past, but they would never forget it.

Gerald broke into their thoughts. 'Now when I press this red button for ignition…'

A faint vibration coursed through the vehicle. The hum of the motor was only just audible. 'To go forward I simply depress the peddle with my right foot, and to reverse, I press the heel of my foot on the peddle directly behind. Both pedals pivot from the same point. The lever on the dash controls acceleration. So you see it's very simple.'

Gerald's gloved hand closed around the acceleration lever and he carefully pushed it forward. The transit vehicle moved forward slowly on its large balloon tyres and down a fixed ramp to the regolith below, which was packed hard by the constant tide of machines running over it.

As he drove, Gerald pointed out a squat domed-roofed building. 'That houses a generator which electrolyses water into hydrogen and oxygen,' he explained. 'Scrubbers filter and circulate air throughout the base, and remove carbon dioxide that is surplus to the requirement of the genetically engineered plants you viewed in the greenhouse gardens yesterday.'

As they trundled along well-worn tracks they passed mobile surface-mining tractors and other machines working the regolith. The Moon wasn't as rich as many asteroids but still there was a decent quantity of manganese and chromium, which were used for alloys. Silicon was also extracted and used as a component in the manufacture of flexiglass. Useful quantities of aluminium, magnesium and titanium for reflective coatings were also mined.

Most of the machines were being operated remotely from the base for safety from solar radiation. Two kilometres out from the base they passed a large building half buried in the regolith. A score of transparent domes encircled the structure, which resembled a semi-submerged whale.

Gerald brought the transit vehicle to a halt. 'That's the fusion plant. It's powered by deuterium, a hydrogen isotope, with helium-3. The charged protons are kept away from the reactor walls with magnetic fields. The Moon has an abundance of helium-3,' he added. 'The Earth none.'

'Why is that?' David asked. He was impressed with the knowledge his father had acquired in the short time he'd been on the Moon.

'The helium-3 comes from the sun, courtesy of the solar wind. It's then soaked up by the titanium in the regolith to a depth of around three metres.'

'Oh look over to the right,' Lisa directed. 'A robot's coming out of the building.'

It turned towards their vehicle and stopped abruptly as if checking and processing what it saw, and then to the delight of all on board, it waved one of its manipulators in greeting.

'I wouldn't be surprised,' Lisa laughed, 'if that robot's got a personality just like our computers.' They waved back and watched the robot make its way to one of the transparent domes. After inspecting it, the robot proceeded to dismantle the dome.

As the vehicle moved off, Amber waved, 'Bye Robby.'

To their surprise the robot sensed the transit vehicle move off. It stopped its task, swivelled around and waved at the departing transporter.

'I wouldn't mind betting that our Robby can talk,' Amber joked.

'It can,' Gerald chuckled. 'It's directed remotely and verbally from the base. But I've been told they can certainly hold a conversation, argue and even moan if they get a particularly difficult task. Swear even!'

Amber giggled. 'And Robby walked funny. As if he was walking barefoot on broken glass.'

'There's a reason for that,' Gerald said. 'They hate doing

maintenance on the surface because the dust gets into their joints. Did you notice the robot didn't kick up any dust?'

'Oh yes, you're right,' Amber said slowly. 'I wonder if Robby moaned about his task?'

'Probably,' Gerald chuckled.

'I hope this Robby, as you have christened him, is not going to be competing with me for your affections?' David whispered to Amber.

Amber turned to David and her eyes crinkled with impish amusement. She patted him on his helmet and then took his gloved hand in hers and squeezed his fingers, but through the thick layers of the glove he barely felt it. 'We'll just have to wait and see.'

The transit vehicle carried on past craters large and small, climbing gentle slopes bathed in reflected Earthlight and down deeply shadowed inclines. It wasn't long before Moonbase dropped out of sight below the horizon behind them. Gerald guided the vehicle down a long slope and brought it to a halt at the bottom so that they were in dark shadow. 'Now look around you,' he gestured.

They raised their heads to the tall dome of sky above, and gazed silently in the magic of the night with expressions of rapture. Earth had dropped out of sight. Thousands of jewels shone with a steady light in the cosmic immensity. So many that it was hard to make out the familiar constellations in the confusion of stars.

Lisa broke the silence. 'Unbelievable!' she whispered reverently. And we've made our first step into the cosmic ocean, she thought to herself. The Moon is our first port of call. Our gateway to the stars.

Chapter Two

Badel opened up the channel to the bacteriology laboratory. 'This is the commander's aide speaking. Put me through to Orador, your team leader.'

'Speaking,' Orador confirmed and felt a wash of fear course through him. He still nursed a vivid memory of his anger charged commander when he had requested specimens from him at his last appointment; it would stay imprinted in his neural network forever.

'Is the commander's medicine ready?' Badel asked.

'Yes,' Orador answered warily.

'Well now would be a good time to deliver it,' the aide suggested. 'He's at a meeting. That's why I contacted you.'

'Very considerate of you,' Orador said, heaving a long sigh of relief. 'The medicine has been ready for a short while I have to confess. I was marshalling my courage to deliver it to him.'

'Can't blame you for that, but get it here as quickly as you can, for my sake as well as his.' The aide chuckled. 'I will tell him you were sorry to miss him.'

'Of course,' Orador said dryly. 'Let me know if there's any improvement in our commander's health over the coming days – discreetly of course.'

'I certainly will.'

*

In their quarters, Gerald and Mary White sat on the edge of their bed. David had requested a meeting with them to discuss a matter of importance. They waited while David's chair directly opposite them personalized to his body configuration.

'Now, David, what is it you wish to discuss?' Gerald prompted.

David swallowed nervously and squared his shoulders. 'I've decided to accept the Foundation's offer to journey with them to the stars.' He could see his father was visibly shocked, but his mother less so.

30

Gerald leaned forward, locking eyes with his son. 'I know the Foundation made this offer to the family, son, but I didn't think for a moment that we would take them up on it.' Gerald's blue eyes narrowed in thought. The silence stretched between them, then he continued. 'I must admit, your mother did mention that you might wish to join your friends in the starship but I dismissed the possibility. I thought our place was here with the rest of the thousand colonists – our own kind.'

'But if we remain on the Moon we would have to endure the sight of poor broken Earth,' David argued, his voice strained. 'We can never go home and the Moon can never be another Earth. But perhaps we can find a new planet? Like Earth used to be.' He saw his father's lips compress in a thin line, his face more drawn than he'd ever remembered. The jowls that had started to collect around his jaw prior to Earth's destruction had disappeared. His father had lost weight but even so, he looked good. Younger than his forty-two years.

A sombre mood descended. 'And when did you make your decision?' Gerald asked coolly.

'While on board the starship. I hope you both decide to join me.'

Mary White put her hand on Gerald's arm and engaged David's attention. 'It's just that your father has been on the Moon a little longer than we have and is settling in well to life on the base. I realise the twins would want to travel on with their parents and Lisa too. But all three are Foundation humans. We thought when it came to the crunch you would choose to be with your own kind.'

Gerald straightened up. 'We are part of history now, son,' he said in a reasoning voice. 'It's a new beginning for us here on the Moon. The chance of finding another Earth must be remote, wouldn't you think?' He leaned forward once more. 'I suggest you consult your computer and find out what the odds would be.'

'I know the chances would be slim but at least we'd be out there amongst the stars searching.' David's eyes were bleak. A curl of unease hit his stomach. It was what he feared. His parents seemed to be dead set on remaining on the Moon. 'Surely it has to be better than spending the rest of our lives on a dead world,' he pleaded.

'Look,' Mary White said, looking at her son and husband in turn. 'I think it would be best if we think about it for a few days before any of us make a final decision.'

*

On Earth volcanism was continuing to pump out carbon dioxide, along with hydrogen laced with chlorine and arsenic. The Foundation estimated that Earth's new atmosphere would end up ten times denser than the old oxygen nitrogen one. Greenhouse cycles had already started. Death immersed the planet. Oceans were evaporating and would eventually begin to boil – Earth would soon be a true twin to Venus. Even now the oceans were becoming toxic from deadly trace elements including mercury and cadmium.

The melting ice caps, the evaporating oceans and the shifting of continents, pitching and heaving on seas of magma, were causing the planet to unbalance itself and wobble with the redistributed mass. And if this wasn't enough, the polarity of Earth's magnetic field was reversing. As a consequence the magnetosphere was compromised, allowing more cosmic rays to reach the planet. Earth was returning to its primordial past.

*

Amber sat nervously waiting in her quarters for David to return from his meeting with his parents. Jarrod and Lisa were with her, giving their support.

Lisa's arm was around her friend's shoulder. 'I'm sure David's parents will choose to come with us. All those stars out there beckon. Who wouldn't?' she encouraged.

'But it's in our genes,' Amber countered. 'We can't help ourselves. We have to go! But the desire won't necessarily be the same for the White's.'

'David feels like we do,' Jarrod said.

'I realise that, but Mr White seems to have settled in so well

32

at Moonbase. I feel he may wish to stay.' Her stomach lurched with the thought of David choosing to remain with his parents on the Moon. 'I'm determined not to press him to go with us. It wouldn't be fair.'

'Attention. David White approaches. Do you wish for him to enter?' the personal computer asked.

'Yes please, Beth,' Amber answered. She rose nervously to her feet and consciously willed her legs to stop shaking.

'I must warn you that he does not look happy,' Beth said, her voice laced with concern. 'Perhaps it would be better to turn him away. You may not want to hear what he has to say.'

Amber forced a bleak smile as she gazed at Beth's sympathetic image on the computer screen. Dark eyes under thick lashes returned her gaze. Beth was blessed with high cheekbones, a beautiful cupid's bow mouth, strong defined chin and long dark tumbling hair. But it was Beth's creation. She had designed the image early in their relationship and had used Amber as her model when Amber's hair had been long.

'Thanks for your concern, Beth, but we have to know whether it's good news or bad.'

'As you wish, my dear.'

Amber's heart sank as David entered. His sad eyes returned her gaze. He smiled bleakly and acknowledged Lisa and Jarrod with a nod.

'It seems my parents, especially my father, are intent on remaining at Moonbase.'

'Oh, David,' she said with a catch in her voice. 'I'm so sorry.' She took his hands in hers, and tilting her head down engaged his deep-set blue eyes. 'Is there any chance of them changing their minds?'

'We're going to view our options for a few days. But I'm not expecting them to leave Moonbase.'

Amber felt wretched. If his parents remained, would David be able to cope and leave them forever? But I mustn't plead with him to break the special bond he has with his parents. Depressing thoughts tumbled through her head. I'm a designer human and will live for a very long time, barring an accident. He's not. He's going to grow old before my eyes while I'm in

33

my paused state and will never look older than twenty-five years.

'Hey there, don't look so sad,' David said forcing a grin. 'I'm still going to leave Moonbase with you. Nothing's going to change that decision. I promise.'

'Well whatever eventuates over the next few days,' Amber said softly, 'I will understand and go along with.'

'My father suggested I consult my computer as to the chances of finding another Earth. How about we ask Beth?'

'Sure,' Amber agreed. 'It's a wonder we hadn't thought of that. I admire your father. He's so switched on. Jarrod and I never really got to know him back on Earth. He was always so busy.'

'I must admit that I've got to know him better myself since we've been on the Moon,' David said. 'Unfortunately for me, he's adapted too well to life on the base.'

Amber sat down on her swivel chair in front of the computer. They all crowded around her. 'Beth. I wish to speak to you please,' she requested.

They waited a few seconds for Beth to generate her presence on the screen.

'How can I help you, my dear?'

'We want to know the chances of finding another Earth-like planet.'

'Goodness me. You're asking me to speculate and I'm reluctant to do that.' Beth's brow knitted. 'Wouldn't you rather listen to some restful music? Or perhaps challenge me to a game of chess?'

'No music or chess thank you, Beth. I realise it involves speculation, but if you could do this for me, I would be very grateful.'

'Very well, Amber. Now this Earth search. Is it just in this galaxy or the whole universe?'

'Just in the Milky Way galaxy please, Beth.' She was surprised Beth could entertain the thought that she might have meant the entire universe.

Beth's generated image looked relieved. 'It's still a huge request, Amber, but I will do my best. As you know, for a planet

34

to support complex life forms it must have surface water. That can only happen if it's a certain distance from its star. This region we call the circumstellar habitable zone. And the star should be a suitable distance from the galactic centre.'

'Why is that?' David asked.

'If it were too far from the centre, the nebula from which the star and any of its planets were born would lack heavy elements. The metallicity of gas from which the stars form declines with distance from the galactic core. And the further from the hub, there is less gas and therefore less star formation.'

'So what about closer in to the galactic centre where there is more metal-rich clouds of gas for planetary systems to evolve?'

'Good question, David. Towards the galactic centre, the number of stars increase. This means there are more close encounters. To add to this, planetary systems forming out of metal-rich clouds will probably contain more comets. Then there is the problem of high-energy radiation in the inner regions of the galaxy – '

'But, Beth,' Jarrod cut in. 'A planet's magnetic field can shield it from particle radiation, and its ozone layer can screen out dangerous electromagnetic radiation.'

'That's true to a point,' Beth countered, 'but the planet's shield can be overwhelmed. If that happens, energetic radiation can ionize the atmosphere and will generate nitrogen oxides to a point where it destroys the ozone layer.'

'It seems that complex life that evolved on Earth must be achingly rare,' Amber stated with an anguished voice.

'I suspect it is,' Beth agreed.

'And then there's the black hole at the centre of the galaxy,' Lisa added.

'Ah, yes,' Beth continued. 'It's more than just a black hole, Lisa. It's a super-massive black hole but thankfully it appears to be dormant. But it could turn on, if a star or star cluster drifts too close to its event horizon. The stars would be sucked in by the gravity tide of the black hole. Then there would be a burst of high-energy electro magnetized particle radiation. You wouldn't want to be near that. All in all, the inner region of the galaxy is not an area to be searching for life. And because there's more stars, there are more frequent supernovas and gamma-ray bursters.'

'This is all very depressing,' Jarrod commented, 'but we know life does evolve in the Milky Way galaxy otherwise we wouldn't be having this discussion.'

'I was coming to that, Jarrod.' Beth's eyes narrowed. Her brow puckered in a frown. 'There's no need to be sarcastic,' she cajoled. 'I'm not responsible for creation of life or the lack of it.'

'I apologise, Beth.'

'Apology accepted. But it's a huge task that Amber requested. You must be patient. Now Earth of course resides in a spiral arm, which lies in a region of the galaxy called the galactic habitable zone. This is in the most likely place to search for complex life forms.'

'This is the region of the galaxy that the starships will explore then?' Amber asked.

'Yes,' confirmed Beth. 'In this region we will search for stars like the sun – around the same age and the same size. Too old a star won't have the necessary elements and planets formed out of the same gas cloud won't either. A very young star may have all the elements in abundance but complex life would not have had time to evolve.'

'And stars that are too large are not an option either,' Jarrod chipped in. 'Even though they have more fuel than a smaller star, they don't live long enough, because they burn their fuel more quickly and so intelligent life wouldn't have time to get started.'

'I see that I've been explaining things you may already know. Please forgive me. And you probably know small stars would be too cool and wouldn't emit enough visible light for complex life to evolve.'

'Could a planet have too much metal?' David asked.

'Yes. Too much metallicity can make terrestrial planets larger and because of this their gravity is stronger, making them rich in volatiles and poorer in topographic relief. This makes them more likely to be completely covered with water. So to sum up, extraterrestrial civilizations seeking new worlds would

36

search for solar systems like yours, David.'

'Have any planets, other than Earth in our solar system, sustained life, ever?' Lisa asked.

'I don't know for sure, so again I can only speculate. The Foundation in time would have explored this possibility. In fact the Moonbase colonists and volunteer Foundation personnel that will remain on the Moon will, in time, do just that. Now, the only planets in the circumstellar habitable zone in this solar system are Venus, Earth and Mars. On Venus, its runaway greenhouse has boiled away all its oceans. Mars used to have liquid water on its surface. Now, that water has drained away, but persists just under the surface. Being a smaller world than Earth, its gravity is less and so most of its atmosphere has leaked away into space. We suspect that complex life would not have had time to evolve.'

'And the gas giants would definitely be out,' David stated.

'Not necessarily, but most likely. Perhaps some creatures could evolve. Jupiter for example has an atmosphere of helium, hydrogen, methane, ammonia and water. It has no solid surface but perhaps organic molecules may be present in the atmosphere. And perhaps life has evolved in these skies, floating like hot-air balloons. Then there are the satellites of these gas giants. Some are almost as big as the planet Mercury. Some are covered in ice, but underground oceans heated by radioactive cores may support some forms of primitive life. It's an exciting prospect for the colony on Moonbase to explore the solar system sometime in the future.'

And then to Amber's dismay, David asked the question she was dreading. But she reasoned he would need to have this knowledge before he made a final determination to remain on Moonbase and explore the solar system, or follow his heart and make the journey to the stars with her.

'How long do you estimate it would take to have a remote chance of finding another Earth?'

'Oh, David. You ask so many fine questions.' Beth's image clouded with sadness. 'I was so hoping that nobody would ask me that in your presence. I suggest you retract the question.'

A curl of unease hit David's stomach. 'I don't wish to

retract the question, Beth, so if you don't mind…'

'Very well then, David. I have been recently programmed to answer this if you or your parents made the request. In fact knowledge pertaining to your question will be revealed to all the colonists shortly; but in the meantime you can let your parents know what I'm about to tell you, but no one else. Have I your word on that?'

'You have my word.' Beth gave him a sorrowful look. His feeling of unease increased.

'My, dear boy. I hadn't anticipated this request. I would have expected your three companions would eventually have been given permission to do that. It is highly unlikely that another Earth-like planet would be found in your lifetime.' Beth paused to let the brutal statement settle and noted the shadow of dismay cross David's face. 'You are aware, I'm sure, that all Foundation personnel appear young?'

'Yes, I have, and when I broach the subject with my three friends I get nowhere. They hedge around, look uncomfortable and change the subject.'

'I understand, David. But you mustn't blame them. The knowledge was privy to Foundation personnel only. Your three friends are going to live for a very long time, as will all Foundation personnel barring accidents. They've been genetically engineered you see. Their genetic systems employ the most effective techniques – '

David cut in, a hard edge to his voice. 'I thought you three were born on Earth.' He swept them with a stony glare. 'I know your parents are alien. But I believed you were regular humans, blessed with great genes.' He looked at each of them accusingly. Amber grabbed his arm, but he wrenched it free.

'You mustn't be angry at your friends, David,' Beth said in a soothing tone. 'They were forbidden to discuss it with regular humans. But it's true. Your three friends were born on Earth, but not in the usual way. They were born in gestation tanks that were constantly monitored. Knowledge and experience were implanted but until recently lay dormant.'

'I knew they had microchip implants but I thought that was what made them so intelligent.' His eyes were wintry. 'I didn't

38

realize that the implants hadn't been switched on. I've been so naïve.'

'Yes, David, and now they have. And it's not all that long ago that they found this out and have had come to terms with it.'

Anger smouldered in David's eyes and he pointedly ignored his three companions. His dream of journeying to the stars was shattered. 'But I thought that it was time warp that made it possible for The Foundation to voyage between the stars?'

'Not that alone, David. A great deal of time is spent well below light-speed. Many areas of the Sagittarius arm warrant investigation you see. And that can be better accomplished at relatively slow speed. So to travel these vast distances requires a long-lived crew. Not only that, the Foundation has other tools. It can be incredibly boring at times in the emptiness of space, so the Foundation has on offer sleep tanks where time can be passed enjoyably in deep sleep. The body almost shuts down completely – near death. But the dream area of the brain is fully functional. You experience dreams that are as real to you as any waking moment. As real as this discussion we are having now in fact.'

'Suspended animation with vivid dreams.'

'That's right, David. And no nightmares guaranteed.'

Despite his anger, he was intrigued. 'Wouldn't muscles deteriorate and bones become brittle with no exercise, because I assume these would be very long sleeps?'

'No. Muscle tone and bone density is preserved electronically.'

'There's no chance then that the Foundation with all its knowledge can lengthen regular humans life?'

Beth's expression brightened at the prospect of lifting David's mood. 'Oh yes we can and I assure you it will be on offer to all the colonists. But first let me explain. Longevity cells have a use-by date. They can divide so many times and then they die. Each cell has an aging clock in its nucleus – a strand of DNA at the end of all chromosomes called telomeres. Each time a cell divides a little of the telomere is used up till eventually it's depleted. The Foundation's technology has been able to defeat the aging clock but it is done prior to birth in the gestation tanks. But in your case David, we can repair age-related damage to organs. And we can boost the immune system. We can double your life expectancy to what it is now. We anticipate that some of the colonists and perhaps yourself may for religious reasons refuse some or all of what we offer.'

'Thank you, Beth, for your information and patience.' The heat of his anger was now giving way to something far colder than a Martian winter. He nodded curtly to his three friends and informed them that he was retreating to his quarters to re-evaluate his options.

*

Amber's dream of David joining her on the starship was becoming a nightmare. It was now almost certain that David would remain on the Moon. She bowed her head. Her vision blurred with unspilled tears as she felt Lisa's comforting arm around her shoulders.

'I was going to ask permission to tell David myself about our longevity.' Amber's dam of tears finally broke and trickled down her cheeks in the low gravity. She brushed them angrily away. 'And if permission wasn't granted, I was going to tell him anyway,' she said defiantly. 'But he's not going to believe that now. And I don't blame him.' Her voice lowered to a murmur. 'But I would never, never, have let him make a final decision without knowing all the facts about us.'

'We know that, Amber,' her brother said in a soothing tone. 'He just needs to be on his own for a while to untangle his thoughts. We have to let him work it through. But I have to warn you. Although I've never mentioned it, I always thought that once David had all the facts, he would have no choice but to remain on the Moon.'

'I know,' she whispered, shaking her head. 'I've been in denial.' Oh David, she thought to herself. You are so like us. The stars beckon and you are starting to talk so eloquently, just like Foundation humans – but you will never be one of us.

Her eyes fell shut beneath dark lashes.

Chapter Three

David lay on his bed, hands cocked behind his head. His dream of blazing a trail to the stars was dead and he would have to come to terms with it. But worse than that, light years would separate him from Amber. He pictured the soft contours of her face, the smooth curve of her leg. And he recalled the scent of her hair, fragrant and exciting and her unusual eloquence. How could he go on without her? Earth was a broken world. Only a thousand of the human race remained. It couldn't get any worse. Why hadn't she told him that she would live so long and remain young till the end of her days? Sure, he was happy for her, but what else has she kept hidden? His eyes prickled with unshed tears, his soul swept along on a tide of despair. He felt the room closing in on him. Restlessly he rose from the bed and strode to the view screen, switched it on and stared out at the stars. They gazed back, mocking him with their steady light.

*

Lisa and Jarrod had departed and now Amber lay alone on her bed, shrouded in sadness. If I could only turn back time, she thought. To be transported back to old Earth, with its nitrogen blue skies, cool forests and majestic mountains. To once more stroll a lonely beach, hand in hand with David. To feel a gentle breeze caress our skin and warm sand beneath our feet. And she missed the chirping of crickets in summer nights, and early morning birdsong in the trees.

But Earth was scoured clean of life. She would sail the sea of stars and witness the wonders without him by her side. She felt her pulse quicken, her anxiety rising. It was a pointless exercise going over it in her mind. Over and over. But she couldn't help it. She was going to lose David. There was no doubt. The hurt in his eyes as he'd left her cabin would haunt her forever.

*

Phillip Wilson, the commander of Moonbase, had the most spacious cabin on the base. Even so it was a crush for the twenty personnel assembled for the briefing that he'd requested. Five sat in chairs facing the commander. The rest huddled shoulder to shoulder behind them.

Behind his expansive desk, Phillip Wilson waited for the assembly to settle. His intelligent dark eyes scanned each face. He was a solidly built man with an olive complexion and dark hair clipped short. He was proud of the men and women assembled for volunteering to remain on the base, and with their skills assist the colonists to survive an otherwise bleak future.

The room went quiet. 'Very soon I will relinquish my command of Moonbase but retain my command of *Orion*.' Phillip Wilson spoke in a measured way that was typical of Foundation and Moonbase personnel. His voice was deep and strong. 'It's been an honour to serve as your commander. What you've done in volunteering to remain with the colonists is admirable and I'm humbled by it. It will be up to you to choose your next commander.' He leaned forward and his chair adjusted to accommodate him. His posture conveyed an impression of urgency. 'But I must warn you to keep a close eye on the colonists. Humans can be treacherous and power mad. Don't allow religious beliefs, politics or jealousies hamper their future and yours. They must abide by the rules your new command will set down. You must deal with any unrest quickly. Isolate troublemakers. It may even prove necessary to modify their behaviour with specialized cranial implants.'

Some of the assembly looked surprised at the commander's last comment. Others nodded their full agreement.

A petite blonde woman sitting directly opposite the commander asked, 'how much do you suggest we disclose to them on longevity, Phillip?'

The base commander didn't appear to mind his first name being used instead of his title. 'You and your new commander must make that decision, Pamela, but I suggest that you disclose only what you are prepared to offer them in age-treatments. But at this stage I wouldn't mention cloning. It could unsettle many of them and cause dissention. When they get to the end of what the treatments can do, I'm sure most will be agreeable to the cloning option.'

'And the childbirth question?' Pam prompted.

'Ah, yes. That's a difficult one. I suggest you educate them on the advantages of adopting the gestation tanks in preference to the primitive way they have practised up till now. But don't force the issue. Allow them to choose.'

The meeting carried on for another hour with discussion on improving the base with the help of the colonists and plans to construct a new starship to replace *Orion*. And then it would be time to explore the solar system. Already the planned starship had a list of possible names, the most popular so far being touted – *Phoenix*. It was important that the colonists had goals. It was the only way for a quality and purposeful existence.

*

'David. I feel your distress and it troubles me.'

David jumped in a nervous reaction to his computer's sudden outburst.

'I am sorry. I see I have startled you. Please forgive me, David.'

'It's not your fault, Bud. I'm a bit strung out at the moment.' He gazed at the computer screen. Bud's blue eyes under a noble brow looked sad. Except for the length of Bud's blonde hair, the image was almost identical to his own. The same strong jaw line and mouth that could turn on a cheeky grin. Bud had generated this image when David had been introduced to Bud on starship *Argo*, when David's hair was longer.

'Explain to me, how you, a computer, can have feelings, Bud?'

'I'm an incredibly sophisticated computer, David.' Bud said unashamedly. 'Impulses in my circuits are programmed to feel empathy and a desire to please. I can feel joy, and I can feel sadness, and with interaction with you, David, I am continually improving myself.'

Despite his dark mood, David smiled. 'Sounds to me like you're bragging,' he teased.

43

'I am just giving you the facts, David. And it hurts me deeply, for you to think of me as a braggart.'

'I apologize. I didn't mean to offend you. I was only teasing. It's what friends do.'

'I have processed teasing into my memory bank. I will endeavour to recognise teasing next time as something friends do. But I would like for you to think of me as just that – a friend. Not as a computer!'

'I'll do my best, Bud. And now I'm going for a walk. I might stroll down to the park.'

'No need to tell me where you're going, David. I know where you are at all times.'

'And how do you manage that?' David asked.

'You have a personalized chip on the left shoulder of all your jumpsuits.'

David laughed. 'I've been accused before of having a chip on my shoulder.'

Bud was puzzled by the idiom. 'I do not understand,' he exclaimed.

'Never mind, Bud. I'll explain the humour of it sometime.'

*

With its weak gravity, walking on the Moon was very different than on Earth. But already the colonists were adapting to it well. David was no exception as he took long loping strides down the well-lit corridor that led to the park. Not all the areas of the base had mobile pathways. The black boots he'd been issued with were at first too large a fit but had surprised him as they'd adjusted quickly to the correct size of each foot automatically. Every contour and every bump on his feet was taken into account. They felt like supple extensions of his own feet. Without a doubt, they were the most comfortable footwear he'd ever worn. And they were quiet. The only echoes off the fused regolith walls came from his footfalls and the rustle of the material of his jumpsuit legs.

It took five minutes to reach the park. The few people in the area nodded politely to David, but made no effort to converse.

He made his way over to a grassed area. The lawn was a uniformly dark green, and he wondered if it was artificial. He knelt down and with the palm of his hand pressed gently against it and felt the springiness of its coarse texture. Still uncertain if the grass was real, he bowed his head and sniffed. The unmistakable scent of chlorophyll finally confirmed to him that it was natural, living grass. He straightened up and ambled over to the park's water feature. On the Moon, to amble is to take little skips and hops. A sort of shuffle and once you get used to it, requires very little energy. But it did look silly to the colonists and would take time to become accustomed to it.

The fountain was playing. It never stopped, he'd been told, except for occasional maintenance. The precious liquid jetted high into the air, its momentum slowing near its peak and then pausing before drifting slowly down like gentle snowflakes in the weak lunar gravity, until finally spilling over lunar rocks in the pool below. Some of the rocks he noticed were partially covered by moss. The planting of exotic grasses around the pool swayed gently in the artificial breeze and reflected well in the dark pool. Like the lawn, the moss and the ornamental grasses were probably real. They would act as natural air-filters and with photosynthesis, remove the carbon dioxide in the air and pump out precious oxygen.

A current of air carrying the scent of coffee and freshly baked pastries assailed David's nose. He ambled over to its source and hesitated at the entrance of a café. The huge and dramatic overscaled glass doors sensed his presence and swung quietly open to reveal a warm, cave-like interior. The café was empty of people. A curved, copper-topped counter dominated the room. The fused regolith walls and ceiling had a smoky ochre sheen to them in contrast to the almost universal grey of the base. Classy copper light fittings added to the ambience of the room.

'Can I help you?' a voice enquired.

David cast a sidelong glance in the direction of the voice. He hadn't noticed the person behind the counter but it wasn't surprising. The man was either kneeling down or was incredibly short; only his head showed above the counter.

'The aroma of coffee and pastries attracted me,' David explained. 'But how do we pay for them? I've no money you see.'

'Not a problem. You must be one of the colonists?' He took in David's nodded agreement. His voice was a pleasant tenor and each word was precisely enunciated – no surprise there. 'Nobody pays, but most of Moonbase personnel is required to do duty in the cafés and shops from time to time. In case you were wondering, I'm an air conditioning specialist genetically engineered for the job. That's why I'm short and slight of frame. I have to be able to crawl through ducts and perform duties where there is very little room to manoeuvre.' His gentle brown eyes engaged David's. 'I'm Mathew, and you are…?'

'David. David White.'

'Oh, yes. I've heard of you and your parents. Through your friendship with Amber and Jarrod Dryden, you and your mother helped persuade the governments of Britain and the USA to trust the Foundation and allow them to attempt to save Earth.'

'Well we did what we could. But I'm sure the Foundation would have attempted to save the planet, acceptance of governments or not.'

'I'm sure you're right, but the Foundation was grateful for your help. Now what would you like to eat and drink?'

David scanned the pastries and cakes behind a glass cabinet and picked out what looked like a custard square. 'And I'll have a black coffee, two sugars.'

'I would suggest a number four coffee as it will be the closest to an Earth brew.'

'That will be fine thanks.'

'If it's not to your liking then I suggest you try a number three or five.' Mathew retrieved a custard square with tongs that looked oversize in his tiny hand, and then filled a mug of steaming black coffee to which he added two cubes of sugar. 'Now, although the coffee's steaming it won't be as hot as you are used to, David.'

'Why is that?'

'The air pressure on Moonbase operates lower than what it was on Earth. The lower the air pressure, the lower the boiling

46

point. But I'm sure you know that. Anyway, good coffee shouldn't be brewed too hot.' His delicate hands lifted the coffee and custard square up to the counter.

David chose a table set against the café's curving wall by the window, with a view that took in the water feature and park. One bite of his custard square confirmed it tasted as delicious as it looked. And the first sip of coffee proved that it was as good as any he had tasted though not as hot as he would have liked. A distant whisper of air conditioning was taken over by a Mozart symphony. But the magnificent composer's composition, the excellent food and drink couldn't lift his depression. Somewhere in the immensity of time and the dark reaches of space, Amber would be lost to him. Forever! His stomach knotted in an agony of despair. Time stretched as over and over he played back in his mind their times together. He brought the mug to his lips and to his surprise found it was empty. He'd eaten his custard square too.

'Another coffee and custard square, David?'

'Yes thanks, Mathew. That number four coffee was great and the custard square was superb.' He made a move to get up.

'No. Stay where you are, David, I'll bring it over.'

A few minutes later, Mathew made his way over to David's table. Although he was diminutive and slim, David noted that Mathew was perfectly proportioned.

'Mind if I join you for a few moments, David?'

'Please do,' David answered, even though he would have preferred solitude.

Mathew sat opposite David and waited the few seconds it took for the chair to personalize to his frame and telescope up to its maximum before speaking. 'I can see that you are depressed, David, and understandably so. But if there's anyway I can help you with information about your new home on the Moon, I'd be happy to do so.'

'That's precisely the problem. My parents and I were given the choice of remaining on the Moon or journeying with the Foundation to discover new worlds. I had chosen the latter until I found that I probably wouldn't live long enough to find a new world like Earth, even with age treatments that would double my life-span. I will grow old. My three closest friends were born at the Foundation and I've been told that they will live for a very long time.'

'I see.' Mathew said slowly. 'I can see your dilemma. It's true that we live for a very long time, but if you wish to be with your friends you should go with them. Don't let this aging problem stop you. Even if you never make planet-fall I guarantee you'll never be bored. There's so much on offer.'

'My parents wish to remain on the Moon, especially my father.'

'Then you do have a problem, David,' he said sympathetically. 'But you still have a little time to view your options. Go to the top. Ask questions. Plead for answers. There's only so much technology can do for you, David. But perhaps that technology may surprise you, if you can persuade those at the top to reveal it.' Mathew's expression changed to one of unease. 'Now I've already said too much, so I'll leave you to your coffee.' As he moved to alight from his chair it telescoped down. He stood up and shuffled back to the counter.

Mathew's advice had caused his despair to retreat just a little. Perhaps his dream could be rekindled? Oh how it hurt to hope.

*

'But in time, David will learn to love the Moon.'

'I'm not so sure Gerald,' Mary White said with a worried frown. 'He's going to miss Amber. She's his balance. It will break his heart.'

'But it will be for the best, surely, now we know that she'll live just about forever. Our life span is very limited in comparison.' He shook his head. 'No. He must remain on the Moon with his own kind. The other option would be too cruel for Amber as well as our son.'

'But if he insists on leaving the Moon?'

'I thought he was coming to terms with remaining at Moonbase. Do you know something I don't?'

'It's just a feeling I have. But you're probably right. I'm

worrying needlessly.'

'Well I've been on the Moon a little longer than David and you, Mary, and I've seen so much more.' He leaned towards his wife and clasped her hands in his. His eyes lost their focus, as if he was looking at something far away. 'I've seen the beauty of a lunar sunrise, witnessed the way the regolith glitters when the sun first hits it. I've seen ancient ringwall mountains and cracked crater floors. And I've seen Mare Nubium and the Ocean of Storms. The Moon has a breathtaking, strange beauty. It's all there just waiting for us. David will make new friends and then he can discover the Moon like I have.'

*

Jarrod Harrison's genetic make up allowed him to be coldly analytical, but it couldn't quell the concern he felt for his twin sister. Amber was hurting. Star travel was not an option for David. Even with life extending age treatments the Foundation would be offering the colonists, their sphere of exploration could only be the Solar System. But if the colonists took the gestation tank option for their progeny, and accepted the full genetic engineering on offer, their children could, one day, travel to the stars.

Lisa had returned to her cabin at his suggestion, so that she could attempt to comfort Amber in some way. But only time could dull her despair, he reasoned. And that wouldn't happen until the starships left the Moon. Perhaps the sooner that happened the better.

*

When Lisa got back to her quarters, Amber was gone.
'Where's Amber, Beth?'
'She's gone to find David. He's in a café next to the park.'
'How do you know where he is?'
'Bud told me when I requested it, Lisa. David has a chip on his shoulder…'
Lisa chuckled. 'I'm sorry to interrupt you, Beth. Please

49

continue.'

'The chip is on the left shoulder of all his jumpsuits. It tells Bud where David is at all times.'

'Very convenient. And I presume I do too?'

'No, Lisa. Your location chip is implanted deep in your brain. So are your friends, Amber and Jarrod. Now, if you could explain your humour earlier, I would be grateful?'

'Well for someone to have a chip on their shoulder means that they are grumpy.'

'Grumpy? I don't understand grumpy.'

'Ill-tempered or grouchy.'

'Oh I understand. But of course I meant for you to take the chip on David's shoulder literally. But thank you for enlightening me, Lisa.'

'It's so sad that David is going to remain on Moonbase. I wish there were something we could do.'

'Well we could offer help to Amber.'

'Oh?'

'We have technology that can steal selected memory from her brain. She could still remember David, but not in any deep romantic way.'

'Stolen memories.' Lisa shook her head. 'There's no way she would agree to that, Beth. No way!'

'Well let us hope it doesn't come to that. But if her depression were to persist she might not have any choice in the matter.'

The sad image of Amber saying her final goodbye to David formed in Lisa's mind.

Amber's misery-filled eyes flooded her brain. David's head was bowed...

Beth's voice broke in. 'Are you going to meet them at the café, Lisa?'

'No,' she said softly. 'It's best they have this time together while they still can.' A deep weariness seized her. The last twenty-four hours had been emotionally draining.

Beth sensed it. 'You need to rest, my dear, to prepare yourself for the days ahead. I suspect you will need all your resilience to support your friends.'

*

David sipped his coffee, contemplating the pain of his past and the uncertainty of his future. Dare he allow himself to hope that perhaps there was some way that he could, or should choose star travel over remaining on the Moon? But would it be fair to Amber? For her to see him grow old before her eyes while she remained forever young. But Mathew had hinted that he shouldn't give up the dream. Go to the top, he had said. Plead for answers. Perhaps there was something the Foundation's high technology could do for him and his parents that hadn't been divulged so far? Something that their computers had been programmed not to reveal.

The custard square tasted uncommonly good, he thought to himself. God, I'm even thinking like Foundation personnel – Uncommonly good! Now why haven't I asked Bud why my three friends and the rest of the Foundation personnel talk so eloquently? His thoughts were broken as he spied a familiar figure dressed in a dark-red jumpsuit, threading her way through the now busy town centre. He felt himself smiling at her. He caught her eye. She waved tentatively, unsure of her reception. He could understand that. His behaviour last time he was with her was unbecoming of him. Downright churlish in fact. His eyes followed her. The over-scaled transparent door to the café opened and she swept in, more confidant of her reception now that David was smiling at her. She made her way over to him and sat down across the table from him.

'I must apologize for my churlish behaviour earlier, Amber. Can you forgive me?'

For a moment she was taken aback by his eloquence and wondered whether he was being sarcastic. She searched his face and saw no hint of it. 'Of course I forgive you. You had every right to be angry, David. But I hope you believe me when I say I intended eventually, before we left the Moon, to discuss the implications of our life expectancy? But you were so looking forward to a future out amongst the stars…'

'I know,' he said with passion. 'I've thought of nothing else. My mind was closed to any future other than the one with you.'

51

Amber leaned over to him, her eyes filling his own. He smelt the sweet scent of her hair. They kissed gently, pulled away slowly, kissed again.

*

Badel breathed a sigh of relief when his commander left for an unscheduled inspection of the laboratory that manufactured food from recycled organic compounds. He opened up a secure channel to bacteriologist and physician Orador, to covertly report on Warstill's digestive problems.

Anxiety furrowed Orador's brow when a colleague informed him that the commander's aide wished to speak to him. Striding briskly to his workstation, he took the call. 'Greetings,' Orador grunted uneasily. 'You are reporting on the commander's health?'

'Yes. As I promised. He is on inspection duty so I thought it opportune to update you. I'm of the opinion that the medication is helping, but it's hard to tell with our commander. He's seldom in a good mood. His loud belching has lessened and his explosive anger tantrums are a little less frequent – '

Orador, dry-mouthed with apprehension cut in. 'This is a secure channel?'

'Yes, yes, of course it is,' Badel reassured.

'I would like to prescribe further medication to our commander, but I can see no way that I could.' His voice lowered to a conspiratorial whisper. 'But I'm relieved that you have noticed an improvement in his digestive problems, and I am sure he would have got back to me if it hadn't been so. He expresses psychopathic tendencies that may be just a simple, chemical imbalance in the brain. But I wouldn't dare suggest that I test him for it.' Orador still nursed a vivid memory of his last encounter with Warstill.

'I can understand your dilemma,' Badel answered sympathetically. 'Now we are on the subject of the commander's head' – it took a deal of control for Badel to suppress a chuckle before continuing. 'Our commander was doing an inspection of the engineering department recently, and unfortunately he bashed his head on a girder –'

Orador cut in. 'He does seem to knock his head a lot. He's always in such a rush.'

'Yes he does,' agreed Badel. 'A female acquaintance of the commander heard of his latest accident and gave him a pink, padded bonnet for him to wear to afford protection.' Again, Badel paused to dampen a chuckle, before continuing. 'I have to tell you: he was not impressed. He told her in no uncertain terms, that he would look ridiculous, and it was not fitting for a commander to wear such a thing.'

The humour was lost on Orador. His attention was focused solely on Warstill's health. 'Thank you for updating me on the commander. As long as he shows improvement I will wait to see him on his next scheduled appointment.'

'In the meantime,' Badel replied in a monotone, 'I will let you know if there are any changes in our just and caring commander.'

Chapter Four

Lisa's eyes flickered open. She'd slept for two hours. A much needed respite from worrying about Amber and David's imminent and permanent separation. She felt refreshed and hoped the feeling would last. But how could it? she asked herself. All too soon she would be worn down once more with emotional turmoil. David was a regular human and aging was wired into the human genome. An all too brief life that was unsuitable for voyaging to the stars. They would remain out of his reach, and that was that. Jarrod was hurting too. She knew he was deeply concerned for his sister's well being. He'd told her he'd never seen Amber so disturbed. Her world was tilting out of balance and there was nothing he could do about it.

Lisa rolled off the bed, rose to her feet and made her way over to the view screen and turned it on. The room darkened as the screen lit up. The Moonbase telescope was aimed at a great star field in the constellation Sagittarius. She let her eyes trace the bands of crystal starlight. Smiling, eyes wide in wonder, she imagined herself drifting on the sea of stars, drinking in the freedom she felt at that moment.

*

David was alone in his quarters. He was glad that Amber had searched him out at the café and patched things up between them. He had wisely restrained himself from repeating to her the sliver of hope that Mathew had awakened in him. Better not to get her hopes up that there might yet be some way that they could remain together. Now, he pondered, who do I see at the top? The base commander? Or should it be the Foundation Director? I'll ask Bud for advice. But it all became academic. Bud's image generated itself on the computer.

'I have a message for you, David. The Foundation Director has arrived at the base and is requesting a meeting with you and your parents. He will see you in one hour at the base commander's quarters. Your father knows the location so it's suggested you join your parents shortly.'

'Do you know what the meeting's about, Bud?'

'No, David. I am not privy to that knowledge.'

Bud's image faded from the screen. David's stomach knotted in anticipation of the questions he would ask the Foundation Director. He felt the tension building. But he would not hold back. His future hinged on the answers.

*

The base commander's secretary, a tall, lean man, smiled politely and ushered the Whites into the commander's quarters. 'If you would kindly take a seat, the Foundation Director and the commander will be with you shortly.'

A flash of cold fear rippled through David. He felt sweat beads on his forehead as he nervously waited. His mother sat next to him on his left, and on her left, his father. On their way to the meeting David had noticed shadows deeply etched around his mother's eyes. He could tell she was worried and he was probably the cause of it. And now he was going to make it worse for her if the answers to his questions made it possible for him to take the road to the stars. All three of them were deep in thought.

The base commander and the Vision Foundation Director swept into the room and sat down behind the commander's expansive desk, directly across from the Whites. Floyd Burke, the Foundation Director was tall, slimly built with fair hair and blue eyes that gave nothing away.

In sharp contrast the base commander, Philip Wilson, had closely cropped dark hair and an olive complexion. His dark eyes scanned the trio opposite and acknowledged Gerald who he'd met once before with a nod.

Floyd Burke straightened in his chair. 'Thank you for coming,' he said politely. 'My colleague, Phillip Wilson, will be sitting in on the meeting.' He turned to Phillip. 'You have met Gerald White before, Commander, but let me introduce you to his wife, Dr Mary White and their son David. As you know they were very supportive of the Foundation when we needed them.'

'I'm honoured to meet you both,' Philip Wilson said in a

deep rich voice with genuine warmth. 'We were devastated that we couldn't save the planet. If we'd only had a little more time...'

'You did what you could and we're very grateful,' Mary White said. 'And with the help of your volunteers who are remaining with the colonists, humankind will have a better chance of surviving its darkest time in history.'

Philip Wilson nodded grimly. 'Yes I'm very proud of my volunteers.'

The Foundation Director leaned forward in his chair. 'The purpose of this meeting is to discuss the offer we made to you. It has been made known to us that the three of you have decided to remain on the Moon.' His gaze rested on David. 'We know that this has been a particularly difficult decision for you to make, David.'

'My decision was made reluctantly and was based on the fact that I wouldn't live long enough to explore other star-systems.' David paused for breath. 'And I didn't care for my friends to witness my aging while they remained young.'

'Based on what you know of our anti-aging technology, David, you made a wise decision,' the Foundation Director said smoothly. 'I have been in discussion with the commander of *Argo*, who as you know is the father of your friends, Amber and Jarrod. We have decided to reveal to the three of you, further information of our technology so that you may re-evaluate your decision to remain on Moonbase.'

'Oh?' David straightened in his chair. A flash of hope surged through him.

'But before we do,' Floyd Burke said, 'you must not divulge this knowledge to any of the colonists.' He gave them each a searching gaze. 'Do I have your word then?'

All three nodded silent acceptance.

'Very well, but I must warn you that the concept may be distasteful.' He paused a moment before continuing. 'When the colonists begin to age, we will be offering the deserving ones the same opportunity. As you know we have offered you anti-aging techniques that can double your life span. And David was right. It still wouldn't be long enough for voyages to the stars. We

56

can't offer you what we ourselves have. That technology is performed in gestation tanks where our children are conceived and born. But we can offer it to any children you may wish in the future – if you choose the artificial birthing tank option. Of course we wouldn't forbid you or the colonists choosing natural childbirth.'

David felt bleak and cold inside. It would be possible for his children to voyage to the stars, but not him or his parents.

'Thank you for the offer,' Gerald said, 'but my wife and I decided years ago not to have any more children.' And he didn't voice it, but it was unlikely they would have chosen the Foundation's birthing science. The concept was too alien.

Floyd nodded. 'I understand, Mr White.' He paused for long seconds. 'Before I broach the next part of our offer I must tell you that it's not the intention of the Foundation to offend any of you.' Floyd looked uneasily at his colleague, the base commander, before continuing. 'We can offer cloning.' There was a stunned silence. He studied the conflicting emotions that played on the faces sitting opposite. Gerald White's eyes narrowed warily and his lips compressed tightly in a thin angry line. Mary White looked interested and that could be understood because of her medical background. And David edged forward in his chair, his face suddenly flushed with hope.

Floyd Burke continued. 'We have stored denucleated eggs from which we can add your own DNA. Prior to cloning we would extract DNA from each of you and store it. Then we would give each of you cranial implants. These implants are not the same as the Foundation personnel have. That procedure was done prior to birth in our gestation tanks. Your cranial implants are very different. They will enable us to download your memories, your personality – your very essence periodically as you live out your extended lifetime and store them. Then when you die these memories and character traits will be selectively chosen and implanted back into your clone. At maturity these selected memories would be completely installed to your clone. This is as much as our technology can do for each of you. We've held nothing back, I promise you. Now I hope we haven't offended you all.'

57

No one said anything for a few moments. A clock on the wall measured the silence.

It was the base commander, Phillip Wilson who finally broke the silence. 'You could make any final decision on cloning at a later date. But we will have to know within twenty-four hours if any of you will be choosing the starship option. With the technology we can offer you, reality need not limit your dreams.'

'Can our clone be cloned again when it reaches the end of its lifetime?' David asked.

'Certainly, Phillip Wilson answered. 'As our technology advanced cloning became obsolete, but before it did, we were successful in cloning each individual eight times. Then for some inexplicable reason all attempts after that failed to survive a ninth cloning.'

'Does a clone live as long as the original individual?' David asked.

'Yes, David. Just as long as the original's extended life span. So eight clonings would equal one thousand two hundred years, and to that you would add the original individual's life span.'

The Foundation Director had been regarding warily, the faces of Dr White and Gerald, while Phillip Wilson had been answering David's questions. He noted Gerald White's head hunched forward, his mouth was set and rigid. Mary White's expression though, gave nothing away.

'Have you any questions, Dr White?' the Foundation Director asked.

Already she had no doubts that David would now choose to leave the Moon. His dream would now become a reality. But her husband beside her was another matter. She would have to tread carefully. 'I'm sure I will think of a number of questions after this meeting. But the question of cloning can be delayed for some considerable time regardless of whether we choose to remain on the Moon or not?'

'That's correct, Dr White. But we do have to know very soon if you wish to accompany us on *Argo*.'

There was an uneasy silence, which was finally broken by Floyd Burke.

'What are your thoughts, Mr White?'

Gerald straightened in his chair. The thought of cloning, cranial implants and children conceived and born in artificial gestation tanks chilled him. But he determined that he would try to be gracious. After all it was the high technology of the Foundation that had saved one thousand of Earth's finest minds he reasoned. 'My family is grateful for your kind offer and everything the Foundation has done for us. We will digest what you have told us and let you know by this time tomorrow?'

'That would be fine,' Floyd Burke agreed. 'There's one more thing I must mention. If you go ahead with cranial implants we can block out unpleasant memories if you so wish.'

The White's returned to David's quarters to discuss the mind blowing offer of the Foundation. David sat on the only chair in the room and faced his parents who sat opposite on his bed.

Gerald White fixed his gaze on his son. 'There's no doubt in my mind and probably your mother's that you are now going to choose to leave the Moon. Am I right?'

'Yes,' he said nervously but resolutely. 'The reality of what the Foundation has offered us has made my dream possible. I hope you'll choose to share that future with me?'

Mary White cut in quickly. She didn't want Gerald answering until she had time to work on him. 'Your father and I will need to discuss it and then get back to you.' She reached over to David and clasped his hands in hers. 'But we understand the offer of the Foundation is compelling and we respect your decision to leave the Moon.'

*

Amber had declined an invitation from Lisa and Jarrod to stroll with them to the park at the centre of town, as she was expecting David to come to her quarters after his meeting with the Foundation Director. She was in no doubt that the director would be requesting the White's to confirm their decision to

59

remain on the Moon. As she lay on her bed, a mood of melancholy descended and settled. Her soul felt as desolate as a lunar landscape. Her lashes were suddenly wet with tears. She curled into a ball and wished for sleep to embrace her with gentle arms and take her away.

*

Hand in hand, Lisa and Jarrod made their way over to a park seat in the town centre. They sat down with arms around each other's shoulders. Lisa wished there was something she could do to lift Jarrod's mood. But with the imminent departure of the three starships they would be leaving David and his parents behind – forever! And as Amber slipped further and further into a pit of despair, Jarrod was becoming increasingly worried about her. Then there was the possibility that she might choose to stay with David on the Moon.

Putting a hand on each side of Jarrod's face, Lisa turned it so that she could engage his eyes. They kissed gently but pulled away when they heard the sound of someone sobbing. They peered behind the seat. A little girl, dressed in a canary-yellow jumpsuit was sitting on the soft grass. Her head was bowed, her shoulders shaking.

Jarrod reached over and lightly touched the little girl's shoulder. Before he could speak she turned and gazed up at him with her tear stained-face.

'I miss my papa. I'll never see him again and I'm sad.' She was nursing a well-thumbed photo and with the directness of a child, she handed it to Jarrod. 'That's my papa.'

Jarrod studied the photo. The man was in his thirties. He had a broad nose, heavy brows, dark hair and strong jaw line. He was smiling. 'Your papa looks a nice man,' Jarrod said as he handed back the photo to the little girl.

'The angels have taken him away.' She blinked away the tears that were blurring her vision. 'One day I will see my papa again when I go to heaven.'

'But that won't be for a very long time,' Jarrod said gently. 'Is your mamma on the Moon?'

'Yes, and she cries a lot. She tries to hide it and I pretend not to notice.'

Wow, Jarrod thought to himself. Compassion and understanding in one so young. And then he remembered he shouldn't be surprised. All the colonists were chosen for their exceptional talents and intelligence.

'I sneaked out of our room while mamma was sleeping so I could be alone to cry. It only upsets her when she sees me cry.'

'That's very thoughtful of you, but if you don't get back to her she may wake and worry where you are.' He gave her a soft smile.

She responded by smiling shyly back. 'My name's Bridgett and I'm seven years old. What is your name?'

'Jarrod, and my friend is Lisa.'

The little girl barely glanced at Lisa. 'Is she your girlfriend?'

'Yes, Bridgett, she is.'

'I like you, Jarrod,' she said candidly. 'Can I be your friend?'

Jarrod was touched. 'Of course you can, but Lisa and I will be leaving the Moon very soon on one of the starships.'

She frowned. 'Where are you going?'

'We are going to search for another Earth-like planet as well as hunt down the aliens that destroyed Earth.'

Bridgett's large dark eyes widened. 'Could mamma and me come with you?'

'I don't think that would be possible, Bridgett.'

'Couldn't you ask the captain of your spaceship? Please, please,' she pleaded.

He glanced uneasily at Lisa. It wasn't like her not to have any input.

Lisa shrugged her shoulders and shook her head. 'I've absolutely no idea what you two have been discussing. I only understood a few words. You've been talking in French!'

'Yes I have,' he suddenly realised. 'Another one of my enhancements, but not one of yours obviously. It must have been triggered as soon as Bridgett spoke.' He quickly explained the situation to Lisa, while the little girl waited patiently.

Bridgett rose to her feet and moved around from the back of the park seat so that she faced Jarrod and Lisa. Her hands were behind her back, her chubby fingers crossed.

Jarrod turned his attention back to the little French girl. 'Now, Bridgett,' he said, reverting back to French. 'It so happens that I have a close connection to the commander of starship *Argo*. I can make a request to him and he in turn can discuss it with the Foundation Director and see if it would be possible for you and your mamma to come with us. But I must warn you that it's not likely that they will agree to it. There are problems that would have to be overcome, and only the Foundation Director is at liberty to reveal them, which I'm sure he will do if he grants an interview with you and your mamma. Of course your mamma may not want to leave the Moon.'

'Oh yes she will,' Bridgett said with conviction. 'She's told me lots and lots of times that she wonders what it would be like to travel on a wave of light and explore the universe with me and papa. It's been a dream of hers. Just like Mr Einstein.'

'Your mamma and you must have special talents to have been chosen as colonists?'

'Mamma is an astrophysicist. She knows lots and lots of things.'

'And what about you, Bridgett?'

'In Paris I went to a special school for gifted children. I find mathematics very interesting and I love music. I play the piano and violin,' she said enthusiastically. 'But I couldn't bring our piano to the Moon – just my violin.'

It was an interesting statistic; Jarrod mused to himself, how music and mathematics often went hand in hand. If you were good at one then you would probably be good at the other. 'Perhaps they have a piano on Moonbase that you can use.'

'Perhaps,' she shrugged. 'Do you know if there's one on your starship?'

'I haven't come across one but there's still a lot of *Argo* that I've yet to see. I can make some inquiries, if you'd like'

'Wait and see if mamma and I can go with you first,' she said practically.

Jarrod was interested to know what her papa did but

thought it wise to wait until she mentioned him again.

'I noticed you spoke English very well, Jarrod. I could tell, you see, because I can speak it a little too.'

Jarrod's eyebrows lifted in surprise. 'That's because I am English, Bridgett.'

'Oh, I thought you were French like me,' she giggled. 'You don't have an accent and you even look French.' She gazed up at him. 'You are kidding me – yes?'

'No,' he chuckled. 'I kid you not! Now lets speak English so Lisa can join in.'

'Okay.' She looked embarrassed. She gave Lisa a shy smile. 'My English … It is not good, Lisa,' she said haltingly. 'If mamma and I go on the spaceship, you and Jarrod can teach me to speak English very good, yes?'

'We'd be happy to Bridgett.' Lisa was captivated by the little girl's accent. And she looked so cute in her little yellow jumpsuit with her long, honey-coloured hair that had so far escaped practical cropping; contrasting her large dark eyes.

'Would you like us to come with you back to your quarters?' Lisa enquired. 'Your mamma might be getting worried.'

'Yes I would like that.' She turned and reached up to Jarrod. 'Carry me please, Jarrod? I don't weigh much on the Moon.'

He stooped down and lifted her to his chest. She pointed directions to her quarters and they started off.

Bridgett nestled her head in the nape of his neck. 'You don't think I'm too young to be your friend do you, Jarrod? I've always got on better with older people.'

'Lisa and I would love to be your friend, Bridgett.' He was feeling tenderness towards the little girl. It was a new experience for him. 'What's your full name?'

'Bridgett Chantal Michaiels.'

'And your mother's full name?'

'Nicolette Jacqueline Michaiels.'

After checking the spelling of Bridgett's surname, Jarrod committed it to memory.

Despite her claim, Bridgett's English was surprisingly

good. She continued to chatter away and shrieked with laughter when Jarrod, from time, leapt up high, almost touching the corridor's ceiling before surrendering to the pull of the weak Lunar gravity.

'Oh, there's mamma.' Bridgett waved towards the figure at the end of the corridor. Jarrod gently lowered her to the ground and she rushed towards her mother.

Nicolette Michaiels waved back and walked towards them with a distinct limp due to a congenital dislocation of her hip that hadn't been caught in time.

As they got close, Jarrod and Lisa could see the expression of relief on her face.

Nicolette was a petite, finely boned woman with a pale complexion – a fragile beauty. Her light-brown hair reached the shoulders of her deep-green jumpsuit. She rested a hand on Bridgett's shoulder. 'I was worried about you, Bridgett,' she scolded gently in French. 'Where have you been?'

'Down at the park. I have met two nice people, Mamma, she said excitedly. 'Jarrod and Lisa. They are from England.'

'I want to thank you both for taking care of my daughter,' she said, reverting to English with a delightful accent. She paused for half a second. 'Jarrod and Lisa?'

'Yes, Madame Michaeils,' Jarrod acknowledged.

'Oh please. Just call me Nikki. I hope she hasn't been a nuisance?'

'Not at all. Quite the contrary in fact. She's been a delight.'

'Mamma,' Bridgett said excitedly. 'Jarrod and Lisa are leaving soon on the spaceship *Argo*,' she said, her words tumbling over each other. 'They are going to look for more planets like Earth and hunt down the nasty aliens who destroyed Earth.' She took a quick breath. 'Mamma, I told them you were not happy on the Moon and you have always dreamt of travelling to the stars. Jarrod said we might be able to go on the spaceship too. So can we? Please, please, Mamma.'

Nicolette's eyes widened in surprise and hope. She turned to Jarrod. 'Is this true? Is there some way that we would be allowed to go with both of you on *Argo*?'

'All I can do is put a request in for you. But would you

64

wish to spend the rest of your lives on a spaceship with very little chance of ever finding another Earth?'

'Oh yes,' she said quickly. 'Without a doubt! Your spaceship is as big as a small world anyway. It would become our home. We could learn so much.' Her eyes clouded. 'And we wouldn't have to view the sad sight of Earth anymore. Bridgett is very young, but even so, she shares my dream.'

'Very well,' said Jarrod. 'I will put in your request and if there is any chance at all of joining us, you will be granted an interview.'

'Oh that would be wonderful.' She turned to Bridgett and hugged her. On impulse she turned to Jarrod and covered his hands in hers. 'We're so grateful to you, Jarrod, for offering us this chance.'

'Well, we wish you the best of luck, Madame...er, Nikki. If your request is successful we will see you on *Argo*. If not, I'm afraid our paths will not cross again.'

Nicolette's eyes began to water as conflicting emotions of sadness and hope played on her face. She hugged Jarrod and then Lisa without speaking.

Then Bridgett stepped forward and hugged Jarrod and Lisa. 'I hope I see you both again,' the little girl said, her voice choking in her throat.

Chapter Five

'Mary, it's not uncommon for children to leave the nest when they reach David's age,' Gerald argued.

'I know that,' she said crossly, 'but at least they were confined to planet Earth for goodness sake. If we stay on the Moon we'll never see our son again! Is that what you want?'

'Of course it's not what I want,' he said testily. 'I'm just hoping David will see sense and remain at Moonbase.'

'It's just not going to happen, Gerald. Put yourself in his place. Would you choose to remain exiled on the Moon? Or would you reach out to the stars with your friends and the woman you love? I think the latter. Don't you?'

'Yes. You're right,' he said resignedly. 'But let's wait a little longer before we make our decision.'

'Gerald, I have to know what your decision will be if David doesn't change his mind. It's tearing me apart! You have to tell me!' She bowed her head and started to weep.

Gerald gently touched her arm. 'We said we'd let the Foundation Director know within twenty-four hours,' Gerald said softly. 'Let's at least wait till then. If David doesn't change his mind in that time, then of course we will join him on *Argo*.'

Mary's anxiety lifted. She dabbed at her tears.

*

'Amber. Wake up, wake up, Amber,' said the insistent voice.

The voice seemed to come to her in a spirit-like form from some remote locale. At first she ignored it, but it persisted. The voice would not let her be. She tried to open her eyelids but they were too heavy and she drifted off once more.

Finally she woke to Beth's urging that she do so. 'You have a visitor. It's David. Do you wish to see him?'

A tide of urgency swept through her. She cleared her throat and licked her dry lips. 'Of course I wish to see him, Beth. Please let him enter.' She rolled off the bed and straightened her creased jumpsuit. Her heart thundered in her ears. The waiting was nearly over.

The door to her quarters opened smoothly. David paused in the doorway, his expression neutral. Then he stepped forward, grinning.

Amber had been holding her breath too long. Now it came rasping out of her in a long, painful sigh. 'I hope that grin means what I think it does?'

'Yes. I will be joining you on *Argo*.'

Her eyes widened. 'Really?'

'Oh, yes. You're stuck with me I'm afraid.'

Amber bowed her head and closed her eyes briefly to hide her emotion.

David moved closer and rested his hands on her shoulders. 'You are all right with that?'

She lifted her head once more. She leaned closer, her eyes filling his. She brushed his cheek. 'Of course I'm all right with it,' she answered, her relief clearly visible. 'But what about the fact that I won't age and you will? Have you come to terms with that?'

'Yes,' he nodded. 'My parents and I have had a meeting with the Foundation Director. They made an offer to us that I cannot refuse.' He paused a brief moment. A trace of worry crossed his face. 'Though what my parents choose to do I can't say.' Then he explained the technology that was revealed to them. 'Much of each lifetime, courtesy of cloning will mean that I will be out of sync with you. In my age treated extended lifetime, I will grow old before your eyes – but slowly, and eventually die. Then I will be reborn as a baby – a baby clone, and my life cycle will start once more.

'But what about your lifetime's memory and your personality?'

'My memories and personality, I was told would gradually, over time be restored. Would you be all right with that?' he asked uncertainly.

'It's more than I could have ever hoped for,' she said with a slowly drawn smile. 'Much, much more!'

67

There was an air of anticipation in the knot of people milling around the town centre. Launch to the stars was just twelve hours away. Only the colonists and a handful of Moonbase volunteers would remain on the Moon. The rest would soon be threading their way through the transit tunnel to board the starship *Orion*. The Foundation was leaving a legacy to Moonbase – *Aquilla*, the orbiting space station and mining vessel *Prospector* to the colonists. *Prospector* would continue to sail the sea of small worlds between Mars and Jupiter, and carefully divert the orbits of selected asteroids to lunar orbit as required, where the colonists would mine them.

David's parents had finally confirmed their acceptance of the Foundation's offer to leave Moonbase and make *Argo* their home. They, along with David, Lisa and the twins, would be on the first of three transporter flights ferrying passengers to *Argo* in closed lunar orbit.

Jarrod had left the confinement of his cabin to stroll around the base one last time. He was anxious to know if his endeavour on behalf of Bridgett Michaiels and her mother had been successful. He'd tried to get confirmation from Basil earlier, to see if any meeting had taken place between them and the Vision Foundation Director, but his computer had no knowledge of any such meeting. His request to communicate with the director or the base commander had been denied. He considered going to Nikki and Bridgett's cabin to see if they'd heard anything, but immediately dismissed the idea. If their request to leave Moonbase had been denied, it wouldn't help the situation by seeing them again. It would be upsetting for all of them.

He was greatly relieved that David and his parents would be joining them on *Argo*. And to see the light back in his sister's eyes once again, lifted his spirits. But for now, his concern was for Bridgett.

*

'What's in the little jar you're packing away, Gerald?'

His face coloured in embarrassment at being caught out. 'It's err … lunar dust,' he said defensively and cleared his throat. 'Sentimental of me, I know, but I just wanted to take a little of it with us. Every time the jar is opened, I will be reminded of the scent of the Moon. It will bring back memories. And who knows. We may never set foot on a solid surface again.'

'You've every right to be a little sentimental. I know that you love the Moon, and you were settling in so well. Now we've forced you to leave,' she said guiltily.

'Mary, there was no choice. I realise that now. We could not be separated from David, after what we've all been through.'

*

Lisa and Jarrod had been on the first ferry load of passengers from the Moon to disembark on *Argo*. An hour later the second ferry had discharged its cargo of personnel, but Bridgett and her mother were not among them.

Lisa and Jarrod anxiously peered out the large view port in *Argo's* observation area and watched the third and final ferry approach. Below, the cratered lunar terrain changed as the great ship orbited. A refuge for mankind on an ancient scarred world. The colonists faced a challenge like no other in the history of the human species. Children born beneath the black sky would never know seasons; couldn't imagine restless oceans or an atmospheric sunset, nor experience the caress of a sweet summer breeze.

All these thoughts went through Jarrod's mind, as he watched the little ferry adjust its alignment to the starship with short puffs of its attitude jets, edging closer and closer until finally docking with the starship. Jarrod felt the faint vibration through the soles of his boots as the mooring latches engaged and *Argo* absorbed the last of the ferry's forward momentum. *Orion* would soon join *Argo* and *Vela* in lunar orbit. Communication between the vessels was by way of Laser Communications Systems (LCO). Twelve hours of final checks would then be carried out and if satisfactory, the starships would blast off into the dark reaches of space. But for now Jarrod was content to remain glued to the view port a few moments longer. After all, they wouldn't be this close to a world again for a very long time. Then he and Lisa would go to the transporter chamber's exit to see if the little French girl and her mother were among the final ferry load of personnel.

*

Orion's double belt of pale green lights began to spin faster and faster and became uninterrupted ribbons of light. The ground beneath the mighty ship began to vibrate, but there was no noise on the airless world. Then *Orion* lifted off its scorched pad on a column of white light – slowly at first, then gradually increasing in speed, easily defying the weak lunar gravity for the short trip to rendezvous orbit with her two sister-ships.

*

'Good morning, David.'

David was sitting on the edge of his bed, alone with his thoughts, recalling how Earth used to be. He turned his head to his computer. 'Good morning, Bud,' he responded. 'Sorry for neglecting you lately. I know how much you like to interact with humans, but there's been so much going on. How are you?'

Bud gave a gracious nod. 'Thank you for asking, David. I am completely operational and my circuits are functioning perfectly, but I have missed your companionship. Could you spare me some of your time, David? There must be many questions you would like to ask me.'

David rose from his bed and strode over to the computer and sank down in the chair, and felt it adjust to accommodate him. Strange he thought to himself how a computer could be lonely. 'I've been involved in my own problems, but now they've been sorted.'

'I am glad to hear that, David.'

'Right. Now … err questions. Let me see.' He paused a moment. 'Ah, yes. I've been meaning to ask you this for a long time.'

'Yes, David?' Bud prompted.

'Except for my three friends, Amber, Jarrod and Lisa, all of the Vision Foundation and Moonbase personnel were born in space.'

'That is correct, David. They were direct descendants of early man from DNA harvested by a visiting alien race. This space faring nation recognised that although early man was primitive, they were nevertheless intelligent. In fact they were in no way inferior to modern man in intellectual potential. They considered them to be an endangered species, and worthy of saving, so another human race was produced far from Earth, and of course their evolution progressed in a different direction than yours, David.'

'Looking like us, they assimilated easily and remained undetected for twenty years, but what I don't understand is how could they speak the languages of Earth? Early man to my knowledge had no language other than perhaps a little rudimentary sign language.'

'For most of their long journey to Earth, they had no knowledge of Earth's languages. It wasn't until one hundred years ago that they first received faint cracklings of early radio broadcasts. Then around sixty years ago they started to receive Earth's first television programs. That's how they learned the languages.'

'Of course. I should have realised. And the television would have shown them how to dress and understand mannerisms.'

'Precisely, David. And now you are going to become a citizen of the cosmos and join your alien brothers and sisters in the exploration of it. How exciting!'

'I agree. Now another question, Bud. How did they navigate starships back to Earth after all those centuries of man's evolution?'

'They knew that Earth's sun was situated on the outskirts of the Sagittarius spiral arm and about halfway from the galactic centre. So that's the direction that they headed for. But of course after all that time they knew the sun and it's planets would have strayed with all the gravitational tugs at its system. They hoped that radio would have been discovered and so direct them to the solar system. As luck would have it, that was the case and they followed the radio waves back to their spiritual home.'

David was totally engrossed in Bud's explanation. Bud's image faded and the Milky Way Galaxy lit up on the screen. David narrowed his eyes against the brightness.

'Now,' Bud's voice instructed. 'Look at the centre of the galaxy then scan to the left. See the small blinking red arrow?'

'Yes. Got it.'

'That's the sun. The planets are too small on this scale to show you.'

'All those stars,' David whispered. 'And that's just one galaxy of millions,' he added.

'Billions,' Bud corrected.

The galaxy of stars slid from the screen and Bud's image returned once more.

'One day, David,' he said solemnly, 'all those galaxies except for our local group that's bound together by gravity will disappear. They are receding at the speed of light from us. With this cosmic acceleration, distant parts of the Universe will disappear forever over what is called the de Sitter horizon. This horizon is the point of no return. Anything beyond it is gone forever. One by one, each galaxy will wink out.' Bud's voice took on an even sombre tone. 'So, David, the space beyond our galactic neighbourhood will become a very cold, lonely and dark place.'

*

Jarrod and Lisa waited anxiously for the transporter room's hatch to open. The minutes stretched. Finally it irised open and personnel assigned to *Argo* filed out. But there was no sign of the little French girl and her mother. They waited another five minutes, then tearing their gaze away from the open hatch they exchanged disappointed glances.

Jarrod shook his head, 'Sadly, it's what I expected. Poor little Bridgett.'

Lisa covered his hand with her own. 'You did your best,' she said softly.

They glanced once more at the open hatch in forlorn hope before making their way slowly back to Jarrod's cabin.

*

The Foundation's evolution progressed in a vastly different direction than Earth's. Although technologically far ahead, the Foundation was in awe of Earth's arts. The Foundation had never developed sculptures or paintings to any great degree unless there was a practical reason to do so. Nor had music and dance advanced to the extent it had on Earth. Their latent interest had been awakened by radio and television broadcasts picked up by their spacecraft scores of years ago, and had guided their mighty ship to Earth's shores.

*

'Two visitors wish to see you, Jarrod. I have checked their identity with Control and have added them to my memory circuits. They are the last of the indigenous humans via Moonbase to be granted residency on *Argo*.'

Jarrod and Lisa's spirits lifted. Dare they hope? 'Their names?' Jarrod stabbed out the question. 'What's their names?'

'Nicolette Jacqueline Michaiels and her daughter Bridgett Chantal Michaiels. Do you wish for them to enter?'

'Yes, yes, yes, Basil. Let them enter,' he said eagerly.

In Argo's artificial lunar gravity, Bridgett reached Jarrod in four loping strides. She hugged him around his legs. 'I am so, so happy,' she said, remembering to speak in English for Lisa's benefit.

'You've been granted your request for residency on *Argo*?' Jarrod's question was directed at Bridgett's mother.

'Yes, and we are so grateful to you for your help in making it possible.'

'Lisa and I waited to see if you were both on the last ferry load of passengers. I'm puzzled as to how we could have missed you?'

Bridgett released her vice grip of Jarrod's legs and was

giving Lisa a hug in the same fashion. 'I was sick, so we did not get off the ferry straight way. Mamma said it was through too much ex … excitement.'

Bridgett released Lisa's legs and shuffled around the cabin. Her face was animated, her hands a flurry of gestures. 'When can you show me over the ship, Jarrod?'

'It's a very big ship and I am only familiar with some of its areas. We have some time before we accelerate out of orbit and head for the stars, so we can start with the observation area. It's one of our favourite spots.'

'Oh look.' Bridgett giggled. 'You are on the computer screen.'

Jarrod turned to the computer, surprised that Basil was still present. 'It's not me, Bridgett. Let me introduce you to, Basil. He looks like me because he modelled himself off my image.'

'I am pleased to meet you, Bridgett Chantal Michaiels. And I am pleased to meet you, Madame Nicolette Jacqueline Michaiels.'

Bridgett and her mother nodded, smiling. 'And we are pleased to meet you, Basil,' Nicolette replied.

'How do you know our names?' Bridgett asked. 'I do not remember our names being mentioned since we arrived at the cabin.'

'You are correct, Bridgett Chantal Michaiels. Your identities were given to me by Control at my request when you arrived at the cabin.'

'You don't have to say all my names, Basil,' she said seriously.

'I am sorry, Mademoiselle Bridgett Chantal Michaiels. How would you like me to address you?'

Bridgett shrieked with laughter. 'Bridgett! Just Bridgett!'

Basil was unsure why Bridgett laughed, but it gave his circuits joy.

'And you can address me as Nikki. All my friends do.'

'You have known me for three minutes and twenty seconds, Nikki and already you have accepted me as a friend. I find that remarkable, and I am delighted. Any questions that you ask me now or in the future, I will answer with infinite patience and understanding.'

'Can I be your friend too, Basil? Please, please!' Bridgett asked.

'I am delighted to be your friend, Bridgett.'

Basil's image faded from the screen. 'You both made a good impression on Basil,' Jarrod remarked.

As the mobile path took them smoothly away from Jarrod's cabin, Bridgett asked, 'will Mamma and I get our own computer?'

'I'm sure you will, Bridgett.'

'Look. That is our cabin,' she pointed. 'It is just five doors down from yours.'

'That's convenient.'

'Nikki laughed. Not too convenient I hope, Jarrod. We must not make a nuisance of ourselves.'

'I'm sure you won't be any nuisance,' Jarrod countered.

Jarrod glanced over his shoulder to Lisa who was standing directly behind him. 'You're very quiet,' he commented.

Lisa chuckled. 'You've all lapsed back into French. But I really don't mind. It's such a beautiful sounding language. Perhaps Bridgett can teach me to speak French?'

'Sorry, Lisa. I keep forgetting to speak English,' Bridgett apologised. 'Forget me. No that's not right. Forgave me.' She looked at Lisa for guidance. 'No?'

'Forgive me is the word you're looking for, Bridgett.'

Bridgett giggled. 'Yes I will teach you French, and you can help me with my English.'

Bridgett and Nikki's eyes were being dragged in every direction, taking in the architecture of the ship with quiet wonder. They'd been told that the Foundation was well behind the Earth in art but Nikki found this hard to believe. *Argo* was a truly magnificent, living breathing sculpture.

Stepping off the pathway at the entrance of the observation area, they paused briefly to allow twin transparent doors to automatically open. They entered the large chamber with its vaulted ceiling. Clear flexiglass spread across one full wall, so clear and pristine that there seemed to be nothing at all between them and the Moon below. Bridgett shuffled nervously towards the glass, dragging her mother who was clasping her hand along with her. Stopping abruptly, she reached out tentatively to touch the glass, to satisfy herself that there really was something between them and the lunar landscape below.

Giuseppe Verdi's opera, *Nabucco*, began to play over the sound system to add to the unreal but exciting atmosphere of the chamber.

'Press yourself against the glass, Bridgett,' Lisa suggested. 'It will feel like you're flying over the Moon.'

'I might fall through the glass,' she said fearfully.

'That can't happen. The glass is extremely tough. Look I'll show you.' Lisa spread-eagled herself against the glass to reassure Bridgett.

Bridgett moved tentatively forward.

'Don't worry,' Jarrod said. 'I will hold you. You can't fall.'

She felt his hands holding her gently. Reassured she stretched out against the glass. Nikki joined her. Below them, a strange barren vista stretched out before them. The ancient lunar mountains were awash with sunlight, and at their base, cast long shadows across a cracked and cratered plain.

Nikki found herself catching her breath at the lunar landscape. She glanced over to Lisa. 'The topography has a strange beauty. And the glass is so clear that it feels there is nothing between us and the Moon below. It's as if there is an invisible force-field holding me up – not the glass.'

'It is definitely glass,' Lisa chuckled. 'It's called flexiglass. It is extremely tough and gets its name because it's actually flexible. Its molecular structure allows its molecules to adjust to whatever pressure is placed upon it, without compromising its strength, or its seal with the metal hull of the ship.'

'Fascinating.' Nikki made a mental note to explore in greater details the molecular structure of the glass with the Foundation scientists.

Bridgett's face was animated. 'It really does feel like we are flying over the Moon,' she said excitedly. 'And it is so beautiful!'

'I'm sure it's not too late for you and your mother to change your minds and return to the Moon if you wish? Even though,' Jarrod pointed out, 'it would make Lisa and me sad.'

'Oh no, no, no,' Bridgett shook her head at the suggestion. 'Mamma and I will not be returning to the Moon,' she said with conviction. She turned to Nikki. 'Isn't that right, Mamma?'

'Yes, dear. Don't fret. Jarrod was just making sure, that's all.'

'And I'm very pleased to hear it,' he said with a slowly drawn smile.

Reassured, Bridgett returned her attention to the Moon below.

It was hard to drag Bridgett and Nikki away from the observation chamber, but time was limited and Jarrod was keen to show them the telescope observatory. They had just one hour left before Nikki and Bridgett had to return to their cabin for a pre-launch briefing and receive their pressure suits.

'How do you know the way?' Lisa asked Jarrod as they strode along a corridor without the assistance of a mobile path. 'You've never been to the telescope observatory before.'

'I had Basil show me a schematic of the ship and he pointed it out.'

'How much further, Jarrod?' Bridgett asked excitedly.

He glanced over his shoulder at Bridgett. 'It's just around the next corner.'

As they turned the bend, the corridor came to an abrupt dead-end. Two silver-metal doors whispered open and they entered the chamber, which was illuminated in dim red light.

There was a bank of monitors at eye level and a lower central display. Jarrod sat down and tapped out a command into the central processing unit.

Lisa gazed over to Nikki and Bridgett with a puzzled frown and shrugged her shoulders, then hunkered down beside Jarrod. 'You seem to know what you're doing, but you've never been in this area before. How come?'

'Memory came surging into my awareness as soon as I entered the room. Everything is familiar. It has to be implanted memory, just like my piloting skills.'

Lisa nodded her understanding, but Nikki and Bridgett sported puzzled looks.

'Where is the telescope?' Bridgett asked.

'It is in another chamber. I will be operating it remotely. I have opened its shutters to the vacuum of space. We will see on the screens what the telescope focuses on.' His fingers danced over the keyboard once more. 'I have set it on a half-hour programme instead of giving it specific instructions. Let's see what it comes up with.'

For a brief moment there was almost total silence broken only by the slight murmur of ventilating air. Then a star-field came into view on the central display – a myriad of suns shining with steady, unblinking light. And then the bank of monitors above the central display came alive with the same view, which was at convenient eye level for Nikki and Lisa, who were both standing. Bridgett, being shorter, gazed at the lower central display.

'Welcome,' said the synthesized voice of the computer. 'You have chosen a random half-hour program. The stars that you see on-screen are part of the Sagittarius star-field and are unmagnified. It's just one of many star-fields in the Milky Way Galaxy. The galaxy's disc is three thousand light-years thick, and one hundred thousand light-years across.'

They took in the starry expanse of sky. It was spectacular but no more than what could be viewed from the Moon with the naked eye. There was expectant silence as they waited for the programme to continue. The star-field faded.

'The next scenes are under high magnification and in real time. Between each scene there will be a brief pause as the telescope is re-directed.'

They could hear the faint working of hydraulics as the telescope sought its target, then silence. At first the image lighting up the monitors was out of focus, then it sharpened into a magnificent sight that all except Bridgett recognised.

The computer's synthesized voice continued. 'This is the *Dumb-Bell Nebula* in *Vulpecula*. It is a sphere of gas ejected by a small, hot blue star at its centre. The star's ultraviolet rays cause the gas to fluoresce colourfully. The central regions contain the most gas and glows hotter and bluer than the thin red outer edges.' Again there was silence as they took in the

78

magnificent spectacle until it faded from the screen.

They all recognised the next telescopic view as it was brought into sharp focus.

'That is the *Orion Nebula*, Mamma,' squealed Bridgett delightedly. 'It is so pretty.'

'Yes, dear, but hush. We mustn't interrupt the computer's description.'

'*Theta Orionis* is the sparkling middle "star" in the sword of *Orion*. But it's not a star. It is a gaseous cloud illuminated by radiation from hot stars embedded in it. It is a star nursery where new stars are being born out of the tenuous interstellar material.'

They gazed silently in awe at the nebula until it faded from the screen and was replaced by a magnificent example of a spiral galaxy.

'Do you recognise it, Bridgett?'

'I think I do, Mamma. Is it the *Andromeda Galaxy*?'

'Yes, dear. It is.'

Jarrod and Lisa exchanged glances. They were impressed that a little girl of such tender years could know so much. But of course, all the thousand souls rescued by the Foundation were especially talented.

The computer continued its lecture. 'The *Andromeda Galaxy* is two million light-years away, acting like a giant counterweight to the *Milky Way Galaxy* and is in the same local group of galaxies. Its tightly wound spiral arms glow blue with the light of massive young stars. Its hub consists of mostly burnt out stars. To the left of the hub and towards the lower right are *Andromeda's* two satellite elliptical galaxies, NGC 205 and NGC 221.

After three minutes *Andromeda* winked out. 'Due to instruction from control the half-hour program cannot be continued,' the dulcet tone of the computer informed them. 'All entertainment and educational areas are now out of bounds due to the scheduled launch of the Foundation starships.'

*

Alone in their cabin, Nikki and Bridgett were immersed in

thought as they waited for their scheduled pre-launch briefing. Their inspection of the Moon in the observation area had been exhilarating, and the foreshortened visit to the ship's telescope chamber had been equally so. But how did Jarrod know how to operate the telescope's complicated controls? Nikki pondered. She gazed over to Bridgett who was studying a beautiful nebula. Its diaphanous filigree of red and blue stretched across the cabin's single wall screen.

Bridgett turned to her mother. 'What's the nebula's name, Mamma?'

'That's the *Veil Nebula* in *Cygnus the Swan*, dear.'

'The blue colour is hotter than the red, just like the *Dumb-Bell Nebula* we saw through the telescope?'

'That's right, Bridgett. The nebula is part of what once must have been the outer layers of an unstable star that exploded around fifty thousand years ago. If I recall correctly, the gas is three hundred billion miles wide and still expanding.'

'Oh, Mamma. You know so much. Do you think I will be clever enough to be an astrophysicist like you?'

'Of course you are clever enough, Bridgett. You can be anything you want to be.' But who is going to teach her? Nikki asked herself. Who will have the time? Jarrod had informed her that Bridgett was the only child on the starship. On any of the three starships in fact. All Earth's remaining children were colonists on the Moon. And soon light years would separate the starships from humankind's last outpost.

A knock on the door announced the arrival of the pre-launch advisor. As there was no computer to instruct the door to open, Bridgett rushed to the door and pressed a green button, just as she'd been shown when they had first been escorted to their quarters. The instructor entered and the door automatically closed after her.

The attractive dark-haired woman introduced herself. 'I'm Mirim,' she smiled at Nikki and Bridgett. 'I've heard so much about you from my son, Jarrod.'

'But…but you're so young,' Nikki said haltingly. 'Surely too young to be Jarrod's mother?'

'I assure you that I am his mother,' she chuckled. 'There

are many things that you and Bridgett will have to come to terms with through the years ahead. One of those things is that no one from the Foundation will ever look old.'

And then it dawned on Nikki. On Moonbase and *Argo* for that matter, she'd never seen anyone who looked old. Jarrod's mother looked like she was in her mid twenties. And she looked stunning in her forest-green jumpsuit.

Mirim broke the stunned silence. 'Well we must press on.' She handed them each their silver pressure suits and requested they put them on. She watched keenly and gave advice when it was needed.

'Now, how does that feel?' Mirim asked.

Bridgett giggled. 'Feels funny.' She clomped awkwardly over to a full-length mirror that was fixed to the wall between their two beds. 'I look like an astronaut.'

'Now put the helmet on, Bridgett, and you really will be an astronaut,' Mirim smiled. 'Leave the visor up, though.'

She did as requested and continued to giggle.

Nikki went through the same procedure with the helmet and heard it click when it locked into place.

These suits you are wearing prevent blood pooling in the extremities of your bodies in high Gs. Close the visors when requested to do so, otherwise leave them open. It only takes a second to close them in an emergency.'

Mirim told them where to report for the pre-launch and explained the chair positions, although not in great detail, as Jarrod would be there to supervise them.

'Why the high Gs?' Nikki asked. 'We are in orbit. I wouldn't have thought it necessary.'

'We wish to intersect the orbits of Jupiter and Saturn and use their gravity-well to save the ship's energy reserves. We are not actually in high G's now, but it feels like it because you've become accustomed to the Moon's gravity. At present, we are at half Earth gravity and gradually increasing it to make it easier for our bodies to adapt to high G's later. You see our window of opportunity requires us to accelerate at high G's to arrive at a predetermined point close to Jupiter. A slingshot effect from the planet's huge gravitational field will accelerate us towards

Saturn, where again we will make use of that planet's gravity-well.'

'But Jupiter is surrounded by a shell of high-energy charged particles,' Nikki challenged with concern. 'Won't that fry the ship's electronics?' And maybe us, she added silently.

'We are certainly aware of the radiation danger but we won't be going close enough for it to damage us or *Argo's* delicate instruments.'

'I apologise, Mirim. Of course I'm sure the crew of *Argo* knows what it's doing.'

'You mustn't apologise. Never be afraid to question anything you're not sure of, especially if you think something might pose a danger. We have a rule – never assume anything! That's how we've been able to survive so long.'

'Well, if you're sure,' Nikki said uncertainly. 'But we don't want to become a nuisance.'

'Of course you won't.' Mirim turned to Bridgett. 'And don't you be afraid to ask all the questions you want,' she said with a slowly drawn smile. 'Anyway you will have your own computer installed in your cabin soon so you will be able to direct most of your questions to her.'

'Our computer's a her?' Bridgett asked.

'That's right. Her name is Beatrice.'

Bridgett laughed so much her eyes began to water. 'That's a grandma name.'

'Don't let her hear you say that,' Mirim warned mildly. 'You might hurt her feelings.'

'Really?'

'Yes, Bridgett. Just treat her like a true friend – a super intelligent friend. She will never get tired of answering questions. The more the better.'

'No problem there,' Nikki chuckled. 'I'm sure my daughter will keep Beatrice very busy.'

Chapter Six

Foundation Director, Floyd Burke frowned anxiously as his eyes swept over the message coming in on his monitor, informing him of major unrest on Moonbase. Demonstrations by the colonists were causing deep concern to the heavily outnumbered Moonbase personnel. Many of the colonists were being persuaded to believe that it was the Foundation that had targeted killer asteroids at Earth; that the world's leaders had been conned into believing it was the Drogs, an old enemy of the Foundation, that were responsible. The individual making these claims and stirring up trouble had been taken into custody and isolated from his followers.

Floyd Burke felt bleak and cold inside. He shook his head in disbelief. Bloody ungrateful sod, he thought to himself. The message continued.

Agent of discord is thirty-two year old New Zealander, Dr Adrian O'Connor BHB MBChB B.Sc. A brilliant academic, he qualified top in both medicine and surgery at Auckland Medical School (recipient of the David Pullar Prize) and gained top student honours in computer information technology at Otago University. After qualifying he spent two years as a junior doctor in Auckland Hospital. Then for the next four years was employed as a troubleshooter for a large medical software company, travelling the world to hospitals that were having medical and administrative difficulties. After identifying their particular problems, he then designed and developed computer software to solve them. For the last two years the New Zealand government recruited him as a computer analyst. A more detailed academic record of Doctor O'Connor is available on request. Message ends. Photo of Dr O'Connor follows.

Floyd Burke stared at the austere presence on his monitor with disbelief. Glacial blue eyes stared back from the central display – mocking. He remembered those eyes well. His anger rose, threatening to overwhelm him. He turned to *Argo's* commander.

'We have trouble with the colonists, Wade.' Floyd

explained the details of the text message. 'The instigator of the unrest, a Dr Adrian O'Connor, has been isolated, and our volunteer Foundation personnel on the Moon request any advice that we can give to them. But first have a look at O'Connor's image on my screen.'

'Recognise him?' Floyd asked.

Wade nodded grimly. 'Unbelievable! It's the New Zealand SIS Director, Mr Black.' He shook his head in disbelief. 'How in the hell did that bastard manage to be selected as a colonist?'

Floyd shook his head. 'He wasn't selected by the Foundation, so he must have been a New Zealand selection. And if the New Zealand Government did as we requested and set up an independent selection panel free of political input, I can see how he slipped through the cracks. Especially as everything was done with great urgency. As you and I were the only ones from the Foundation to have met the man, the photo in his dossier would have meant nothing to our own inspectors.' Floyd scrolled back on his computer to Dr O'Connor's dossier.

Wade quickly read through the details. 'Do you think all this is true?'

'Most likely. That's how he got selected. He's obviously a brilliant academic. Missing in his dossier is his alias – Black, and the fact that he was the New Zealand SIS Director.'

It all seemed so long ago when they had met the man, but in fact it was only a few short weeks. He was dangerous. At a meeting of world leaders he'd done everything possible to discredit the Foundation. He sowed the seeds of suspicion by claiming that the Foundation themselves were responsible for targeting the asteroids at Earth – not a so called enemy fleet that Earth's own astronomers had confirmed were bound for Earth. Accepting there was a fleet, he argued that it most certainly would be Foundation cruisers.

Could this be the beginning of the end for the colonists? A feeling of deep despair washed through the Foundation Director. Something had to be done quickly before it got out of hand. He turned to Wade. 'Cancel our launch. Advise Moonbase to shuttle O'Connor to *Argo* as soon as possible. We will deal with him here.'

'Our window of opportunity to harness Jupiter and Saturn's gravity-well is very tight,' Wade said uneasily.

'I'm well aware of that. But for the colony to have any chance, we must remove this dangerous individual from it. He will be coming with us. We will isolate him while we explore our options.'

*

The message over the ship's address system was brief. It advised that launch to the stars was postponed for a further twelve hours due to another colonist being granted residency on *Argo*. No other information had been forthcoming.

'I wonder if the colonist will be a child or a grownup?' Bridgett asked excitedly.

'I've no idea, Bridgett,' her mother answered, but she hoped it would be someone near her daughter's age.

Nikki mulled over the repercussions of a delayed launch. She wondered if the starships would have to accelerate at high G's for a longer period, to allow harnessing of Jupiter and Saturn's gravity-fields. If so, it was not something she was looking forward to, as that entailed a longer period in her pressure suit. For the brief time she had spent in her suit earlier, she'd felt restricted and claustrophobic.

The cabin's vid-phone electronic chimes broke into her troubled thoughts. She picked up. A rich star field in Sagittarius faded from the wall screen and was replaced by Mirim Dryden's image.

'I hope you and Bridgett are settling in? We apologise for the launch delay.'

'We are both fine, thank you,' Nikki responded.

'Unfortunately because of the delay, pressure suits will have to be worn for a longer period. I couldn't help noticing when we fitted your suit earlier that you seemed a little strung out. Are you claustrophobic?'

Nikki had to appear strong before her daughter. 'A little, but I'll be fine,' she managed. She was surprised that Mirim had noticed her discomfort. She'd tried not to let it show. 'The suit itself wasn't too bad, even though it was very restricting. It hit me when the helmet clicked in place.' She recalled the tide of panic that engulfed her once the helmet was sealed. 'I did manage to clamp down on my panic though.' Sure you will, she silently added. 'So I'm sure I will get used to it. At least Bridgett seemed okay.'

Mirim smiled. 'Yes she seemed to take it in her stride. We can sedate you just before you suit-up if you like?'

'I don't think that will be necessary.'

'Well if you change your mind let me know. In the meantime all the leisure and recreation areas are closed and will remain so for some time. Although the launch has been delayed,' she explained, 'we still hope to depart earlier than the deadline if possible.' Mirim's gaze flicked over to Bridgett. 'My daughter and her friend, David, are in Jarrod's cabin. They would love to meet you both, and we do need to vacate your quarters so that we can install your computer.'

'Oh yes, Mamma. Let's go meet them please, Mamma, please!'

'Of course, dear. Go and brush your hair. Quickly now.'

Bridgett turned to Mirim. 'Will Beatrice be here when we get back?'

'Yes, she will be installed, I promise. But I must warn you. When she's on-screen for the first time she will generate a likeness to either you or your mamma.'

'Well I hope she looks like me, because there are no other children on the ship.'

'Then you must make sure that you enter the cabin before your mamma.' She exchanged glances with Nikki who nodded her acceptance of the suggestion.

*

O'Connor's calm expression masked an inner tension. He should have bided his time; he chided himself. Waited until the Foundation cruisers were long gone before he showed his hand. He knew that now. He wondered what his fate would be? A cold finger of fear brushed his spine. Perhaps they planned to jettison

86

him on route to the stars. Shuddering, he pictured his body tumbling over and over somewhere in the cold dark reaches of space. Or maybe he would be rendered down as fertilizer. Of course. It must be the latter, he reasoned. He couldn't imagine them wanting to waste anything so valuable – the iron and copper in his blood, the calcium in his bones. Surely he told himself, they must have gardens on board as a food source and air purifier. They would welcome his nutrients.

Securely belted in, he waited with little enthusiasm for the ferry to lift off from its scorched launching pad to rendezvous with *Argo*. Two Foundation volunteers, one on his right and another seated opposite, closely guarded him.

*

Two *Argo* troopers escorted Dr O'Connor briskly through the entrance of the Foundation Director's quarters. Dressed in a burnt-orange jumpsuit, he walked tall, his chilling presence still fully intact.

Floyd Burke and Wade Dryden's emotions were buried beneath masks of studied calm as they waited for Dr O'Connor to be seated. Floyd gestured to the two troopers to sit in chairs either side of O'Connor.

For a brief time while being escorted to the director's quarters O'Connor's sense of wonder had overcome his fear. He couldn't help but admire the ship's architecture, its curving walls, vaulted ceilings, mobile paths and the soft glow of hidden lighting.

But now his fear returned. As he sank into the chair, he heard a faint purr as it adjusted to the contours of his lanky frame.

Floyd Burke leaned forward in his chair. 'So we meet again, Mr Black. Or is it Dr O'Connor? How do we address you?'

'O'Connor,' he answered tersely.

'We've studied your dossier. We suspect that its details are correct?'

'They are. That is why I was chosen as a colonist.'

87

'Very impressive credentials. And you have no living dependents?'

'No. My parents passed away when I was ten years old. I was an only child. An aunt raised me. Now she's dead like the rest of the human race,' he added bitterly. 'And before you ask, I never married, have no children, and yes, I'm heterosexual.'

'But you omitted the fact that you worked as the head of the New Zealand SIS under the name of Black.'

'Yes of course it would not show on my record,' he said impatiently. 'After all, it was the Secret Service.'

Floyd straightened in his chair, engaging O'Connor's chilly blue eyes. 'You've caused deep suspicion to sour the relationship between the colonists and volunteer Moonbase personnel. Our people are sacrificing themselves by remaining on the Moon to help the colony's very survival. Now your destructive interference has sown the seeds of doubt amongst them. It's going to be difficult to regain that trust.'

'My heart bleeds,' O'Connor sneered. 'It really does.'

Wade spoke for the first time, his anger taking over. 'You're an ungrateful sod! We did everything we could to save your planet. It's a great pity that you were chosen as a deserving colonist.'

'I don't know why you will not admit that it was a fleet of Foundation cruisers that were responsible for destroying the Earth,' O'Connor countered. 'I'm a prisoner for god's sake. What harm could it do to tell me the truth.'

'You are in protective custody, that is true,' Floyd agreed. 'Your future is basically in your hands though. Over the short term we will do everything in our power to persuade you of the truth. The Drogs are our enemy. They and they alone were responsible for destroying the Earth!'

'I'm sure I won't be persuaded to believe that rubbish,' O'Connor growled. 'Eventually you will execute me. Of that I am sure. But I'm curious. What method will you employ?' he asked defiantly.

'You won't be executed,' Floyd answered. 'And you will not be returning to Moonbase to cause further unrest. You are coming with us, and if we fail to gain your trust, then you will leave us with no option. You will be subjected to a programme of mind-altering technology.'

'Ah, it is torture then,' he said sourly. 'I might have guessed.'

'There's no torture involved whatsoever. We will modify your memory and blot out your distrust of the Foundation, and simply replace it with information that is truthful about our enemy, the Drogs, and us.'

'My God! You're going to download my brain and reload it with false memories,' he said in horror. 'Everything I've achieved, all my knowledge will be lost to me. It won't be me.' He leaned forward and added bitterly. 'My very essence will be gone! I'd rather be dead.'

'It won't be like that at all,' Floyd countered. 'It will still be you. We will allow you to keep knowledge that is not harmful to us. Your memory will be edited and sections that could cause the Foundation problems will be removed. But none of this need happen if we can get through that entrenched distrust you have of the Foundation.'

O'Connor remained silent – shocked at what lengths the Foundation would stoop to.

'You are now going to be escorted to your cabin to reflect on your options.'

Floyd nodded to the troopers. 'Take him away.'

*

'Amber is so beautiful, isn't she, Mamma?' Bridgett spoke in English. The more she practised the more she would be able to impress Jarrod.

'Yes, dear. And David seemed nice didn't he?'

Bridgett nodded in enthusiastic agreement. 'His eyes were so blue, Mamma. Did you notice?'

Nikki burst out laughing. She couldn't help herself. Not much got past her little girl. 'His blue eyes were accentuated by his blue jumpsuit, dear.'

'I don't understand that word acc ... accentuated, Mamma.'

'It means emphasised.' Nikki shook her head. 'No that's

another long word you won't understand...'

'Oh yes I do,' Bridgett said proudly, much to the surprise of her mother. 'It means that his blue jumpsuit made his blue eyes more noticeable.'

Bridgett patted her daughter's head. 'You're so clever. Your English is so good.'

'Don't be condescending, Mamma,' she said seriously. Then an impish grin spread over her face when she registered the shock on her mother's face. She'd been waiting for just the right moment to surprise Nikki with the word *condescending* that she had learnt just a few hours before. Each time she and Lisa helped each other with French and English, Bridgett requested Lisa to teach her one really long word.

They stepped off the path to enter their cabin. Bridgett turned to her mother. 'Let me go first so our computer can be a little girl.' She hesitated a moment. 'I'm sorry, Mamma. Perhaps you would like to go first? Maybe one little girl's enough for you? I really don't mind.'

'That's nice of you to ask, but I think another little girl is just what we do need.' Nikki brushed Bridgett's cheek gently. 'She will be good company for you.'

Bridgett smiled and turned to their cabin door and was surprised when it whispered open without their access code being entered. She skipped into the cabin, realising that the new computer was probably responsible.

'Greetings, Bridgett Chantal Michaiels,' the computer announced in a deep sensuous voice. 'I am Beatrice. I have been fully installed and my circuits are fully functional. I am an audiovisual computer so you need only to speak your commands to me. The screen lit up with flickering silver light. 'One moment, Bridgett Chantal Michiels. I will generate my presence onto the screen.'

As she watched with eager anticipation, the screen's flickering silver light changed to swirls of colour like an artist's palette; then it took the form of a head and shoulders silhouette at first before finally fleshing out to a three dimensional image of Beatrice. An image almost identical to Bridgett.

A broad smile spread across Bridgett's face. 'You can come

in now, Mamma.' She sat down in the new computer chair, which was upholstered in a matt-black leather-like material and felt it adjust snugly to her body.

Nikki stood behind Bridgett, her hands resting gently on her daughter's shoulders. 'Beatrice's hair is cropped short,' she commented. 'Other than that she looks just like you, Bridgett.'

'Greetings Nicolette Jacqueline Michiels. I hope my presence pleases you and your daughter. Your comment about the length of hair is noted. I anticipated that your daughter's long curls will shortly be cropped short, as is the fashion on *Argo*.'

Bridgett cut in. 'I don't mind your cropped hair at all, Beatrice,' she giggled. She glanced over her shoulder at her mother, who was doing her best to contain her laughter also, but with little success. Words were not necessary. Both knew what the other found so hilarious.

Beatrice looked puzzled. 'You both find me amusing. Why is that?'

As Bridgett couldn't stop giggling, Nikki explained. 'It's just that you are a little girl on screen, but you speak like a grown woman with a deep silky voice. Your voice I must say is exquisite – just out of place for a little girl.'

'You would like me to change it?' Beatrice asked.

'Oh no, no, no,' Bridgett squealed, before Nikki could answer. She turned to her mother for her reaction.

'Well I don't mind, Beatrice,' she said shaking her head. 'Keep the voice by all means.'

'Very well,' Beatrice said smoothly. 'If it brings you both joy. Then there is no reason to change. Now, there are important details for me to explain to you both.'

'Yes, Beatrice?' prompted Nikki.

'Over the coming weeks I will be fine-tuning my circuits to allow our relationship to grow into a truly wonderful friendship. The more we interact with each other the sooner that will happen.'

'I'm sure you're going to be a great help to us both,' Nikki said. 'There's so much for us to learn, so many questions that we will want to ask you.'

'Then feel free to do so at any time. Now I must advise you

both to rest while you can. Once *Argo* breaks lunar orbit she will be accelerating at high G's for a considerable time, and there will be some discomfort.'

Don't remind me, Nikki thought to herself. She felt weary, so Bridgett must too. 'If we sleep we may not hear an order to report to our launch area.'

'I will not let that happen. You will be woken, I promise.'

*

Dr Adrian O'Connor gazed around his sparsely furnished cabin. Its starkness was broken only by a brightly coloured quilt of intense red and blue stripes, which covered the single bed, huddled in the corner of the room. A solitary small table and chair was fixed to the floor in the opposite corner. Above it, a wall screen acted as a view port showing in real time the scene outside the ship's flawless hull. Dominating the scene at that moment was a large brightly glowing orb. It was Earth reflecting back, all the light it received from the sun. O'Connor pictured how dark it must be under the shroud of contaminated atmosphere. All life had been extinguished, he told himself. There could be no doubt. And he knew who was responsible. The embers of his anger re-ignited. His eyes narrowed in fury.

He tore his gaze away from the view port and pushed down on his anger. It was counter-productive to a clear head. He had to be cool and calculating. Sitting on the side of the bed, his eyes explored his quarters. To his left he traced the outline of a door that he had missed on his first cursory inspection. But no wonder he had missed it first time around. It was the same metallic grey as the rest of the room and there was no door handle or obvious mechanism to open it. He rose from the bed and strode towards what he hoped would be a bathroom to relieve his uncomfortably full bladder. As he approached, the door rose vertically and disappeared into the ceiling. It was indeed a small bathroom, though he couldn't fathom what the functions of some of the various buttons and levers might be.

Chapter Seven

The artificial gravity on *Argo* had gradually increased to 1G in preparation for its launch from Moon orbit. Even so, Nicolette and Bridgett were coping with it well. The latest bulletin had estimated that launch to the stars was just four hours away.

'Oh, Mamma, I am so excited.' Bridgett clasped her chubby fingers together and rocked forward in her chair. 'I am looking forward to seeing Jupiter and Saturn. It's sad we won't be seeing Mars, though.'

'Yes it is, dear. It won't be in a convenient position in its orbit for us to view.'

Bridgett gave an audible sigh. 'Yes, I know that, Mamma.'

'Sorry, dear. Of course you do.'

The door to their cabin slid open unannounced, and a squat, dumpy machine no taller than Bridgett trundled in, towing a trolley of cleaning equipment. It swivelled to face Nikki and Bridgett. 'Greetings to you both,' it said in a dulcet tone. 'My name is Spick. I am your cleaning robot.'

Bridgett giggled. She couldn't help herself. She was about to say something when another robot entered the cabin. The only discernable difference between the two robots was the different coloured hoops that circled their middle, emphasizing their dumpiness.

'And this is my partner, Span – and late as usual.'

'That's because I'm more thorough than you with my cleaning duties,' she protested. 'That, is why it takes me a little longer.'

Nikki stifled a giggle as she heard the second robot's name.

'Now you will have noticed,' said Spick, 'that I have a blue hoop around my middle and Span a pink. This is for identity purposes only.'

'And I am Nikki and this is my daughter – '

Spick cut in. 'We already know your names, Nikki and Bridgett, unless of course you have changed them since our recent programming?'

'No, Spick, we haven't.'

'Thank goodness, I hate to be reprogrammed,' he grumbled. 'Now we will check over your cabin and tidy up. You humans make such a lot of mess. I don't know how you would manage without us.'

Bridgett was shaking with laughter. Spick sure was a grump, but funny grumpy.

'I will start with the beds,' Spick said.

'No you won't,' Span countered. 'It is my turn to do beds. You can do the dusting. Anyway you don't make beds as neat as I do.'

'Yes I do,' he protested. 'And stop showing us up in front of the humans.'

'You are doing that all by yourself.'

'No I am not,' Spick argued.

'Enough, Spick! Just get on with your dusting.'

With that, Spick went quiet. His manipulators hung by his side, his head swivelled downwards.

'My apologies to you both,' Span said in a conspiratorial whisper. 'Spick is still operational. He is just sulking. I will make a start on the beds.'

As Span trundled off, Nikki tried to coax Spick out of his bad mood. She reached over and patted the top of his black, shiny head. It felt warm and smooth to her touch. 'I've made a mental note that it's your turn to do the beds next time,' she said in a conciliatory tone.

With that, Spick slowly lifted his head. 'You see what I have to live with,' he complained. 'She is so crabby. Always gets her own way. It's just not fair.'

'So you will do the dusting for us, Spick?'

'I suppose so,' he said resignedly. He beckoned Nikki to come closer and whispered, 'The blue hoop around my middle also means I am the boss of Span,' he said, contradicting his earlier statement.

'I heard that!' Span said angrily. 'He tells untruths when it suits him. We are supposed to work as a team. Neither of us is boss of the other!'

'You see what I have to put up with, Nikki. But before I get on with my work I have a question, if I may?'

'Yes, Spick.'

'I have noticed that Bridgett laughs a lot. I have not had experience with children before. Is it normal for your young to laugh so much?'

'Well at the moment she is happy, but not always.'

'Mamma, I can speak for myself if you don't mind.'

'Of course, dear.'

Bridgett turned her attention to Spick. 'I am very excited about our launch to the stars, which is in a few hours. But I am also happy to have the company of you and Span. I think you are both very nice. I hope to see you lots and lots of times.'

It was the first time anyone had said that they appreciated the cleaning robots' company. It made his circuits tingle with joy, a sensation that occurred most infrequently. Perhaps these humans from Earth would treat him better than the genetically enhanced Foundation crew. Not that they had been mistreated in any way by the Foundation. It was just that so far Bridgett and Nikki seemed nicer somehow. Softer and kinder perhaps? But time would tell.

'Spick. Are you all right?' Bridgett asked, her voice laced with concern. It had been a long silence. The little robot had just stood there motionless.

'I am sorry, Bridgett. It was just that my circuits were tingling with joy when you said Span and I were nice, and that you would like to see us frequently. Well there are two ways you can see more of us over and above our daily scheduled tasks. You can make a lot of mess. That would mean you could request us to clean your cabin more often. But I have to say that would not make us happy. But,' he said craftily, 'you could pretend your cabin was untidy and call us.'

Bridgett shrieked with laughter. 'Sneaky, sneaky, sneaky! But I love it.'

Points of light all over the head of the robot flashed in joy. He rocked from side to side and waved his two manipulators around with abandon.

Span who had overheard the entire conversation was acting in a similar manner.

Nikki also shook with laughter that she could contain no longer.

After the squat little robots left, Bridgett felt a sharp pang of guilt. She turned to Nikki. 'Mamma, I should be feeling sad. Papa, the human race, and all the creatures of Earth are dead. All gone!' Her eyes suddenly shimmered with unshed tears.

'Dear, it's alright to be happy, just as it's alright to be sad,' she explained, reaching out and hugging her daughter. 'We must cherish the happy times without guilt and accept the sad moments. Papa would understand. He wouldn't want you sad all the time.'

*

With thirty minutes to launch, the co-ordinates were programmed into *Argo's* navigational computer – the engines and structural integrity fields set to maximum.

David was now strapped securely to his acceleration couch, outfitted in his pressure suit and helmet with faceplate open. He and Jarrod had a short time ago, helped a fully kitted out Nikki and Bridgett into their launch positions. Bridgett was excited about the upcoming launch, even though she'd been briefed about the unpleasant G forces they would have to endure. But Nikki, he'd noticed, seemed very nervous and was valiantly trying her best to hide it.

He turned his head towards Amber on the couch to his immediate right. She returned his gaze with her remarkable, deep, infinitely dark eyes.

'Hey. You look good,' he said softly.

She chuckled. 'How can you tell? All you can see is my eyes.'

'That's enough, I assure you. I can picture you easily without all that gear you're wearing.'

'I'm not sure how I should take that comment,' she said with mock indignation.

David felt himself redden with embarrassment and was glad of the protection of the helmet. 'What … I mean is,' he stammered, 'I pictured you in your jumpsuit. That dark red one as a matter of fact.'

'Well I will take your word for it, David,' she teased.

*

Nikki could feel the pulse of her fear throughout her body. Being encased in the restricting pressure suit and strapped to the couch, she could literally feel the claustrophobia bubbling away in her tummy. But she knew the suit was necessary to stop blood pooling in the extremities. The helmet pressing on her scull wasn't helping. How was she ever going to stand it when the faceplate was closed?

All on board had their pressure suits attached to biomedical sensors. Their heart rate, blood pressure, breathing rate and internal temperature were being monitored and fed into a central processing unit.

She wished now she'd taken a tranquilliser as Mirim had suggested earlier. Then she heard the clomp of boots. They were headed in her direction – moving quickly. They stopped at her couch. She looked up at the helmeted figure and recognized those dark eyes immediately.

'I have been keeping a close eye on your medical readouts,' Mirim said, 'and I can see you are in a very distressed state.' She talked very softly so as not to alarm Bridgett who was on the couch to the right of Nikki. 'I strongly recommend you take this tranquilliser, Nikki.'

'I'm sorry to cause all this bother,' Nikki said in a strained voice, 'and yes please to the pill.'

Mirim quickly released Nikki's safety harness, then removed her helmet. She helped Nikki raise herself to a sitting position and then handed her a little white pill and a small glass of water. Normally a painless injection was all that was needed for sedation, but with her pressure suit on it was impractical to do so. The injection would have also been faster acting than the pill.

After swallowing the pill, Mirim helped Nikki refit and secure her helmet, then Nikki reclined back onto her couch and Mirim quickly strapped her in.

'Now you have nothing to worry about, Nikki,' she said in a soothing tone. 'Just try and relax and let the pill do its work. Now I must dash and prepare for launch.'

When the sound of Mirim's footsteps faded away, Bridgett asked with concern, 'Are you alright, Mamma?'

'Of course, dear,' she replied, trying to keep her voice steady. 'I've just taken a little pill to calm me. It's just that I'm overexcited you see.'

'Then … you're not scared, Mamma?'

'Of course not, dear. Just thrilled at the big adventure ahead of us.' Of course you are not scared, a voice in her mind said. You're just totally, bloody, terrified!

Then came the announcement she was dreading.

'Close faceplates and keep heads still and facing the ceiling for the duration of the launch,' the computer synthesized voice demanded. 'No more talking. Five minutes to launch.'

Nikki closed her faceplate. A whimper of fear escaped her lips. She closed her eyes and tried to let her mind drift away but it was no good. She opened them once more and noticed the view screen on the ceiling had come to life. It showed the Moon. It was in real-time – not a computer projection. And she thought of the colonists they would be leaving behind. Their children would be born under a dark sky. The gentle gravity of the Moon would mean they would have lighter bones, slimmer bodies and they would be tall – very tall. But they would never experience a clear blue sky, an atmospheric sunset or sunrise. Never feel the gentle caress of a summer breeze. Never dip their toes in a salty ocean or hear the lapping of the sea on a sandy shore.

The view of the Moon slid away to be replaced by a telescopic view of Earth – again in real time. But it wasn't the Earth she remembered. No longer a blue and white world. Now it was just a bright sphere of reflecting sunlight. And beneath the shrouded world, not a single living creature stirred in the total darkness.

It was depressing to gaze at her old home world. She would prefer to remember it how it used to be – a world teeming with life.

Thankfully the broken planet slid from view to be replaced

by the Moon once more. A barren, quiet world. A world of strange beauty. A world antagonistic to life, where the efficiency of machines recreated conditions vital to the survival of the colonists. She wished them well.

A clock came up on the bottom left hand side of the screen as the final countdown to launch began. Sixty seconds, fifty-nine, fifty eight…

*

Reclining on his acceleration couch in the dining area, Jarrod felt a tingle in his spine as he stared up at the ceiling screen, and pondered what wonders they would discover? But his anticipation changed to one of concern when he thought of little Bridgett. The high G's would be very uncomfortable and painful for her – downright frightening, in fact, until, the point where she blacked out, which would not be until after her mother did; because Bridgett's heart had a shorter distance to pump blood to the brain. This was why indigenous Earth astronauts were always short – less chance of losing consciousness during high G forces.

The artificial gravity, set at 1G, suddenly switched off. Only the couch harnesses prevented Jarrod from floating off in the zero gravity. The clock in the ceiling view screen blinked out. *Argo* was now officially launched. There was no sudden lurch from orbit, but a few seconds later Jarrod could feel the gentle pressure of micro gravity kicking in. Another five minutes and it had returned to 1G. The Moon looked down impassively, still with no discernable difference in its diameter.

Directly opposite Jarrod, uneasiness enveloped Nikki like a suffocating shroud. Heavy fingers clutched at her as the gravity from *Argo's* acceleration increased. Now it was distinctly uncomfortable. She hoped Bridgett was handling the situation better than she was, and comforted herself in the knowledge that Bridgett wasn't claustrophobic.

Already the Moon on the ceiling screen had shrunk to the size of a golf ball.

And as the minutes ticked by, the G forces increased

markedly. Nikki's chest began to ache. It took a great conscious effort to breathe. Black flecks swam before her eyes. Her cramping belly threatened to heave. Perhaps this was a mistake, she told herself. Perhaps she and Bridgett should have made their home on the Moon. Too late now.

And still the ship continued to accelerate – faster and faster.

She was experiencing vision distortion created by her eyeballs being pressed into her sockets. Everything darkened, except for a circle of light directly ahead. She was experiencing tunnel vision, just as they had been told would happen in their launch pre-brief. Now it was a real agony to breathe. She felt like she was drowning.

Then mercifully the circle of light blinked out as she lost consciousness.

As the minutes ticked by, Gerald White lost consciousness, and was closely followed by Dr White, David, and finally Bridgett.

Jarrod, Amber and Lisa though, would remain conscious for the entire period of high G's, as their genetically modified haemoglobin molecules processed oxygen more efficiently. But they were feeling a high level of discomfort.

The Moon, now just a tiny dot on the screen, finally blinked out and was replaced by a computer projection of the Milky Way galaxy.

The mighty ship powered on, along with her sister ships, *Vela* and *Orion*, outwards from the fusion furnace of the sun, to the gas-giant planets, Jupiter and Saturn.

Amber went through the pre-brief in her mind, which had stated that it was highly unlikely, that any Foundation personnel would black out. More of a concern was how David and the rest of the indigenous humans would handle the continuous high G forces. The pre-brief had informed them that, although they would feel a great discomfort and lose consciousness, it was unlikely to cause long-term harm. But still an ever-present concern enveloped her.

How much longer would they have to be pinned to their couches? Amber had lost all track of time. She wished the clock on the ceiling screen had remained on.

After four hours, the acceleration began to lessen. Imperceptibly at first, but after ten minutes Jarrod became aware of it, even though the G force remained high. He tried to lift his arm but it proved impossible. He would remain pinned to his couch a little longer but was buoyed by the fact that soon they would be back in 1G once more.

It was still strangely quiet. The only sounds he could hear were the creaking of the couches as their weight lightened and the gentle whisper of ventilating air. It carried with it the scent of Earth, as the air was processed through the plants in the agriculture area of the ship. It would be a constant reminder of how Earth used to be. His hatred for the Drogs was always there, bubbling beneath the surface. But now he felt the anger well up deep within him, and with sudden insight, he pondered the possibility that intelligence could be a rare commodity in the cosmos. Perhaps it was the Drogs' mission to destroy it whenever they discovered it, so that they could be the supreme intelligence of the galaxy.

Well, he knew what his mission was. And he knew what his father's was. They would hunt down the evil creatures – every last one of them. He scowled and his mouth turned down into a hard line.

After long minutes and to everyone's relief, the gravity on board was now a comfortable 1G where it would remain until they reached the vicinity of Jupiter. Then the three starships would conserve their energy reserves by hitching a free ride with the tug of the giant planet's gravity-well. But for now, only the readout on the navigational computers showed that the spaceships were moving.

Bridgett was the first of the indigenous humans to regain consciousness. The last thing she remembered was being crushed, and then everything went dark except for a' circle of light directly overhead – then nothing.

Her tummy was a little sore and apart from feeling a little nauseous she was none the worse for the ordeal. The view screen directly above her informed her in text, that it was safe to open the faceplate of her helmet and release her safety harness. She did this and the acceleration couch reverted to its chair position.

It felt good to be upright again. A wall screen directly opposite her gave further instructions, informing her that she could remove her pressure suit when she felt up to it.

She sighed with relief. Life for now was back to normal. Well, as normal as it could be for a little French girl en-route to the stars.

Chapter Eight

Robot troopers, Hugo and Titus, stirred and flexed their manipulators. It was the first movement they had made in years, ever since their final test run after their manufacture at the Vision Foundation back on Earth. Over two metres tall and jet-black, they were a formidable presence. Four powerful manipulators sprouted from their armoured bodies, one of them terminating in a wide-angle laser weapon, the other three ending in blunt, powerful fingers capable of ripping metal plates to shreds.

Their immediate duties had been programmed, and they trundled off towards the doorway which irised open at their approach.

*

Dr Adrian O'Connor lay sound asleep stretched out on his back and did not hear the door to his apartment whisper open. The two robot troopers trundled in quietly and stationed themselves either side of the bed. One of Hugo's manipulators whipped out, seizing O'Connor's burnt-orange jumpsuit collar with stubby digits, lifting him up until the doctor's face was level with two optical sensors at the top of the robot's body.

'What the hell!' O'Connor muttered in shock as he came awake and took in the menacing form of Hugo.

'Good, you are awake,' growled the robot. Hugo released his grip and O'Connor fell back sprawling onto the bed. 'Come with us. You eat meals with rest of humans. Behave or Hugo kills. Understood?'

With conflicting emotions of rage and terror playing upon his face, he raised himself from the bed. Play it safe, a voice inside his head counselled. 'I'll just use the bathroom and wash my hands, if that is okay?' he asked uneasily.

'Two minutes,' Hugo stressed, 'or Hugo drag you out,' he said with grim simplicity, while pointing his laser projector at him.

Grumpy bastard, O'Connor thought to himself as he rushed away.

Upon their entrance into the dining area, the room grew silent as the two robots escorted their prisoner to an unoccupied table directly to the left of table ten, which was occupied by David, Lisa, Bridgett, her mother Nicollette and the twins.

'Damn!' David exclaimed harshly. 'How in the hell did he manage to get on board?'

'You know this man, yes?' Nikki asked, registering the loathing clearly expressed on David's face.

'I certainly do. He's an old enemy of ours. He did everything in his power to dissuade the nations of Earth from trusting the Vision Foundation's offer of help.' He relayed all of his experiences of the man he knew as Mr Black.

Bridgett tugged at the sleeve of Nikki's jumpsuit to gain her attention.

'Yes, dear?' and took in at once her daughter's frightened expression.

Uneasiness was creasing the skin between Bridgett's eyebrows. 'I'm scared of those big, black, robots, Mamma. I – '

The robots had acute hearing, and Titus who was closest to table ten, let his attention wander to that area. He swivelled and looked down at Bridgett. 'We guard prisoner. You not worry, little human,' he said in a powerful bass voice. 'If you misbehave, then you be scared,' he warned.

'Titus!' Hugo bellowed. 'Pay attention to prisoner.'

Chastised, Titus swivelled back to his former position while nodding his acceptance of the reprimand.

O'Connor was silent as he waited for the robots' next instructions.

'Prisoner order food from central display. Hugo shows how'.

O'Connor shook his head. 'That won't be necessary.' He tapped out his request from the menu on the display panel set flush in the centre of the table.

Hugo turned to Titus. 'Titus fetch food for prisoner. This time Titus not let his attention wander.'

Titus trundled off muttering that he wasn't designed to

104

carry plates and fetch food. He was a warrior, not a servant.

The meal was delivered to O'Connor, and despite the menacing presence of the robots, he tucked in, and found the food surprisingly good.

*

Weeks sped into months. With the unaided eye, Jupiter, fifth child of the Sun, was now the size of a golf ball. Already its gravity was having a tenuous influence on *Argo*.

Jarrod entered the ship's service hangar alone. Amber and Lisa had declined his invitation to join him. They didn't want to see the machine that might, someday take him on a dangerous mission. But he was impatient to find out what progress the ship's engineers were making on his Interceptor's restoration, and was pleasantly surprised. Material for the construction had been processed in *Argo's* zero gravity mill. The Interceptor's body was coated with heat resistant polymers with high hydrogen content. Hydrogen atoms prevent nuclear fragmentation, having just one proton in its nucleus. So when dangerous high-energy particles hit there is not the concern of a scatter of particles. Transparent polymers high in hydrogen were also used in the manufacture of the Interceptor's screen and the pilot's helmet-visor. A team of engineers was carefully removing the spider's web of alloy that cradled the flawless hull of the sleek, dark, fighter-craft – a sleeping eagle poised for action.

'You're further ahead than I anticipated,' Jarrod commented to a nearby engineer.

The stocky man turned, his face registering recognition as he saw Jarrod. 'We sure are,' the engineer said with pride. 'The team has been dedicated to see its completion as early as possible.' The hand clutching a dirty cloth was squeezed into a tight fist. 'We are as keen as you to be fully prepared for battle. If we ever meet up with them again, that scum won't know what hit em.'

'Can't argue with that,' Jarrod agreed. 'When will it be ready for a test flight?'

The engineer smiled. 'A test flight isn't necessary. All the tests are carried out right here in the hanger. You will be the first to actually fly it, and you certainly deserve to.' Admiration coloured his voice. 'You did a fine job in your last encounter with the Drogs.'

'Not good enough, though,' Jarrod countered. 'It didn't stop me getting blown out of the sky. I was just so bloody lucky!'

'Granted. You were lucky, but you were up against overwhelming odds. The Foundation's fortunate to have such a fine Interceptor pilot.'

Jarrod shrugged modestly. 'Well, thanks for that.'

*

Bridgett watched the computer screen fill with an image almost identical to herself.

Beatrice looked sad as she regarded her little human friend. '*Bonjour, Bridgett. Comment allez*-vous?' she asked in her silky, feminine voice.

'*Tres bien, merci, Beatrice. Et vous?*'

'*Tres bien, Bridgett.*' But there was sadness in Beatrice's voice.

'I'd rather speak English if you don't mind, Beatrice. My English needs practice.'

'Certainly, Bridgett. I have missed you. I thought that perhaps you had forgotten me…maybe made new friends.'

'Oh no, Beatrice,' she said reassuringly. 'I would never do that … I promise.' Then she remembered the cleaning robots. 'Sorry. I have made friends with our two cleaning robots…but you are still my friend, and I will not forget you. Promise.'

Beatrice's expression cleared. She smiled softly. 'I am relieved to hear that. How can I help you?'

'Now that Jupiter is getting close, I have been wondering why we've not seen any asteroids?' She'd asked her mother earlier and although Nicolette knew the reason, she thought it would be nice for her daughter to ask Beatrice. With so much going on she suspected that Beatrice might be feeling neglected.

'The Foundation's starships are careful to avoid the

106

asteroids, and being much smaller than planets they have not been suitable for you to observe. But you have not missed much. Compared to planets, asteroids are rather boring.'

Bridgett thought to herself, that the one that destroyed her planet was far from boring. 'I am so looking forward to seeing Jupiter up close. When will that be?'

'Closest approach will be in forty-one days, but you will not be able to see it. You will be on your acceleration couch and wearing your pressure suit, experiencing high G's.'

'That is sad. I was so looking forward to it.'

'Let me link you to one of the ship's telescope so you can see it close up right now?'

'*Oui*…yes please, Beatrice, I would love that.'

'Very well, my dear. Just give me a moment to see which telescope is free and I will link up with it.'

Beatrice's image disappeared in a cloud of pixels to be replaced seconds later by a stunning view of Jupiter. Bridgett, wide-eyed, studied its dominating presence almost filling the screen in all its glory. Complex cloud patterns caused by the gas giant turning on its axis every ten hours raced around the planet in colours, salmon-pink, yellow, blue and brown. The Great Red Spot – a large storm bigger than the Earth, stared out to space like a giant, baleful eye. Bridgett gazed back in wonder. And then she noticed a strange pink glow at the planet's North Pole and asked Beatrice to explain the phenomena.

'That is the planet's aurora,' Beatrice explained. 'It is caused by a combination of the solar wind and excited gases that surround Jupiter's magnetic field. Unlike Earth, both Jupiter and Saturn's aurora is pink because of a concentration of hydrogen gas. They do not have a greenish aurora because there is a lack of oxygen.'

'So if we glimpse a green aurora on any planet we may discover in the future,' Bridgett reasoned with extreme clarity of perception, 'it would show a presence of oxygen and so a strong possibility of life.'

'Precisely, Bridgett. On Earth, oxygen was the essence of human existence.' Beatrice continued to voice-over the telescopic scene on-screen. 'Jupiter is a giant world with a huge atmosphere, Bridgett.'

'Yes I know, Beatrice, and thank you for letting me see it close up.'

'You are welcome, my dear. I will tell you a little about the planet. Its atmosphere is made mainly of hydrogen and helium, and its solid surface is so deep that no sunlight can pierce it. At the surface the sky is inky-black. No stars! No sunrises! No sunsets! The only illumination ever, would be from bolts of lightning in the atmosphere. Jupiter emits from its interior around the same amount of heat as it receives from the sun. If the planet had been bigger it would have *turned on* as a star. Earth would have had two suns.'

'*Sacre-bleu!*' she exclaimed, lapsing back into French in her excitement. 'I did not know that. And I think I can make out Jupiter's rings.'

'Yes, Bridgett. All four of the giant planets have rings. Jupiter's are tenuous…do you understand the word tenuous?'

'Well I have never heard that word before, but my English …it is not good,' she said modestly, 'but perhaps it means thin, because that is what they are…yes?'

Beatrice continued. 'You are correct, Bridgett. These thin rings are made of mainly dark, mostly small particles. In comparison, Saturn's splendid rings are made of mainly frozen water.'

'Oh, look! I can see a satellite and its shadow crossing Jupiter,' Bridgett squealed in delight.

Beatrice instructed the telescope to focus on the satellite.

'In a few moments the telescope will bring it on screen to you, Bridgett.'

The screen darkened then brightened, displaying the satellite. The image was at such a crisp resolution that it was like looking straight into space through a glassless window.

Bridgett gazed in fascination at the boiling cauldron of orange, reds and yellow on the surface of Jupiter's innermost Galilean moon.

'That's Io, Bridgett. Its density is about the same as rock, and it's volcanically very active, so its surface features are constantly changing. In fact it's the most volcanically active world in the solar system. It would be a topographer's nightmare.'

'I do not understand the word to … to … togra –?'

Beatrice came to the rescue. 'A topographer is someone that does maps of planets. On Io, the landscape changes so rapidly it would not be long before the map would become out of date.'

'I understand. Thank you, Beatrice. It's a very red world!'

'Yes, it's redder than Mars. Each of the four Galilean satellites are almost the size of Mercury. Europa's density is around the same as Io's, but the outer two, Ganymede and Callisto, have a far lower density, halfway between rock and ice. It is suspected that there may be underground oceans of water on these two moons. This is a project that Moonbase will no doubt pursue in detail in the future. But first they will have to build a starship, then the solar system will become their backyard.'

Beatrice's lecture continued with little interruption from a captivated Bridgett. She described the features of the Galilean satellites as they came into view.

Callisto with countless craters resembled a glass ball. Ganymede had many impact craters, but most had been mysteriously ploughed over in some way. There were ridges and mysterious light-coloured streaks on its surface.

But the moon Europa had no craters or mountains; its surface completely covered by an ice crust, possibly 100 kilometres thick, which overlaid the moon's silicate interior. Ice fractures covered the satellite's surface in a confusion of dark lines.

Beatrice briefly touched on the remainder of Jupiter's significant moons. Adrastea, Amalthea and Thebe followed Metis, the closest moon to Jupiter. Then the innermost of the Galilean satellites, Io, Europa, Ganymede and Callisto. The silken voice of Beatrice made them all seem like magical worlds, just waiting to be explored – 'Leda, Himalia, Lysithea, Elara, Ananke, Carme, Pasiphae, Sinope…'

*

The Foundation's three cruisers were gaining speed on the downhill run towards Jupiter. From time to time, engines fired nominally for trajectory corrections; otherwise it was a free energy ride – courtesy of the giant planet's gravity-well.

The gravity was increasing rapidly, but was well within *Argo's* structural limits. Even so, the mighty ship shook alarmingly. Of more concern was the status of the indigenous humans.

A suited up Bridgett was terrified. It was worse than the high G's she experienced when Argo launched from Moon orbit, to enable the cruiser to catch and harness Jupiter and Saturn's gravity-wells. Her restraint belt threatened to cut her in half. Now her tiny frame weighed eighty-two kilos – and rising. Her pulse was rapid. Her eyelids, heavy as lead weights remained closed. Her chest ached – each breath an agonizing triumph of will.

And then, mercifully – blackness.

All the indigenous humans were hooked up to medical sensors and in the high G's even the Foundation personnel were incapacitated to a degree. Robot medics were on standby, and in an emergency were programmed to respond immediately and take appropriate action.

A plasma shroud was building up around the three cruisers. Ship to ship LCO communication systems were down and would remain down until the cruisers escaped Jupiter's radiation belts. But it was expected. No damage to the systems was anticipated.

And so the mighty ships continued on – faster and faster, to a future more extraordinary than even the Foundation could imagine.

*

Particle and field detectors indicated *Argo* had cleared the giant planet's radiation belts. *Vela* and *Orion* had also safely negotiated Jupiter's lethal radiation belts and escaped the incredible tug of the planet's gravity. All LCO communication systems and circuitry throughout the three cruisers were checked. All were fully operational.

110

Argo's dim lighting aided the fiction that it was early evening. Artificial gravity was set to lunar G's rather than Earth's to conserve energy. All acceleration couches were now in the upright chair position. Pressure suits could now be removed.

Bridgett remained seated. Her head was bowed. Nicolette could tell she was crying and quickly rose to her feet to comfort her daughter. She put a comforting arm around her daughter's shoulders, then removed Bridgett's helmet.

Bridgett lifted her tear stained face to Nicolette. 'I thought we were all going to die, Mamma. My chest ached and I could hardly breathe. I think I must have fainted.'

'We all did, dear. But it's over now.'

'No it's not, Mamma. We still have Saturn yet.'

'But Saturn's gravity is not as great as Jupiter's. So we are over the worst, and we survived that.'

'Yes, Mamma, I understand that.' She wiped her tears away with the back of her hand. 'Anyway, I should not be a crybaby. We are so lucky to be on this starship. But I miss Papa so much.' She wished she could retrieve his photo from her jumpsuit pocket, but that wasn't possible until the pressure suit was removed. She rose to her feet. 'Let us go to our cabin, Mamma and take these suits off.'

Nicolette could see the fatigue clearly visible on her daughter's face. They shuffled off in the low gravity to their cabins and a well-earned sleep.

*

Titus trundled down the stationery pathway on his pre-programmed task. All pathways would be immobile for the foreseeable future as exercise was encouraged in the low gravity setting. It would help stop calcium leaching from the bones and muscle atrophy – especially for the indigenous humans on board. They had all been issued with exercise regimes, which they were encouraged to keep to. There were, of course, regenerative beds where muscular tone could be achieved electronically for anyone who became seriously unfit.

111

Bridgett was alone, stretching her legs as she shuffled along in the low artificial gravity. It was part of her exercise programme. She turned the corner the same time Titus did from the opposite direction.

She craned her head and gazed in fright at the robot towering above her, blocking her way.

Titus stared down at Bridgett for a finite moment. Except for the time he'd met Bridgett in the restaurant area, he had only ever come in contact with fully-grown adults. 'Why are you so tiny, little human?' he asked in his frightening synthesized voice.

'I am still a child,' she explained nervously. 'All human children are tiny, but we grow taller as we get older.'

Titus didn't acknowledge her statement. He wished to study her more closely, so he reached down with two of his manipulators and lifted her gently till her face was level with his optical sensors. He studied the soft contours of her face. 'How old little human be when full-grown?'

The robot's voice sounded harsh to Bridgett's ears. She tasted the dry fear in her throat. Her energy fled as her brain sought protection, nearly causing her to faint.

Titus was puzzled at her silence. He shook her gently. 'Speak, little human. Speak now!' His deep voice boomed, echoing harshly off the corridor walls.

'I ... I am scared. You scare me. Could you let me down please?'

'Titus only scare bad people – not programmed to hurt good people.' He lowered her gently to the ground.

'Thank you.' She sensed the robot meant her no harm. 'When I am around fourteen or fifteen years – that's Earth years, I will be a fully-grown adult. I am the only child on *Argo*,' she added. 'Bridgett is my name, and I'm pleased to meet you,' even though she thought to herself, scared to meet you might have been more appropriate. 'And I remember your name. You were the robot that got told off for talking to me in the restaurant.'

'Other robot is Hugo – very scary robot. Always saying Titus easily distracted. Hugo always angry, always threatening to shut down Titus's circuits.'

'Well it seems I have distracted you again, and I'm sorry. I

112

hope you will not get into trouble?'

'Titus not mention to Hugo meeting with Bridgett – then no trouble.'

Bridgett smiled at the robot's logic, then turned at the sound of someone shuffling down the passageway and gazed in astonishment.

'Bridgett tell big lie!' Titus boomed. 'Bridgett not only child on ship.'

She turned and looked up at Titus. 'Well I thought I was the only child, but I am happy that I am not.'

'Everything all right here?' the diminutive figure asked.

'Yes, but I just told Titus … err, the robot, that I was the only child on board.'

'Well, yes you are,' he said in a pleasant tenor voice.

'But you tiny – no bigger than Bridgett,' Titus challenged. 'Must be child!'

'I am an adult, I assure you. My name is Mathew and I'm genetically engineered to be short and slim because I'm an air-conditioning specialist. This allows me to crawl through ducts where there is little room to manoeuvre.'

Bridgett tried unsuccessfully to hide her disappointment.

'I suspect you were hoping I was about your age, Bridgett.'

'Well yes. I was surprised to see someone my height for a change. At times I get a sore neck always looking up at people. But I am pleased to meet you, Mathew.'

'And I'm pleased to meet you, Bridgett. There's only a handful of personnel on *Argo* that are my height, and now you have added to that small number.'

'Well I won't always be this height.'

'No,' Titus bellowed. 'Little human grow tall – not stay small like genetically engineered air-conditioning specialist.'

'I'm aware of that, Titus,' Mathew chuckled. 'But tell me. Do you always talk with a loud voice?'

'Titus talk loud for very good reason. Loud scary voice frighten bad people.'

'But Bridgett and myself are good people,' he said gently, 'so there's no need to shout.'

'Perhaps good people – perhaps bad. Titus not sure. I have

113

important task – tiny people step aside.'

Mathew and Bridgett quickly moved aside as the robot advanced, its treads whirring noisily in the corridor's confined space.

Mathew regarded Bridgett with his gentle brown eyes. He was well aware that Bridgett, along with her mother and the Whites, were the only indigenous humans on board. Then he remembered O'Connor was too – the troublemaker from Moonbase.

'Are you and your mother still happy to be on *Argo* rather than remaining on the Moon?' he asked as they shuffled down the pathway.

'Oh, yes. It would have been hard to remain on the Moon and be so close to Earth, knowing that we could never return home.' There was sadness in her voice, but also determination.

The little French girl captivated Mathew and he adored her accent. He wished he could listen to her speak for longer but he had tasks to complete and so took his leave.

Bridgett continued on her way after checking her pedometer that was strapped to her yellow jumpsuit. She still had two kilometres to complete of her daily exercise regime.

Chapter Nine

The door whispered open. In the dim light of the cabin, Titus muffled the noise from his drive tracks, just as Hugo had instructed him to do. Looming over the sleeping figure, two manipulators shot out, grabbing O'Connor's orange jumpsuit. He shook the man roughly. 'Bad person wake now,' he said in his most menacing voice.

O'Connor's unfocused eyes opened in fright, his heart beating like an express train. He'd been wrapped in a pleasant dream of old Earth. Now he was back in his nightmare reality.

'Get up now,' Titus ordered. 'Foundation Director wishes meeting.'

O'Connor, his breath coming in ragged gasps, angrily tossed his blanket aside and swung his legs over the edge of the bed.

'O'Connor too slow. Get to feet now!'

'When is this meeting then?' he asked tightly, rising to his feet.

'Ten minutes ago. O'Connor already late!'

'Well that's not my fault,' O'Connor protested. 'You were late getting here.'

Titus thumped O'Connor on the shins with one of his lower manipulators. 'Titus blame O'Connor.'

O'Connor's face scrunched in pain. He could feel the heat of his fury pulse through his body.

Blunt, metal fingers grasped each side of O'Connor's face. Titus turned up O'Connor's terrified face so that he stared up at the robot's optical sensors.

O'Connor had no doubt that Titus could squash his head like a ripe melon.

'Titus kick in shins to hurry O'Connor,' he explained as if talking to a child. He released his vice-grip of the hapless O'Connor.

'I ... I need to go to the bathroom.'

'No time – late for meeting.' He shoved O'Connor towards the open door and manipulated him in the direction he wanted him to go.

'I know where the Director's office is,' O'Connor complained.

'Good. Titus right behind you. If too slow, Titus rolls over and crush!'

O'Connor needed no persuasion.

*

Floyd Burke, The Vision Foundation Director buzzed his secretary. 'My meeting with Doctor O'Connor is well overdue,' he stated with a trace of impatience creeping into his voice. 'Get onto security and check on it please, Joseph.'

'No need to, sir. He's just arrived.'

'Good. Send him straight in please.'

Joseph glanced up at O'Connor and the robot escort. 'The Director will see you now,' he said as he keyed in the code to open the director's door.

'Dr O'Connor, take a seat please.' Floyd Burke gestured to a chair opposite him.

O'Connor sank into the proffered chair. Titus stood directly behind him within easy reach of his manipulators.

'Now that you have had time to reflect, Dr O'Connor,' his voice was cool, 'I hope that your view of us has changed.'

O'Connor squirmed under the steely gaze of the director. 'I'm keeping an open mind. I'm still not convinced that Drogs exist and were responsible for Earth's demise.'

The director was silent for long seconds. 'I would have thought that a man with your undoubted intelligence would have realised by now, that the Foundation did everything in its power to save Earth.' Forcing himself not to allow a note of frustration to creep into his voice, he continued. 'Surely by now you can see that?'

'As I said, I'm keeping an open mind,' he answered evenly. 'Perhaps it's the environment of the Secret Service over many years that has caused me to distrust the Foundation.' He leant forward in his chair. His voice turned silken. 'If I was allowed to have the freedom of the ship, it would help me re-evaluate my

116

stand on the subject of trust.'

There was a long silent moment while Floyd Burke regarded O'Connor. 'Very well, Doctor O'Connor, I'm prepared to allow you limited freedom of the ship. A robot will be your constant companion, and remember we have security cameras throughout the ship. You will be carefully monitored.'

'Of course, sir. I understand that is necessary,' he said reasonably.

Floyd Burke's expression hardened. 'And let me warn you, Doctor O'Connor. Unless we gain your trust we will have no option but to download your brain. Memories that are negative to the Foundation's interest will be erased – forever! Knowledge that is useful to the company will be retained.' He saw expressions of fear and anger cross O'Connor's face.

O'Connor clamped down on a desire to snap back in anger. After all, the meeting had gone about as well as he could have expected. His plans were on course. And now, at least he would get some degree of freedom.

Floyd judged that now, he could soften the threat a little. 'As you would know, Doctor O'Connor, memories consist of stored series of electric impulses. They are not part of the genetic code. Your very essence would remain.'

'Yes I am certainly aware of that,' he said carefully.

'Anyway, hopefully all this won't be necessary. Now the robot will escort you back to your room where you will remain for a short time while we reprogram the robot.' He keyed in the door code and it whispered open for O'Connor and Titus to leave.

'Titus not happy! Not agree with Foundation Director,' he grumbled as they made their way back to O'Connor's quarters. 'O'Connor – agent of discord – should be reprogrammed,' he grumbled. 'Not Titus.'

O'Connor's footfalls echoed dimly off the featureless, passageway walls. He turned to the robot but was careful not to slow down. No way did he want an excuse for a dumb robot to roll over and crush him. 'I'm sure the Director knows best,' he said, smiling thinly.

A human would have recognised O'Connor's smile as feral.

*

After many discussions with his parents, nothing had changed David's mind. He would accept the Foundation's offer of cranial implant and age treatments that would more than double his life expectancy. And upon his eventual death he agreed to be cloned. Of course he knew he had the option at any time to back out of being cloned, but why would he want to. The stars and all their mysteries beckoned, so he had a deep need of that precious commodity *time*!

He was all scrubbed up in a well-lit surgical theatre, nervously awaiting his cranial implant. The theatre was spacious with an array of complex electronic equipment. Three clear upright gestation tanks stood in the far corner of the room, along with three clear regenerative beds – all empty. His mother, Doctor White, was suitably attired in sterile gown, slippers, mask and headgear. As well as having concern for her son, she was also fascinated by the Foundation's technology and had gained permission to observe the procedure.

David and Doctor White were surprised to learn that surgical robots would be performing the implant. Foundation personnel had assured them that they were highly skilled machines and had put them at ease. And it was a very simple procedure.

When David was fully anaesthetized, a tall, slim, and incredibly flexible surgical robot quietly and efficiently set about the procedure. It extended a delicate manipulator with thin, metal fingers, which held a scalpel to David's head and began to cut.

Another surgical robot was on hand for the purpose of explaining and answering all Mary White's questions, as well as providing back up for the other robot surgeon.

'I noticed earlier that a few of David's scalp hairs were packaged along with fingernail cuttings?'

'That was to extract DNA and store it in the Life Bank for when we need it.' The robot's voice was a smooth baritone. 'Human hair consists of keratinzed cells. Hormones are involved in the cyclic follicular activity. The cells in the hair and

118

fingernails retain the genetic code more effectively than soft body tissue.'

'Your DNA technology must be very advanced.'

In answer, the surgical robot gave a small nod.

'I presume the intravenous drip in his arm is feeding him antibiotics?'

'No. Antibiotics are a very primitive medical treatment and are entirely unnecessary. We are reversing free radical damage with antioxidants and vitamins. He's also receiving beneficial scavengers that will remove any dormant infectious agents. And thrombocytes – blood platelets, combined with molecular enhancement technology now course through David's system. They will swarm to any wound that David might sustain in the future to fight infection and repair any trauma. David will still age, but now it will be much slower. When he eventually dies we will clone a new David unless instructed otherwise.'

'Very impressive technology.' She tried to ignore the noise of the drill as it bored into David's skull to a depth the same thickness of the implant. 'Will the cranial transplant show on his scalp?' She'd been shown the implant earlier and was surprised that it was no larger than a standard watch battery.

'It won't show. There are no terminals for us to plug into. Its internal energy will last David's extended lifetime. My colleague is now folding back David's scalp over the implant, and within sixty seconds, all tissue damage will be repaired by David's new immune system.'

'And when do you download his memories?'

'My colleague is doing it right now.'

She saw the robot's delicate fingers dancing over a keyboard and saw him watch a screen come to life beside David's bed. It was a confusion of colour and symbols that made no sense to Mary. After two short seconds the screen blinked off.

'All done,' the robot said simply.

Mary's eyes widened. 'That's an incredibly short time to download a copy of his lifetime's knowledge and memory.'

'A brain is like a computer disk,' he explained. 'It can receive a lifetime's knowledge and memory in a few seconds. All David's data will be stored and eventually be restored to

David's clone. Of course from time to time we will need to update David's memory. I strongly recommend that all indigenous humans on board have the same procedure.'

The operating surgical robot removed David's intravenous drip and checked the area of the scalp, which had been cut away to receive the implant. He nodded in satisfaction and for the first time in Mary's presence he looked over to her and spoke. 'Another very fine procedure accomplished. My success rate remains at one hundred percent,' he said immodestly 'Patient will be well pleased with resultant enhancement.'

'Thank you for your care of my son and your fine work.'

'Thank you, Doctor White. I love my work. It's what I was designed to do.' His voice was an identical reassuring, smooth baritone to his colleague. 'Now David will be fully recovered in a few minutes. If you would like, now that you're here, I can perform the same procedure on you.'

Mary chuckled at the surgical robot drumming up business. 'No thank you. I would like to discuss it further with my husband, but let me assure you that I'm almost certain that I will undergo the procedure.'

The tall, slim robot gave a small nod. 'Then I will look forward to seeing you again soon, Doctor White.'

David began to emerge from the anaesthetic. Voices were murmuring, but too softly to understand. He slowly opened his eyelids. A bright, blurred shape hovered over him and he became aware of his hand being held. As his vision sharpened he finally recognised his mother peering down at him.

Concern creased her brow. She saw his eyes widen as he turned his gaze from her to sweep the room. He remained mute … yet he appeared wide-awake.

David returned his gaze to his mother again. His mouth was working but he uttered no words.

Mary's expression could not fully conceal an undercurrent of anxiety. 'Speak to me, son!'

His mouth was working but still no words escaped his lips. He squeezed his mother's hand in an attempt to allay her fear. His senses were completely overwhelmed, but he managed a half smile. Every scent, every image, and now every sound, so intense. He just felt so bloody good. It was as if his body was flooded with endorphins. He was acutely aware of every crease, and every fold in his mother's gown.

Mary White turned to the robot that had done the operation. 'Something's wrong,' she said fearfully. 'He's unable to speak! Is he going to be all right?'

'Of course, Doctor White, I assure you,' he said soothingly. 'All his senses are heightened and he's just coming to terms with it.'

'Thank goodness. You've seen this reaction before then?'

'Well … no. I haven't seen it on any of my patients before but there's a very good reason for that.'

'And that is?' Mary prompted.

'This was my very first operation – '

'But I distinctly remember you telling me that it was another fine procedure accomplished,' she reminded him. 'And you claimed your success rate was one hundred percent!'

'I assure you, dear lady, that I have done the procedure eleven times prior to David's operation, and each with faultless precision. David just happened to be the first living being. All the others were inanimate dummies.'

My God, she said silently. I wish I'd known that.

As if reading her mind the other robot said, 'I was keeping a close eye on procedures, Doctor White and I assure you my colleague did a fine job. You have nothing to worry about.'

She turned her attention back to her son.

'Who … are you?' David stammered. 'Are you a … nurse?'

She failed to see the mischievous glint in his eyes.

Mary glared at the robot who'd done the procedure. 'Nothing to worry about!' she challenged in an angry voice.

'Mother, stop worrying. I was only kidding you. I'm sorry. It was mean of me to scare you like that.'

Mary blinked back tears. 'David! Don't ever scare me like that again,' she scolded. She looked down at him for a silent moment. Her expression of relief needed no words.

'I'm sorry, Mum. I was actually speechless for awhile,' he said remorsefully. 'And when I felt I could speak, I just couldn't help teasing you. Sorry.'

Mary leant down and hugged David. 'I will forgive you this time,' she whispered, 'but never scare me like that again.'

She moved away when the surgical robot that had carried out the procedure approached the other side of the bed. With slender, pale, titanium alloy fingers, he tapped out a command on the keyboard beside the bed. He watched as a report on the computer screen showed the status of David's pulse rate, breathing rate, body temperature and blood pressure. All were perfectly normal for a young healthy human.

Mary and David both knew that the enhancement would never be as advanced as the twins or Lisa's. To David, though, it would certainly feel like nothing short of miraculous.

*

David, Bridgett, Lisa and the twins raised their eyes to the vaulted ceiling of the recreation chamber. They'd reserved it earlier for their exclusive use – and it was confusing. The ceiling could be the floor for all intents and purposes – or a wall could be the floor or ceiling. There simply is no up or down in zero gravity, even though their stomachs told them they were falling.

They'd familiarised themselves earlier by viewing a short film showing the fun things that could be experienced in the weightless environment.

Vivaldi's *The Four Seasons* playing on the sound system dramatically broke the silence. The chamber was spacious, around half the length of a football field and twenty-five metres wide, and well lit with hidden, shadow-less lighting. It was gravity shielded from the rest of the ship, as was the manufacturing and pharmaceutical compartments. They'd been advised to tackle simple exercises first, and then progress to the more difficult tasks as their confidence grew. The film had ended by thanking them for their interest, and encouraging them to use the facility whenever possible, for physical and mental well-being.

At each end of the chamber, and halfway to the ceiling, a wide platform protruded; and they fully intended to make use of it, as they progressed from the simple, to more complex exercises. Recessed handholds were peppered over walls and ceiling. Bridgett was keen to begin at the most difficult exercise, but Jarrod persuaded her it would be unwise until she acquired more muscle tone.

Although they hung on to a railing, their bodies floated around with abandon. Their laughter echoed loudly off the walls and ceiling – even over Vivaldi's masterpiece.

The film had encouraged beginners to practise flexing knees and pushing off walls, floor, or ceiling to glide to target areas. But pushing off too hard could result in hitting the target area with a thud and possible injury. Conversely, too weak a push and it could take an infinite amount of time to reach your destination. This is why pressurised nitrogen gas canisters had to be carried at all times. A well-aimed squirt of gas would propel you to your destination.

Amber, it was decided would lead off with the first task. Holding onto the hitching rail, which felt cool to her touch, she faced the entrance wall. In her other hand she held the pressurised nitrogen gas cylinder. It was around the size of a paint spray can.

She let go of the railing and gave a two second blast of nitrogen. She floated off and after a few seconds rolled her shoulder, just as the film had advised. This action gently spun her around to face the approaching wall. A short distance from the wall she managed a swimmer's tumble turn, and hit the wall with flexed knees. She pushed off like an arrow, to return to her starting point.

She had pushed too hard. To compensate, she gave a one second blast of gas at the fast approaching wall to slow her down. It worked perfectly. She lifted her arms to the ceiling and her body followed in a graceful curve, so that she presented her feet to the wall. Just a feather touch of her boots and she grabbed the hitching rail. To her embarrassment they all clapped.

'It was beginner's luck,' she said modestly, looking at each of them in turn. 'That is all it was. It was far from perfect anyway. The exercise was to use the pressure-can once only. I used it a second time to slow down. Whoever goes next,' she warned, 'be careful not to push off too hard on the return length.'

Heeding her advice they practised, and became increasingly graceful and then moved onto more complex exercises as the film had advised – tumbling, rolling and gliding with arms to their sides. The only thing that stopped them tumbling or rolling forever in zero gravity was strategic squirts of their nitrogen canisters. Surprisingly none of them felt the least bit queasy in the weightless environment.

Then, full of confidence, they decided to attempt the ultimate exercise. Pushing off, they glided towards one of the platforms, ten metres above them – or was it below them? Jarrod and Amber reached the platform in one go.

David and Lisa overshot it, but swam down to the platform by using handgrips that were set into the walls and ceiling.

Bridgett misjudged and came up short but managed to grab a handgrip and used it to propel herself gracefully to the platform. Each of them had their pressure canister in a pouch at their side. To prevent floating away, they slipped their feet into stirrups that were dotted over the platform. When moving around the platform, they were careful to have at least one foot anchored in a stirrup at all times.

'I definitely want to have a try please, Jarrod,' Bridgett pleaded. Without waiting for a reply she added, 'I know I'm not as strong as a grown up, but I have been doing all my exercises including pushdowns … I mean pushups. Look.' She flexed her biceps. 'Can you not see how big and strong my muscles are?' Her honey-coloured hair that normally curled around her shoulders floated in every direction. She gazed up at Jarrod, her large, dark eyes willing him to agree to her request.

Jarrod gave her an uncertain smile, then turning to David, Lisa and his sister, he arched his eyebrows in question.

Amber shrugged her shoulders. 'Well we can help if she gets into difficulties, I suppose, but will there be any equipment in her size? After all she's the only child on board and it might not have been anticipated that her size would be needed.'

As quick as a whip Bridgett informed them that there were air-conditioning experts on board that were no bigger than she was.

'That's right,' David agreed, remembering Mathew, and the

helpful advice that he had given him.

'Well let's look and see then,' Jarrod volunteered. He negotiated his way to the storage door that was set into the wall, making sure he had at least one foot in a stirrup at all times. Sliding open the yellow concertina door revealed ten sets of folded wings, all the same size hung neatly on the wall facing them, as well as two smaller sets.

Bridgett was correct in her assumption. 'Yes! Yes! Yes!' she cried out and jumped for joy. Her tiny feet slipped out of the adult sized restraints and she shot off like a rocket in the direction of the ceiling. Slipping his feet out of the restraints, David stretched out, and grabbed Bridgett's legs. Then he too began to drift away with Bridgett in tow.

Jarrod held onto a handhold and with his free hand grabbed Lisa's left hand as she slipped her feet out of her restraints and pushed off. Reaching out, she managed to snare one of David's ankles, allowing Jarrod to pull the human chain back to the platform once more.

But there really was no danger. They all felt a little foolish. The age-old fear of falling was imprinted on their brains and they'd all acted instinctively.

One by one, they carefully donned their wings – each helping the other – each wing slightly longer than an arm-span. Constructed out of a smooth, black rubber-like material, they were semi rigid and fastened to their arms by thick elastic loops. The leading edge of each wing was thicker than the trailing edge – the engineering and design, modelled from an eagle's wing. With arms spread wide, the wing's surface lay parallel to the floor with arms fastened directly behind – much the same as competitive swimmers trained with paddles strapped to the palms of their hands to increase arm and upper body strength.

Vivaldi's *The Four Seasons* ended. There was a pause, then Holst's *The Planets* played from concealed speakers. Jarrod pressed a large orange switch to alter the zero gravity to a one sixth Earth gravity environment. Then he reset the air conditioning directional flow, just as the film had instructed. This would compensate for the lift the wings would give. If this wasn't done they would all end up on the ceiling.

Slipping his feet out of the restraints, David pushed off the platform. His outstretched wings caught the eddying currents of air generated by the air conditioning. Caught in an endorphin rush, he grinned. He was an eagle – gliding – flying with weightless grace. Dipping a wing he glided to his left and then in an opposite action, soared to his right.

Since his cranial implant, he was seeing things with extreme clarity of perception. Every scent, every scene and every sound, so much more intense.

Now he'd dropped below the height of the upcoming platform. It was coming up fast. He flapped his wings – once, twice, to get more height. It took a surprising amount of effort to do so. His speed increased, but now he was only a metre from the ceiling – the platform far below him. Crashing into the wall with a sickening thud he managed to grab a handhold and hung on grimly through a haze of pain and embarrassment. Waiting a few moments to compose himself and the pain to abate; then using the handholds, he pulled himself down to the platform, to the polite applause from the other side of the chamber.

Bridgett on her first and only attempt didn't have the strength to flap her wings, just as Jarrod had feared. Nevertheless she glided gracefully to the other side and grabbed a handhold a metre below the platform. Even with wings she managed to make her way back to the platform above with David's help.

Their confidence grew with each flight across the chamber - soaring with skill and grace to compliment Holst's *The Planets* masterpiece.

But their arms and upper body were starting to ache from the unfamiliar exercise of flying. Bridgett unstrapped her wings and using handholds, made her way down to the chamber's entrance.

Lisa, David and Amber flew across the chamber one last time to stow their wings. Jarrod followed with Bridgett's wings folded between his legs. After stowing the wings he readjusted the gravity to zero and reset the air conditioning, then they pushed off the platform to join Bridgett at the entrance.

Bridgett gazed at each of them in turn, and burst out laughing.

As they looked at each other, they too began to laugh. Their faces had puffed up in zero gravity because of a redistribution of body fluids.

Chapter Ten

Ever since David's cranial implant ten months ago, he sometimes found it difficult to sleep – his brain too active and bursting with thoughts and ideas to settle. And tonight was one of those nights. It was exhilarating, but sometimes it could be deeply depressing.

He cocked his hands behind his head. Tonight, instead of trying to sleep he would surrender to wakefulness and give his thoughts free range. In the long years ahead, he wondered where their journey would take them. What strange celestial shore might eventually become their home? Probably a planet stranger than he could ever imagine.

His mind wandered back to the first time he'd met Amber, and how she had taken his breath away with her beauty. He'd thought her too beautiful for him – as unattainable as the moons of Saturn. Fate had brought them together, and for awhile he'd feared destiny would keep them apart.

He remembered his old driftwood town – their strolls on the beach, the salt-scented winds and the steady call of the surf. But now the beach was no more. And they were leaving the shores of Earth far behind. They would never return – ever! He felt an unsettling wash of depression, but countered it by reminding himself that his parents as well as his dearest friends were with him on *Argo*.

His thoughts went back to his brief time on the Moon. He remembered the excursion they made in a transit vehicle over the Moon's lonely terrain. And he recalled gazing up in the magic of the night at an amazing starfield. The black sky was ablaze with stars – multicoloured jewels in the cosmic sea. And now he was sailing that vast ocean of stars.

He was one of the luckiest indigenous humans in the universe.

At last he closed his eyes and allowed himself to drift away.

*

Bridgett gazed through the flexiglass of *Argo's* viewing blister. She was puzzled. The rings of Saturn had disappeared. Yesterday they had been clearly visible to her naked eye.

A few days previous she had peered through the ship's telescope at the spectacular rings, shining from the light of the distant sun – each icy particle, large and small, glowing like diamonds in the dark sky.

But today she could still make out the atmospheric bands racing across the planet's disc – but no rings.

Bridgett turned to Jarrod. 'What has happened to Saturn's rings?'

'They are still there, Bridgett. The orientation of the ship has brought them edge on, that's all, and they are not thick enough from this distance for you to see them.'

She giggled. 'I am just a silly little French girl. I should have realised.'

Jarrod ruffled her hair and chuckled. 'Every fifteen years or so the rings are edge on from Earth as well.' But now of course it didn't matter, he thought to himself bitterly – there would be no one on Earth to view the rings ever again.

The Foundation cruisers were now only two weeks away from the tug of Saturn's gravity-well, which would accelerate them on another free energy ride. The high G's would be tough on the crew, and especially so on the indigenous humans, but less so than with Jupiter's frenetic encounter.

Commander Floyd Burke sat at the master controls facing a curving bank of consoles. Computer screens flickered showing each area of the ship, the status of every system. His eyes rested a moment on each screen and were well pleased. All systems were performing satisfactorily.

He keyed in instructions and watched the screen directly in front of him fill with images representing the Drog cruisers. A superimposed grid located the ships precisely, and readouts at the bottom right hand corner of the screen ticked away their distance, confirming the enemy were still accelerating away from the Foundation vessels at a tremendous rate.

Energy conservation on the Foundation starships had been excellent. Energy had only been consumed at the launch from

Moon orbit, and continued on for a few hours to attain the speed necessary to catch the free energy rides from the gas giants. Once past Saturn the stardrives would be engaged to pursue the Drogs in earnest.

The Drogs had also made use of the gas giant's gravity-wells; but they had also continued to use their on board propulsion engines. This meant that they would be using precious fuel reserves. They were gambling that they would be so far away from the Foundation cruisers, that they would be undetectable. Then in the vastness of space, it would be virtually impossible for the Foundation to seek them out.

Perhaps the Drogs' tactic would prove to be a successful one.

*

The door whispered open, and the two cleaning robots entered with their trolley of cleaning equipment in tow. Bridgett and Nicolette rose from their chairs to greet them.

Spick trundled over to Bridgett, his manipulators reaching up to her.

'What on Earth are you doing, Spick?' Span asked.

'I am going to give Bridgett a hug.'

'Only humans give hugs,' she reprimanded. 'I think you need reprogramming, Spick. You are a cleaning robot – nothing more, nothing less.'

Spick felt a sulk coming on but managed to suppress it.

Span turned to Bridgett and Nicolette. 'Please excuse my co-worker. I do hope he has not offended you both. He seems to be suffering an identity crisis.'

Nicolette chuckled. 'I assure you that we are happy for you to hug us if you so wish.'

Spick needed no encouragement. He wrapped his manipulators around Bridgett, just like he had seen Amber and Jarrod do when he had been cleaning their quarters.

Bridgett shrieked with laughter and hugged the squat little robot back and patted his warm, smooth, head that had lit up with points of light as his circuits tingled with joy.

'Release the hug and back off immediately, Spick,' Span ordered. 'We have important work to do.'

Spick released his hold of Bridgett. The points of lights on his dome faded – the tingling of his circuits ceased. He swivelled around to face Span. 'You sure are one grumpy robot. It is you that needs reprogramming – not me.'

'Stop this arguing in front of the humans,' she snapped, 'you are showing us up.'

Spick gave a sigh, just like the humans did from time to time. 'Very well, but remember it is my turn to do the beds.'

'I know that,' she said crossly. 'And the sooner it is done the better.'

Spick made his way to the beds. He was a little perplexed. When he and Span argued it seemed to make the humans very happy – especially Bridgett who laughed the most.

Meanwhile Span busied herself with the vacuuming. She plugged in a flexible hose to one of four outlets in the cabin then pressed a red button. This opened up the hose through the hull of the ship, to a tiny fraction of the available vacuum of space.

*

Bridgett and friends crowded into the observatory to view Saturn through the telescope. Never again would they be this close to view the elegant planet. *Argo* would get closer, but then they would be in their pressure suits and strapped to their acceleration couches experiencing high G's, unable to view the closest approach.

The jewel of the solar system blew them away. No photos had prepared them for the awesome sight of Saturn in the black sky. *Argo* was now above the plane of the rings that marked the subtle harmony of gravity in a magnificent display. The divisions of the rings were clearly visible – especially the major ring-gap – the Cassini's Division.

The rings cast a deep shadow on the speeding clouds of Saturn. They witnessed the transit of one of Saturn's many moons, Enceladus, upon the face of the planet. Enceladus – a very white world with many ancient impact craters, that curiously were all on one side of the moon. On its other side some strange melting event had eliminated all the craters.

Then they studied Titan, Saturn's largest moon – its mysterious tawny coloured atmosphere of nitrogen and methane shrouded its surface. Normally a moon wouldn't be able to hold onto an atmosphere; but in Titan's case, the upper atmosphere was so cold that the molecules didn't move fast enough to escape Titan's gravity-well.

They had time to observe the moons Tethys and Dion. They studied briefly Iapetus – a world of complex organic matter in an orbit exterior to Titan's. Then Rhea, a world saturated with craters and tiny Phoebe, with a diameter of just 150 kilometres. An unusual world because of its highly inclined and retrograde orbit of Saturn.

But there were many more moons that they didn't have time to study – Atlas, Pandora, Epimetheus, Janus, Mimas, Telesto, Calypso, Helene, Hyperion ...

All had black skies except Titan.

*

Once free of Saturn's gravity-well the Foundation fleet engaged their stardrives and accelerated at high G's. After three hours of great discomfort, the ships reduced the stardrive output to ten percent, to allow an acceleration of 1G. Even this acceleration proved to be tiring for a few days, after spending most of their journey so far at considerably less than 1G.

Five months' ship-time later, at 1G acceleration, the Foundation fleet had left Saturn far behind – all on board, well aware that Saturn was the last planet of Sol's family that they would ever see again. Uranus, Neptune and Pluto were at a point in their lonely orbits that were far away from the starships' flight paths.

*

For three hours, Wade Dryden, commander of *Argo* had endeavoured to locate the Drog fleet.

132

But they were beyond the range of the starship's search technology. *Argo* would, he decided remain on its present flight path. With any luck the enemy would come in scanning range if *Argo's* speed was greater, and if the Drogs' flight path remained unchanged.

But that was not at all likely.

*

A further nine months ship time passed and the Foundation starships were still accelerating at 1G. They had cleared the orbits of Neptune and Pluto and were now passing through the Kuiper Belt of comets – vast, dark icebergs drifting in lonely orbit around distant Sol – lying dormant; waiting patiently for some passing celestial body to disrupt their orbit. Of those chosen, some would be ejected from the family of the Sun, never to return. Others would have a grander destiny and become spectacular comets as they fell inward towards Sol – celebrating its warmth as the atoms of gas and melting water stream out behind in a glorious ghostly tail for millions of kilometres.

All this time, Doctor O'Connor had been careful to appear to be coming around to the Foundation's way of thinking. The tactic was allowing him greater freedom to explore the ship and the motives of its builders. But it was frustrating to be continually shadowed by a dumb robot.

A request he had made earlier to tour *Argo's* garden area had been granted.

His throat tightened in a wave of sadness as the pungent, chlorophyll scented air assailed his senses, reminding him of home. His gaze slowly swept row upon row of hydroponic crop tanks. Further distant in the vast chamber, a variety of fruit trees including citrus grew. They appeared to be thriving under the artificial sunlight and the gently gurgling nutrient fluid. As well as a food source, the damp, humid air boosted the ship's air supply with oxygen through the process of photosynthesis by trees and crops. The same process helped filter out the waste carbon dioxide that the crew exhaled.

Brooding anger still simmered inside him. It was always

there, bubbling below the surface. Nothing the Foundation had explained to him had convinced him of the fiction that the Drogs, an enemy alien race, were responsible for human's tenure on Earth ending. The majority of colonists on the Moon and the few humans on board *Argo* trusted the Foundation. But he couldn't stand by while lies became truth by repetition.

Two robots attended the garden complex. No Foundation personnel were evident.

'Perhaps we should move it along, Doctor O'Connor. We have been granted just a half-hour inspection,' Titus said in a voice devoid of inflection. Since his reprogramming many months ago the robot's persona was a great deal less aggressive.

'Of course, and thank you for reminding me, Titus,' O'Connor said formally. From experience he was treating the robot with an outward show of respect. Although the robot's demeanour was more benign, he could still turn menacing on occasion.

They would be selecting random avenues of crops, as the chamber was too vast to inspect all of it in the time allowed.

As he ambled down the first avenue, Titus's attention wandered to one of the garden robots who was studying a panel of dials which gave out readings of temperature, humidity and nutrient acidity levels.

Exploiting the moment, O'Connor hunkered down and pretended to inspect the anchoring system of a tomato plant. The strong scent of tomato permeated the air, but was not unpleasant. His burnt orange jumpsuit stood out like a beacon to the almost universal green of the crops, as did the large red tomatoes hanging from the plant. He scooped a handful of damp pebbles and grit that was part of the plant's anchoring system, then straightened and continued on down the metal-grated pathway – Titus followed a discreet distance behind. A green reservoir of reticulating, nutrient, fluid stood at the end of each avenue – insurance against catastrophic failure, which could happen if a pump failed, or there was a blockage. Better to lose one avenue of precious crops than have a total crop failure.

As O'Connor reached the end of the lane he managed to drop a little of his cache of stones and grit into the open nutrient reservoir without the robot noticing. He repeated the vandalism on a further three reservoirs undetected.

The remainder of the pebbles and grit he discarded into a fifth reservoir, and he smirked in satisfaction. But his satisfaction was abruptly interrupted as he felt himself being lifted by the scruff of his neck. He felt his pulse quicken, his fear rising.

Titus released his grip and unceremoniously dumped O'Connor who fell in a crumpled heap on the metal grating, knocking the wind out of him. The robot stared down at the pain wracked O'Connor for a finite moment – then two manipulators telescoped down. Grabbing O'Connor with powerful stubby fingers, Titus jerked O'Connor violently up till he was facing the robot's optical sensors.

'Titus disappointed at O'Connor's act of sabotage,' he said simply. 'Now Titus deliver O'Connor to Foundation Director for punishment.' This time to O'Connor's relief, the robot lowered him to the ground.

Before they moved off, Titus programmed in instructions to the garden robots to check and repair as necessary, any faulty reticulation systems.

The robot's programming some months ago had probably saved O'Connor from injury. Titus was just a few paces behind O'Connor as they headed towards the Foundation Director's quarters. To try and escape was futile. With the robot's tremendous acceleration he would be quickly caught.

His face froze in a bitter mask as he contemplated his fate at the hands of the Foundation Director.

*

Months of uninterrupted 1G acceleration had allowed *Argo* to reach the incredible 2/3 sub-light speed. Now the Foundation starships were sailing above the plane of the Oort Comet Cloud – a trillion icy worlds orbiting the distant Sun, which now appeared as a very bright star.

With her face pressed against the viewing blister, Bridgett peered out at the jewelled vista in astonishment. The sky was ablaze with rubies. Curiosity knit her brow as she turned to Jarrod. 'Why are all the stars red?' she asked.

Jarrod rose from his chair and strode four paces to where Bridgett stood. He stared down at her for a silent moment and smiled. '*Argo* is travelling away from the stars at a good fraction of the speed of light, and so the light from the stars has changed to a lower frequency towards red. It's known as the Doppler effect. It causes the stars to be red-shifted.' He searched her face for understanding.

'I thought the Doppler effect was just to do with sound only; like when a train approaches, the sound waves are different from when it passes you.'

'The Doppler effect, Bridgett concerns both sound and light.'

'Then if we looked at the stars through the ship's forward viewing blister they would be a different colour, because we'd be travelling fast towards them,' she reasoned. 'So what colour would they be,' Jarrod?'

Jarrod shook his head in amazement at little Bridgett's agile mind – so clever! And so young! 'They would be blue-tinged, because the light would be a higher frequency … blue-shifted.'

Bridgett nodded and returned her attention back to the star field. They reminded her of a beautiful ruby necklace her papa had given Mamma for her birthday two years previous. Her throat tightened and she felt a prickle of tears, as once more grief's cold fingers reached for her. Dear Papa – she missed him so much.

Jarrod returned to his chair next to David, and to a new topic of discussion – Moonbase.

'Now the speed of the ship has increased dramatically,' David remarked, 'time must be slowing down for us, but it certainly doesn't feel like it.'

'Yes relativistic travel is a strange concept,' Amber chipped in. 'The rate at which time flows is variable. It just depends entirely on the speed of the observer.' Her eyes went distant. 'All the children at Moonbase will now be adults, but to us, shipboard time, only months have passed.'

'Mind boggling,' David commented. He gazed over at her

perfect beauty that time would never fade. And only time would tell how they both would cope as he himself aged, died, and, was then reborn as a baby clone.

'Moonbase may well have constructed their starship by now,' Amber remarked.

'Hopefully along with fighter craft,' Jarrod added.

*

Although the Moon has useful quantities of material, it isn't as rich as many of the asteroids. And so the Foundation mining vessel *Prospector* sailing the sea of small worlds, diverted one that was rich in materials to low Moon orbit for the colony to mine. Wordy texts would continue between the Foundation and Moonbase for as long as practical.

*

Floyd Burke, the Foundation Director, shook his head in frustration. O'Connor was exhausting his tolerance for confrontation. 'Most of us, Doctor O'Connor were of the opinion that you were keeping an open mind on the excellent intentions that the Foundation had for Earth.' He leant forward in his chair. 'It's tragic that our efforts to save the planet were unsuccessful, but we did our best.' There was deep sadness in his voice. 'Removing your disruptive influence from the lunar colony has improved the chances of its survival and gives us some comfort. But we are disappointed in your act of sabotage and for that you must be punished.' He looked into O'Connor's chilly, blue eyes, searching for a sign of repentance – he saw none. 'Have you anything to say in your defence?'

'Yes I do, sir,' he said uneasily. 'My act of vandalism was an aberration.' He paused a moment. 'I don't know what came over me. I admit that I'm far from convinced of the professed intentions of the Foundation.' His voice turned silken. 'If, in the fullness of time, I find that my mistrust of the Foundation is unfounded, then I will humbly apologize. But in the meantime all I can promise you is that I will try to keep an open mind.'

Floyd Burke stared down at O'Connor. 'I will give you a choice of punishment. You will be taken to your quarters, and rationed to one meal a day for a week. Freedom to wander the ship with a robot escort will be withdrawn. Further more, as we also rely on our crops for good quality air, your cabin's air will be slowly withdrawn to a point of great distress to you. Then after a week, with the steady build-up of carbon dioxide, we trust you may have a deep respect for our crops.'

Floyd continued. 'But you do have a second choice. One, which I hope you will choose. We can simply give you a cranial implant and download and remove all the negativity you feel towards the Foundation.'

Without hesitation, O'Connor chose the first option.

A short time after the dismissal of O'Connor, Floyd Burke summoned Wade and Simon for a meeting – the topic being O'Connor.

Floyd explained to them both the two choices he'd given O'Connor.

'It's unfortunate that he didn't choose the cranial implant, so on reflection, I've decided that he will have one anyway.' He saw them both nod in relieved agreement. 'We can't have a loose canon on the ship. I feel sure his paranoia of the Foundation is too deeply embedded to ever be removed over the coming years. Do you both agree?'

Wade leaned forward in his chair. 'I think it's a wise decision. It's not as if he hasn't been given every opportunity to mend his ways.'

The director glanced to his left and arched his eyebrows. 'Simon?'

'O'Connor is a dangerous man in his present state, and I must say how relieved I am with your decision, sir.'

'I am pleased that you both agree with me. All along, I didn't expect O'Connor to change, but I hoped he would.' He clasped his fingers together and leaned back in his chair. 'Now, Simon, I will leave you to arrange the procedure and this is how I want it done.' He folded his arms and leant forward in his chair. 'He's never to know he's had the implant!' He paused a moment before continuing. 'He will be expecting his punishment of course, so give him one meal a day, and over a period of two days, reduce the oxygen level to a degree where he's uncomfortable. Then anaesthetize him with gas via the air-conditioning. Take him away for his cranial implant and edit his downloaded thoughts and memories that are counter to the Foundation's best interests. Unfortunately, we will have to give him a degree of molecular enhancement so that his scalp heals quickly – but that's all. Further on, if he proves to be a good citizen, we will give him what he thinks will be a cranial implant – then we can give him a full enhancement. Any comments?'

Simon and Wade agreed that the plan of cold logic was an excellent one.

*

The brain in many ways is like a computer, and like a computer, if it's programmed to forget something, it does. The information is completely erased.

Chapter Eleven

O'Connor's cranial microchip implantation had been carried out satisfactorily. While allowing a mild memory of distrust of the Foundation to remain, false memory legitimising the Foundation's claims now overlaid that former distrust. He was returned to his cabin at week's end, and his intravenous feed of nutrients was curtailed, and the anaesthetic withdrawn.

Coming out of the anaesthetic haze, O'Connor became aware of something cold and metallic holding his hand. He opened his eyes slowly. With his vision mist-shrouded, he blinked several times to refocus. His eyes widened. A tall slim robot stood by his bed, peering down at him.

'Welcome back to the conscious world, Doctor O'Connor. You blacked out because of the low oxygen content of your cabin,' the robot lied. 'You have been unconscious for days, but I have made sure that you were not in any danger,' he said smoothly.

'What ... what sort of robot are you?' he mumbled.

'I am a surgical robot,' he said proudly.

'Well the only danger around here,' he said weakly, 'is that mountain of nuts and bolts behind you.' He pointed to Titus.

'Titus is a very fine warrior robot,' the surgical robot countered. 'He is here to see that you come to no harm.'

'Of course he is,' O'Connor echoed with heavy sarcasm. 'Now if you don't mind I would like you to release my hand.'

The surgical robot concurred with his patient's request, and O'Connor was sure if it was possible for the robot, it would have given him a patient little smile.

Withdrawing from the side of the bed, the surgical robot said, 'I will leave you now in the excellent care of Titus. You are now free to roam the ship at his discretion – '

'Yes, just you and me,' Titus cut in. 'Like old times.'

O'Connor answered with a scowl.

*

Eighteen months shipboard time had passed since leaving Moon orbit. The fleet of Foundation cruisers had now left the Oort Comet Cloud behind. *Argo* was now three times further from the Sun than Pluto. Here the pressure of interstellar electrons and protons is greater than the tiny pressure from the solar wind, an area of space known as the heliopause – 100,000 AU's from the Sun, which was now one and a half light years distant.

Wade Dryden sat at the bridge. The curving bank of computer screens was reporting the status of each system of the ship, showing everything was functioning satisfactorily.

His fingers danced over his keyboard for one final check. His expectations were low, his hopes high. A superimposed grid lit up the screen. No Drog vessels showed up on the grid. He turned to Simon. 'Well that just about does it,' he said shaking his head. 'We will have to abandon our enemy search.' He sighed. 'Cut *Argo's* acceleration to 1/6 G. We won't take up the shortfall of gravity by artificially raising it to 1G to conserve energy.'

Even at the lower acceleration *Argo's* speed was still increasing to an appreciable fraction of the speed of light.

*

Because the ship's gravity was now equivalent to the Moon, there was an increased exercise regime in place – necessary to prevent calcium leaching from the bones and muscle atrophy. It wasn't a regime that was set in stone, and was left to each individual to police his programme. Regular medical readouts would show up any slackers.

In *Argo's* gym, Lisa and Jarrod had finished their warm up and stretching exercises. They harnessed themselves to treadmills with robust rubber cords that substituted the lower setting of the ship's gravity. This forced them to support their own mass. Setting their watches, they started off in a slow walk, straining against the revolving belt. After three minutes they increased their pace, embracing the added discomfort right through to the inevitable pain. Their aching bodies protested as

141

old tissue broke down, but would be replaced by new, stronger muscle.

Meanwhile, David, Amber and Bridgett were doing upper body exercises. With feet anchored securely to the floor they were hunched over, and rhythmically pulling spring-loaded cords attached to the wall.

No one spoke, the silence broken only by intermittent gasps and groans between gritting teeth. Eventually they swapped apparatus to give other muscle groups their required workout.

After a warm down on completion of their workouts they grabbed towels from a dispenser on the wall and slowly dried the pooled sweat soaking their bodies. Exhaustion was overcoming any desire to talk. When done they dropped the towels into a laundry bin to be automatically laundered – the sweat would be recycled to be consumed once more by crew.

Retrieving their swimming gear from their lockers, they made their way to the warm, humid swimming pool chamber adjacent to the gym. The twenty-metre pool had three lanes.

It would be a new experience for them. They'd used the pool many times before, but that was in 1G. Now that the ship's gravity was set at 1/6 G, it was going to be interesting to see how the water behaved.

Jarrod was the first out of the changing shed. The others quickly followed. As the pool was just over Bridgett's head she wore air filled armbands.

'You go first, David,' Jarrod suggested, 'and we'll see how the water behaves.'

David nodded agreement and dived in. They all laughed as they witnessed the abnormal height of the waves, and the dreamlike slowness that they moved across the pool from David's point of entry.

Joining David, they quickly adjusted their swimming technique to suit the unusual action of the water.

After half an hour of the highly unusual swimming session, and many involuntary mouthfuls of water they flagged it away. It was an interesting experience, but they all agreed that they preferred to swim in normal gravity.

*

Lisa and Jarrod were just about to tap out their midday meal order when Bridgett and her mother entered the dining area. Bridgett, resplendent in a freshly laundered, canary-yellow jumpsuit, wore a grin from ear to ear. A name patch was embroidered on her suit to the right of her heart. It read *Bridgett Michaiels – Space Cadet.* Above this were sewn astronaut's wings. 'Notice anything different about me?' she asked proudly.

'Not that I can notice,' Jarrod said slowly. 'Wait a minute, you've had your hair restyled and it suits you.'

Bridgett shook her head in a negative response. Her smile faded and she turned to Lisa for her input.

'I thought it was a new hair style too,' she kidded.

Bridgett caught their joking expressions at last. She bowed her head and covered her eyes with her hand and pretended to weep. She rolled her eyes up, and through a gap between her fingers she saw the look of concern on their faces.

'Bridgett we were only kidding and we are sorry.' Jarrod hesitated ... 'we didn't mean to upset you.'

Bridgett raised her head. Her expression brightened. 'Got you both,' she giggled. 'I was just kidding back.'

Nicolett and Bridgett eased themselves into seats opposite Jarrod and Lisa. Nicolett was grateful to the thoughtful soul responsible for the handiwork on Bridgett's jumpsuit. It had lifted a mood of melancholy that had descended on her daughter earlier.

Then David and his parents arrived for their midday meal. Almost immediately they spied Bridgett's embroidered name, title and astronaut's wings.

'Very impressive, Bridgett,' Gerald effused. 'And such fine embroidery. You certainly deserve your wings. David told me how well you managed in the zero G chamber.'

'Thank you,' she said modestly.

David crouched down beside her and shook her hand. 'Well done, Bridgett.'

'Yes well done,' Mary White echoed, patting Bridgett's back.

143

Doctor O'Connor was far from happy when he entered the dining area accompanied by the intimidating robot, Hugo. O'Connor would have preferred Titus, but he was being reprogrammed. This was his first meal since coming out of anaesthetic and he felt a little strange. All was not well – something wasn't right. He remembered sabotaging the crop chamber, but for the life of him he couldn't understand why he would do such a thing. He sat down and gazed to his right at table ten. Seven pairs of stony eyes returned his gaze. Man, he thought to himself, they hold a grudge a long time. I gave them a hard time back on Earth, but now everything's been resolved. They were right. And I was wrong not to trust the Vision Foundation, and that should be the end of it.

Gerald felt something pressing uncomfortably in a pocket of his jumpsuit.

Mary noticed his fidgeting. 'What is it, dear?'

'Just a minute and I'll tell you,' he said as he retrieved the object from his pocket, and looked down at his hand with embarrassment.

Bridgett was curious. 'What is in the bottle, Mr White?'

'Ah … it's a bottle of lunar dust …just a souvenir. That's all it is.'

'Can I look at it?'

'Of course you can, Bridgett.' He was glad that no one appeared to think his little bottle of dust was a strange keepsake. He passed it over to the little French girl.

'Can I open it, Mr White?' she asked. 'I would like to see if it's still got the same smell … scent,' she corrected herself, being prideful of her English. She saw him nod in agreement. Her face scrunched up as she attempted to unscrew the lid.

Her mother reached over to her. 'Let me do that for you, dear.'

Just as her mother's hand reached for the bottle the lid suddenly unscrewed. Half of the contents spilled out onto the table. Fine particles of electrostatically charged lunar dust billowed out to be picked up by a current of air. The scent of wood smoke permeated the area. Most of the air-born dust would be filtered out by the air conditioning. All at table ten and in close proximity would breath in a tiny amount of the fine dust – but it was of no consequence.

And a miniscule amount would dust Hugo's circuitry.

'*Je regrette*,' Bridgett exclaimed.

'We are so sorry, Gerald,' Nicolette apologised. 'It was entirely my fault. If I hadn't reached for the bottle I'm sure it wouldn't have spilt.' She brushed as much dust as she could back into the jar. One of the dining area's cleaning robots would deal with the remainder later.

'No need to apologise,' Gerald said. 'Accidents happen. No harm done. Anyway we hardly lost any of the dust.'

'Can we order now, Mamma?'

'Of course you can, dear.' She was about to key in her order when mayhem erupted at O'Connor's table.

Hugo's manipulators swung violently in all directions. Microscopic particles of dust had been sucked into his circuits by his cooling fan. The compromised circuitry was instructing him that the ship was under attack. His head swivelled, searching the immediate area with his optical facilities for an enemy presence – seeking any unusual life form that had somehow breached *Argo's* security.

Hugo peered down at table ten. He'd found an enemy infiltrator. One of the humans seated was so tiny compared to the rest – a dead giveaway. With a single vicious motion, a manipulator telescoped out grabbing the front of Bridgett's yellow jumpsuit.

A piercing scream escaped her lips. 'Let me go! Let me go!' she cried out at the robot towering above her.

Cries of fear and outrage erupted around the restaurant. Hugo paid no heed. Sweeping away all attempts of those at table ten to free Bridgett from his vice-grip, he lifted the little French girl to the level of his optical sensors.

The oscillating pitch of a siren rose above the pandemonium in response to the monitored display on the bridge's central control.

'It is over,' the robot said simply as it regarded Bridgett's frightened eyes. 'Hugo take enemy to recycling machine to be rendered down for fertiliser.'

Her mother's screaming was the last sound that Bridgett heard before her brain sought protection by shutting down, and she fainted away.

O'Connor looked down at his hands and saw they were clenched into fists. Shaking his head, he couldn't contain himself any longer. He would not stand by while the little French girl's life was in peril. All the pent-up anger that he'd bottled up against the way Hugo had treated him had to be released.

In a single movement, O'Connor launched himself off his chair onto the back of the robot – his lean hard face wild eyed with rage. Clinging on for dear life with one arm around the robot's shoulder, and in clarity born of a crisis, he reached around the robot's head with his free arm, and covered the robot's optical sensors with his hand.

Blinded, the robot still clung onto the little girl. Another manipulator that terminated in a wide-angled laser projector hung at the robot's side, and thankfully, so far hadn't been operational. But the other two manipulators flailed around in deadly confusion, connecting with dinner plates and cutlery. In the low gravity the missiles flew across the dining area. Some intersected each other's orbits – and some impacted soft flesh.

The robot swivelled violently to the right, then to the left to shake off a determined O'Connor – the action proved unsuccessful.

Stubby metal fingers grasped the offending hand and tore it away from its optical facilities and squeezed.

O'Connor cried out in excruciating pain as his hand crushed in a mess of broken fingers and bloody flesh. The robot released the mangled hand, and O'Connor, with great presence of mind, and through an all-encompassing pain, managed to reach up once more, and smear the robot's optical sensors with blood and tissue from his injured hand.

And still O'Connor hung on.

Angry and frustrated with his impaired vision, and the cause of it still clinging to his back, Hugo accelerated backwards towards the wall of the restaurant.

O'Connor let out a scream as he slammed into the wall, sandwiched between the wall and the robot's back.

Hugo jerked forward. O'Connor slumped in an unconscious heap to the ground.

Jarrod tried to wrestle Bridgett from the robot's grasp. A manipulator shot out giving him a jarring thump on his left temple, sending him sprawling backwards. Blood seeped from his head wound.

Hugo reached down to the blurred shape. Stubby fingers bathed in O'Connor's blood seized Jarrod's jumpsuit, jerking him upwards, then slamming him against the wall.

With the wind knocked out of him and agony lancing throughout his body, Jarrod fought to stay conscious.

Lisa raced over to him and kneeling down cradled him in her arms, her concern clearly visible on her face.

He tried to reassure her, but no words came to him. His eyes lost their focus as he surrendered to the darkness. His genetically enhanced immune system swung into action. Thrombocytes – blood platelets swarmed to his head wound to repair the trauma.

David staggered forward from a blow to the back of his head, as he too tried to free Bridgett's limp body from the robot's grip. On legs of rubber, his momentum finally stalled as he collapsed over table ten. The oblivion of unconsciousness reached out for him – claiming him as he slipped into its dark embrace.

The restaurant was now more like a war zone. With no regard to the chaos he'd created, the confused and dangerous robot's misted vision located the exit and he trundled off, still clutching Bridgett.

In *Argo's* low gravity setting, the six members of the elite assault team bounded down the corridor towards the dining area, their footfalls echoing dully off the walls. They were a formidable force, outfitted in armour from head to toe – their helmets complete with dark protective visors. The strange armour was bathed in shifting colour as it took on the background hues of the immediate environment. Any reasonable distance from an enemy the camouflage would be very effective.

Team leader, Paul Mason raised a hand to halt his men as Hugo advanced up the corridor, still clutching Bridgett's limp

147

body. 'Stand perfectly still,' Paul ordered his men in a raspy voice. 'And stand tall,' he added. 'With the robot's impaired vision, we don't want him to think we are tiny aliens like the little girl.'

Hugo slowed as he approached the assault team. They were just a blur through his optical sensors. Friend or foe he wondered. He came to a stop, ten metres from the group.

'Move to one side,' he bellowed.

'We can see your vision sensors are impaired otherwise you would recognise that we are your allies,' Paul said. 'Let me say that you have done a fine job in detecting and neutralizing an enemy agent.'

'Hugo not sure if you are friend or enemy,' he said in a booming voice.

'Let me assure you that we are Foundation personnel. We have not drawn our weapons against you because we have no intention of engaging you in battle. Now if you will allow me, I will clean your optical sensors so that you can see us better.'

'Very well, Hugo allow. Any false move and Hugo kill.'

Paul Mason carefully withdrew a cloth from a compartment at the side of his armour that he used to clean his own visor. Hunkering down he sprang up gently so as not to alarm Hugo. Wrapping an arm around the robot's neck, he proceeded to clean the optical sensors. He glanced down with concern at the little French girl. He was relieved to see the rise and fall of her chest. He was in no doubt that a flexing of the robot's stubby fingers would end her life. He would have to use all his skill and patience to negotiate her release. Satisfied that he'd cleaned the lenses as best he could, he scrambled down. Later the robot's optical facilities would be given a more comprehensive clean. And the circuits would be checked out to see what caused the robot's confused and dangerous behaviour.

'Now, great warrior robot, can you see now that we are a Foundation assault team?'

'Hugo can see that now. Move to one side so Hugo can finish mission.'

'What does that involve, great warrior?'

'Taking enemy to be rendered down for fertiliser.'

148

Paul Mason suppressed a shudder of revulsion. 'Let us do that for you brave, Hugo. You've done enough for one day,' more than enough you crazy son of a bitch, he added silently. 'It would be an honour for one of my men to do this menial task for you.'

Without a word, Hugo gave a small bow and deposited Bridgett to the floor.

Paul waved one of his men forward. 'Take her away and complete brave Hugo's mission.'

The trooper bent over Bridgett and carefully lifted her. Turning on his heel he strode out as quickly as he could in the low gravity. Fortunately the hospital was in the same direction as the recycling area and wouldn't raise the suspicion of Hugo.

*

O'Connor had regained consciousness and became aware of a surgical robot by his bed studying information on his medical readouts. Trauma to his head had caused a severe concussion. But already the bruising on his head had disappeared, and would be explained away by the Foundation. His injured hand was another matter. Because of this it was more heavily bandaged than was necessary. Already the healing process was well on the way due to his genetically enhanced immune system that he was unaware he possessed. And his hand would remain bandaged longer than necessary to avoid raising the suspicions of O'Connor, himself, a medical doctor.

'Was I concussed?' he asked the surgical robot.

'Welcome back to the conscious world, Doctor O'Connor. Yes, and I must compliment you on your rapid recovery.'

'How long have I been out?

'Just over an hour.'

'I'm puzzled. My head doesn't hurt at all.'

'Yes, as I said, a remarkable recovery.' The surgical robot was well aware that O'Connor was not to know of his cranial implant.

'And my hand was badly mashed but it doesn't feel like it?'

'That's because of our wonderful painkillers,' the surgical

149

robot effused, 'that are coursing through your system. You would be well aware, Doctor, if pain can be avoided, or lessened, it speeds up the healing process.'

'Yes I'm aware of that, but I know that I had many of my fingers broken.'

'Oh no, Doctor. You're mistaken,' the robot lied. 'It would have been a very painful experience for you but I assure you no bones were broken.'

O'Connor conceded the point with a nod. 'Was the little girl rescued from that brute of a robot?' The surgical robot pointed to the bed next to O'Connor's. He turned his head and was surprised to see Bridgett. She lay very still. The only movement she made was the shallow rise and fall of her chest. Her mother was beside the bed, holding her daughter's hand, gazing down at her with concern.

'She is suffering shock and is sedated,' the surgical robot explained. 'It was such a traumatic event for the little girl. Three ribs were cracked and she's heavily strapped, but the outlook is good.' It was a pity all the humans didn't have cranial implants and an enhanced immune system the robot mused.

Nicolette looked up and smiled at O'Connor. It was a rare experience for him. She came over to his bed, and he noted her slight limp. Gazing down at him, she said, 'I cannot thank you enough for trying to save my daughter and risking your life for her,' she said in her delightful French accent.

'I ... I did what I could,' he stammered – 'everyone did.' His pulse quickened as he took in Nicolette's large dark eyes, porcelain complexion and silky light-brown hair that curled around her shoulders.

'You were so brave and so clever. Through all the pain of your poor injured hand you did not give up. Smearing the robot's vision was a big factor of my daughter being rescued. Doctor O'Connor let me introduce myself. I am Nicolette Michaiels. My friends call me Nikki, and that is what you shall call me.'

The force of her personality washed over him. He could feel a warm rush of blood throughout his body, and was sure she would notice his face redden in a blush. Something that he hadn't done since his teenage years. Since those early years he'd always been in total control.

'And … you … must call me, Adrian.'

She silently regarded him for a moment, then, on impulse, clasped his good hand in hers, and leaning down, kissed both his cheeks.

He picked up the scent of her body, fragrant and exciting. It took all his willpower not to reach out and pull her to him.

It would be years before he set eyes on her again.

*

Hugo was checked out and to the astonishment of the technicians, they found the cause of the robot's bizarre and dangerous behaviour – lunar dust. They disconnected the robot's higher functions, cleaned the circuits, his optical sensors, and did a thorough reprogramming.

Hugo was back!

The lunar dust was traced to the dining area.

In his cabin, a remorseful Gerald sat on the side of his bed, his head bowed. He'd slept little over-night as his mind churned over the terrifying episode with the robot. He paid no regard to his battered and bruised body from attempts he'd made to free Bridgett from the robot's grasp; the guilt simmered inside him.

Mary stood by his bed, resting a hand on his shoulder. She felt his pain. 'You mustn't blame yourself, dear. It was an unfortunate accident.'

Raising his head, he gazed up at her with red-rimmed eyes. 'I should never have brought the lunar dust on board,' he said, his voice croaky, tinged with strain. 'I knew it had a reputation of getting into electrical equipment. I should have had more sense,' he scolded. 'And because of my bloody sentimentality so many were injured.'

An image of Bridgett's limp body in the clutches of the robot rekindled in Gerald's mind. He shuddered. And now Bridgett is lying injured and traumatised in a hospital bed – all because of him! He'd gained little comfort when Mirim had told him that the Foundation should have anticipated that someone

151

might have wanted to take a little of the Moon with them. And then Nicollette had insisted she was to blame. If she hadn't reached for the bottle there wouldn't have been a spillage of lunar dust. But none of their claims of responsibility could assuage his guilt.

And it could have been much worse! He let out a tense sigh and fixed Mary with a bleak gaze.

'Well it's over now, Gerald,' she said gently. 'Bridgett will recover quickly, and the lunar dust has been jettisoned to space. We just have to put all this behind us.'

'Yes. I know that you're right. I just need a little time to come to terms with it.' He was silent a long moment as his thoughts went to all of those brave souls who'd tried to rescue Bridgett. One stood out in his mind. 'O'Connor's actions were commendable – I even feel sorry for him.'

'Yes, he was very brave taking on the robot with no regard to the danger to himself. It was so unexpected.'

*

On Nicolette's next visit to her daughter's bedside she looked over to O'Connor's bed. It was empty. A surgical robot informed her that he'd been discharged and was resting in his cabin. She felt a sliver of disappointment at not seeing him, and immediately chastised herself. After all it was great that he was well enough to be discharged.

Two days later Bridgett was recovering well from her injuries, both physical and mental trauma. The reason for the robot's dangerous behaviour was explained to her.

'It was my fault, Mamma, not the robot.'

'It was an unfortunate accident, dear, and if anyone's to blame it's me for reaching for the bottle just as you opened it. Anyway the lunar dust has been jettisoned to space so nothing like this can happen again.'

'What happened to the robot?'

'It is being repaired and reprogrammed.'

'Can my friends visit me soon? I am feeling much better, so they won't make me tired.'

'I will make inquiries.'

The next day Bridgett had a continual stream of visitors.

And later that day, Dr O'Connor visited her, and was disappointed that Nicolette wasn't present at her daughter's bedside. He stared down at Bridgett. She was sleeping and that's a good thing, he told himself – sleep is a great healer. He reached down and adjusted the blankets around her shoulders and quietly left the room.

Chapter Twelve

Five years ship time had passed since leaving Moon orbit. The three mighty Foundation cruisers powered on, faster and faster through the eternal void, accelerating at 1/6 G. Bridgett was now twelve years old. Like her mamma, she had a fine-boned, aristocratic face, and had retained her bubbly personality.

Since the lunar dust episode, Dr O'Connor had been spending his time on the other two cruisers, *Vela* and *Orion*, even though he'd pleaded on numerous occasions to be returned to *Argo*. He was being further assessed to see if he was developing fresh symptoms of paranoid behaviour. But with no paranoia apparent, he was shipped back to *Argo* in a five-berth shuttle that was shared between the three cruisers.

*

Simon placed a palm to a small identification screen. The iridescent-green metallic door slid silently open and he ushered the group in. Only Amber, Jarrod and Lisa had been there before when the unusual circumstances of their birth had been revealed – a short time before Earth's destruction. David and his parents knew about the chamber and its various functions though.

They stood around Simon with expressions of curiosity.

Simon wasted no time. 'As you all know, a human's life is too fleeting for interstellar travel. Even so, with the exception of Doctor O'Connor, you all chose to journey on to the stars with the Foundation – '

'And let me tell you,' Nicolette said, 'that we are grateful. Remaining on the Moon with broken planet Earth in the sky would have been a constant sadness. And here on *Argo* there's so much to see, so much to learn.'

'Well I am happy to hear that.' He gazed over at Bridgett and smiled. The last time he'd seen her she was just a delightful child. Now she was almost fully-grown, on the brink of womanhood.

'Your education has been going well?' Simon asked.

154

'Mamma teaches me a lot, and my computer, Beatrice, is a wonderful teacher too,' she said enthusiastically. 'And thank you and the Foundation for your present to me on my birthday yesterday. Now I can resume my music again.'

Jarrod had enquired of his father months earlier if there was any way a piano could be constructed on board for Bridgett. To his delight his father had told him that he saw no reason why it couldn't. Plans for an electronic piano were in the ship's library, and the engineers had completed their task of constructing replacement Interceptors that were lost in battle.

And so the piano was constructed.

Simon went on. 'Now the reason for this meeting. The three upright tanks to your left are gestation tanks where our children are born.' He noted the shock etched on the faces of Nicolette, Bridgett and Doctor O'Connor, but continued on. 'I will briefly explain the functions of all the machines in the chamber, then any questions you may have, you can ask your computers or Jarrod, Amber or Lisa later.'

It was a touchy subject and he was relieved there were no interruptions during his explanation of the gestation tanks, and to their credit no questions were forthcoming. Their computers would attend to them later.

Simon continued in a resonate baritone. 'The Foundation is prepared to offer you extended lifetimes, and by that I mean double your expected lifetime. I am not alluding to relativistic time, just your shipboard apparent aging. Of course this doesn't concern Amber, Jarrod or Lisa,' and explained that all the Foundation humans lived for an indefinitely long time and never looked older than twenty-five years.

For a long, silent moment, Simon gazed at the group ... letting his words sink in. 'David has already accepted our offer of extending his life and has an enhanced immune system installed. Further more we made an offer to him that upon his death we would clone him, which he has accepted.'

O'Connor, Nikki and Bridgett's eyes widened – stunned at the mention of cloning, but again they remained silent, not wanting to interrupt the flow of information.

'David has a cranial implant and through this we have

downloaded his lifetime of memories, knowledge and experiences. Regular downloading will be needed to keep our records up to date. Upon his eventual death they will be transferred in quantum amounts to his clone. You see, even with your extended lifetime that we offer you, it is far too brief for star travel and the search for a new Earth.' He paused for breath, and resumed at a slower pace. 'So our offer to you is the same as what David has agreed to already. Doctor White and Gerald White are aware of their son's acceptance and are still making up their minds whether to accept the same. Of course you could agree to just doubling your lifetime and make a decision about cloning later on. In the meantime it would be prudent to have your DNA stored in our Life Bank.'

'But you will need more than our DNA to make clones,' O'Connor argued.

'Of course, Doctor O'Connor. We have human de-nucleated eggs in our Life Bank.'

'And when our clone eventually dies, you will be able to clone us again and again?'

'Not indefinitely.' He explained that they could clone each of them eight times. A ninth cloning always failed for some inexplicable reason.

'Now, no more questions. Your computers have all been programmed to explain any questions you might have. One of you will have to share your computer with Doctor O'Connor.'

'Adrian can share ours,' Nikki chipped in, smiling warmly at O'Connor.

'Very good.' Simon gestured to the other twenty vessels, and explained that they were regenerative beds. 'At present there are nine empty vessels. Foundation personnel that are not needed for the day to day running of the ship occupy the rest. This way we can help conserve the ship's valuable resources. An identical chamber to this has a further twenty regenerative beds and three artificial wombs. Our surgery too, has three birthing tanks and three regenerative beds.'

'A total of just nine birthing tanks? Is that all?' Doctor O'Connor asked.

'Yes, Doctor. You see we live for a very long time.'

'Yes, of course, and I'm very curious as to why that is. Could you enlighten us about that phenomenon?'

Simon gave a wry smile. 'Your curiosity is understandable, Doctor O'Connor, but I am not at liberty to divulge that information at this time. Now I digress. The vacant regenerative beds are at your disposal if you so choose; otherwise Foundation personnel will fill them. He touched briefly on the various functions of the beds, and encouraged them to digest the information and consult with their computers for more detail and the advantage of electing deep sleep.

O'Connor was still totally unaware of his enhanced immune system and cranial implant.

O'Connor accompanied Nikki to her cabin to allow a more in-depth understanding from her computer of what the Foundation was offering. They were alone, as Bridgett had gone to Jarrod's cabin with Lisa and David to discuss with them their understanding of deep sleep and cloning.

'Alien technology implanted into our head! Downloading our memories and experiences! Cloning! Deep sleep! My mind is spinning. I don't know whether to rejoice or be repelled by the offer. What about you, Nikki?'

'I have to confess I am excited. Just imagine, Adrian,' she lowered her tone to lend significance to her words. 'Our life expectancy will double, then we can live on in our clones – eight more extended lifetimes, all made even longer if we accept deep sleep. Think of the adventure and the discoveries that could unfold in that time.' She turned to her computer. 'Beatrice,' she commanded.

Nikki sat down and waited for Beatrice to generate her presence.

'How can I help you, my dear?' Beatrice asked in her sultry voice.

O'Connor, who was gazing at the screen over Nikki's shoulder, couldn't help himself. He burst out laughing. Beatrice was the image of Bridgett when she was just a little girl. And the sensuous voice was so out of place.

'Please excuse my companion, Beatrice. He does not mean to offend.'

'No offence taken, my dear. You have some questions for me?'

'We fully understand the cloning and immune enhancement that has been offered to us, but I would appreciate you going over the details of deep sleep.'

'In your case, as an indigenous human, your body struggles with nature, and unfortunately it is an uneven struggle. The deep sleep vessels are regenerative. They preserve and reduce wear and tear on your bodies. The whole body slows down to near death, but the machine makes sure that death does not occur. Chemical brain activity is measured and cellular reconstruction is carried out to damaged areas.'

'But what about the problem of muscles, atrophy, and calcium leaching from our bones into the bloodstream with prolonged inactivity?' Nicolette enquired.

'Muscle tone and bone density is preserved electronically.'

Nicolette nodded her understanding.

Beatrice carried on. 'Even though the brain all but shuts down, the dream area is fully functional. Your dreams will be vivid and pleasant. Before you are immersed in the tanks you can select what type of dreams you would prefer.'

'Well thank you for being so helpful, Beatrice.'

'Not at all, my dear.'

Beatrice's image faded from the screen.

Nikki turned to O'Connor. 'A bit scary about the body nearly shutting down completely.'

'Well, when we sleep the body does shut down to a certain extent. I don't think it's anything to worry about,' he reassured.

'What would you choose to dream about, Adrian?'

His eyes went distant and he was silent for a moment. 'In my dreams I would like to discover a new planet with a blue nitrogen sky graced with lacy white clouds. I would stroll in a cool forest, swim in a warm ocean … lay down in a soft meadow … with Nicolette by my side.'

'Oh, Adrian, how lovely of you to want to include me in your dreams,' she said softly. She wasn't sure but she thought she caught a blush before he looked down and studied his hands.

O'Connor felt his face redden. The moment stretched. He

158

glanced sidelong at her.

Her lips were parted. She held his gaze for a finite moment, then pulled him to her so their lips could meet. She leaned her cheek against his and clung to him hard, warmly.

For a few minutes there was little spoken, but much enchantment.

*

The Foundation vessels were just three days away from the edge of a large, dark, gas and dust cloud. No course corrections would be necessary to avoid it, as their present course would just clear it.

Simon's eyes widened as he hunched over his scanner display. 'Well, well, well,' he said in a loud baritone. 'What have we here?'

The bridge fell silent. The systems analyst, Angela Shriver glanced to her right to Simon. Her dark sculptured eyebrows arched in question above sea-green eyes.

The navigation officer, Angus Macandrew's scanning of a large star-field in Sagittarius, was interrupted as he gazed to his left at Simon's focus of attention.

Commander Wade Dryden who had just entered the bridge, leaned over the back of Simon's chair and studied the blip on the display screen. 'Sharpen up the image please, Simon,' he ordered crisply.

Simon's fingers keyed in a command to the image intensifier.

As the blip came into sharp focus, there was no doubt. It was a solitary Drog cruiser with its propulsion system engaged, the ionised green glow of its exhaust clearly visible.

Simon smiled as he pictured in his mind the three Foundation cruisers and their compliment of Interceptors swooping down like hawks attacking a helpless prey. He looked expectantly over his shoulder at the commander for an order to set a new course to do just that.

Wade read Simon's unspoken expectation, but shook his head slowly. 'It could be an ambush,' he said, his voice a low rumble. 'A Drog armada could be easily concealed in that cloud ahead,' he explained. 'We won't take the bait.' He ordered a course change for *Argo* with instructions for *Vela* and *Orion* to follow.

The three cruisers swung away to the new course setting that would take them well away from the curtain of gas and dust, and all it might be concealing.

*

On board the Drog cruiser, Axel gazed at his display screen with bitter disappointment as the Foundation cruisers vectored away. So much planning had gone into the mission. He'd been shadowing the Foundation cruisers from his forward position without a hint of being detected by them – until now, and that had been deliberate. Contact to his fleet had been kept to a minimum and sent by tight laser beam so as to avoid detection – and now at the last moment the wily Foundation fleet hadn't taken the bait. These Foundation humans are survivors, he thought to himself. And they were tough – a worthy adversary. He even admired them grudgingly. 'Oh well,' he grunted to himself, 'we will just revert to our reserve plan.' The enemy was not tough enough for what he knew was in store for them.

The thought gave him great satisfaction.

*

The molecular gas cloud was too vast to warrant scanning for enemy vessels, but after a week the surprisingly dense, molecular cloud had been left well behind, and with it the threat of an ambush. For thirty minutes discreet bursts from the Foundation cruisers attitude jets were returning the vessels to their original course.

Back on course, propulsion was cut to zero. Artificial gravity was set at lunar G. Even coasting the vessels maintained a considerable fraction of the speed of light in the cold darkness. There was nothing ahead to hinder their progress.

Well – nothing that the Foundation anticipated.

*

The Drog cruiser under the command of Axel, continued to accelerate so as not to fall too far behind the Foundation vessels, and matching the Foundation's course change with discrete blasts of its attitude jets. Axel felt no concern at the Foundation's course setting. It was still well within the parameters of where they now wished the three cruisers to be headed. He would just have to be patient. Communication with his fleet in the gas cloud would continue by way of a tight laser beam, and for security, kept to a minimum.

*

Doctor White and Gerald had accepted the offer of doubling their life expectancy and cranial implantation. Their memories would be downloaded regularly to keep up to date. Their DNA was stored in the Life Bank and they would decide at a later date about the cloning offer. It was then that Simon warned them that if for any reason they could not finally make up their minds, they would be automatically cloned upon their death. Then a tactful offer was made to them both about rejuvenation therapy. After a complete medical check they would be given cell regeneration and hormone enhancement. Of course they both accepted.

Eventually all the indigenous humans accepted deep sleep for a period of just six months. They thought it their duty to conserve the ship's resources. Anyway they would be helping themselves extend their lives along with rejuvenation therapies. As their hair and nails would continue to grow in deep sleep, they would be trimmed and harvested for DNA by surgical robots and stored in the Life Bank.

*

'Mongrels! You destroyed our world,' Jarrod raged, 'murdered our people.' Once again he was in the cockpit of his Interceptor, swooping down on an enemy fighter.

He woke up with a start, his body steeped in sweat. Images of Earth's final days in his dream were still fresh in his waking mind. He was still a prisoner of his nightmares. Squeezing his eyes shut, he tried to drive the vision from his mind. But he could not erase his dreams, just as he could not blot out the memories of what the Drogs had done to his world. It had been the greatest challenge humankind had ever faced. But the awful truth was, Earth was now no more than a volcanic nightmare of a world, totally unfit for habitation. Only a thousand souls had survived the holocaust.

He threw off his blanket and swung his body off his bunk and filled the basin beside the bed with water. Cupping the cold liquid in his hands, he drenched his face, then stared at his reflection in the mirror above the basin. A face etched with hatred returned his gaze with burning eyes that had witnessed too much in one so young.

He shook off his dark mood and remembered that his good friend David, who was still in deep sleep, would be awakened in just two more days.

Unbidden, Jarrod felt a strong urge to visit the service hanger to check out his Interceptor. He needed to touch the smooth space-black hull – to sit in the cockpit and gaze at the instruments and dream of the time he would fulfil his destiny.

Lisa would always sense those times that he would be compelled to visit his Interceptor. He would become introspective. Any conversation she had with him would be closed. A simple yes or no would be all she could get out of him.

Jarrod would always politely invite her to come with him to the hangar, but she knew he really needed to be alone. He would never press her to come, and if he ever did she would refuse. And in these times a dark depressing air would surround her. She couldn't bear to think of the machine – the dark angel that would scorch out of the belly of the starship and place him in grave danger, as he engaged the enemy once more.

*

After six months of deep sleep, Bridgett was returning to

full consciousness with the gentle urgings of a surgical robot.

As she opened her eyes she couldn't make out the shape hovering above her bed; but gradually as her vision cleared she recognized the surgical robot.

'Oh, my dear, good evening and welcome back to the conscious world. You will be feeling so refreshed after your deep sleep.'

'*Bonsoir*, she answered instinctively in French. '*Pourriez-vous parler plus lentement, s'll vous plaif?*'

'You want me to talk more slowly? Or would you like me to speak in the French language?' The surgical robot was confused.

'Oh, I am sorry. English is fine. I'm just a bit light headed that's all.'

'Understandable, my dear.'

'Is my mamma awake yet?'

'She will be shortly.'

'What about Jarrod?' she asked.

'Jarrod and Amber did not go into deep sleep. There were only the six beds unoccupied at the time, and they were reserved for the six indigenous humans.'

'Oh that's right. But Jarrod and Amber were born on Earth so they are really indig … indigenous,' she managed to finally get out.

'That is true, but we do not think of them in that way, because they are genetically enhanced humans like their parents who were not born on Earth. But this is a point we could argue for a very long time. Would you like to?'

Bridgett chuckled. 'No. I fully understand that they are special.'

'And so are you, my dear.'

*

Simon leaned forward in his chair as he focused on blips that had just appeared on his scanner screen. 'A meteor shower out here?' he muttered to himself. Very unlikely, he answered himself silently as he keyed in the image intensifier. The blips sharpened, and now he could make out a strange incandescent glow enveloped the "meteors". But out in the great void between the stars meteors or comets would be dark blobs. They wouldn't have an incandescent glow. That could only happen when the heat from a nearby star caused them to out-gas. 'What the hell are you?' he asked, his voice loud enough for Angela Shriver to hear.

The systems analyst straightened in her chair and slid a glance over to Simon. 'What's up, Simon?'

A flash of cold fear ran through him as he noticed the blips were subtly changing course – spreading out. They could only be spacecraft – a bloody lot of spacecraft.

'About fifty or so spacecraft ahead,' he choked out.

'Are you sure, Simon?'

'I am sure,' he said tightly. 'Most of them are changing direction. They have to be craft of some kind.' He felt bleak and cold inside.

'How soon till they are in range of our weapons?'

His fingers danced over his keyboard and the answer came up on his screen almost immediately. He read out the information to Angela. 'Our present course will bring their fleet of fifty-two craft in range of our weapons in thirty days.' He turned to Angela and fixed her with a bleak gaze. And we will be in range of their weapons, he added silently.

It was then that he had the awful premonition. Once more his fingers danced over the keyboard. Forty-nine blips behind *Argo*. He didn't need to sharpen the image.

Angela Shriver registered Simon's look of horror. She felt her throat tightening. 'There is another fleet behind us?'

He nodded confirmation. 'Be careful for what you wish for,' he said bitterly. 'It seems the hunter has become the hunted. I never expected that the Drogs had so many cruisers.'

'Perhaps it's not a Drog fleet,' Angela countered. 'Perhaps it could be a friendly space-faring race.' She had a thought. Her eyes widened. 'Perhaps it could be our creators?'

'I think not. All our records showed that they usually travelled in pairs.'

Not one soul on the Foundation cruisers had ever met their

164

creators. Only the original crew would have, but after being cloned eight times, they had passed away many millennia ago. But through their brilliant research they had been able to defeat the aging clock. Unfortunately it was not for them, but was their legacy to their children.

Chapter Thirteen

'You are probably right, Simon,' the commander said tightly as he leaned over Simon's shoulder looking at the latest images on the screen. 'They are most likely Drog cruisers, and our craft have too much momentum to make a drastic course change. It would be ineffective anyway,' he explained, his voice a low rumble. 'Soon the enemy will completely encircle us. There is no way we can escape the net they have set for us.'

'Continue on our present course then, Commander?'

'Yes, Simon. We will run the gauntlet.'

*

Wade motioned his son to an armchair opposite to his and Mirim's. Their quarters were similar to Jarrod's, but half as spacious again. It was well lit with shadowless lighting and had a workspace consisting of two personal computers with desks and chairs. Directly opposite the computers, a large wall screen was lit up with a view of the Pleiades in the constellation Taurus – bright young stars swimming in tendrils of blue light.

As Jarrod's chair adjusted to his body, he registered his parents' sombre expression and the tension heavy in the air.

After a lengthening moment, Wade leaned forward, his hands tightly clasped and said, 'son, the Foundation is in need of your services.'

Jarrod jerked forward in his chair. 'To pilot an Interceptor?' he asked excitedly.

'Yes, we do,' Wade said simply.

Jarrod felt an adrenaline rush. At last, he thought to himself. At last! He grinned, his eyes hard.

Wade fixed his son with a bleak gaze. 'We have sailed into a Drog ambush I'm afraid, and as commander I take full responsibility for our dilemma.'

'But we always hoped to catch up with the Drogs and deliver revenge.'

Mirim, who had been silent until now, laid a hand on

Wade's arm. She straightened in her chair and fixed her son with a sad gaze. 'Jarrod, this is a battle we cannot win.' Her voice was low and fearful. 'The Drog fleet ahead is fifty warships strong, with almost the same number behind us. All too soon they will encircle us. Our calculations tell us that we cannot change our course significantly at the speed we are going, nor can we outrun their cleverly set trap.'

'Your mother is right, son,' Wade said, failing to hide the unease that edged into his voice. 'We must attack and breach their blockade at a single point with everything we have, and attempt to slip through. Only then can we outrun them.'

'Cut and run,' Jarrod muttered as he lowered his eyes. He shook his head. It wasn't the image he'd carried around all these years since the destruction of Earth. But he knew his parents were right. Yes, cut and run he repeated to himself silently, and live to fight another day.

Mirim gazed over to her son. Her lashes were suddenly wet with tears. She hurriedly brushed them away.

Jarrod raised himself from his chair and reaching out embraced her. Then after shaking his father's hand, he turned on his heel, and in four silent strides, reached the door and exited.

Mirim could feel a deep frozen fear at her core. She turned to Wade. 'We are sending our son to a certain death.' Her dam of tears finally burst and she sobbed.

Wade cradled her in his arms. He cleared his throat. 'Nothing is certain, Mirim,' he said softly, trying not to allow a despairing note to creep into his voice.

∗

Amber regarded her twin across the restaurant table. His face was a little more drawn than usual and he looked troubled; she could feel it.

'You're very quiet this morning, Jarrod.'

'Sorry. I was thinking about my Interceptor and going over its controls and gauges in my mind,' he said slowly. 'You know I go quiet when thinking about my machine,' he explained.

'Yes I certainly do,' she said, reassured that there was

nothing to worry about. Or was her brother hiding something from her? He sure does look sombre.

Lisa who was also sitting across from Jarrod was relieved to hear it was nothing more than one of Jarrod's quiet times. Very soon she was sure, he would go to the hangar and visit his beloved machine once more and get it out of his system. She smiled inwardly. Just as well I'm not a jealous type. She started into her meal, and as always, tried not to think that some of the food might well have passed through bodies many times before – eating food through the loop was a thought she always tried to repress. She grimaced. Oh well she told herself. Just tuck in and try not to think about it.

It was then that the message blared out over the ship's speaker system informing them of the imminent attack by two large Drog fleets.

Lisa and Amber gazed over at Jarrod as the message continued. Both now realised why he had been so quiet. As a combat pilot, he had already been briefed.

The chilling message informed that the battle with the enemy would commence in approximately twenty-nine days.

Gasps and murmurs filled the room.

A paralysis of fear gripped Lisa. She felt her throat tightening. Her mouth opened as if to speak, but no words came.

'You should have told us, Jarrod,' Amber said, as bleakness flooded her mind.

The tension built up, radiating around the room. For a brief moment, the murmurs in the restaurant died down. It was unnaturally quiet. The impact of reality of an imminent attack was numbing.

Lisa's wracking sobs broke the brittle silence. She propelled herself from her chair and threw herself at Jarrod, wrapping her arms tightly around his neck. 'I won't let them take you,' she cried. 'Not again. I won't!'

Jarrod took her in his arms. 'It's my responsibility to pilot the Interceptor,' he said with gentle directness. He cradled her head and stroked her hair. 'Listen to me,' he said softly. 'Nothing can change that.'

Jarrod shot a gaze over Lisa's shoulder to Amber.

Her sad eyes returned his gaze. 'We know you have no choice,' she said, as she tried to suppress the fluttering wings of black fear pulsing through her.

*

Doctor O'Connor was lying on his bunk resting, listening to a Mozart symphony when the dreadful news flash cut in. He listened in stunned silence. When the bulletin ended he jerked to a sitting position and swung his legs angrily over the side of the bunk.

'Just great. Bloody great!' he swore angrily. 'I've just found the woman of my dreams and now I'm going to lose her.' But it's worse for Nikki he scolded himself silently. She had Bridgett to worry about. She will be devastated.

Restlessly he got to his feet, strode three paces to his left, and stood in front of his wall screen, hands clenched tightly behind him. Out of habit he hunched forward and gazed at the projection of the great nebula in Orion. He stared at it for a few short seconds, but the splendid sight did nothing for him. He straightened and felt the cold stirring of defeat. There was just no way the Foundation cruisers could take on such a large fleet. No way!

Returning to his bunk he sat down and dropped his head in his hands. This can't be happening, he told himself.

*

Joseph stood before the group gathered in Simon's spacious quarters and surveyed them silently for a few moments. His face was a mask of calm, but his emotion was buried deep. It was a most unpleasant task that he'd been delegated to do. The group was seated and an expectant silence descended as they awaited the briefing.

'Thank you all for attending this urgent meeting. Normally Simon would be addressing you, but he is with the commander working out a battle strategy.' He looked over to David and gestured for him to come and stand beside him.

Although invited to the meeting it didn't really affect Lisa, Amber and Jarrod, as their alien enhancement was locked in.

Lisa was wearing a freshly laundered forest-green jumpsuit, in stark contrast to her ashen face. She was mildly sedated and still in deep shock. Her eyes were red-rimmed and her posture conveyed utter dejection. She appeared shrunken – in a crumpled daze, as she clung onto Jarrod with all the energy she could muster.

Joseph laid a hand on David's shoulder and went on. 'Most or all of you will know that David has undergone our life extending techniques along with a cranial implant. His memories and experiences have been downloaded regularly and stored. Upon his eventual death he will be cloned and memories and experiences will be discreetly downloaded into his brain from infancy to adulthood.' He glanced over to Mary and Gerald White. 'David's parents have accepted the life extension but have yet to decide on a cranial implant and cloning.' He leant forward. 'I strongly advise all of you here to let us extend your present life expectancy and allow us to give you all a cranial implant. You must instruct me at this meeting if you don't wish to be cloned; otherwise you will be cloned if you do not survive the upcoming battle.' In all probability none of us will survive the battle ahead, he told himself. 'But there is a problem.' He paused for effect and looked at each of them in turn before continuing on. 'Your clone will resemble you exactly as you all did as a baby, right through infancy to adulthood.' He lowered his tone to lend significance to his words. 'But they will not be you! The clone can only be you if we download your experiences, your very essence into your clone. So I strongly urge you to all to receive a cranial implant as well as the life extending techniques that are on offer.' He searched their faces briefly and continued on in an urgent tone. 'And I really do need to know right away before we engage the enemy. Even if our ship does survive, some of you may not,' he said with brutal bluntness.

Nicolette raised her hand. 'My daughter Bridgett and I were discussing cloning just yesterday and we have chosen to live on in our clone, and to that end we accept cranial implants.'

'I'm pleased to hear that, Nicolette. What about the rest of you?' His voice softened. 'I am sorry that it is necessary to rush you like this,' he added.

Nicolette turned to O'Connor who was standing next to her. She squeezed his hand and implored him to accept the Foundation's offer.

He gazed down at Nikki and smiled tenderly. 'How could I refuse an offer to share many lifetimes with you,' he said gallantly. Raising his hand, he indicated to Joseph his acceptance of all that was on offer.

Joseph gazed over to Doctor White and Gerald.

Mary turned to Gerald. 'I'm going to accept the cranial implant and the cloning,' she whispered. 'We may not survive the upcoming battle. Better to live on in our clones with our son. Please!' she entreated. 'Accept the offer, Gerald. If not for you then do it for me.'

'A blending of alien technology is abhorrent to me,' he whispered so as not to offend Joseph. 'But I really don't have a choice.' He smiled tenderly down at her.

She brushed his cheek. 'Thank you, my darling.'

They nodded their acceptance to Joseph.

Joseph gave an inaudible sigh of relief. He could not understand why anybody would take so long to accept the Foundation's gift of time.

'Except for Amber, Lisa and Jarrod, please follow me to the surgery,' Joseph instructed. 'Our surgical robots are ready and waiting in anticipation of your acceptance.'

Gerald's eyes widened; shocked at the speed Joseph was moving them along for their cranial implant and memory download.

On their way to the surgery, Joseph explained in detail, the procedure they would undergo.

There were no questions. Some were surprised how little time was needed to receive the implant and subsequent download of all their life's experiences and memories.

*

171

'Well we could save energy if we cut the artificial gravity entirely, Commander.'

'That would create more problems than it would solve, Simon. No, the gravity setting will remain unchanged.'

They were in Wade's quarters, strategising battle plans. Wade leant forward in his chair, elbows resting on the tabletop across from Simon. 'For the meantime we will maintain our present course and our projected time of arrival at the blockade. One day out we will accelerate our three cruisers' stardrives to their maximum safety limit. Our angle of incursion will change, and I'm hoping this manoeuvre will take the Drogs by surprise. We will be upon them quicker than they had anticipated, and they will be forced to reposition their cruisers at very short notice. This will allow a short window of time when we will have less Drog cruisers to deal with. With a tremendous amount of luck, we will engage a lower concentration of enemy cruisers – a short sharp battle that may allow us to pass through their net. If we can do that, I know that we can outrun them.' He paused for comment from Simon.

Simon was horrified with part of the strategy. 'But, Commander, the indigenous humans will not survive the high G's!'

'Perhaps they can,' Wade countered. 'I have been going over our forefathers' history to see if they had a technique for surviving high G's – a time long ago, before they discovered virtual immortality and the ability for their progeny and themselves to withstand high G's.' He straightened in his chair. 'All their records show that they were fortunate in never having to endure dangerously high acceleration, but nevertheless they were prepared to a limited extent in case they did. Their contingency plan was that most of the crew would take their chances with the high G's while a select few would be protected. They would be lowered into sleep tanks and put into deep sleep. And this is what I propose we do with the indigenous humans.'

Simon expression was puzzled. 'But, sir, deep sleep will not protect them?'

'Of course not, Simon. There is more than deep sleep involved. Their lungs will be drained of air, and then gradually

172

filled with a special oxygenated, saturated solution that will keep their lungs and chests expanded. Of course breathing in the normal way will cease – the primitive area of the brain that controls breathing would be isolated. Surgical robots will be programmed to perform the procedure and I do not anticipate any problems.' He straightened in his chair and continued. 'Really they are lucky in a way. If *Argo* is blown away they won't know anything about it. But I digress. They will be helmeted of course to protect their eyes, nasal passages and the delicate mechanisms of the inner ear. The sleep tanks will be closed and sealed except for a hose with a one-way valve connected to an exterior reservoir. Another special liquid will be pumped into the sleep tanks from the reservoir until it reaches a predetermined pressure. After thirty minutes the liquid's properties will change dramatically. It will become viscous, and so cushion their bodies from the high G's. After the battle, air will be allowed to enter the sleep tank by simply disconnecting the hose that had been used to fill the sleep tanks. This will allow the liquid's viscosity to reduce once more to that of water. The hose will be then reconnected and the one-way valve reversed to allow the liquid to be pumped back into the external reservoir. The liquid in their lungs will then be sucked out, and the pathway to the brain will be reopened to allow normal breathing.'

'I would like to go over one point with you, Commander. How long will the liquid in the lungs remain oxygenated?'

'Twenty-four hours, and that will be sufficient.' He gave Simon a searching gaze, his dark eyes hard. 'By then we will either have broken the enemy's blockade or been blown out of the sky. A few hours before our weapons are in range of the enemy they will be lowered into the tanks and the initial procedure will be commenced. Shortly after that, our three cruisers will accelerate as much as our safety margins allow. When we engage the enemy we will break the blockade or become a short-lived star,' he said bluntly.

Simon was impressed. Well, with everything except the strong possibility of being blown out of the sky. Wade always seemed to be one step ahead of everybody else – an innovative commander. Of that he was in no doubt. If anyone can get us out alive it's got to be him.

'This meeting is adjourned, Simon. I have to run over this plan with the Foundation Director, then I will get back to you.'

*

'I'm impressed with the strategy you and Simon have come up with,' the Foundation Director, Floyd Burke said. 'I realize our chances of survival are slim, but now there is hope.'

'There is another point I would like to discuss with you, sir.'

'Yes,' Floyd prompted.

'Commander of *Orion*, Phillip Wilson, has made what I think is a useful suggestion. They have a number of long-range research probes on board. They also have explosives stored, ready for future geological research. He wishes to attach the explosives and infrared flares to the probes and launch them towards the enemy fleet to compromise their radar. The probes would be exploded by way of attached timers. It could create a useful diversion.'

At the great distance that separated the enemy from the Foundation cruisers, laser cannons were ineffective. Even though they were tight laser beams, over such a distance they would still gradually spread to a wide, ineffective beam of light.

'I agree. It could cause confusion to the enemy.'

'I will tell him to go ahead then, Floyd.' Wade paused for half a second before continuing. 'I do have another concern about the high acceleration on one of the indigenous humans. The French woman, Nicolette Michaiels is claustrophobic. She may not agree to the immersion procedure.'

'Offer sedation.'

'Even then she may not give her permission.'

'Then anaesthetize her through her cabin's air vent along with her daughter and anyone else in the group if necessary,' Floyd Burke said bluntly. 'Universal acceptance would be preferable, but might not be possible. We will do what is best for them. One way or another they will all under-go the procedure.

And do not inform them of the procedure until you have to. We don't want them fretting any longer than necessary.'

*

Lisa was still on medication to ease her anxiety. She lay on her bunk waiting for the latest administered sedation to take effect. She squeezed her eyes tightly shut, endeavouring to drive the fearsome vision from her mind. But she could not shake the feeling that Jarrod's next mission would be his last. She would never see him again. Her head began to swim as mercifully the powerful sedative kicked in and she surrendered to the blessed darkness.

*

'It's just as David explained it, Gerald. With the enhancement, I'm thinking more clearly and analytically and it's exhilarating.'

'And you, my dear, look more beautiful than I can ever remember.'

'Don't tease me,' Gerald,' she reprimanded lightly. 'Your eyesight is now so sharp you can't help but notice every line on my face.'

'Character lines, that's all they are,' he bantered. 'But don't forget that the regeneration therapies they gave us will take some days to take full effect.'

'True, Gerald,' she said. In a sudden mood swing to deep despair, she said, 'but what good will it do if *Argo* is destroyed.'

Gerald could see the pain in her eyes. 'We must remain positive, Mary.' But now awful visions of the upcoming battles were now playing out in his own mind.

Chapter Fourteen

Simon hunched over the screen as it filled with the images of enemy cruisers ahead. A superimposed grid located the fleet with precise accuracy, and readouts at the bottom of the screen monitored the closing distances from the Foundation cruisers.

The enemy was swarming to the area they had calculated the three Foundation cruisers would be in just five days time.

Simon smiled. Gaps in the blockade were already becoming apparent in the area where the Foundation would hope to penetrate – twelve hours earlier than the Drogs anticipated.

The enemy would realise as soon as the Foundation cruisers accelerated that the forecast incursion point would have to be revised, and they would scramble as quickly as possible to plug the gaps in their blockade.

*

'But we are not designed to stand such acceleration,' O'Connor protested. They were back in Simon's quarters for an urgent meeting convened by Joseph. Again Joseph was unhappily filling in for Simon.

'I am aware of that, Doctor O'Connor, but I assure you we can get around that.'

Joseph explained the procedure that their commander had unearthed by searching the distant past – a procedure formulated by the Foundation's former crew. He continued on, and as the horror of the procedure hit home, their faces turned ashen but Joseph pressed on to the bitter end.

There was a stunned silence. Not one of the group was enamoured by the idea of being in a tank, covered in gel, and their lungs filled with liquid. Nicolette could feel a rising tide of panic. No way could she go through with the procedure. She felt herself begin to shake and was grateful for Adrian O'Connor's arm around her waist supporting her. She knew what she must do.

'We will sedate you all of course,' Joseph hesitated. 'Or we can fully anaesthetize you if necessary – '

Mary White cut in. 'I'm sure all of us will need to be fully anaesthetized,' she said. 'Perhaps a show of hands?'

A murmur of agreement coursed around the room. Nicolette raised her hand like all the rest, but she knew in her heart what she must request, but it would be out of earshot of Bridgett.

'Very well then. We will meet here in two hours and I will escort you to the sleep tanks.' He watched them start to file out except for three of the group who hung back.

'Take Bridgett to our quarters please, Adrian,' Nikki whispered. 'There's something I want to clarify with Joseph. I'll be with you shortly.'

O'Connor responded with a nod. Although reluctant to leave Nikki's side, he rested his hand on Bridgett's shoulder and led her away.

'A moment of your time please, Joseph?'

'Of course, Nicolette,' he said uneasily. He knew the group's acceptance had been too easy.

'I cannot go through with it,' she said, shaking her head. 'I am sorry, I just can't. I appreciate your offer. I will take my chances with the high G's.'

'But you will not survive,' Joseph protested, 'and it will be an agonising death, and that the Foundation cannot accept.'

'Very well, Joseph. Then in that case I request euthanasia.'

Joseph was stunned at her suggestion.

Nikki went on. 'Then of course if our ship survives the battle, I could live on in my clone.'

'But you would be a baby. How would your daughter react to that?'

'She is nearly a woman now,' she countered. 'She will understand when you explain my claustrophobia, and that I really had no choice.'

'You still have a few hours to consider this drastic step.'

Nikki shook her head. 'I have made up my mind,' she said resolutely. 'I know the Foundation may not grant me euthanasia, and I appreciate their right to refuse.'

'Very well, Nicollette. Your request is granted. Do you wish to inform your daughter?'

'No, Joseph. I do not want her to know anything about it. I will inform Doctor O'Connor but no one else.' Nikki was surprised her wish had been granted, that Joseph had capitulated so quickly, and that he had the authority to do so.

'As you wish, but as I said, you still have time to change your mind.'

Nikki didn't argue the point. She nodded and thanked Joseph for his understanding and kindness and took her leave.

*

At Bridgett's request, O'Connor had escorted her to Jarrod's cabin so she could wish him well for his upcoming mission. And now Nikki was back in her quarters explaining her decision of euthanasia to him.

O'Connor was mortified. 'You can't be serious. You can't do this to Bridgett and myself. You just can't!'

She stood close to him, face upturned. 'I have made up my mind, Adrian. Nothing can change it.' Her eyes burnt into his, her gaze unwavering.

'But you would be anaesthetized,' he reasoned. 'You won't be aware of your claustrophobia.'

'The thought of it is enough.' She shuddered. 'I am just barely holding on as it is. Bridgett must not get wind of this.' She gazed up at him, her eyes filled with despair and in a voice barely above a whisper she continued. 'Of course she may never know if our ship is destroyed.'

A thread of panic entered his voice. 'I can see there's nothing I can say that will change your mind.'

Her sad eyes rested on him. 'I will be reborn in my clone,' she said with resolve. 'Bridgett will raise me. You will wait for me, Adrian?' she pleaded, her voice choking in her throat.

He fixed her with a bleak gaze. 'Of course I will,' he responded, his voice a croak. At last he tore his gaze away from her, as cold despair swept over him.

Gazing up at him she could feel his anguish. It was the darkest time of her life. Reaching up, she placed a hand to each side of his face and turned it so he had to meet her gaze. 'I am

178

so, so sorry to burden you with the knowledge of my intent, Adrian, and I know you will keep a protective eye on Bridgett.'

With a bewildered shake of his head he looked down and felt pinned in place by the intensity of her gaze and enchanting beauty. 'I will protect her with my life,' he said simply.

And she knew he meant it. She buried her head on his chest and when the tears came she could not quell them.

*

Jarrod caught a glimpse of himself reflected in the screen of the Interceptor. A despairing air enveloped him – a darkness haunted his eyes. He glanced down at the clock digits ticking away at the bottom corner of his screen. Thirty minutes to launch. He comforted himself with the knowledge that at least the White's, Bridgett and Nicolette would soon be in deep sleep, along with O'Connor – all oblivious to the battle ahead. His parents, Amber and Lisa were a different matter. They would live every minute of the battle right up to the time they broke the blockade – or were blown out of the sky.

Just an hour ago he'd had his last memory download before struggling into his pressure suit and endured the distressing farewells. Lisa had clung to him sobbing and had to be literally prized from him before he could take the long walk to the hangar and his awaiting Interceptor. But now he was glad of this compulsory quiet time to psyche himself up for the battle ahead.

And in response his mood changed. Although the odds of survival were poor, he couldn't help deny a sense of exhilaration – a tingling in his spine. And felt a deal of guilt that he should be experiencing such a feeling.

*

Nicolette glanced over to her daughter on a gurney next to her. 'Do not worry, dear. Soon we will all be in deep sleep, long before we are immersed in the tanks.' To her ear, her voice sounded far from comforting, but it was the best she could do. And my own sleep will be just a little deeper than yours she

179

added silently.

'I'm nervous of course, but I know it's all for the best. See you when I awaken, Mamma.'

'Yes, dear. See you soon.'

'This won't hurt a bit,' the surgical robot said smoothly as he leant over and administered the injection to Nicollette.

A floating feeling for a few short seconds. Then the light faded from her eyes.

*

Warstill turned to his aide. 'Open up a channel to the leading enemy cruiser,' he barked. 'Get me their commander. And for goodness sake speak the language.' He gave his aide a stony gaze. 'You learnt the language as I ordered?'

'Yes, sir,' he answered nervously. A hint of pride coloured his voice. 'I studied many of Earth's languages through their radio and television transmissions.'

'Good. Get on with it then and impress them with your skill.'

*

All the air in *Argo's* hangar had been sucked out and stored. The three Interceptor pilots now relied on the pressurised environment of their cockpits. Jarrod scanned his instrumentation in a final check. A blinking green light at the bottom left off his display screen ticked off the last minutes before launch.

'Leader One to Ceptor Three. Come in, Ceptor Three.'

'Copy, Leader One. All systems green.'

'Very good, Ceptor Three. Stand by for launch.'

In the confinement of the cockpit, and the constriction of the pressure suit, his body avoided overheating by way of a power pack that cooled the fabric of his suit with a built in temperature control.

The steady green light on his display screen cut out to be replaced by a flashing orange light. He was caught in an endorphin flow, and in his adrenaline high, a second seemed an hour.

The wide hangar door opened silently in the airless environment, and in the prearranged sequence, Interceptor Two catapulted out into the cold infinity of the galaxy. Seconds later the craft's chemical propulsion system engaged. A sudden flood of energy lit up the facing side of *Argo* before the Interceptor was swallowed up in the black void.

Jarrod instinctively braced himself for his own imminent, savage launch. The orange light on his display turned a solid red. He gazed down at his screen as it ticked off the remaining seconds. His dark eyes gleamed, and then he sank hard back into his chair as his fighter craft catapulted violently, but smoothly on its cradle to embrace the darkness. Seconds later the on board computers commanded the chemical propulsion drive to engage. He sank even further into his chair. His pressure suit prevented his blood pooling in the extremities, and his genetically modified haemoglobin molecules processed oxygen extremely efficiently, preventing him from blacking out. He was required to reach the Drog fleet as quickly as possible, to prevent the enemy regrouping to the Foundation's revised incursion point.

His screen informed him that Joseph's Interceptor One had also launched – soon to be joined by six fighter craft from *Orion* and *Vela*. He was experiencing temporary vision distortion created by his eyeballs being pressed into their sockets by the tremendous thrust of his Interceptor.

Five minutes later when clear of *Argo*, the Interceptor's chemical propulsion system shut down and the craft's stardrive cut in. Any earlier it would have fried *Argo*.

At such a distance from the enemy, it was highly unlikely that the tiny, slim fighter-craft would be detected in the vast void – at least for a considerable time. And when the Foundation cruisers accelerated, it was hoped the green ion-glow of the cruisers would distract the enemy radar from the Interceptors.

*

Wade was at his post on the bridge to receive an incoming

transmission. '*Argo*'s commander speaking,' Wade said gruffly. 'Our screen is blank. Identify yourself.'

'I am Warstill, the Drog fleet commander,' he stated in a deep, base voice. 'I will get back to you. Stand by.'

With an angry shake of his head, Warstill bawled out his aide for forgetting to procure picture transmission. It was no way to impress the enemy and he watched sternly as the aide quickly remedied the oversight.

Wade's blank screen came to life. He cast a cold eye on the loathsome face of the enemy. The creature's fur-covered ears were huge to catch faint sounds in their home planet's thin atmosphere. It had forward facing hunter's eyes and a long flexible snout, which retracted in the cold for protection. Below the snout the creature's low-slung jaw was huge, with carnivore teeth.

'My message to you is simple,' Warstill said in a low rasping voice. 'Surrender your three cruisers to our command. Resistance is futile. We wish to learn of your technology and the reason for your longevity. Share this with us and we will spare your lives.'

Wade narrowed his eyes and clamped down on his raw anger. 'It is not in our nature to surrender,' he said, a hard edge to his voice. 'And we have no need to. We have recently developed a weapon of awesome destruction, beyond your imagination. We are looking forward to the confrontation,' he lied. 'Your transmission to us has now identified your cruiser and it will be constantly tracked.' He lowered his voice to lend significance to his words. 'It will, I promise you, be the first to experience the wrath of the Foundation!'

Warstill felt a cold chill course down his spine. The Foundation Commander sounded so confident. He's bluffing, a voice in his mind said. He quickly brushed the fear aside and regained his composure. Yes, it had to be a bluff. Two could play that game. 'And we too, Commander have recently developed terrible weapons beyond your imagination, and your ship, *Argo* will be the first to be annihilated.' His voice turned conciliatory. 'But our offer of surrender will remain open for a further two hours. After that if you do not surrender to us, I suggest you make your peace with your god.'

Warstill abruptly cut the transmission. Talking to the Foundation's commander had an unsettling effect on him. He could not understand why they would choose death over enslavement.

*

Amber lay on her acceleration couch in the tight embrace of her restraint harness. In her pressure suit she was as prepared as she could be for the imminent acceleration, eyes closed, breathing deeply, alone with her thoughts. Two hours earlier she had embraced Jarrod, and the harsh reality was that it would probably be for the very last time. The Foundation Interceptors would do everything possible to keep their starships incursion points clear of enemy cruisers – at all costs!

She was all cried out – empty of tears as bleakness flooded her mind. She heaved a tense sigh, as the synthetic voice of a computer announced over the ship's speaker system, a programmed acceleration would begin in sixty seconds.

*

On board his cruiser, Warstill was bawling out his three battle strategists. 'Not one of you anticipated that the Foundation cruisers would accelerate. Now we have to scramble our ships to another area altogether.' He scorched them with a furious gaze. None of them would meet his eyes.

'Look at me when I speak to you,' he demanded.

They reluctantly obeyed and lifted their heads. One of them was visibly shaking.

'Permission to speak, Commander?' another of the strategists asked nervously.

Warstill acknowledged Vabor with a curt nod.

'We did not think they could survive such a savage acceleration, sir.'

'You just didn't think!' Warstill bellowed. His anger gave way to something far colder than the freezing ocean of space. He

183

looked at them each in turn. 'If any Foundation cruiser breaches our blockade, one of you will be paying with your head! Now get out of my sight and recalculate their incursion point.'

*

Green rivers of raw energy surged out of the Foundation cruisers as they accelerated towards the enemy.

Simon was pinned to his chair by the tremendous acceleration. The mighty ship shook and vibrated and he wondered if the ship's structure and its titanium girders could cope. But the engineering was superb, he reassured himself, and all their calculations had reported that the ship could indeed cope. More of a concern was the consumption of valuable energy. With the high acceleration, and the resultant dramatic increase in mass of all aboard, there was nothing he could do except gaze at the blurred vision of his computer screen, as the acceleration scrunched his eyeballs out of shape. For the time being, everything on board was under control of the computers, and would remain so until the ship cut its acceleration.

On his central display, his compromised vision could still make out the superimposed grid, showing that the enemy cruisers were well aware of the Foundation's strategy, and were already marshalling their ships to where they expected the Foundation would attempt to break the blockade. Because they were going at a slower speed than the Foundation cruisers, it did allow them to change direction, although ponderously.

For the Foundation cruisers though, it was virtually impossible to change direction at such a high velocity. Their incursion point was set. And for some time, the three cruisers were entirely in the hands of their computers.

*

'So far so good,' Jarrod muttered to himself as he surveyed his central display. The Drog armada was apparently unaware of the Interceptors otherwise they would have launched their own fighters. The Foundation cruisers and Interceptors had superior tracking technology than the Drogs, but soon the enemy would inevitably be aware of the Interceptors arrowing in towards them.

Jarrod's Interceptor's acceleration suddenly cut out. For a nanosecond his stomach lurched, then he remembered his craft was pre-programmed to do just that. From now on, the craft would be completely under his control. To continue to accelerate would sacrifice the manoeuvrability of the Interceptor, and of course drain valuable energy and so compromise the effectiveness of the weapon pods.

The readouts on the screen continued to tick away the closing distance from the enemy cruisers.

*

Warstill stiffened in his chair on the bridge of his cruiser when nine incoming blips in tight formation registered dead centre on his central display. They had to be Foundation fighters. But he'd expected them. Seconds later there was total confusion on the bridge as a further thirty blips showed up at the right of screen.

'Get over here now!' Warstill hollered to his three strategists. He swivelled his chair away from his monitor to confront them.

They scrambled to their commander and gathered around him, well aware of the reason for their commander's displeasure. The total of thirty-nine blips on the strategists' own computer screens had alarmed them. It was totally unexpected – nine fighters, yes, but what were the other thirty blips?

'Explain these thirty blips at right of screen,' he demanded.

'We will need time to investigate them, Commander,' the bravest of the three answered in a strained voice.

'Do it and report back to me,' he snapped, in a low, angry rumble, 'and tell me how you plan to deal with them,' he added.

With sudden furious energy Warstill rose from his chair and stormed out of the bridge.

*

With the speed of *Argo*, and Doppler Shift, radio transmissions from Moonbase were now almost non-existent. The communication officer was persevering, but was rewarded infrequently. On those rare occasions a message was received, the reception was poor and fading.

And the messages were generations old.

Chapter Fifteen

Joseph opened up the channel to his team. 'Leader One to squad. Shortly we will be showing up on the enemy scanners, and they will launch their fighter craft. Do everything in your power to keep engagement to a minimum. Our mission is to keep the incursion point as free as possible of enemy cruisers.' Easier said than done, he added silently. 'Acknowledge please.'

Acknowledgement was duly received and final communication systems and navigation alignment checks were carried out as they continued on.

Minutes later ten enemy fighters stabbed out of the belly of the nearest enemy cruiser. Soon they would be joined by many more as the other giant warships closed in.

*

At Warstill's appearance, the bridge fell silent. He had a stylish way of dressing. His loose fitting sleeveless, peacock blue tunic reached to his knees and was secured to his waist by a jewel encrusted leather belt. A crimson cape draped his wide shoulders. He was deep through the chest, and weighing in at 300 kilos he was a dominating presence. His chair sighed in protest as he settled into it. He gazed angrily at his display screen. The Foundation Interceptors along with thirty unidentified blips remained on screen – thirty mocking points of hard light. Are these the terrible weapons that the commander of the Foundation cruiser so confidently alluded to? he asked himself.

And the time had long passed for their surrender.

The tension built up, radiating around the bridge.

Suddenly Warstill swivelled his chair away from his display screen and hollered for his strategists to join him.

Scrambling from their workstations, they gathered around their commander in a tight semicircle, dry mouthed and nervous.

'Your proposed strategy?' he barked.

Vabor, the bravest of the trio responded. 'Well, sir,' if the enemy cruisers continue to accelerate, they will compromise their shielding and deplete their energy reserve needed for weaponry. We judge they will cut their acceleration very soon. We have a provisionary incursion point and will fine-tune it as soon as their acceleration ceases and their speed is stable. In the meantime the three of us are in agreement that eight of our nearest cruisers, including our own, should head for the estimated incursion point. If you would allow me to use your computer for a moment, sir.'

Warstill grunted agreement and watched Vabor key in instructions. A super imposed grid appeared on the screen showing the images of the Foundation cruisers and Interceptors, and their exact location and distance from their own battleships. The strategist pointed to the provisionary incursion point where the eight cruisers should head for.

'That's settled then,' Warstill said impatiently, 'but how do you propose to deal with these other thirty blips?'

'Our cruisers closest to them will deal with them as soon as they come within range of our cannons. They can't be crewed because they are too small. Perhaps they are a diversionary tactic. Perhaps – '

'And a very successful tactic,' Warstill cut in angrily. 'I had anticipated that we would have had a far greater number of our ships to repel their charge of our blockade. Now a number of our ships are to be diverted to deal with these thirty missiles!' His voice was a low, menacing rumble. 'How many of our cruisers do you propose to divert?'

'Just four, sir.'

Warstill's displeasure focused entirely upon the poor strategist. 'Just four! Just four you say! Four of our valuable cruisers that could have helped secure our blockade and destroy the enemy totally,' he raged.

Vabor took an involuntary step backwards as Warstill's wrath poured over him.

There was a long silence finally broken by Warstill. 'Very well,' he said sharply, 'continue to monitor the situation and take appropriate action.' He lowered his tone – it was full of menace. 'Remember if any of the enemy breach our blockade one of you will loose his head!' He looked at each of them in turn.

Their misery-filled eyes returned the commander's gaze as they waited to be dismissed.

*

Simon breathed a sigh of relief as the heavy fingers of acceleration released him from their fierce grip. The haze of pain that had clouded his vision quickly passed. The computer screen above his head switched off. Now the ship once more was under the control of the crew. His couch returned to the chair position. His central display lit up, showing that four of the twelve closest enemy cruisers were separating, showing that their concern for the probes had distracted them. Simon's smile was tempered by the reality that the other eight Drog cruisers still posed a formidable force to deal with. Added to that, ten enemy fighters from each cruiser meant a total of eighty fighters. Ten had already been launched.

A brief weightlessness was replaced by artificial gravity set to lunar G's to conserve energy.

It would be another two hours before he could enter target coordinates into the navigational computers.

*

Nicollette awoke with a start, but her eyes remained closed, her leaden lids refusing her feeble attempts to lift them. All energy had fled.

And something was stealing her breath away. The residual fluid left in her lungs was making its presence felt. She felt she was drowning. A sudden and violent spasm of coughing rattled in her chest.

She felt awful. Her chest ached. She couldn't recall getting sick. Her attention was drawn to a murmur of voices that were too soft to understand and she wearily dismissed them. Even in the gentle artificial gravity, heaviness pervaded her body. She was cold and became aware she was almost naked and covered by a single blanket. Who had undressed her? And why was she in this surgical ward?

Something tugged at her mind. Something wasn't quite right. Her body tensed as memory surfaced. She'd refused the immersion procedure and had died. Now she must be a baby clone, she told herself. Her eyes opened wide in confusion. But she was reasoning like an adult and that couldn't be. With a surge of adrenaline, she found the energy to withdraw her hands from under the blanket. She studied them carefully, turning them over and noticing the scar on her left palm incurred as a child when chopping wood. They were adult hands.

Joseph had tricked her. He'd ignored her request of euthanasia. She shuddered at the thought of the immersion procedure that she must have gone through. For a moment her lips compressed in a thin angry line. But her mind relented. The immersion was over. Perhaps it really was for the best, she reasoned. Rather than scold Joseph, perhaps I should thank him.

Then reality stabbed at her. She would probably never meet up with him again. Brave Joseph would now be in great danger, preparing the way ahead for the cruisers to follow. He would most likely sacrifice himself so that the Foundation cruisers could break the blockade.

Tears pooled in her eyes and refused to fall in the ship's gentle gravity. She lay back on her bed and closed her eyes exhausted. Concern for her daughter and Adrian O'Connor fought for her attention. It was then that she heard footsteps approaching her bed. Through the tears she saw it was Mirim.

Mirim lay freshly laundered clothes on the end of the bed and leant over and covered Nicollette's hands with her own.

'You are the first to awaken, Nicollette. Let me put your mind at rest. Your daughter is fine. She's still sleeping but her vital signs are strong and so is the rest of the group.'

'Thank you, Mirim.' Nicollette's voice was dry and papery like an old woman's.

'Please forgive us for not granting your wish of euthanasia,' she said uncertainly. 'The act is forbidden. We preserve life at all cost. Joseph could not grant your request, but he thought it a kindness to let you think we would.'

'His intentions were excellent, and now it's over I am glad

to have my life back.'

'I am relieved to hear that, Nikki. Now rest up for an hour to speed your recovery, then return to your cabin and put on your pressure suit as we will be accelerating once more as we near the enemy blockade.' She saw a look of concern cross Nikki's face. 'I assure you it will not require the immersion procedure. Your pressure suit will afford you enough protection but it will be uncomfortable.'

Nikki could feel her body tensing. 'Can I have a panic pill?'

Mirim smiled at the French woman's turn of phrase. 'Of course,' Mirim said smoothly. 'We will give you a painless injection instead of a pill before you suit up. Now rest up for a little while,' she urged.

*

O'Connor awoke with a violent wracking cough. He instinctively sat up so as not to choke. His whole body was a haze of pain, clouding his vision. His chest ached, causing him to wince with each painful breath. Then his whole body tensed as his memory came surging to his awareness. It hit him like a physical blow. Nicollette would now be dead! His eyes filled with despair as he lay back on the couch. Closing his eyes he could picture her enchanting face, her angelic beauty and her delightful accent. He recalled the scent of her body, fragrant and exciting. A voice in his mind told him that she was not gone – she would live on in her clone.

Mirim Dryden who'd arrived at his bedside interrupted his thoughts.

'You are the second of the group to awaken, Doctor O'Connor.'

He opened his eyes reluctantly. He was in no mood for a verbal exchange.

Mirim gazed down at him. She was smiling.

She had no right to smile, he told himself. 'How did you know I was awake?' he croaked.

'I was reading your vital signs on these gauges next to your bed,' she explained. 'All of the group are doing well and will awaken shortly.'

O'Connor sighed, regretting the tone he'd taken. He inhaled, and let his breath out slowly. 'How is Bridgett doing?'

'Her vital signs are fine, and her mother is already awake.'

'Her mother! Nicollette is awake!' His brow drew together in perplexity. 'She changed her mind?'

Mirim's eyebrows arched. 'You knew of her request then?'

'Yes.' He closed his eyes briefly to hide his emotion. 'Thank goodness she changed her mind.'

'No. She did not change her mind. We went ahead with the immersion procedure anyway. Not very democratic of us I know.'

O'Connor held Mirim's gaze. 'I'll not argue. You did right.' He paused for breath. 'I'm so very glad you did.' The relief was clearly visible on his face.

Mirim smiled, but her expression could not fully conceal an undercurrent of anxiety. It was then that O'Connor remembered her son Jarrod was on a dangerous mission to take on the might of the Drog fleet.

*

The aide approached warily towards his commander and waited respectively to be acknowledged.

'Yes?' Warstill snapped, without looking up.

'A report has just come in that another seventy missiles are showing on our scanners heading towards our entire fleet in all directions,' the aide said nervously, his mouth dry with fear of his commander's reaction. 'Our three strategists wish for you to join them on the bridge to discuss this latest development.'

'Wish you say!' Rage coloured Warstill's face a deep purple as he gazed up at his aide. 'They will wish they were never born when I finish with them!'

The aide prayed for nothing better than to flee from his commander's anger.

'Communicate to them I'll be with them shortly.' Let them stew awhile, he thought to himself. Let them reflect on their incompetence. 'Dismissed,' he spat out.

The aide nodded, turned and scurried out of his commander's cabin as quickly as respect would allow.

Everyone on the bridge heard Warstill before they could see him. Though the corridor leading to bridge was heavily carpeted, Warstill's distinctive, thumping gait echoed off the walls, despite wearing cushioned leather sandals. Entering the bridge area, he strode past the three strategists that stood respectively to one side to allow him access to his workstation. Settling into his chair he gazed at his central display. A confusion of blips confirmed his aide's report.

He swivelled his chair and fixed his strategists with a red gaze. He could clearly see fear ripple across their faces.

'Explain this latest development!' Warstill bellowed.

A paralysis of fear gripped all but one of the strategists. 'We have conferred with our weapon's specialist. She says the missiles are primitive technology and they pose no threat to our mighty fleet. Our cruisers can easily destroy them.'

'Then she's a fool,' Warstill hissed. 'She is underestimating the Foundation.' His deep-set red eyes burnt like hot coals. 'Am I the only one who respects their capability?'

'We do respect their capabilities,' the bolder of the three strategists countered.

Warstill's gaze flicked over to the two, non-verbal strategists who'd found something of interest to study on the thickly carpeted floor. He took their silence as a sign of weakness and returned his attention back to Vabor once more.

'Do you think then,' he said, clearly enunciating his words, 'this worthy adversary would launch primitive weapons in the vastness of space with the hope of destroying our cruisers?'

'I understand your point, sir,' he said with an edge of desperation in his voice. 'They have something more subtle in mind?'

'Precisely.' He shook his head. 'Perhaps they are no more than a diversionary tactic as you first suggested. But I strongly suspect they're more than that,' he said with an irritated shake of his head. Warstill leant forward on his chair. 'The three of you are exhausting my tolerance for your ineptitude,' he said with dangerous calm. 'All of you were chosen as strategists because

193

of your high intelligence, but now, sadly that intelligence seems to have fled.'

Warstill craned his head and looked at the ceiling as if seeking a divine explanation of the Foundation's tactics. His fleet had conquered the Foundation colony on the planet known as Earth. The indigenous human's finite tenure on the planet had ended also, and was an added bonus – they could have caused a threat in the distant future as their technology grew. They were obviously an intelligent race to have discovered radio and television technology, but foolish to allow their signals to leak into space and become beacons to the mighty Drog fleet.

Now their world was a cold and empty place – totally unsuitable for life.

But still the smart Foundation colony had been able to successfully retreat to the stars in their tiny fleet of three cruisers. Even worse! They had won that right by destroying valuable Drog cruisers and coming through the fierce battle relatively unscathed.

One of the non-vocal strategists was studying the central display over his commander's shoulder. It was his sudden intake of breath that broke the brittle silence.

Warstill followed the strategist's gaze and saw a confusion of star-bright blips now crowding the entire screen. He blinked in disbelief.

The first of the Foundation missiles had disgorged its payload of infrared flares, scattering them in a vast cloud.

Warstill was consumed with indecision. A curl of unease hit his stomach. It was hard to measure these wily humans in Drog terms he lamented to himself. And to make things worse, he could smell the sweat of fear emanating from his useless strategists. He shut his eyes to blot out the mocking images on screen. 'Abort intercept of the first thirty missiles,' he ordered. 'Our four cruisers are to return to the projected Foundation incursion point as quickly as possible.'

*

The strategy of Philip Wilson, the commander of *Orion* was

brilliant. As the effectiveness of the radar blocking infrared flares faded another missile would disgorge its payload of flares. Each missile carried a small atomic device that *Orion* had stored on board for future seismic exploration and planetary research. Fifteen minutes after disgorging its flares each missile would detonate in a nuclear explosion, complete with an electromagnetic pulse to further confuse the enemy.

The Foundation cruisers engaged their stardrives for a short ten-minute burst so they would arrive at the incursion point earlier.

In his pressure suit, David sank hard back into his acceleration couch. His eyeballs pressed back into his eye-sockets causing everything to become a blur. But this time under the sharp acceleration he managed to stay conscious – for now.

The influence of Amber, Jarrod and the Foundation had made a profound change in him. And with his cranial implant he was thinking more clearly and analysing everything around him. Rich rivers of thoughts surged through his mind.

Unbidden, an image of Moonbase came to him. He pictured the colonists living in their rough-hewn tunnels that laced the complex. The base was deep enough to afford protection against fierce, solar radiation and wild swings of temperature both day and night. He made a mental note to work out later how much he'd aged compared to the colonists. The original colonists would have all died of old age of course, he reasoned, but their clones would survive them. Relativistic equations, he told himself, show that time slows down as speed increases. But objects having mass can't travel at the speed of light, as their mass would become infinite. So his own body could travel close to the speed of light, but never quite attain it. Now if we can just survive the blockade ahead, he thought, what wonders will we uncover? Upon what celestial shore might we come to rest? It was his last coherent thought.

As the acceleration increased his mind began to scramble. His peripheral vision diminished. Only a tight circle of light directly ahead remained. Finally, that too disappeared as unconsciousness claimed him.

As *Argo's* speed increased, blue shift began to stain the

stars ahead. In the vast ocean of space random atoms from time to time sparkled as they hit the outer skin's deflection shield. On board, time had slowed to a crawl. Outside the cruiser though, the universe continued to age.

Chapter Sixteen

Ten enemy fighters were closing fast. Jarrod received clearance to engage the leading enemy fighter.

As his NAV system plotted an intercept course, he felt the adrenaline pulse through his body. Targeting was close to locking on.

The other Interceptors peeled off formation as they positioned themselves to attack the enemy.

In the confinement of the cockpit, Jarrod's suit's built in cooling system was keeping him cool. He glanced at digits in the lower right corner of the screen, ticking off the closing distance to his target.

Targeting locked on. Jarrod flicked off the safety cover from the laser cannon's firing mechanism and pressed the trigger.

A beam of potent energy stabbed out, but a nanosecond earlier the Drog fighter had cut to the left.

Jarrod's lips tightened in a thin angry line. 'Valuable energy wasted,' he muttered. He banked his Interceptor to starboard and pursued.

Again, the target was locked on, but too briefly. The enemy fighter went into a steep climb.

Jarrod followed – straight up. He was coping with the heavy G forces – just! His enhanced haemoglobin molecules were processing oxygen to their very limit and prevented him from passing out. Even so, he felt his awareness slow. The target locked on. With desperate concentration and infinite slowness, his hand inched towards the laser cannon trigger. With awareness slowed to that of an indigenous human everything seemed to be in slow motion. He pressed the cannon's button.

The beam of energy cut into the darkness, finding its target. Pilot and machine blossomed into an intense multi-coloured cloud.

Death had not lingered.

Jarrod levelled out, and as his brain cleared, he slid a glance out of his cockpit at the battle below. He dearly wished he could assist, but his orders were specific. Hit and run. Engage one target only. Destroy it and move on to the incursion point. To this end he spun his craft through eighty degrees to port and felt the smooth thrust of the Interceptor as it accelerated away. Minutes later his headset crackled.

'Ceptor Eight to Ceptor Three. Respond please.'

'Copy,' Jarrod replied.

'I've made one kill and am now following your flight path, Ceptor Three.'

'Good work, Ceptor Eight.'

'Sadly I have to report we lost Ceptor Nine to enemy fire.'

Jarrod inhaled, and let his breath out slowly. 'Let us make sure he did not die in vain,' he said with a hard edge to his voice.

*

At last the three Foundation cruisers cut their acceleration. On board *Argo* there was brief weightlessness before gentle artificial gravity kicked in. The medical sensors built into David's chair recognised he was returning to consciousness and gently returned his acceleration couch to the chair position.

The first thing he did was read the latest bulletin on the room's large wall screen. It reported eight enemy fighters had been destroyed, but at a terrible cost. Interceptor Nine and Interceptor Six had been lost to enemy fire. The remaining seven Interceptors were speeding towards a much greater confrontation. They had a deadline to meet, and they had to make it on time. Seven tiny craft to take on the might of the Drog fleet.

It was a harsh reality. The Interceptors had won the brief battle, but could ill afford the loss of two pilots and their valuable craft.

David was grateful Jarrod was still alive, but he shook his head. His eyes filled with despair. None of the Interceptors could survive the conflict ahead. Of that he was sure. He shuddered as he pictured the gigantic enemy cruisers bearing down on the tiny pencil-slim Interceptors.

It was a dark and fearsome vision.

Perhaps it would have been wiser to have remained on the Moon. He felt a stirring of guilt. Because of him, his parents had elected to be outward bound to the stars, rather than live on the Moon without him. And now they were in grave danger. But he'd been impaled on a dilemma. Yes, he could have chosen to live on the Moon, but a life without Amber was unthinkable. He'd always felt so inadequate next to her willowy long-legged beauty. But she'd seen something in him that had attracted her. It was remarkable that she'd returned his feelings. Now it could all end with the blockade ahead.

Let it go, he told his restless mind. Let it go.

*

In his quarters, Warstill could feel the air tightening around him. What was the Foundation up to? What was their forest of radar blocking devices hiding? Then it came to him. He swivelled his chair away from his expansive desk and in a single urgent movement rose from his chair. Five strides. An impatient pause to wait for the door to open, and he stormed out.

His startled aide scrambled to his feet respectfully.

'Let my strategists know I'm on my way to the bridge,' Warstill snapped.

The strategists stood apprehensively at Warstill's workstation, steeling themselves for another torrid session with their commander. Already they could hear his heavy footfalls echoing in the corridor leading to the bridge.

Each thundering footstep grew in volume until suddenly they ceased while Warstill waited impatiently for the door to open.

A whimper of fear escaped the most timid of the strategists.

Tension radiated around the bridge.

Warstill strode past his strategists. Reaching out with a meaty paw he swivelled his chair around, flicked his crimson cape away from his powerful shoulders and settled his impressive weight into the chair.

He fixed his strategists with a hard gaze.

199

'We were about to arrange a meeting with you ourselves, sir. We...'

Warstill waved the strategist to silence. 'I couldn't stand by while you three wasted more valuable time trying to understand The Foundation's tactics,' he grumbled. 'Therefore,' he said with heavy condescension, 'I have taken it upon myself to do your job for you. It's my belief that the Foundation cruisers have accelerated again under cover of their radar blocking flares, so in my opinion they will arrive at the incursion point earlier. How long they will accelerate for is unknown of course. Until they register on our scanners once more, I propose we accelerate our cruisers to maximum to the incursion area. As soon as we have their cruisers on screen again we can fine-tune our speed to secure the blockade.' He could feel their minds working. 'Yes I know it will be a drain on energy reserves. It's a gamble. Any comments?' he invited.

The strategists looked at each other. None was brave enough to let Warstill know that the plan he had come up with was almost identical to theirs. But they all knew that if their commander's plan failed, he would hold the strategists to blame. One of them might lose his head.

Warstill hunched forward in his chair and searched their faces for a brief moment 'I will take your silence as full agreement. Action my plan immediately.'

They regarded their commander with cold, scared, eyes and acknowledged him with a nod and small bow.

*

Eyes wide in a continual endorphin high, everything to Jarrod had a sharp-edged look to it. The stars in the cold, eternal night ahead were blue-tinged jewels set in black velvet. He glanced at his screen. Still no Drog fighters.

And the seven Interceptors continued on. Seven lethal-killing machines, with seven resolute pilots nursing a terrible hatred for the enemy ahead.

*

The forest of radar blocking flares thinned and finally snuffed out. Even though the Foundation cruisers short burst of acceleration had ceased, their speed had not. Now Simon's central display showed the way ahead was still clear of enemy cruisers. He called up a one hundred and eighty-degree detailed sweep, forward of the Interceptors.

'Damn,' he swore. The Drogs had anticipated the Foundation's strategy – but obviously not straight away. The periphery of his screen was filled with the images of eight enemy cruisers, somewhat spread out. So the Foundation's strategy was at least partially successful. A superimposed grid showed the closing distances of each enemy cruiser. It would be another hour before they were in practical range of each other's cannons.

*

After recovering fully from the immersion procedure there had been little time for the group of indigenous humans to reunite. But now they had been granted forty minutes reprieve from their acceleration couches to move around and mingle with each other. Pressure suits had to remain on – faceplates open.

David clomped over to his parents who were seated on their couches that were now in the upright position. Guilt at the danger facing his parents had been eating away at him.

David gazed down at his parents and noted the palpable weariness in their faces. 'You should have both remained on Moonbase. It's my fault that you didn't, and I'm sorry. I've placed you both in grave danger.'

Gerald leaned forward in his chair and gazed up at his son. 'It's not your fault at all, son. It was our decision to be here. The blockade ahead is a harsh, formidable reality, I know. But we mustn't forget the potent capability of the Foundation weaponry.'

'Your father's right,' Mary White said. Her eyes narrowed with concern as she leaned towards David. 'We chose to be with you, and it wasn't a difficult choice to make.' Her tone gentled. 'Our future is shrouded in uncertainty, I know, but at least we

201

can face it together.' She reached over and brushed his cheek
softly.

*

The seven remaining Interceptors initiated a minimal course
change to align themselves with the enemy cruisers. Jarrod's
face was washed green in the glow of his instrument panel. The
soft light emphasized his chiselled jaw. As he gazed down at his
central display, a superimposed grid showed the precise location
of the eight Drog cruisers and readouts ticking away their
distance.

How many enemy would he take out? he asked himself
before his Interceptor was consumed by enemy fire. He was
under no illusion. There was very little chance of him piloting
his Interceptor back to *Argo's* womb – back to his family,
friends and Lisa. He was destined to die young. He let out a
tense sigh. His thoughts were unsettling. It was then that his
central display showed up a second wave of twenty enemy
fighters' launch from the bellies of their cruisers.

His helmet headphones crackled. 'Leader One to
Interceptor Three. Prepare to engage enemy fighters at your
discretion.'

'Copy, Leader One.'

Ten minutes later the seven Interceptors peeled off
formation to engage their selected targets.

Jarrod was glacially cold as he flicked off the safety cover
of his laser cannon. Now his chosen enemy fighter was closing
fast. It was in his cannon's cross hairs. His heightened senses
and reflexes responded. He had no hesitation. The energy beam
stabbed out. The enemy fighter erupted in an expanding shell of
brilliant yellow and orange light.

Jarrod cut to the left avoiding three enemy fighters that
were closing fast.

Lethal pulses of energy beamed out of the three fighters.
None found their target.

Jarrod's cockpit lit up as his Interceptor sliced through the
outer edges of the remnant cloud of the fighter he'd taken out.

202

He pulled his craft into a steep climb into the eternal darkness. With his vision tunnelling in the high G's, he looped his craft in a tight arc. Accelerating into a steep dive then levelling out, he climbed sharply once more. The manoeuvre took him behind the three enemy fighters. He had the trailing fighter locked on. A potent energy beam scorched out of the Interceptor taking out the power plant in the fighter's rear, sending the craft tumbling into the void – forever. It would be a slow and painful death for the Drog pilot.

Jarrod rewarded himself with a smile. He knew he was now supposed to speed towards the Drog cruisers, but giving into his instinct to make another kill, he swung his Interceptor to port and gave chase to an enemy fighter.

Once more he had an enemy fighter in his cannon's cross hairs. The laser cannon's lethal energy beam spat out, slicing through the tail section, but with little apparent damage. Nevertheless the pilot would be subjected to a painfully slow death, as the atmospheric pressure was gradually lost through the punctured hull. The pilot would be asphyxiated. Just as oxygen is the essence of human existence, so it was for the Drogs.

Jarrod clamped down on his compelling instinct to continue the conflict with the enemy fighters. He was acutely aware of the main mission. And he knew it would almost certainly be his final conflict. While fleeing the remaining Drog fighters, he realigned his Interceptor to the formidable incoming Drog cruisers. Only then did he realise that he was the last Interceptor to do so. The remaining Drog fighters would give chase – he had no doubt. But the surviving Interceptors would outrun the fighters, giving them a window of time to take on the might of the closest battle cruiser.

Jarrod would learn that eight enemy fighters had been taken out, but Interceptor Five had been destroyed. Now the wolf pack of six Interceptors would take on the might of the huge cruiser.

*

Faces lengthened as they read the bulletin on the wall screen. Even though the Interceptors had acquitted themselves well, they had lost another pilot and Interceptor. Lisa was relieved to see Jarrod had survived – but for how much longer she asked herself? She stood close to Amber and put her arm around her friend's shoulder. She could feel her trembling.

A sense of impending doom enveloped her senses. Even if the starships succeeded in breaching the blockade, she was sure none of the Interceptors would survive. She knew Amber would be thinking the same. An overwhelming depression settled. She was finding it hard to breathe – her senses acute to the fact that Jarrod would not survive the battle ahead. Only in dreams would she walk with him again. She turned her eyes away from the screen and bowed her head.

*

'Another eight fighters destroyed,' Warstill grumbled as he turned away from his computer screen at his workstation on the bridge. He swivelled his chair around and gazed up at his three strategists. 'It's a disgrace!'

Their heads were bowed, studying their feet. Fear thickened the air.

Warstill hunched forward. 'Look at me when I'm speaking,' he hissed.

They raised their heads reluctantly and met Warstill's chilling gaze.

'Which of you are going to tell me what your strategy is now!'

As usual, Vabor, the least timid of the strategists spoke. 'Sir, we advise the launch of another twenty fighter craft from two of our other cruisers to intercept them,' he said in a respectful tone. 'Our twelve surviving cruisers from the last skirmish will block their retreat.'

'Retreat! They've got no intention of retreating,' he bellowed. 'They will be dead set on slowing us down so their cruisers can slip through our blockade. They will fight to the death.' He straightened in his chair. 'Your plan to launch another twenty fighters is a stupid one. Our mighty cruisers will meet them head on, along with our pursuing twelve fighters. We will blow them away.'

*

Jarrod scolded himself for giving away to his instinct to take out another fighter. The real battle was ahead. He knew that. And he was five long minutes behind his comrades in the battle that had already commenced – he should have been with them. Not good enough, he told himself. The foreboding light show from the action ahead was clearly visible as the Interceptors attempted to shepherd the leading cruiser away from the direction of the incursion point.

At last Jarrod joined the fray, narrowly avoiding an energy bolt. The Interceptors were swarming like angry wasps – stinging the Drog cruiser's defensive shield with their laser cannons. And for now the Interceptors superior manoeuvrability was saving them from lethal pulses of energy bolts being fired from the huge enemy cruiser.

There was no communication between the Interceptors. It was unnecessary. Each pilot knew what he had to do in the silent, deadly conflict.

As the battle continued, still no Interceptors were lost to enemy fire, partly because of the skill of the pilots and a tremendous amount of luck. Even so, the huge Drog cruiser broke through the Foundation's thin battle line.

Jarrod was about to give chase when his earphones crackled. 'Leader One to Interceptors. Do not pursue. We have gained a little time for our own cruisers and drained some of the Drog cruiser's energy.' The tenor of his voice rose. 'I have the next incoming cruiser on screen, and so will you. That is where we have to set our course.'

On board Interceptor Three, Jarrod knew if they could balance up the number of Drog cruisers to three or four or even five to confront the Foundation cruisers they may not attack. He knew the Drogs preferred to have an overwhelming number of attack vessels at their disposal.

*

Sitting at his workstation on the bridge, Warstill's expression was hard, cold and threatening. There was a heavy silence. Everyone knew the commander was far from happy.

Warstill grunted in frustration. Not one solitary kill, he told himself. Our ship was combat ready. There could be no excuse.

Some heads would roll!

Chapter Seventeen

So engrossed in the wall screen's latest bulletin in the dining area, Amber didn't hear her mother approach. With her nerves so frazzled, she recoiled when Mirim placed a hand on her shoulder.

'I am sorry, dear,' Mirim said gently. 'I wanted to share the good news with you. No more Interceptors lost. It is better than we expected, and they have managed to delay an enemy cruiser and drain some of its energy.'

'Nevertheless,' Amber countered, 'won't the Drog cruiser reach the incursion point before we do?'

'Probably, Amber, but we can deal with a lot more than a solitary enemy cruiser. They will have to have many more cruisers arrive before they take us on,' she reassured her daughter.

'But our own Interceptors' energy is not unlimited.'

'Mirim nodded. 'True, dear. Before their energy is spent, they will rendezvous with our cruisers beyond the incursion point.' She knew the probability of the Interceptors returning to safe harbour was extremely slim, but she did her best to conceal her anxiety.

Amber gazed back at Mirim. Her mother's intentions were excellent, but she was not fooling anyone. She blinked her eyes slowly, solemnly, but didn't say a word.

*

The stars looked down impassively on the pencil-slim Interceptors as they sped through the darkness, to their next enemy encounter. Realistically Jarrod knew this would be the final part of their mission. Energy reserves would be almost depleted. Any surviving Interceptors would need their remaining reserve of energy to return to their own cruisers that hopefully would have slipped through the blockade.

His earphones crackled once more. 'Leader One to Interceptors. Enemy cruiser will be in range in three minutes.

Break formation and engage the enemy at your discretion. Good luck.'

Jarrod peeled his craft to port then levelled out. Each blast of his cannons he knew would slow the enemy cruiser, albeit minimally. No need to get the huge craft in the cannon's cross hairs. You could not miss such a large target.

*

Bridgett and Nikki joined Amber, Lisa and David in the dining area. Pressure suits were still being worn. Their chairs were facing the wall screen as they waited nervously for the next bulletin. Bridgett hero worshiped Jarrod and desperately hoped for his safe return.

Meanwhile Mirim had reluctantly left the dining area on urgent business.

Amber had always been protective of Bridgett and she put a comforting arm around her shoulders.

No one spoke. The only sound was the whisper of the ventilating system.

A sense of impending doom enveloped Bridgett. Adults had tried to hide the fact that it was unlikely any of the Interceptors would be returning. But she was twelve years old. She could read adults' body language and facial expressions.

And the silence stretched.

At last the latest report came up on the screen, informing that the Interceptors had engaged the second enemy cruiser.

Bridgett hunched forward in her chair, as did Amber. Bridgett could still feel her friend's arm around her shoulders, but squeezing more tightly now. Even through the bulk of the suit, she could feel Amber trembling.

Nikki covered her daughter's gloved hand with her own as they all gazed with deep trepidation at the screen. The message faded from the screen, but now that the Interceptors had engaged the enemy cruiser there would be regular updates.

So they waited and they waited.

*

For five long minutes, the battle raged. Again the Interceptors were avoiding enemy fire. The Interceptors returned fire – every needle of light finding the huge enemy cruiser's defensive shield.

If we could take out just this one cruiser, the odds would improve the chances of the Foundation breaking the blockade. Jarrod immediately dismissed the foolish notion. How could the Interceptors destroy such a powerful adversary? The orders were to slow down, divert the enemy cruisers – nothing more. Get real! he silently scolded.

An enemy beam lit up Jarrod's cockpit. A fraction lower and it would have cut him in two. He banked to port then rolled his craft once – twice, then straight up and over and returned a pulse of three laser bolts at the cruiser's defensive shield.

So far, so good. The cruiser was using up valuable energy, but so were the Interceptors.

The darting and diving Interceptors were making it difficult for the enemy's cannons. Jarrod's earphones crackled into life.

'Leader One to Interceptors. Enemy fighters fast approaching. Deal with them at your discretion.'

Twelve fighters from the original squadron of twenty were almost in range. Jarrod cut to the left and did a 180-degree turn. He had them on screen. He cut to the right, then to the left, to make his Interceptor a difficult target for the enemy cruiser that was now behind him. The leading fighter was locked on but almost immediately it dipped away.

Jarrod swore through clenched teeth. 'Mongrel.' He dipped the Interceptor's nose and pursued the fighter. Once more the enemy craft was in the cross hairs. Jarrod's safety catch was still flipped off the firing switch. He pressed the laser cannon's trigger.

The beam flared out. It punched through the nose of the fighter with little apparent damage.

'Damn,' Jarrod swore. 'Not good enough. Another waste of valuable energy.'

He was about to manoeuvre his Interceptor to line the target up once more, but realised it wasn't necessary. The fighter began to trail smoke from its nose section. It quickly spread towards the cockpit.

The Drog pilot was victim to an internal fire caused by damaged circuitry.

Jarrod knew the fire would suck up all the oxygen. The pilot would be asphyxiated then roasted. Jarrod allowed himself to smile.

Or perhaps he would be roasted alive before he suffocated – even better.

He slid a glance to his left. Another Interceptor had joined him. His comrade went into a sudden dive to avoid three fighters zeroing in.

Jarrod pulled his Interceptor into a steep climb, lancing high into the vault of the heavens towards Aldebaran, a K- type, orange star in the Taurus constellation. A few long seconds into his climb he levelled out briefly, then looping his craft in a tight arc, went into a sharp dive – levelling out, it took him directly behind the three enemy fighters in pursuit of his comrade.

Jarrod aligned his craft directly behind the trailing fighter. Target locked on. Direct hit!

Consumed by the lethal beam, the enemy fighter blossomed into a beautiful flower of red and orange roiling light. Like the Interceptors, the fighters had no shielding. All their energy was needed for speed and weaponry.

Jarrod rocked and dipped his craft like a leaf in the wind to avoid enemy fire from both the huge cruiser and enemy fighters. Up to now the strategy was proving to be very successful.

He gave chase to another of the fighter craft that was in pursuit of his comrade.

Jarrod had the target locked on. The energy beam cut through the fighter in a blaze of scorching light.

Jarrod quickly repositioned his Interceptor once more to trail directly behind another fighter.

Too late! The enemy fighter destroyed a fleeing Interceptor in a blaze of super-heated atoms.

Jarrod looked on in horror. Anger quickly followed. His lips compressed into a thin, bitter line.

Again he had the enemy fighter locked on. Lethal light lanced out. It took the fighter out in a radiance of raw energy.

Jarrod's earphones crackled.

'Leader One to, Interceptor Three. You and I are the only ones left. We are all done here, son,' he said urgently. 'Your energy reserves will be low. Return to *Argo*.'

Jarrod was horrified that all but two of the Interceptors had been taken out. They had been doing so well; he was starting to hope that some of them might even make it back to their cruisers.

'Interceptor Three to, Leader One. You are breaking up,' Jarrod lied. 'Repeat message.'

'If you can hear this, son. Get out of there! Return to *Argo*,' he implored. 'Repeat. Return to *Argo*! Please respond!'

A primitive hostile instinct consumed Jarrod.

'Perhaps there is a way a solitary Interceptor can take out the cruiser,' he whispered to himself.

Instead of retreating, he cut to the left and aligned his craft in the massive cruiser's flight path – ignoring Joseph's continued pleas to retreat. Accelerating to maximum he set his cannon onto automatic and pressed the firing switch.

Destructive energy pulsed out, pointing to the exact spot where he hoped to strike the giant craft – if he could just be spared for a few long seconds from being destroyed by enemy fire!

Brilliant flashes of enemy beams cut through the darkness, slashing the night with fire.

His cockpit continually lit up as the enemy realised his intention.

He had disobeyed orders, but he knew he would not be around to be reprimanded. If he could just take out the cruiser it might allow the Foundation cruisers to slip through the blockade – everyone he loved might be safe. He would leave them with a legacy of grief, and for that he was sorry. But it was a worthwhile sacrifice, he reassured himself.

Faces rolled through his mind. Amber, Lisa, the love of his life, his parents, Bridgett, Nikki, David…

Joseph's instinct was to return to the battle, but there was nothing he could do now! He felt wretched. Conflicting emotions washed through him – desperate sadness mixed with anger.

It was obvious that Jarrod had disobeyed a direct order.

Joseph watched on helpless as Interceptor Three tore through the enemy's weakened shield. A great concussion of light erupted, drenching the darkness in a cloud of intense colours. The Interceptor had penetrated the cruiser's power plant.

Joseph shook his head in awe of the bravery of his young charge. He had crippled the enemy cruiser – perhaps not mortally. But it would be one less cruiser that would reach the blockade.

Joseph felt a prickle of tears for all the brave Interceptor pilots that had perished. He felt a deal of guilt that he would be the only one to survive. And Jarrod! It was such a shock to find out that he was a maverick. A very brave maverick!

He sighed sadly as he accelerated towards a rendezvous point. If the Foundation cruisers were destroyed, he and his Interceptor would ply the star lanes of The Milky Way forever!

*

On *Argo*, the wall screen flickered to life with its dreadful message. Only Interceptor One had survived.

Anguished cries reverberated around the room.

Grief thickened the air.

Now the last trace of hope Amber had been nursing for her brother had fled.

Tomorrow was his birthday. He would have been just twenty-four. He'd been destined to die young.

Her throat tightened as she felt grief's cold fingers. 'Oh, Jarrod, Jarrod,' she whispered to herself as tears spilled down her cheeks. She found it hard to pull her gaze away from the chilling message. Mercifully her eyes lost their focus. It was then that the sound of sobbing broke through her fog of grief. She swivelled her chair away from the screen and turned to Bridgett. Nicolette was trying to comfort her daughter as best she could. O'Connor was by her side.

Bridgett's misery filled eyes turned to Amber 'My dearest friend in the whole universe is gone,' Bridgett said, her voice choking in her throat. It was just like the time her Papa had been taken and it hurt so much.

Amber's mouth parted as if to speak, but no words escaped her lips. No words could be adequate to assuage the pain of their loss. All she could do was embrace her friend.

Lisa sat with her head in her hands. The chilling message was imprinted firmly in her mind. It was so hard to accept that Jarrod had perished. He was gone and it left her bleak and cold inside. At that moment she wished she could embrace death too. Perhaps she would not be sad for long she told herself. If they couldn't break the blockade ahead they would all perish.

A gong sounded, alerting another incoming report. Once more, tear stained faces turned to the wall screen. It was a short message. It explained how Jarrod, against orders had sacrificed himself to take out an enemy cruiser.

Gasps and murmurs filled the room. The youngest Interceptor pilot who had only lived a handful of years had made the ultimate sacrifice.

As the message faded from the screen, Lisa pictured the tiny Interceptor hurtling towards the huge enemy cruiser, all the while narrowly missing the enemy's cannons – finally penetrating the cruiser's shielding and crashing in a holocaust of flames. For a brief moment anger took over. Her eyes turned wintry. What was he thinking? Didn't he know that it was far and beyond what anyone expected of him? And didn't he know I'd never get over him?

She squeezed her eyes tightly shut as she tried to drive the awful vision from her mind. It hurt so much to give him up.

David's face was clouded with grief – his sadness too deep for tears. He looked over to Amber who was hugging Bridgett. Her helmet framed her sad eyes that shimmered with tears. It nearly broke his heart. What could he say to her? How could he comfort her? He would wait until his trembling ebbed – then he would try.

Again the gong preceded another message. This time it was verbal as well as on screen. They were to remain in their pressure suits and be restrained in their acceleration couches, but in the chair position. There would be no acceleration, but they needed to be prepared for the blockade ahead.

On the bridge Wade's grief threatened to overwhelm him – devastated that his son had been cut down so young. Just a quick look at life was all he'd had. But he clamped down on his grief and prepared himself for the battle ahead. *Argo* would not be deviating from its programmed flight path. At the tremendous speed it was travelling, an attempt to manoeuvre the craft would cause more problems than it could solve. No. The plan was a simple one. Full shielding would be engaged. The Foundation cruisers would fire upon the enemy cruisers when in range of their cannons. If an enemy cruiser got in the way too bad! They would annihilate each other.

Orion and *Vela* were not accelerating so they were conserving fuel. *Argo* though was using a little energy to slow down – but not enough to disturb passengers and crew. This was necessary to enable a successful pick up of Interceptor One. On the other hand Joseph was accelerating his craft to maximum, to allow a successful docking with *Argo* way beyond the incursion point. It was his only chance. The Foundation would not risk all three cruisers to slow down, and because *Argo* was decelerating, it was unnecessary to have the artificial gravity switched on. The deceleration was giving its own form of gravity.

If *Argo* was destroyed, Joseph would sail the infinite sea of space for eternity.

Chapter Eighteen

Warstill's eyes burned with fury. He'd planned to have at least twenty-five cruisers to secure the blockade. Then his expectation was cut to eight due to those confounded infrared flares. Now a crazy Foundation pilot had crippled a valuable cruiser that would now take no part in the blockade, cutting the number to seven. He did not like the odds.

Everyone on the bridge had their heads down and their eyes fixed nervously on their screens, avoiding eye contact with their commander.

Warstill shook his head in frustration. 'Strategists!' he bellowed in a basso profundo voice that carried to every corner of the bridge and beyond.

The three strategists scrambled to Warstill's workstation and waited tensely for his wrath to pour over them.

Remaining in his chair, Warstill gazed up at the strategists, scorching them with a furious look. 'Well,' he rasped. 'Do we abort? Or do we engage the enemy?'

As usual, the bravest of the three unfortunate strategists was about to speak, but Warstll waved him to silence.

He turned to the other strategists, his expression cold and threatening. 'Let me hear from you two for a change.'

'We a...a...abort.' one strategist stuttered. 'From experience the only way to defeat this enemy is ... err ... to have an overwhelming superiority of numbers.'

Warstill nodded and turned to the other strategist who was visibly trembling.

'I ... concur with my colleague, sir,' he managed to mumble.

'Wrong! Wrong! Wrong!' Warstill railed. 'We have gone to great lengths to mount this mission. We cannot abandon it.' Anger turned his face a deep purple. 'Your ineptitude has made it much more difficult than it should have been.' He hunched forward in his chair. 'Now listen to me,' his voice a low rumble. 'Our seven cruisers must accelerate beyond the blockade point.' He went on. 'Because the Foundation cruisers are travelling at a tremendous velocity, they will of course catch up to us, but it means it will afford us a little more time when they will be in range of our cannons. They will not be changing their flight path at their speed.'

'But, sir, with respect,' Vabor, the boldest of the three strategists said, 'it will be energy draining.'

Warstill grunted. 'It will be a short confrontation because of their tremendous velocity. We will destroy them in that short window of time, or they will escape.' He fixed each of the strategists in turn with a chilling gaze. In a voice no louder than the purr of a tiger, he said, 'if the latter is the case there will be consequences.'

*

Weapons specialist, Hilary Jensen sat at her station and called up the weapons display. She did a quick but thorough check. The nearest Drog cruiser was almost at extreme range of *Argo's* cannons. She noted that the enemy cruisers were accelerating away from the incursion point, but she doubted they were in retreat because they were still in close proximity to the Foundation cruisers' flight path. She suspected they were trying to gain a little more time to have the Foundation cruisers in range of their cannons for a longer period. She nodded. Unfortunately it was a good ploy by the Drogs.

Argo had dropped back a little from her sister ships, now that she was decelerating. *Vela* and *Orion* would be the first to fire their weapons at the enemy.

Seconds later, lethal light scorched out of *Vela* and *Orion* into the freezing, eternal night, seeking out the enemy. They found their target – impacting on the closest enemy cruiser's defensive shield. All the Foundation cruisers it was decided would be concentrating on that one unfortunate enemy cruiser – no matter what! And the Foundation cruisers would absorb the enemy's fire as best they could. This way there was a chance they could take out one enemy cruiser before they attempted to breach the blockade.

Fire was returned, impacting on the leading Foundation cruisers.

On *Argo*, Hilary Jensen hunched over her display. She pressed a key to arm the lasers and focused on the target. Her hand poised over the firing key, waiting for the target to come within range. Seconds later she pressed the key. A needle of light penetrated the darkness. There was no doubt. It would impact the singled out Drog cruiser that had lost the roll of the dice.

The Drogs could choose to target just one Foundation cruiser also, but that could make it possible for the cruisers to break the blockade. This, Warstill would not entertain.

The closer the protagonists got to each other, the intensity of fire increased.

Argo rocked and shuddered as enemy beams impacted its shielding. The craft's attitude jets fired in frantic sequences trying to maintain stability. Each impact was slowing *Argo's* momentum minimally. As a result, the valuable energy needed by *Argo* to decelerate to allow a rendezvous with Joseph had lessened.

Strapped securely to their chairs, all aboard *Argo* were sustaining severe bruising from their restraining harnesses. Anguished cries reverberated through the ship.

Lisa took no heed. Alone with her grief, her world had already crashed and burned. Her eyes glistened with unshed tears. How can I go on without you, Jarrod? she silently asked. Losing you is tearing me apart.

It was the darkest time of her life. In her mind she could see him clearly, his chiselled cheekbones, his riveting dark eyes, and his eloquence that he was so proud of. Yes. Jarrod would live inside her head as long as she lived.

Finally she allowed her tears to fall.

Amber was hurting too, but for now was all cried out. Her face was a frozen, sad and bitter mask. But underlying the sadness there was anger. Jarrod had no right to disobey orders – no right to be a hero! He had done it for those that he loved – taken out a cruiser to improve the odds. Well my, dear brother, she silently said. If we survive the next short while, it will probably be because of you. You have fulfilled your powerful destiny – but you have left us with a cruel, legacy of grief.

The stars looked down with no regard for the raging battle. Wade sat strapped to his chair at his station on the bridge directing operations. There was a palpable sadness in his features.

Pulses of tight laser beams from *Argo's* cannons were finding their target time after time. But a worrying situation had developed. The solitary enemy cruiser that was taking all the hits from the Foundation cruisers had positioned itself directly in *Argo's* flight path. Obviously a tactic ordered by the Drog commander. They were prepared to sacrifice their cruiser if it could take out *Argo*.

Wade turned to Simon. 'If the enemy cruiser ahead survives our cannon fire much longer we will be done for.' His lips compressed in a tight angry line. 'At least we will take an enemy cruiser with us,' he added.

'The enemy cruiser's defensive shield must degrade soon,' Simon said, trying to keep his voice upbeat.

They looked at each other uneasily, then turned back to their screens.

In a frozen instant the enemy cruiser's defensive shield was neutralised. The unprotected hull was no defence against the combined fire from the three Foundation cruisers. The mortally wounded enemy cruiser was shunted out of *Argo's* flight path. Seconds later it erupted in a pillar of fire.

Wade sighed inwardly as he studied his screen.

Moments later everyone on the bridge looked up as unnatural brightness flooded though the view ports.

The enemy cruiser had violently exploded, becoming a short-lived star. The roiling cloud blanketed the way ahead.

A few long minutes later, *Argo* sliced through the outer edge of the orange and blue cloud of super heated atoms. The starship rocked and vibrated as enemy fire impacted its defensive shield.

Minutes later *Vela* and *Orion* reported to *Argo* that they had broken through the barricade and were now out of range of the enemy's cannons. All on the bridge gave a muted cheer, being respectful of Wade's loss. Now the full attention of the enemy's cannons focused on the solitary Foundation cruiser. The mighty starship rocked, swayed and vibrated as enemy beams impacted its shielding. Attitude jets fired continuously trying to maintain stability.

Argo sped past the blockade but was still under heavy fire from Drog cannons.

A piercing siren wailed out. An enemy laser bolt had breached *Argo's* defensive shield.

Wade called up a damage report and waited anxiously. Moments later the report showed three of the craft's attitude jets had been damaged. The enemy laser had punctured the hull and that area had been sealed off automatically from the rest of the ship. Wade sighed with relief. It could have been a lot worse. Then anxiety knifed through him as he remembered he still had to pick up Interceptor One. That made repairing the attitude jets an urgent priority. He would get Mathew onto it as soon as possible.

Argo's shielding was weakening due to its heavy demand on the ship's energy supply.

Wade silently reprimanded himself. He should have been alert to the weakening shielding. He called up weapons specialist, Hilary Jensen to cease firing – something he should have done much earlier. All energy would now be diverted to shielding.

Five minutes more of intense enemy fire and they were out of range of the Drog cannons. We have made it, he told himself. But for Jarrod's sacrifice, it's doubtful we would have.

All three cruisers had broken the blockade with damage restricted to *Argo* alone. But Interceptor One was the only Interceptor out of a total of nine that had survived. And it was going to require a desperate rescue mission to save it.

*

Warstill was furious. The mission to destroy the three Foundation cruisers was a dreadful failure and his strategists must take the blame. He knew what he had to do. He swivelled 180 degrees and launched himself violently off his chair. His three strategists recoiled in fear. They had never seen their commander's face so purple – such was his rage.

Warstill brushed past them and stormed towards the exit. Turning his head back towards the hapless strategists, and without breaking stride, he snarled, 'I'll be back!'

*

On *Argo*, a verbal report announced that the blockade had been successfully breached. There was a muted cheer. The message went on to describe the status of the attitude jets. In the meantime pressure suits could be removed, but they would have to return to their acceleration couches within the hour. It was hoped by then the attitude jets would be repaired. Then an attempt could be made to rescue Interceptor One. It would be tricky because of the high velocity of the starship. *Argo* was still decelerating at 1G in preparation of the rescue mission, so a generated artificial gravity was unnecessary.

Interceptor One was accelerating at an uncomfortable 4 G's. By the time *Argo* was close, Joseph hoped their speeds would be close to matching for a successful rescue. He was overjoyed when the message came through that all three cruisers had broken the barricade. If the pickup was unsuccessful, he could at least die with that comforting knowledge.

Back on *Argo* Mathew was squeezing through the access tunnel leading to the area of damage, grabbing a handhold with one hand and pushing a trolley with the other. The handholds were set into the walls and spaced strategically along the length of the tunnel. He was suited-up, because once he had entered the access tunnel, it had closed on him and was drained of air to match the damaged area of concern that was open to the vacuum of space. He had done his pre-breathe of oxygen to purge nitrogen from his blood stream. This was necessary because his suit could not be pressurised as much as *Argo's* air pressure, as it would become too rigid. But his pre-breathe should have been two hours – not the ten minutes that he'd had because of the emergency. There would certainly be consequences. He would suffer a condition known as the bends – a frothing of the remaining nitrogen in his bloodstream because of the short pre-breathe. He knew it could kill him.

Pushing the trolley of tools and replacement parts that might be needed, he noted the trolley was not running as freely as it should. Probably a missed maintenance, he grumbled to himself, but there was nothing he could do about it now.

The suit's air had a metallic scent to it, which was perfectly normal. Sweat beaded his brow as he struggled in the confined crawl space. If the repair had not been so urgent, a service robot could have been programmed to do the job.

Finally he came to the end of the tunnel, which was closed off by the automatic shut down of the damaged area, as it was open to the vacuum of space. He reached over the trolley with difficulty. His eyes stung as sweat finally breached the barrier of his eyebrows. He swore as he pushed a button at the side of the emergency hatch. It opened and he moved on through. At least the area was spacious enough for the diminutive Mathew to stand up.

For a brief few seconds he took in the sight of a magnificent star field through the torn hull. He wondered if there could be another Earth orbiting a sun-like star, sailing the rich star field.

Dragging his eyes away from the spectacle reluctantly, he applied the brake on the trolley by pushing on a lever at the side, just below the toolbox. Then he tapped out a command on the control panel on his left arm to increase the suit's built in cooling. He had misjudged how hot it was going to be in the tunnel, and the crawl space was so restrictive it would have been difficult to access the suit's control panel any earlier.

The tools were made of titanium, because if repairs ever had to be made near the stardrive's super conducting magnets, it would be highly dangerous to use steel tools.

He sighed as he inspected the extent of the damage, but it could have been a lot worse. There was no time to lose, so without pause he set about repairs. He opened up the case to reveal an impressive array of tools, yet all he needed was a suitable hammer. He struck the buckled hull repeatedly until it was back as near as possible to its former position. The attitude jets that were attached to the damaged hull were now roughly back in their correct position. He would fine-tune their angles in relation to the hull later.

Mathew's earphones crackled. 'How much longer, Mathew?' Wade asked urgently.

'I have only just started the repairs, sir.' He failed to hide a trace of annoyance creeping into his voice.

'I am aware of that, Mathew. There is not much time,' he said, stating the obvious. 'Joseph is counting on us. Give me a time estimate for the repairs so I can increase our deceleration if necessary.'

'Twenty minutes should do it, sir,' he said a little more harshly than he'd intended.

'Thank you, Mathew. I know I can count on you.'

Mathew got back to the task in hand. 'If I didn't have interruptions I would be able to get the job done that much quicker,' he grumbled to himself. He immediately regretted the harshness of his statement. Wade had just lost his son. And Jarrod was almost certainly the reason that *Argo* had breached the blockade.

He grabbed the plasma torch from the toolbox. It looked huge in his tiny hand.

He was sure Wade would have picked up on the terseness that had crept into his voice. He would apologise to him later – if he survived the bends!

Lighting the hand held plasma torch by flicking a switch, he immediately began to weld the ripped edges of the torn panels at a molecular level. Ten minutes later the task was completed. The panel beating was not pretty, but he felt pleased with the repairs. He reconnected the electrical wires that had ripped away from the attitude jets when the hull had been penetrated.

Reaching for a ring spanner he began the task of adjusting the angle of thrust of each attitude jet. Using the tool, he turned the eccentric cam in a clockwise direction. 'Damn,' Mathew muttered. An indicator light directly above the cam's adjusting nut remained a solid red. He turned the nut anti clockwise little by little. Finally the indicator light changed to green.

Mathew repeated the adjustment of the other two attitude

jets successfully, and reported to Control that the job was completed.

Sighing with relief, he re-packed his tool-case, released the brake and pushed it into the access tunnel. Hunkering down he crawled into the access tunnel. With one hand he grabbed a handhold, pulling himself forward as far as he could go while pushing the trolley with his other hand. Changing hands at the next handhold, he pushed the trolley ahead of him once more. Is it getting harder to push? he silently asked. Or am I just weary?

But it was becoming a monumental effort. Something was not right!

It was taking all his strength to move the trolley – and it was taking too much time!

His stomach lurched. The trolley wouldn't budge! He was trapped in the tunnel. He rested a moment and concentrated on regulating his breathing, inhaling deeply and exhaling slowly.

He managed to get a foot on one of the handholds behind him. He gripped the trolley with his right hand, while his left hand grabbed a handhold. With a supreme effort he pulled on the handhold, and pushed with his foot on the handhold behind him with all his strength.

The trolley wouldn't budge!

His body was steeped in sweat. 'What the bloody hell do I do now?' he asked himself. Don't panic a voice inside his head counselled. Contact Control.

With a great effort he managed to back up the tunnel enough to free his arms to allow him to access the suit's radio.

'Mathew to Control. Come in Control.'

Wade answered. 'Yes, Mathew?'

'I have a situation, sir. The trolley is stuck in the tunnel.' Mathew explained the unsuccessful technique he had been using to no avail.

'Okay, Mathew, here is what we will do,' he said in a calming tone, and explained each step of the procedure they would be using.

Five minutes later, the tunnel was repressurised and reopened. An engineer then proceeded to insert a long metal pole into the tunnel. Every few minutes he twisted the pole, and it telescoped out, allowing him to extend it further into the tunnel. Repeating the action once more, the pole finally contacted the trolley. A few minutes of manipulation and it snagged a hole at the front of the trolley which was there for that very purpose. It was the first time that the technique had ever been used – the first time it had ever been needed.

The engineer grabbed the handle and by radio instructed Mathew to attempt to get the trolley moving. The engineer assisted by pulling the robust pole as hard as he could. The trolley remained stubborn to the end, but slowly, with a high pitched screeching of protest it reluctantly slid slowly out of the tunnel.

As soon as Mathew vacated the tunnel, his helmet was removed and oxygen was administered through a mask. Then two surgical robots lifted him onto a gurney and rushed him to a decompression chamber for urgent treatment.

A check was done on the repairs, and the air pressure showed that it was successfully sealed from the vacuum of space. Another brief test showed that the reaction thrusters were performing perfectly.

A large red label was stuck to the trolley, stating that it was not to be used till further notice. Later it would be found that the brake's release mechanism was faulty.

Some service robot was going to get a rap over its titanium alloy knuckles.

Chapter Nineteen

Joseph checked the status of energy reserves. Five percent remained. He cut the acceleration immediately. The meagre energy reserve would be needed to link up with *Argo* later. He was informed that repairs to *Argo's* attitude jets had been completed successfully, and was heartened by the news. Meanwhile his Interceptor continued to speed through the void, but now without the oppressiveness of acceleration.

Shadows were deeply etched around Joseph's eyes. He felt desperately empty. Once more his thoughts went back to his brave Interceptor pilots now all perished. It was expected of course, but he'd survived! And the sense of guilt remained with him – always would, he suspected.

Jarrod had disobeyed orders and sacrificed himself. How could he face his parents? Unbidden, a thought came to him. Perhaps it would be easier if rendezvous with *Argo* proved impossible? Perhaps he could make that happen. He could cut to port with his remaining energy and accelerate into the eternal night and embrace death. His body could ride the star lanes forever. Not a bad place to die. For a brief moment his spirits lifted with the crazy notion. No! a voice in his mind scolded. He must allow *Argo* to pick up its one remaining Interceptor and experienced pilot, if it was at all possible.

With nothing to do but wait he turned his attention to the confusion of blue tinged stars ahead. He tried to pick out the familiar constellations but it was impossible. Being so far from Earth, the vantage point was drastically altered. The old familiar patterns had changed and were totally unrecognisable.

Even though *Argo* was decelerating, she was still going appreciably faster than the Interceptor was. While Joseph was pondering the field of bright blue gems in his Interceptor, back on *Argo*, crew and passengers were instructed to return to their stations and prepare for a pick up of the sole surviving Interceptor. Pressure suits would not have to be worn.

Amber was the first to enter the dimly lit restaurant area with David by her side. The pale-pearl greyness of dawn began to appear in the synthetic sky above. Her face was ashen, in stark contrast to the black jumpsuit she wore.

David's eyes narrowed with concern. His arm rested lightly on her shoulders, and he wondered whether he should have chosen to wear a black jumpsuit out of respect.

He sat her down on her chair and strapped her in.

She smiled up at him, but her expression could not conceal her sadness. 'Thank you, David,' her voice barely above a whisper. She lowered her gaze and stared at the blank wall screen – the memory of its cruel message still entrenched in her soul.

David looked down at her with a worried frown. He sensed she needed to be alone with her sadness. For now, there was nothing he could do – nothing anyone could do for her. He moved away to his own chair and strapped himself in.

People were filing in silently and seating themselves down in an orderly fashion. David was relieved to see that none were wearing black jumpsuits. Lisa was among them. Her eyes were filled with hopelessness. David could see she was barely holding it together. Bridgett was behind Lisa, accompanied by her mother and Adrian O'Connor. The last ones to file in were Mary and Gerald White.

The hush continued. The air was thick with grief.

On the bridge Wade gazed at his central display. A superimposed grid showed the exact location of the Interceptor and *Argo's* position in relation to it. Readouts at the bottom of the screen ticked away the distance separating the two craft.

While the attitude thrusters had been out of action, *Argo* had been unable to trim her flight path in relation to the other two cruisers. It couldn't be helped. And because of the rescue mission, *Argo* would make no attempt to alter her present flight path.

The decision would later cause a grave consequence.

It was decided it would be far simpler for Joseph's tiny Interceptor to manoeuvre rather than the huge cruiser. To add weight to the decision, the Interceptor's velocity was for now, still appreciably slower than *Argo*.

Wade opened up communication with Interceptor One.

'*Argo* to Interceptor One. Come in, Joseph.'

'Copy, sir.'

'You need to change course now, and stay on line.'

'Very good, sir.'

'Okay. Bearing zero five zero, Joseph.'

Wade studied his screen. The blip on screen representing the Interceptor clearly showed the course correction.

'Come in, Joseph.'

'Sir.'

'Please lift your craft twenty-eight degrees.'

'Yes, sir.'

Wade studied the screen. 'Good, Joseph. Now level out and maintain your flight path. Accelerate at 1G for five minutes and wait for further instructions. Over.'

'Yes, sir.'

*

Ordered to the environmental chamber by Warstill, the three strategists nervously awaited their commander's presence. The mission had been a dismal failure. They knew they would carry the blame, even though Warstill had overseen the whole mission. The decisions were his alone. Nevertheless it would be the strategists who would be punished. The very fact that they were to assemble in the environment chamber was disquieting.

They heard him thumping down the corridor that led to the chamber. The footsteps ceased outside the entrance. Even before the door had slid fully open, Warstill burst through.

The sight of their commander resplendent in ceremonial dress was enough to make even the bravest of the three strategists tremble. There was little doubt in their minds that one or all of them were going to be executed and rendered down into fertiliser.

It could not be worse!

In his ceremonial, gleaming armour he looked every inch a fearsome warrior. His wore an anodized meteorite steel breastplate over his royal-blue tunic. Matching wide embossed steel bracelets adorned his thick wrists. A leather helmet emphasised his huge head. Supple leather boots ended halfway up his powerful calves. A bejewelled scabbard was home to a magnificent steel sword encrusted with gold mountings. The fearsome weapon had a double-cutting edge as well as a stabbing point.

Warstill's sensitive flexible snout picked up the scent of fear as he strode in and came to a halt in front of them. His gaze slowly swept each face. He smiled. The smile was blood chilling.

Warstill noticed Vabar, his more verbal strategist was holding up his comrade, Gusgus, who was trembling uncontrollably. It confirmed what he had always thought of that particular, useless specimen. Yes they would be better off without him.

'Well I have made up my mind.' He paused and studied each face. 'I was of a mind to punish you all, but I've decided to be lenient.' Again that blood chilling smile. 'Just one of you will be paying with his life.'

'Sir. Permission to speak?'

Warstill was taken aback. Of course it was Vabar requesting permission to speak; even so, he didn't think even Vabar would have drawn attention to himself. Begrudgingly he admired his bravery.

'Permission granted, but be quick.'

'With respect, sir, I would have thought our weapons specialist is as much to blame as we are.' He did a small bow. 'And thank you for letting me speak.'

'I have not forgotten her misguided advice. I have something else in store for her. Do not concern yourself about it.' In his mind he could see the weapons specialist. She was far too attractive to be terminated.

Warstill turned his attention back to what he regarded as the weakest link – the least valuable of the three.

'I have chosen you, Gusgus. You will be punished for the collective ineptitude of all three of you.'

Gusgus visibly crumpled.

Warstill ordered the other two fortunate strategists to escort the victim to a large wooden butcher's block that took pride of place in the middle of the environment chamber. Gusgus resisted all the way to the block while continually pleading for his life.

'Sir. Permission to speak?' the verbal strategist asked.

Warstill hiked his shaggy brows. 'What is it now, Vabar?' His voice was an intimidating low rasp.

'Gusgus is a brilliant strategist. He never talks much, but when he does, it is always worthwhile listening. He … '

'Enough!' Warstill screamed. 'I have made my choice.' He fixed the strategist with a red gaze, his voice a sinister hiss. 'Unless you want to take his place, Vabor?'

'No, sir.'

'Good then.' He focused his attention back to the shaking strategist. 'Have you any last words, Gusgus?' His voice was a monotone.

Although still shaking, Gusgus had not pleaded for his life for a full minute. He knew it was hopeless. He would beg no more. He straightened up and looked at Warstill, his gaze unwavering. 'You are the one who should take the blame. It was your tactics that failed us. You are a bad and cruel leader.'

'Enough!' Warstill screamed.

'I will not be silent. Nobody likes you.'

'I am not interested in being liked – just respected,' he bellowed.

'You are not respected,' the victim spat out. 'Just feared.'

'You have never had much to say for yourself before,' Warstill snarled. 'Now I can't shut you up. Well we will soon fix that!'

With that Warstill strode over to a freestanding cloak-stand.

In the short time it took Warstill to retrieve three pairs of red coveralls, the two strategists tried to comfort their comrade as best they could. They were surprised and proud at how he had stood up to their commander.

'Put these on to protect your clothing,' Warstill ordered the two strategists guarding Gusgus. 'One of you at a time,' he said warily, mindful of the possibility of mutiny.

Gusgus still trembled. He had no control about that, but he remained resolute. He would beg no more. He would not give his commander the satisfaction. He would leave this life a true warrior.

As soon as the two strategists were suitably attired in their protective clothing, Warstill withdrew his sword from its scabbard and placed the gleaming blade carefully on the block at its furthermost point from the three strategists as a precaution. He donned his coverall, all the while keeping his eyes on the trio. Grabbing his sword, he motioned the strategists either side of the trembling Drog to lower him face down onto the block. He looked on and was surprised, and a little disappointed that the victim did not resist. It would have been more enjoyable if he had done so, but at least he was trembling.

Warstill laid the cold blade on the strategist's neck. With both hands he slowly lifted the sword above his own head.

Warstill smiled. His eyes glazed over. In one single vicious motion he wielded the heavy sword down. The head separated from the trunk. Blood gushed into the air from the still beating heart. The strategists lifted their comrade's headless body into an upright position.

The severed head had rolled ninety degrees on the bloody block.

For a brief moment of consciousness the brain was still functioning.

Gusgus's head gazed up in horror at his bloodied trunk.

Then darkness.

*

'*Argo* to Interceptor One. Respond please, Joseph.'

'Copy, sir.'

'In eight minutes we will overtake you. Then it will be up to you to accelerate to catch us, and match *Argo's* speed so you can return safely to us. What is your energy status?'

'Two percent, sir.' He heard the commander's sharp intake of breath.

If his attempt to return to *Argo* failed, there was no other Interceptor on board the starship to rescue him. *Argo* did have other craft, but they were surface to orbit ferries, totally incapable of reaching the speed of an Interceptor. His craft would be his coffin, and together they would sail the galactic ocean forever.

'Good luck, Joseph,' Wade said softly and closed the channel.

'Decelerate another ten percent, Simon. I just hope it's enough. Joseph's perilously low in energy.'

Eight minutes later and even though still decelerating, *Argo* overtook and sped past the Interceptor.

Joseph accelerated his Interceptor with his remaining energy reserve. *Argo* was already out of visual range. He gazed at his central display and the blip that represented the starship ahead, then down to the bottom of the screen that showed the separation between the two craft. After two minutes of acceleration he was pleased to see that at least his distance from *Argo* was now stable.

Another three minutes of acceleration and readouts showed he was closing on *Argo*.

A warning message in orange came up on the screen, stating energy reserves were at a critical level – one percent remaining.

'Do not give out on me now,' Joseph pleaded. He hadn't expected to survive – none of the Interceptor pilots had. But now he was so close to *Argo*, it would be a cruel blow for the energy reserves to cut out.

Readouts on the screen showed separation from the decelerating starship was shrinking a little faster now.

There was no more communication between the two craft. It was up to Joseph's skill and a deal of luck now.

His spirits rose. He had a visual on the starship.

Again the message came on screen – this time in red. Energy levels were critically low. He dragged his eyes away from the screen and its chilling message. His mouth set in a thin line of determination.

Now that *Argo* was clearly visible ahead he would ignore the screen.

If his energy reserves ran out now he knew his craft would not slow. It would overtake *Argo*, but with no energy supply he would be unable to operate his attitude jets or his breaking jets and so, would be unable to return to the belly of the starship.

He smiled grimly as he promised himself he would give the cruiser a symbolic wave before being swallowed up by the dark ocean.

*

In the hyperbaric chamber Mathew was fighting for his life – a direct result of his pre-breathe of pure oxygen being foreshortened.

At normal air pressure, nitrogen and other gases are exhaled or dissolved in the blood or tissue.

A frothing of the remaining nitrogen and other gases in Mathew's bloodstream was a potentially fatal condition. Every joint in his body ached, and his skin was covered in a blotchy rash. He felt weak and weary, and to add to this, his stomach was cramping.

In the chamber the air pressure was gradually increasing then decreasing around his body, which encouraged gas bubbles to dissolve.

Mathew's body watch could do nothing to help his decompression sickness, but after a few hours he began to feel better. He even managed to smile at the attendant robots when they looked through the chamber's porthole to check on him. This in spite of the fact that he was hooked up to instruments that were recording every aspect of his condition, and being monitored by the surgical robots outside the chamber.

Due to the correct treatment being administered early, Mathew's symptoms began to disappear. A message over the chamber's speakers confirmed what he already knew. Treatment would continue for approximately another hour, then he would be assessed once more. If his condition warranted it, he would be allowed to return to normal duties. Although if any emergency required attention in the vacuum of space, he knew he would not be asked to do it for at least twenty-four hours. That was the time it took after treatment to be fully recovered.

*

After continuous acceleration, Joseph could now see the

open hatch of *Argo's* launching bay ahead. Cutting his acceleration and trimming his flight path minimally with his attitude jets, he began his braking manoeuvre.

He felt his pulse quicken, his anxiety rising. His breaking jets were consuming the last dregs of energy. *Argo's* open hatch loomed ahead, beckoning. The Interceptor's velocity was still too great! 'Don't give out on me now,' Joseph pleaded. 'Just a few minutes more, please!' But energy reserves only lasted another twenty seconds.

He swore. There was nothing he could do. With the energy cells depleted he couldn't alter his flight path, couldn't brake, and couldn't accelerate away from the cruiser ahead. He would not allow his Interceptor to cripple, or even worse, destroy the cruiser ahead. His only option was to self-destruct. His hand reached for the switch below the instrument panel to arm the device – hesitated – then he decided to communicate his intentions to the cruiser ahead.

'No, Joseph! We acknowledge the margin for you to survive a rendezvous is slim. We have activated a force-field net and set it to maximum. Calculations show that you will not damage *Argo* and there is a slim chance you might survive. Therefore we order you not to self-destruct. You will hit the energy net at 524kms an hour – which is the difference between the speed of *Argo* and your craft. Good luck, Joseph.'

'Thank you, sir. I will carry out your order.'

The open hatch was coming up fast – too fast! The force-field net bubbled out beyond the hangar's entrance in preparation of swallowing Interceptor One, and dampening its forward momentum.

Joseph instinctively shut his eyes. The Interceptor slammed into the force field net. Exposed to such high G forces, Joseph was mercifully rendered unconscious. The Interceptor finally came to a halt as it crashed into the hangar wall. Now its work was done, the force field shut down.

The large launching hatch closed behind the Interceptor. Air jetted into the vacuum of the hangar and sound with it.

The force field had done well, but it still had been unable to absorb all the forward impetus of the Interceptor. The craft had slammed into the specially designed spring-loaded hangar wall that helped to cushion the Interceptor's impact. It caused no damage to the wall, but the nose of the craft was badly crumpled. But it had been engineered to do just that – crumple on impact and lessen the force of the impact. So a combination of the force field, the spring-loaded wall and the Interceptor's crumple zone, had allowed Joseph to survive the crash.

An hour later Joseph regained consciousness in *Argo's* main hospital ward. Joseph was superbly fit from a robust fitness regime. His well toned, hardened muscles had played a part in his survival. And his body watch system had swung into action. Thrombocytes – blood platelets combined with molecular enhancement swarmed to the areas of trauma to repair damage.

Chapter Twenty

Lisa's condition was somewhere between numbness and reality. She needed to be alone. Amber had gone to her parent's cabin at their request, and Lisa took the opportunity to excuse herself from her friends to return to her cabin.

Stumbling her way to the cabin, she was a picture of white-faced despair. It just wasn't fair, she told herself. Joseph had returned safely. Jarrod could have too! Just a quick look at life was all he'd had.

Reaching her cabin, the door quietly opened, and making her way shakily to the bed, she sank to her knees. Laying her head on the bed she broke down and sobbed. It's so hard to give him up, she told herself. How can anyone take his place?

They can't a mocking voice inside her head answered.

But what else could she do?

Left to hold a broken dream, she would witness the wonders of star travel without him by her side.

Through the tears and the hollow pain of grief, a thought came to her. Amber's eyes were an echo of Jarrod's. Now every time she made eye contact with her friend, she would be reminded of him.

The thought was unsettling.

*

Bridgett and Nikki looked up as the door of their cabin opened. Spick and Span entered with a trolley of cleaning equipment in tow. After so many years of cleaning duties the only way Bridgett and Nikki could visually tell them apart was by way of coloured hoops that circled their midsections. Of course, once they started to talk their differing personalities shone through.

When Bridgett first met them, she was not much taller than they were. Now she towered over the dumpy cleaning robots.

Spick trundled over to Bridgett; his manipulators spread wide.

Bridgett stooped down to receive her customary hug.

'I am so very sorry your good friend Jarrod is no longer with us,' Spick said softly.

'Thank you, Spick. It is a very sad time. I am going to miss him.' She felt a prickle of tears but managed to retain her composure. Time enough later when she was alone for tears. She didn't want to start her mother off. She patted the robot's smooth shiny dome.

Spick turned to Nikki and gave her a hug too.

To Bridgett's surprise, Span trundled over and gave her a hug. She had never done that before. Span had always frowned upon Spick's display of affection. Only humans hugged. They were robots and she'd never ceased to remind Spick of that simple fact.

'Sorry for your loss, Bridgett,' she said.

'Thank you, Span.'

Then it was Nikki's turn for a hug from Span. Nikki broke down. Tears spilled down her cheeks. 'I am so sorry,' she apologised to the squat little robot. 'It was through Jarrod's kindness and understanding that we are here at all,' she explained. 'He was a dear, dear friend.'

Span backed off and looked at Spick for direction.

They gazed at each other helplessly. Spick shook his dome. 'Let us get on with our cleaning,' he whispered.

With her mother now crying, Bridgett finally allowed her own tears to fall. She strode over to her mother and embraced her.

Twenty minutes later the cleaning robots had completed their task. Bridgett, now composed, hunkered down beside the robots and gave them both a hug. 'We love you both very much. You know that, don't you?'

'Yes we do,' they both replied in unison.

Spick took the lead. 'We are sorry that we were not able to cry with you. It's like Span always reminds me of. We are just robots. Always will be,' he said dejectedly. 'We are not even warrior robots – just cleaning robots.' His manipulators hung by his side, his head bowed.

'You are both more than that,' Bridgett hugged them again.

'You are both our dear friends – always will be, I promise. We adore you both.'

'Thank you,' they both replied and trundled out the door.

It was the first time the robots had refrained from arguing between themselves out of respect for Bridgett and Nikki's sadness. It was not lost on Bridgett and Nikki.

*

For a little over two hours, no random atoms had impacted *Argo's* deflective shield – a fact that had gone unnoticed by the crew.

Wade sat at his usual place on the bridge with its curving bank of monitors. Two hours earlier, he had set a course to link up with *Vela* and *Orion* and had been attempting to communicate with the two cruisers. A fault analysis check finally reported an anomaly. The tight communication laser beam was curving away from the target cruisers. The reason for it was not apparent.

Wade shook his head in perplexity and ordered systems analyst, Angela Shriver, to investigate the cause.

She regarded her commander for a few short seconds. Her unusual sea-green eyes registered her puzzlement. She dipped her chin in acknowledgement. 'Yes, sir.'

A vibration through the ship was faint, at the very edge of awareness.

Wade then did a routine check on *Argo's* course setting that he'd ordered earlier. His eyes widened as he hunched forward in his chair. *Argo* had drifted to port. What the hell was Simon playing at?

He asked Simon to explain.

'Our navigation officer set the course earlier as you instructed, sir, and I rechecked the settings. I am at a loss to know how, or why we have veered to port.' A curl of unease whispered up his spine. His long fingers danced over the keyboard as he called up the navigation systems. It confirmed his commander's claim. He quickly reset the course to Wade's earlier setting.

In recognition of the instructions the portside attitude jets fired frantically to realign *Argo's* course – vigorously attempting to generate a lateral vector. But something wasn't right. Vibrations could now be felt throughout the entire ship, in stark contrast to its normally smooth operation.

Argo responded sluggishly. It was taking too long! With infinite slowness the craft changed course – minimally.

'Should we engage the stardrive?' Simon asked.

'No, Simon. Our energy reserve is low. If we engaged the stardrive, we would have to discontinue operating our attitude jets. Our only hope, it seems, lies with the attitude jets continual operation.'

The portside jets remained firing, but were not making any impression. In fact the ship was slowly veering back to port. The little that they had gained was now lost.

'Angela.'

'Sir.'

'Have you managed to find a reason for the communication's problem?'

'No, sir. I'm sorry.'

'Well leave it for now. Find out what is causing our ship to veer to port.'

Angela acknowledged the order and set about her task with urgency.

Wade felt the cruiser lurch again. Everyone on board would have. *Argo* was losing the battle!

Angela scrolled through the navigation systems and paused when *Argo's* position came up on the screen, confirming the cruiser's drift to port. She felt the commander's eyes upon her as she scrolled through the status of all the navigational and related systems.

Argo lurched — even greater this time and the cruiser shook and groaned from the stress. The attitude jets were losing the unequal struggle.

All eyes were on Angela. She felt a deep frozen fear at her core, and suddenly stopped scrolling. She turned to Wade and tried to keep her voice calm, but with little success. 'Some invisible force is pulling in *Argo*.'

'Yes, we know that Angela,' he retorted tersely.

She could see Wade was waiting for her to elaborate with thinly disguised impatience. 'Well... err,' her voice wavered and became uncertain. 'Well, something exotic in origin.'

'A black hole?'

'Yes,' she replied, the fear plain in her voice.

'But we've seen no evidence of it,' Wade countered.

'We did miss something,' she said ominously. 'For a considerable time our craft hasn't registered any random atoms hitting our defensive shield. Whatever is sucking us into its web must have swept up any stray atoms in its area of influence.

All three were experiencing a flood of adrenaline to their cerebral cortex, jolting their heart rates – commanding their brains to fight or flee, but they could do neither. Nature's monster had them in her web.

'See if you can get the positions of *Vela* and *Orion* on screen please, Angela.'

'Yes, sir.' She tapped in a command. Nothing! She repeated the command. Still no response and advised Wade of the failure to get a reading.

'I am not surprised,' he said with a worried frown. 'Nothing is getting through this damn gravitational field we are in.'

The ship gave another severe lurch. 'Jesus! Je...' Simon choked back a second expletive. This time the cruiser stayed tilted.

'Except for the lack of random atoms hitting our deflection shield,' Wade said, 'there was no evidence of a black hole in the vicinity.'

'Perhaps it's been inactive and turned on as we drew close to its event horizon,' Simon volunteered.

'Yes. I think you are right, Simon.'

'A view of the area directly ahead might reveal something?' Simon suggested.

Wade nodded agreement and rose from his chair with difficulty on the sloping deck and leaned over Simon's shoulder.

At first they noticed nothing unusual in the field of stars. Then simultaneously they spied an unusual area of space – a faint halo of phosphorescence surrounding a well of darkness. It confirmed their strong suspicions.

'So unexpected to discover a black hole in this vicinity of the galaxy,' Simon stated bitterly. 'In the hub with all the old, burnt out stars, yes – but not out here in the Sagittarius spiral arm.'

'Yes,' Wade agreed, the muscles bunching hard in his firm lean jaw. 'Totally, bloody, unexpected! We are accelerating into a black hole – a cosmic drain.' He wrenched his eyes away from Simon's screen, and awkwardly returned to his workstation. He wished Mirim could have been on the bridge with him as the end drew near.

'Should everyone report to their launch positions?'

'No time, Simon.'

'We're done for then.' Simon's voice was a little slurred due to the effects of the gravity- field.

'Yes,' Simon. 'We have run out of luck – run out of time.'

*

Millions of years had passed since the mass of immense density had embraced anything larger than a few stray atoms. Nature's creation had caused a flaw in space-time within its influence – the event horizon. And at the centre of the spinning accretion disc, the singularity – a mathematical point where all space and time are infinitely distorted. A place where humankind's laws of quantum mechanics and physics break down.

Normally a black hole can be detected by its gravitational influence of nearby stars. But a solitary black hole is the most dangerous of all. *Argo's* radar hadn't detected it because the scanning beams had been swallowed up by the hole. With no reflected signal the conclusion was that there was nothing ahead of the cruiser.

*

In her cabin, Bridgett was sprawled face down on the steeply sloping floor, desperately clinging her bed's cold metal rail to prevent slamming into the wall opposite. The alarm was plain in her voice. 'Mamma, what is happening to the ship?'

For a frozen moment Nikki was unable to speak and was glad her daughter couldn't see the fear on her face. Clamping down on that fear, she swallowed and tried to keep her voice calm. 'It is just a course change, Bridgett.' Nikki's bunk was on the opposite side to her daughter's and she was pressed up hard against the wall, which was preventing her from injury. 'Keep holding onto your bed, dear,' she implored. 'I am sure the ship will stabilise soon.' Wish it were true, she added silently. It couldn't be a planned major course change as they would have had a prior warning and be strapped in on their acceleration couches.

Bridgett managed a glance over her shoulder to seek reassurance but caught Nikki's ashen expression. Pretending relief from Nikki's words, she remained silent.

Unaware of Bridgett's gaze, Nikki's face was a mask of abject fear.

After what seemed an infinitely long interval there was a sudden lessening of the gravity field and the ship gradually righted itself.

Their expressions cleared, but it would be a brief respite – both unaware that they were being pulled into a desert of darkness.

Gazing at their wall screen at the view directly ahead of the ship was disquieting. What was going on? Nikki wondered. Not a solitary, solemn star to light the way – just a pit of darkness.

A chilling text came on to relieve the darkened screen. It told them that the end was near. They were being pulled into a black hole. The message advised that they should make their peace with their god.

Nikki registered Bridgett's look of horror. 'The message is clearly wrong, dear. It will shortly be updated,' she reassured. '*Argo* is on an even keel and the gravity almost back to normal. There is nothing to worry about.' But is it? she silently asked. The message faded from the screen and was replaced once more by the darkness ahead. They continued to look at the screen, expecting a new message to confirm their belief that all was well.

With the ship level and the gravity less intense, Nikki made her way to Bridgett's bed. They embraced each other in relief while they waited for more information to come on screen.

But Nikki was puzzled. How could the ship right itself and the gravity relax its powerful grip? It didn't make sense. Perhaps *Argo* had managed to generate a powerful enough lateral vector and overcome the black hole's influence? Yes, that must be it, she reassured herself. Her mind began to banish the last vestiges of her fear, and as the tension began to ease from her chest, she brushed her daughter's cheek with a kiss and gently broke their embrace.

Bridgett heaved a sigh of relief.

But minutes later, gravity's heavy fingers returned. Nature's monster would not be denied. Nikki grabbed Bridgett and they managed to scramble to Nikki's bed, where it would be safer as *Argo* began to tilt to port once more. Frozen with fear they embraced each other, silently, desperately. Long moments later, Bridgett became aware of a gossamer-like tingling on her hands and face, as her body began to stretch because of the tidal effect of the black hole.

A few short minutes later they were pressed hard up against the wall. Bridgett's heartbeat slowed as it pumped against the increasingly powerful gravity-field. She was experiencing vision distortion as her eyeballs scrunched out of shape. Trying to regulate her breathing was becoming impossible. Now it was just as difficult to exhale as it was to inhale. Each breath a triumph of will.

Exotic particles pulsed around *Argo*. The entire ship creaked and groaned.

A stabbing pain in Bridgett's ears was all consuming. She wished she could lift her hands to her ears to help alleviate the pain, but her arms were leaden. She thought desperately that swallowing might help, but no! The cruel gravity-field would not allow it. She could not speak – and in her pain she could not cry out.

Argo's lights flickered and died. All computer and electronic devices cut out. The ship was now in total darkness, but only for a minute or two.

Flowers of flickering light – copper and silver relieved the darkness. Most on board put it down to sensory deprivation – their eyes playing tricks. With complete silence your ears will hear phantom sounds. And when deprived of sight, your eyes will let you see things that are not there. In short, your sensory mechanisms need something to do, otherwise they will get up to mischief.

Mamma and I will be with you and the angels soon, Papa. It was Bridgett's last coherent thought.

One by one, everyone on board blacked out – the indigenous humans first, followed by the Foundation humans.

Space-time was curving around the mass of infinite density.

Chapter Twenty One

Amber, Lisa and the crew gazed up in wonder at the magic, curving canopy of stars – a sight that would live with them forever. Their gaze traced the curve of sparkling gems down the walls and continuing on far below them. The colours were spellbinding in their intensity.

They were in a tunnel of stars.

It felt like they were standing on a solid floor, but if they were it was completely invisible.

Wide-eyed in wonder, Amber turned to Lisa. 'Could this really be heaven?'

'It could be,' Lisa answered, 'but I don't believe it.' She hesitated a moment, then continued. 'Yet we could not have survived a journey into a black hole.'

'If it's not heaven, where is our ship?'

They looked at each other in complete puzzlement.

Their attention was jolted by a gentle, woman's voice from some indeterminate point. 'Welcome travellers, you have stumbled upon the *Starway*.'

There was a stunned silence for long seconds.

A pale mist floated above them and gradually coalesced. For a few heartbeats the beautiful human figure was translucent, but she gained solidity. Even so, they could still see right through her.

From an invisible podium, she smiled down at the assembly. She wore a lacy, pale blue, transparent gown. A light current of air blew a diaphanous cape away from her shoulders and her golden hair streamed out behind her.

'Are we still alive?' Floyd Burke, the Foundation Director asked the translucent figure.

'Yes,' she assured him.

'What have you done with our ship?' Floyd asked.

'Don't concern yourself,' she said in a pleasant singsong voice closely akin to an Irish accent. 'Your ship has been disassembled down to its constituent atoms and will be reassembled at the *Starway's* exit.'

Another stunned silence.

It was *Argo's* commander that broke the spell of bewildered silence. 'How could you possibly do that?'

She gave Wade a patient little smile. 'All you need to do for now is believe it,' she said.

'How do you know our language?' someone asked.

'That's because we are part of you now and are interacting with your minds.' She returned her focus to Wade. 'We know everything about you, Commander, and planet Earth.' She gazed down with her angelic smile and continued on. 'From now on we hope to be permanently bonded with you, but please don't be concerned – it will be a symbiotic relationship.'

Wade would check out the relationship later, but now he had a more pressing question. 'How could we possibly survive a black hole? Our understanding has always been that nothing could escape its influence – even light.'

'Without our help and guidance you would not have survived. But I can tell you that your belief is not quite correct. Quantum fluctuations let energy escape at the event horizon in the form of radiated particles. As you have theorised, the event horizon is spherical and encloses a spinning accretion disc, and at its centre, the singularity. So for the most part you are correct. The angle of your approach to the black hole, along with the velocity of your ship was fortuitous. It allowed your craft to orbit the black hole at the very edge of the accretion disc. But eventually you would have been drawn into its embrace before completing a full orbit. However, there was enough time for us to intercept you and draw you into our own powerful gravity-field. You will no doubt remember a brief respite from the black hole's rampant tidal force, when our own gravity-field was in balance with it?'

Wade smiled wryly. 'We remember it well.'

'Without our intervention you would have perished.'

'So if our angle of incursion in relation to the black hole had been more oblique, you would not have been able to save us?'

'Precisely, Commander.' She continued on. 'The flickering lights you would have glimpsed when your ship's systems shut

245

down were us. I am just a combination of many of those lights brought together so that we could manifest ourselves in your likeness. We felt this way, it would be easier to share dialogue with each other.'

'Fairy lights,' someone whispered.

'I thought she was an angel,' someone countered.

'Why did you see fit to intervene and save us?' Wade asked.

'We know everything about you, Commander and everyone on board your cruiser. As I mentioned before, we are part of you now. As well, we have accessed and downloaded totally, all of your starship's computers and processed it. This information has reinforced what we already knew through our interaction with all of you. You are worthy of our help and guidance. You are a restless race and are difficult to satisfy. When a particular scientific problem or mystery is solved you will quickly move onto the next. These are some of the qualities that have allowed us to select you. As well we have found you to have valour, compassion, kindness and many other fine attributes.'

'Why should you care?' Floyd Burke asked.

She smiled. 'We need your help?'

Floyd was taken aback. An entity such as she, with the awesome power to dampen the effects of a black hole, was herself asking for help. Unbelievable!

'We have need of your ship and your military expertise. It is a task to which we believe you are uniquely suited.' She paused a moment to lend weight to her statement. 'When you take charge of your ship, Commander, you will find you are in an unfamiliar zone of the cosmos.'

'And what zone is that then?'

'We will give your curiosity free rein to work that out, as we need to keep all your faculties sharp and keen. Solving it without our help will be so much more rewarding. But I must tell you that some things you may discover are beyond the limits of scientific inquiry – beyond explanation.'

'Well, if you say so.' Wade didn't want to be ungracious. After all the entity had saved them all.

'The zone of the cosmos you will exit into is out of balance.

To put it simply a marauding race's influence is spreading out of control.'

Could not be worse than the Drogs, Wade reminded himself.

While the meeting with the entity continued, Amber was busy scanning the press of people. Where were David and his parents? she asked herself. And where were Bridgett, Nikki and Doctor O'Connor? Something was wrong! She could feel it.

The entity must have picked up on her concern, or perhaps it was just a coincidence. It was she who broached the chilling fact that involved the missing group of six.

'Sadly we have an unfortunate situation. For reasons that for the moment escape us, six of you did not have a locked-in life force.' She passed a sober glance around the assembly before continuing. 'We have made them as comfortable as we can, and they are poised at the tunnel's exit awaiting the arrival of your cruiser.'

Amber's body stiffened – a pulse of anxiety coursed through her. It had to be the indigenous humans the entity was alluding to. They were the only ones whose life span was so short.

'What is wrong with them?' Amber asked, fearfully.

'Without the locked in life force they have suffered massive cellular degeneration.' She gazed down at Amber who was clearly upset. 'I am so sorry,' she said gently.

Amber turned to Lisa for support. 'First my brother, now David and our friends,' she whispered. For the moment she was numb, but she knew all too soon the tears would fall.

Lisa remained silent, not trusting herself to speak. She saw darkness haunting Amber's eyes. Reaching over, she gave her friend a comforting embrace. As she did so, six faces rolled through her head. How would they look now? Would she recognise them? It didn't bear thinking about. Her eyes watered but she clamped down on her deep sadness. She needed to be strong for Amber.

A heavy silence fell across the assembly.

Amber turned to the ghostly entity. 'Can we go to them?'

'Of course,' she said softly, and pointed to the direction

they should take. 'It's not far.'

'Thank you,' Lisa acknowledged for both of them.

They threaded their way through the crowd that sympathetically parted for them.

As they disappeared around the curving tunnel, a curtain of incandescent haze drew itself across the tunnel's stars.

Argo's crew gazed up at the entity for explanation.

'That is your starship's constituent atoms heading for the tunnel's exit,' she explained. She picked out Wade in the crowd. 'You will be able to return to your command shortly.'

Meanwhile ten minutes was all it took for Amber and Lisa to reach what they thought must be the exit: a circle of pulsing colour – electric-blue and vibrant yellow. For a few moments their six friends were lost in the background of swirling colours. But it was understandable. All but one of the six was suspended in the air with no visible sign of support. They were lying prostrate at a height a bed would be, seemingly unencumbered by gravity. Perhaps they were lying on invisible beds, Amber and Lisa reasoned, just as they were standing on an invisible floor.

A stooped, rail thin, elderly figure, was keeping a lonely vigil over the other five. Cloaked from head to toe in a loose fitting, pale green gown, only her head and arms were bare. She looked up as Amber and Lisa approached, but failing sight prevented her from recognising her two friends.

Amber thought the stooping figure was probably the most mobile of the six friends and therefore the youngest.

'Bridgett?' Amber enquired.

'Yes,' she said in a thin, papery voice. With effort she lifted a thin skeletal hand covered in age spots and beckoned them closer.

Even though they had been forewarned, Amber and Lisa were shocked. Bridgett had been cheated out of womanhood and sent plunging into old age. Her once honey-coloured hair was now snow-white, long and lank. Her skin was wrinkled and sallow and stretched tightly over her cheekbones. Her dark, aged watery eyes had lost their sharpness and had retreated into the caverns of her skull.

'Ah, yes, Amber and Lisa. I can see you both now,' she said with a faint trace of her delightful accent of old. 'I am so glad you have not been afflicted with rapid aging as I have.'

'We are so sorry, Bridgett.' Amber gently embraced her friend's fragile frame while all the while steeling herself to look upon David.

Overwhelmed with pity, Lisa's cheeks were wet with tears as she too, softly hugged Bridgett.

'There, there, Lisa, don't upset yourself,' Bridgett said bravely. 'I have been caught up in the confusion of past and present, but I am coping. But I am afraid; Mamma and all the others are slipping away.'

She hesitated before continuing in a voice barely above a whisper. 'Perhaps it is for the best.'

Amber and Lisa remained silent for a few moments. They did not feel they could contradict Bridgett. Perhaps she was right. Perhaps it would be kinder if none of the five sleeping figures regained consciousness.

Lisa and Amber had noticed that Bridgett's mind had fared better than her frail body. She was coping bravely and seemed to have accepted the cruel reality.

With trepidation, Lisa and Amber turned and gazed down at the five elderly figures that appeared in a state of levitation. Like Bridgett, they were wearing the same type of green garments. They had no blankets covering them.

Amber scanned the sleeping figures with horror. They were all shrunken with age – even more than Bridgett was. It was obvious that David would be one of the three that were sporting long, bushy, grey beards. And then she noted that one was shorter than the other two bearded figures. No need to ask Bridgett. It had to be David. Steeling herself she gently touched his arm. 'David?'

There was no response. 'David.' she repeated a little more loudly.

His lids slowly opened. Once the colour of a summer sky, his eyes were now a washed-out blue. He blinked and gazed up at her.

Now she recognised him, and it broke her heart. She knew

one day that she would witness him aging, but that was after a full and long extended lifetime, courtesy of the Foundation's aging treatments – not just what to her seemed only a few hours. David was cheated! She was cheated! She asked herself, did he know he had aged? She should have asked Bridgett if he knew.

David licked his dry lips. His mouth opened as if to speak, but no words came. He coughed to clear his throat and tried again. His bloodless lips quivered, his voice was slurred. 'Amber, is … that you?' He lifted a frail, hand and gestured her to bend closer towards him.

'Yes it is, my darling.' The intensity of her pity was overwhelming. An inner voice told her that she was fortunate that he was conscious, and that she would be able to farewell him before he passed away, but it was little consolation. David had lost the treasure of time.

'Now I can see you better,' he said in a dry brittle voice. 'My eyes … are not as sharp as they were I am afraid.' His breath was faint and shallow, but he managed a brave smile – just a faint echo of old. 'But I must say you have aged well,' he joked.

He knows he has aged, she realised. Amber felt cold and frozen to her core. Part of her was dying. Leaning down she cradled his face in her hands. She felt her throat tightening. Her eyes blurred with tears. Unable to speak for the moment, she brushed his thinning grey hair away from his face and kissed his wrinkled brow.

'I thought I must have caught a virus when I awoke earlier.' David paused to catch his breath. 'Then I noticed my aged arms and hands and realised my whole body had deteriorated into old age.' A trace of bitterness coloured his voice. 'I have not had an opportunity to look in a mirror, and I've no desire to do so.' He paused once more to catch his breath before continuing. 'I was shocked when Bridgett identified herself to me … and explained that my parents, Nikki and Doctor O'Connor had not awoken and were also stricken with rapid aging.'

Amber noted that like Bridgett, David's frail body seemed too old for his surprisingly alert mind.

'I don't like you to see me this way. I … must look like a

wrinkled, dried up prune.'

She brushed his cheek. 'However you look will not change my love for you, David,' she said in a hushed voice.

David was tired. So tired. He felt he was beyond the limits of exhaustion. 'I am so lucky to have known you, Amber,' he rasped. 'So, so lucky.' His thin bloodless lips smiled faintly. His eyes flickered over to Lisa and back to Amber. 'My regards to Lisa. Tell her when I have rested, you can both explain to me this strange place we are in.' He didn't voice it but he dearly hoped he would not awaken. His heavy lids closed as his mind and body sought the refuge of sleep.

Amber leant over and kissed his brow once more. She continued to gaze at his wasted frame.

She was losing him and was acutely aware that he might not awaken.

Lisa interrupted her dark thoughts. 'Bridgett wants to rest now and wishes us to leave for awhile.'

Bridgett knew that her friends were overwhelmed at the situation they were witnessing. They needed to retreat from the awful scene. And it was true – she was weary.

Amber turned to Bridgett. 'How do you know where your bed is?' she asked.

Bridgett looked puzzled. She pointed to her bed that was clearly visible to her. Even her old eyes could see that. She moved shakily to one side and sat on the side of the bed. 'You cannot see my bed?'

'Well no!'

'Lisa, can you see my bed?'

'No, Bridgett,' she answered. 'Perhaps it is in some time stream, and is out of phase with Lisa's and my consciousness?'

'Perhaps it is,' Bridgett countered, 'but I am too weary to speculate. At the moment my bed looks very inviting, and I must add, it is the most comfortable bed I have ever slept in.' She gave a faint smile. 'Just what these old bones need.'

They watched as Bridgett lay back, placing her head on an invisible pillow.

'Now you must excuse me while I rest.'

'Of course,' Amber replied and touched Bridgett's shoulder gently.

Amber turned to David's sleeping form, and leaning down, brushed his cheek with a soft kiss, so as not to wake him. Although his breathing was shallow and rapid, he looked peaceful. Perhaps in his dreams he might be young again. She hoped so. Straightening, she felt Lisa's comforting arm around her shoulders. As she turned to make her way back through the tunnel of stars, she took one more glance at David over her shoulder. She could not shake a feeling that she would never see him alive again.

Once her friends were out of sight, Bridgett sat up carefully, and slowly swung her legs over the side of her bed. Her excuse to her friends that she was weary was true. But she needed to be alone in case she broke down, and she did not want to inflict that on her friends who had been through such a lot. And she needed to stay awake in case her Mamma or the others awoke. They would need all the comfort she could give them.

Bridgett felt she was drowning in her sea of broken dreams. She dropped her head in her hands and at last allowed her tears to fall. The years that they had lost could never be found.

Heads bowed, Lisa and Amber strode out in silence – leaving the dreadful, sad scene behind them. A memory flashed through Lisa's mind. The only time she had ever seen anyone as ashen as David was when she was a little girl. She had discovered John Davies, one of her earlier foster parents, dead on the lounge floor of a heart attack.

They joined *Argo's* crew. Upturned faces concentrated intently on every word that passed the entity's lips.

There was a brief pause, so weapons specialist Hilary Jensen was able at last to ask her question. 'Why did our ship have to be broken down to its constituent atoms?'

'That is because the tunnel's area of influence is unable to accommodate such a large vessel. If it hadn't been broken down it would have disappeared into the black hole.' The entity paused a moment while she regarded Hilary, taking in her dark eyes, fine bone structure and closely cropped dark hair. 'Nothing would have survived the gravitational tide and radiation flux of the black hole.' A pause, then. 'So we could not allow that. We have been waiting an infinitely long time for a worthy space-faring race to come within our sphere of influence.'

'Are we the first then?' Wade asked.

The entity took long seconds to answer. She looked troubled as she returned Wade's gaze. 'You are not the first. Just a handful of space-faring races have passed through the tunnel. Many millennia have passed since the race before you came through.' After a lengthening moment she continued. 'We allowed this, but we should not have! We judged them to be worthy of saving. It was a dreadful mistake. Because of us, an area of the cosmos is now out of balance. We need your help to address this deteriorating situation.'

'But we are just one ship,' Wade said.

'Granted, but we can help. Previously some of us blended with each race for a short time so that we could share dialogue and understanding with them. Before they exited the tunnel, we in turn migrated back to our own environment. After our dreadful judgment we determined that if another race we thought worthy came along, we would form a symbiotic relationship with them permanently, as we will with you.' She paused a moment. 'Well, if you allow it,' she corrected. 'If you agree, your ship and crew will be an extremely potent force.'

'And if we refuse?'

'We will break our symbiotic bond with you. It will only be permanent if you so choose.'

'And you can return us back where we came from, but distant enough from the black hole for our safety?'

'I am sorry. That is not possible. We can only return you to the black hole's area of influence.'

'Not possible because you don't want to? Or is it just really not possible?'

'It's beyond our power to return you to a safe distance from the black hole. But if you agree to our offer of symbiosis and exit the tunnel to another zone of the cosmos, you will never be able to return from whence you came. It is a one-way tunnel. Those of us who remain blended with you will be reluctantly accepting exile. They too will never be able to return to their home.'

We really have no choice then but to go along with what the entity wishes, Wade thought to himself.

'That is right, Commander.'

It was disconcerting that the entity had answered Wade as he had not vocalised his thoughts.

'Yes, I am in your head,' she reminded him.

The entity continued. 'We are resolute in our resolve to blend with you permanently. Never again will our judgement of what appears to be a worthy race be the sole reason to allow safe passage through the tunnel. We require permanent blending as insurance against making another dreadful mistake.'

'I understand your concern. Can you let us think about it and get back to you?'

'Of course, Commander, and I will discuss in more detail about the blending at the end of this meeting.' She swept the assembly with her eyes. 'Meanwhile are there any more questions or concerns that any of you have?'

Lisa jumped in. 'Did all the previous space faring races you allowed through the tunnel have a locked in life force?'

'Indeed they did. It has been our experience that civilizations capable of travelling the vast distances between the stars had already solved the longevity problem. It's what we expected – up to now. With our interaction with you, we now know there can be exceptions.'

Immortality – the ultimate secret – the ultimate prize. Wade knew that there was nothing the Drogs desired more – nothing they wouldn't do to get it.

The entity swept a gaze around the assembly before continuing. 'If you had been like the indigenous humans that you were attempting to bring to technological and emotional maturity, we would not, now be sharing dialogue. We would not have intervened.' She paused to let her words sink in, and continued. 'They tolerated poverty, atrocities, war and an uneven spread of the planet's wealth – and worse. They were rapidly degrading the viability of the planet to sustain future generations.'

Wade saw a couple of his crew about to protest at the harshness of the entity's statement. He gained their attention, shook his head and waved them to silence. It would not serve any good purpose to argue humankind's history. He certainly didn't want to upset her. Then he remembered that the entity would know what the crewmembers were about to say. If *Argo's* crew agreed to the blending, they would have to trust that it would not steal their humanity from them. Of course they would think over the entity's offer, but unless it was more repugnant than death, he was sure that they would go ahead with it.

And so the questions continued.

Chapter Twenty Two

A hush fell over the assembly. They were exhausted with so many questions, their minds overloaded with facts. But sometimes, hard logic seemed out of place in the strange environment. And their necks were getting a little painful from craning up at the diaphanous creature.

'Now I have answered your questions for the moment, let me explain our blending that we hope you will to accept.' She continued in a friendly, coaxing voice. 'Once our blending is permanent, we will endeavour not to be an overly intrusive presence. Your mind will, in time accept us, and for the most part you will forget that you are even blended – just like now.'

There were murmurs around the chamber. Many had already forgotten that they were temporarily blended.

She smiled and gave a gracious nod. 'For the most part we will just be a voice in your head giving sage advice. On other occasions we will be a more overt presence – there to help avoid hidden danger, and help protect you against that danger – if we can. You will need us, just as we need you to help restore the balance of the cosmos that you will be entering. And above all, we need to be with you as insurance that you will not turn rogue on us, as the last race we allowed through did.'

'And what do we call you if we accept?' someone asked.

She chuckled. 'I thought that would have been obvious. You can call us your guardian angels.'

Nervous laughter rippled through the room. Wade was relieved. The entity possessed a sense of humour; it helped him believe the entity meant them no harm, and it could assist a symbiotic union to work.

As *Argo's* commander, Wade knew that it was his call to decide whether or not to accept blending. It was not a difficult decision to make. Death by way of a black hole, or life united with a strange alien entity. Death of course was not an option.

As a courtesy he turned to the Foundation Director and told him of his decision. The director was in full agreement.

The entity didn't wait for Wade to vocalise his decision to

her. 'I am so pleased you choose to blend with us, Commander. As I said before, we will be as unobtrusive as possible.'

'If you could give me a moment, I would like to address my crew.'

'Of course, Commander.'

He raised his voice to reach the ears of all his crew. 'If any of you choose death to the option of being blended, would you please raise you hand and call out your name.'

There was a long silence. It was what he'd expected. After all it couldn't be worse than death he reassured himself. He felt better that at least he'd given them the choice. Nobody could blame him in the future for allowing the blending. Though it wasn't necessary, he turned to the entity and nodded his crew's acceptance.

The entity pointed the way to the exit – the direction that Lisa and Amber had taken earlier. Before they started off, she warned them that they would be aware of the full and permanent blending – a not unpleasant moment, she assured them.

Her enchanting face smiled down at them, one last time. 'I wish you well,' she said and effervesced away.

A murmur of surprise spread around the chamber at her sudden disappearance. Faces gazed at each other in puzzlement. And they waited with trepidation for the permanent union of a strange alien race. A race made of pure energy left over from the collapse of an unstable star.

Wade felt a rich current of energy course through him. As the entity had assured them, it was painless and not an unpleasant sensation. He could tell by the expressions of his crew in close proximity to him, that they were experiencing the same as him. A dozen seconds later he was instructed politely by his mind's alien companion, to lead the way to the tunnel's exit.

Wade and the Foundation Director threaded their way though the press of crew as instructed, and linked up with Mirim. She was wearing a space-black jumpsuit. Her face was drawn and colourless. As he took her hand, he could clearly see the grief of losing Jarrod mirrored in her eyes.

Mirim smiled bravely. 'Have you seen Amber?'

'Yes. She's with Lisa. Don't worry. She's coping.'

Wade turned to his crew and waved them to follow him.

Uneasiness enveloped the crew. Some made jokes, but the humour was strained.

When they reached the strange exit, Wade looked around and was puzzled.

'Do not be concerned,' his guardian angel whispered in his mind. 'The six invalids are in the hospital wing of your ship. Surgical robots are attending them.'

'Thank, you,' Wade said softly and a little self-consciously. He looked at the Foundation Director whose nod told him that it was a question he'd also silently asked his own angel.

'Just step into the circle of colour. No harm will come to you, I promise.'

The exit was sufficiently large to accommodate three at a time comfortably.

Wade remembered an old rule of his, that for the most part he'd always followed. *Don't cross the line you can't come back on.* Well now he had no choice. He tested with the toe of his boot. There was no resistance. A tingling sensation pulsed through his body. It was painless and not unpleasant.

Mirim and the director did the same.

Still hand in hand, Wade and Mirim stepped through the pulsating wall of energy.

They gazed up. The stars above, below and to the side all turned red and darted away. They wondered at the reason for the red-shift. Now they were in another tunnel of ghostly white mist that was rising from below them. It was blanketing around them. They couldn't even see their feet.

'Look straight ahead, Commander,' his angel told him in his mind. 'You will be able to make out a faint wash of red mist in the distance. That is your final exit that will allow us to board our starship.'

Wade noted the inclusive words, *us* and *our*. His angel was certainly making herself at home. He heard his angel chuckle at his musing. 'And you are making me very welcome, Commander.'

Behind Wade, the crew was backing up. Some were poised halfway through the second exit and it looked bizarre: a leg here, an arm and a foot there, to the amusement of the crew that could see the phenomenon. A crewmember remarked jokingly, that they were keeping their options open in two worlds.

As Wade, Mirim and Floyd Burke moved off, the bottleneck eased. Wade advanced with dreamlike slowness. It was all he could manage. He slid a glance to Mirim and Floyd and noticed that they were affected the same way.

'Do not be concerned, Commander,' his angel told him. 'The environment of the tunnel is affecting your mobility. It is nothing to worry about.'

With an absence of elegant movement, they trudged on with infinite slowness. Wade was impatient to get back to his ship. Only there, with the responsibility of command would he be able to disengage his emotion for the loss of his son, albeit it briefly. After what seemed thirty minutes to Wade, but was in fact was only five, did he notice a brightening of the red mist in the distance.

Another four minutes later, Wade, Mirim and Floyd finally reached the exit. Once they stepped through it they could never return. They would take all their emotional baggage and deep sadness with them. The circular exit appeared to be an exact replica of the earlier one, except that it was bathed in a foreboding pulsating fiery red, right through to soft hues of pink. Hope it's not the gates of hell, Wade thought to himself. He heard his guardian angel chuckle.

Wade squeezed Mirim's hand. He didn't wait for his angel to tell him the obvious. They strode right on through and were immediately followed by Floyd and the leading crewmembers. They found themselves in a small, ivory coloured chamber that led straight to *Argo's* boarding ramp. The mysterious fog had vanished, and what they could see of their craft was heartening. The view was limited by the size of the small chamber that was pressed hard up against *Argo's* hull, to form a perfect seal from the vacuum of space. The ship looked pristine and shiny – like brand new.

'Remarkable,' Floyd commented to Wade and Mirim. 'Rendered down to its constituent atoms and then reassembled. What amazing technology.' He paused a second, and in a whisper added, 'or magic.'

Wade nodded agreement. He wished his son could have seen the entity's remarkable achievement. He felt a vicious stab of grief. He knew Mirim would be thinking the same. He turned to her, and could see she was quietly weeping. There was nothing he could do except lay a comforting arm around her shoulders and lead her up the boarding ramp.

Floyd respectfully stood to one side, allowing them to board the ship first. His heart went out to them and their sad loss.

At the entrance, Wade and Mirim paused a moment and gazed back, expecting the crew to be right behind them; but Floyd was holding them back, to allow Mirim and Wade a few moments alone, to take in the wonder of the resurrected starship. Wade gave a wave in acknowledgement and appreciation at the gesture. Mirim stepped closer to Wade as they turned on their heel and disappeared into the belly of the starship.

They hopped on a mobile pathway that would take them to the bridge area. They gazed around, inspecting systems as they went. The whisper of ventilating air with its scent of infused chlorophyll reminded them of old Earth and was reassuring. Obviously something was growing in the garden area. The lighting so far was functioning satisfactorily and artificial gravity seemed to be set at a comfortable 0.5G. But the real test would be how the computers performed.

Nearing the bridge area they could make out the flickering screens of the curving bank of computer monitors. Moments later they stepped off the mobile pathway and made their way to the bridge. At first glance everything appeared to be operating, as it should. Wade and Mirim sat down at their workstations and began to check the status of every area of the ship, the pulse of every system.

Minutes later they were joined by systems specialists, who in normal circumstances would take about thirty minutes to do a thorough check of their particular field of expertise and responsibility.

Everything was going smoothly until the navigation specialist, Angus Macandrew, commented to Wade, that his navigation systems made no sense.

'Stick with it Angus,' Wade encouraged. 'Recheck each system and get back to me.'

'Yes, Commander.'

Systems analyst, Angela Shriver's dark eyebrows arched in puzzlement. What she was seeing could not be right. Better do a recheck, she told herself otherwise her commander would request one.

Wade turned to Simon. 'Now we are out of the black hole's influence, I would like you to see if we can communicate with *Vela* and *Orion*.'

'It could take some time, Commander, as we don't know what sector of the galaxy we are in. They could be light years distant.'

'I'm aware of that, Simon. Just set the transmission to automatically do 360 degree sweeps every hour or so.'

'Yes, Commander.'

Angela Shriver had finished her analysis and was impatient to unburden herself to her commander. She rose from her chair and made her way to Wade's workstation.

'Sir.'

Wade swivelled around on his chair and gazed up. 'Yes, Angela?'

She engaged the commander with her distinctive sea-green eyes. 'I must have some circuitry problem with the hangar area. A scan shows that the area is completely full. Instead of just one Interceptor, there are now three.' She saw Wade was about to interrupt but pressed on. 'And further to that, the report states that there are two armoured terrain vehicles, parked in tandem as well as two landing craft.'

'Well we know that can't be right.' He sighed. 'Wish it were though. Do a recheck, Angela, and get back to me.'

'I already have done, sir.'

His mind's personal companion interrupted before he could get back to his fault analysis specialist. 'There is nothing wrong with the system's circuitry, Commander.'

'There has to be,' he retorted. 'We only have one surviving Interceptor.' He gestured to Angela Shriver by pointing to his head, that he was conversing to his angel. Angela nodded her understanding.

'Not any more, Commander,' his angel said. 'The status report is accurate.' She chuckled. 'We could not expect you to perform with an under strength capability.'

'How could you construct all those craft?'

'I assure you, it was quite within our capability. We had your solitary Interceptor for a pattern to work with. We just duplicated the same pattern of atoms in the same sequence. And getting the material for their construction was not a problem. Eons ago, we waylaid small planetoids rich in metals, minerals and water ice, instead of allowing them to be wastefully sucked into the black hole.'

'And what about the other craft?'

'Patterns were kept from previous space faring races that we allowed passage through the tunnel. We manufactured what we thought would most suit you.'

'I will check it out. And thank you.'

Wade turned to Angela to explain. She had only heard his words, in the two-way conversation. He related in full what his angel had told him.

Wide eyed, she responded. 'Unbelievable!'

'Come on, Angela. Let us go see for ourselves.' In his mind he heard his angel chuckle. He turned to Mirim and gestured for her to accompany him as well. He immediately regretted his offer. The Interceptors would remind her of Jarrod. But everything around them would be a constant reminder of him. There could be no escape from it.

It took six minutes to get to the hangar. They paused a moment and gazed around in amazement. Three sparkling, space-black, Interceptors were parked side by side, and presumably ready for action. They walked over to the three, elegant fighter craft. It was impossible to tell which was Joseph's original Interceptor. Wade ran his hand over the smooth hull of what he thought might just be Joseph's craft. He reasoned this because it was parked in the same spot engineers had left it, after repairing damage from Joseph's crash landing. And the entity might just be of a mind to have parked Joseph's Interceptor in its original position.

After an enthusiastic inspection their eyes turned to the metallic-green, single-seater, terrain vehicles. They appeared impressively brutal and lethal, and equipped with detection gear and what appeared to be light laser armament. The four large wheels with their thick treaded tires they would find out later were air-filled.

Wade scaled a two rung ladder attached to the side of the nearest vehicle for a closer inspection. He pulled a lever on the single hatch to gain entry but there was no response. He tried turning the lever to the left and then the right, but still no response. His entity would know how the mechanism worked, but she was remaining unobtrusive. Then pushing the lever the hatch slowly opened, which was fortuitous as it allowed Wade time to duck out of the way. He should've been standing on the lower rung and waited for the hatch to open fully before climbing to the next rung, and would inform his engineers about the simple procedure.

He crouched down and entered the cabin and slid onto the seat, which was upholstered in a pale green, leather-like material. The cabin lit up in a soft green light and the hatch closed automatically. A ripple of concern coursed through him. He hoped he would be able to work out how to get out, but quickly dismissed his foolishness. It was no time to get claustrophobic. He felt the seat form to the contours of his body, and noted it needed only minimal adjustment to do so. They sure like the colour green, he told himself. The instrument panel with its alien symbols was illuminated in a wash of subdued green. And yes, steering the vehicle was by way of a verdant green, steering wheel, which was a comfortable distance from Wade's body. He wrapped his fingers around the wheel and it felt just the right thickness for his fingers. Well now he knew a couple of things about the alien race that had designed the machine, besides being keen on the colour green of course. They must have similar hands and digits to humans. Their arm length must be around the same length too, because of the comfortable distance of the steering wheel from Wade's body. And they would be physically around the same size as he, because of the seat design, and the size of the cabin. Well the engineers will be kept busy sorting out more technical problems – the instrumentation, and propulsion systems of the vehicle, but they would have to wait until planet-fall, before they could test-drive it.

'Now how do I get out of here?' he whispered. He focused on a lever like the one he used to open the hatch. He pulled the lever and the hatch slowly opened. He allowed himself a small smile of satisfaction. As he exited he noticed a safety harness hanging on the door pillar. Very sensible, he noted.

'Angela, Mirim, do you want to inspect the machine?'

They both shook their heads in a negative response with a hint of amusement on their faces. In Wade's absence they had joked about men and their toys.

They moved onto the lander craft that were designed totally differently from each other. One had a dumpy metallic-green hull, while the other was appreciably longer, and streamlined. Wade figured the dumpy one would be a transporter to airless worlds. The other would be for flying in space and through the atmosphere of worlds so blessed with that valuable commodity – air.

Wade turned to Angela and Mirim. 'These craft could be very handy machines.'

'Yes,' Angela agreed. 'Better to risk a lander craft on a strange planet, than our starship with all its crew.'

Argo had a three seater, surface to orbit ferry that had been infrequently used. The Foundation's larger personnel carriers had all been based on Earth and the Moon.

It wasn't necessary to enter the alien dumpy craft. They peered inside one of six large view ports on the nearest shuttle. There were ten seats for passengers, and one for the pilot, upholstered in the same green fabric as the terrain vehicle, and equipped with safety harnesses. Directly behind the passengers' seats was a cargo area, which would easily house a terrain vehicle as well as other incidentals. And at the rear of the craft, a generous hatch to allow access to the cargo area. As no one had entered the cabin, the instrumentation was not lit up.

Wade decided that the engineers and prospective pilots would work out the instrumentation and how to fly the machine.

He didn't want to spoil it for them.

The other lander was streamlined, and Wade checked it over next, in a similar fashion. Colour schemes were the same as the dumpy lander. No surprise there. But the colour green was restful on the eyes. The slim craft had seating for one pilot and six personnel. On one side was a large hatch that led directly into a cargo bay – again with enough room to house one terrain vehicle. Access for the pilot and crew was by way of the same hatch. Wade reasoned that the wings would probably be aeroelastic to allow wing warping when flying in an atmosphere. Deflection of leading and trailing edges would change the wings' profile. This would help to manoeuvre the craft and undoubtedly reduce vibration. Peering through a small window, Wade could see that there were two sets of controls. One set would probably be for flying in space and the other in atmosphere. The craft reminded him in many ways of the shuttle the Foundation had designed and left for the Foundation community on the Moon. Like the dumpy lander, he would leave everything for the engineers and pilot to investigate more thoroughly.

'Very wise,' the angel in his mind agreed. 'It will be a considerable time before you make planet-fall, and in regard to the terrain vehicle testing, it will be a welcome diversion for the crew that you detail that responsibility.'

'I am glad you approve,' Wade replied. He saw Angela and Mirim looked a little puzzled, but they smiled understanding when he pointed to his head.

His angel continued. 'All the other space-faring craft that passed through the tunnel were either too large or too small.'

'How large? And how small?'

'One race was four times the size of a human, and their body configuration was far removed from that of your own. And so of course their fighter craft and shuttles on board their starship were of gargantuan proportions. On the other hand, the smallest in stature of the races that passed through, were no larger than your hand, and were very different in appearance from a human.' The angel chuckled. 'They had wings and are similar to the human's fantasy of a fairy in appearance. Their starship was about the size of the dumpy lander you inspected, so you can imagine the dimension of their fighter craft and shuttle.'

Wade nodded. 'The Foundation have always been of the opinion, that all alien life must be diverse and would be unlikely to resemble a human.' Wade slid a glance to Mirim and Angela who were listening to the one-way conversation. Again they nodded their understanding as they waited patiently for the discussion to end. They appreciated that initially there would be many such discussions – many things to understand – many problems to be solved.

Chapter Twenty Three

Navigation specialist, Angus Macandrew, was at a loss. He understood the uncertainties of interstellar navigation, but even so, he had absolutely no idea what sector of the Milky Way Galaxy they were in. They were lost! The readout numbers and curving graph lines made no sense. The navigational computers were stubbornly informing him, that where *Argo* was stationed did not exist.

'But it has to exist, because we are bloody well parked here,' he swore in a low whisper so as not to draw the attention of his fellow technical specialists. His commander would be back at his station soon and would be expecting him to have the problem sorted. In frustration he rose from his chair and strode to the nearest view port, twenty paces behind his workstation.

The expanse of crystal starlight took his breath away and calmed him. With a broad grin of delight, he lifted his eyes a few degrees to his left. A diaphanous filigree of red, white and blue, filled his vision. His eyes traced the lacy nebula across the sky. Stars were clearly visible through the tenuous gas and dust that once was the outer shell of an unstable star. The out rushing gas was emitting blue light, in contrast to the trailing gas, glowing in white and red.

He dropped his eyes to a magnificent, rich, star-field below. All thought of his navigational problems had fled his consciousness as he witnessed the wonder of night sky before him.

*

In *Argo's* surgical ward, Bridgett had just awoken. She slowly rose from her bed, anxious to check on her mother and the rest of the unfortunate group. A haze of pain from her joints rewarded her for her concern. Old age is so cruel, she told herself. A surgical robot hastened to her side to assist her. She shook her head stubbornly, and waved him away. 'Thank you, I can manage. But tell me, how is my mother and the others in our group doing?'

'As well as can be expected. While you were sleeping, all of you were administered your final aging treatments.'

In a thin, reedy voice, she asked, 'can we expect any improvement, then?'

'It is possible that you might,' he said kindly, 'but unlikely for the others, I'm afraid, but we were duty-bound to try. Aging is wired into the human genome, you see … '

'Yes, yes, I'm aware of that,' she said impatiently, and a little more harshly than she intended. 'And thank you for all your help and concern,' she said more softly. 'Now I wish to be alone with Mamma.'

As the surgical robot trundled off, she turned to her mamma's bed that was next to her own and gazed down at the shrunken figure. The skin was stretched tight over Nikki's aristocratic, finely boned face. She was connected up to feeding tubes and a monitor that continually checked her vital signs.

'Oh, Mamma … Mamma.' Her voice was a low murmur. It did not rise in volume, but grew more agitated. 'Please wake up so I can tell you how much I love you, and allow me to say goodbye.' Bridgett squeezed her eyes tightly shut. She had wished she had never awoken, so it was cruel and selfish to wish her mother to do so, and at that moment, was relieved her mamma had not responded to her selfish pleas.

Bridget heaved a long sigh. 'I am sorry, Mamma. Do not listen to me. Just keep sleeping – be in peace.' She stroked Nikki's forehead tenderly. It felt dry and cool to her touch. She looked at Nikki's chest to confirm she was still breathing, but at the sound of arguing, she looked up. Recognising the voices, she managed a dry chuckle.

'I want to talk to her first.'

'You always talk to Bridgett first. Now it is my turn!'

The surgical robot in charge of the ward moved swiftly to intercept the cleaning robots.

Spik and Span halted in their tracks when confronted by the tall surgical robot.

'Have you permission to visit this ward?' the surgical robot asked in a stentorian tone.

'We were working in the area,' Spik lied, 'so we decided to visit our good friends, Nikki and Bridgett, who we were told were unwell.'

'Without permission I cannot allow you to be in this ward,' the surgical robot said haughtily.

The cleaning robots hung their heads in disappointment.

'Oh let them through please,' Bridgett intervened in her thin papery voice. 'They can't do any harm, and it's true, they are my dear friends.'

The cleaning robots glanced at each other, and if they'd been human, would have had puzzled expressions on their faces. Spick whispered, 'who is this kind elderly person, Span?'

'I have no idea. She is very nice to lie about us being her friend, just so we can get to see Bridgett and Nikki.'

The surgical robot grudgingly allowed the cleaning robots through. 'Only Bridgett is awake, so do not tire her,' he warned.

Spick and Span trundled off to thank the kind elderly lady for encouraging the surgical robot to allow them through.

Bridgett gave the cleaning robots a warm smile and was pleased to see they didn't appear to have come to any harm. 'It is so nice to see you both again, Spick and Span.'

Surprised that she knew their names, they decided to humour her. 'And it is nice to see you,' Spick replied. 'I was wondering...'

'Do I get a hug from you both?'

The two squat robots glanced at each other in confusion, then trundled closer to give her a perfunctory hug.

'Would you be so kind as to tell us where Bridgett Michaiel's bed is please?' Spick asked.

That's when she realised the robots didn't recognise her. And who could blame them. Bridgett sat down carefully on her bed, as her legs were getting tired and shaky from standing too long. 'This is my bed. I am Bridgett.' She relayed briefly what had happened to the group of indigenous humans.

The robots were further confused, as it appeared that Bridgett was in a sitting position with no visible means of support. And they could see no hope in Bridgett's expression. 'Oh, we are so sorry,' Spick said sadly. 'We were only told that you and your mamma were unwell.' He started to advance towards Bridgett. So did Spam. Not wanting to argue in front of Bridgett, he allowed Spam to hug their poor, dear friend before doing so himself.

'Mamma and all the others are unlikely to awaken,' she informed the shocked robots. 'Though it appears that I have a little time till I succumb to unconsciousness, and finally death,' she explained with gentle directness. 'There is nothing more the Foundation can do for us. But please, do not be sad. It is such a joy for me to see you both again.'

Even though Bridgett was in a sitting position, the dumpy robots still had to look up at her, and for the moment, both were unusually quiet.

Bridgett rested a frail hand on each of the robot's shiny, black domes – they were smooth and warm, just like she remembered. Often she'd been teased about investing her emotion in the little robots; unlike the Foundation crew, who could not entertain the thought of ever sharing dialogue with robots other than direct functional commands. She gestured to the view port fifteen paces away. 'Could you both assist me to view the stars once more?' she asked, looking at them each in turn.

'Of course we will,' the robots answered in unison, and helped her to rise from her bed.

'You must not feel pity for me,' Bridgett entreated. 'I have seen more in my short life than any other indigenous human in history.'

The three friends slowly and carefully made their way to the viewing port.

Since her final aging treatment, her eyesight had improved markedly, but it took a minute for them to focus. Bridgett felt a shimmer of tears as she gazed at the splendour before her. She was in total awe. A billion beacons of light in every colour of the spectrum, shone with a steady light. Her lips blossomed into a smile. Stars as far as her old eyes could see, and a misty, lacy nebula of red, white and blue stretched across the sky. She felt light-headed. She had been holding her breath, and consciously exhaled. She remembered what David had mentioned many times. He had dreamt of floating among the stars, just like her mamma had. When Mamma finally passes away, she would request that she be set adrift of the ship to float amongst the stars. Mamma would like that.

And later on, before her own awareness faded, she would request to be suited up, and with a full tank of air be set adrift from *Argo*, into a fairyland of stars. Then when her air was low she would drift off to sleep – forever!

She alone would have chosen her time to die.

And she alone would have chosen her place to die.

Like her mamma, she would drift forever in the great cosmic ocean. The thought was comforting.

Bridgett's legs were tiring, but in her rapture she was finding it difficult to pull her gaze away from the panorama before her. But the pain in her weary legs finally won out, and with the assistance of her two robot friends, she returned to her bed.

*

As Angus Macandrew reluctantly made his way back to his workstation, he had a thought. Somehow that nebula seemed familiar. It reminded him of the *Veil Nebula* in the constellation *Cygnus the Swan*. That nebula, if he remembered correctly, was around 360 billion kilometres wide and careering outwards at around 400,000 km's an hour. Sure, it didn't look exactly the same, nor would it. *Argo's* vantage point was now vastly changed, so of course it would look different. He would check it out.

Sitting at his station his fingers danced over the keyboard, commanding the navigational computers recheck *Argo's* position. A star map lit up on his central screen as the computer searched. The star map faded from the screen a few seconds later to be replaced by a map of another sector of the galaxy. Time after time, maps lit up and faded. Thirty minutes later the exasperating message in text came on his screen.

WHERE *ARGO* IS PARKED DOES NOT EXIST.

He shook his head and swore under his breath. He knew

they were somewhere. It was impossible to be nowhere. 'Why can you not get that,' he hissed at his screen. He edged forward in his chair and commanded the navigation computers to do another search. This time, specifically in the vicinity of the *Veil Nebula*. A star map of the area came on screen – with a negative result. Angus jerked in surprise when the navigation computer unexpectedly repeated the text message verbally. Everyone within earshot was now informed that *Argo* was parked in an area that did not exist.

Systems analyst, Angela Shriver, was now back at her post and chuckled. 'Are you lost, Angus?'

He gave her a grim smile. 'Well if the navigator is lost, it means we are in big trouble,' he retorted with irritation laced with embarrassment.

'Sorry, Angus. Forgive me. I just couldn't help myself,' she said contritely.

Angus jerked in surprise a second time in just two minutes. His personal angel spoke to him softly in his mind. 'The nebula you suspected was the *Veil Nebula* is actually the remnant echo of an unstable star that eventually collapsed into a black hole – like the monster that dragged you into its sphere of influence.'

'Thank you for that information, but I still have no idea where we are.' Out of the corner of his eye he could see that Angela was wondering whom he was talking to. He pointed to his head which was fast becoming the accepted sign that conversation with an entity was going on.

'Think of it as an entertaining challenge. I assure you that the ship is in no danger, and I know all your life you have loved puzzles. There are many systems checks to do before your commander will be satisfied that *Argo* is ready for launch. So why not wait until then and involve yourself in this navigational challenge?'

'Of course you are right, angel,' he said softly, relieved that there was no urgency, and no absolute requirement that he alone needed to find out where they were.

Angela Shriver's acute hearing picked up on the navigator's comment. 'You have never called me angel before, Angus.' She fluttered her eyelids and tilted her chin. 'How sweet,' she teased.

272

Angus turned to her and rolled his eyes and grinned. But he had to admit that her unusual sea-green eyes had an unsettling effect on him – always did and probably always would.

Angela wasn't sure, but she thought she caught a blush from Angus before his attention returned to his screen.

Back in the surgical ward, Bridgett was resting. She was imagining herself drifting out of her body to float amongst the stars, just as David had imagined, eons ago. Spik and Span had left with a promise to sneak back to the ward if at all possible the next day.

Shipboard time was 4pm and the artificial sunlight had dimmed from its midday peak. Artificial gravity was set to 0.5G's for the comfort of the aged humans. Less gravity meant less strain on the heart and circulation system. That and the cell regeneration drugs were postponing their time to die. But there was no quality of life except for Bridgett.

Two hours passed, and Bridgett awoke to the sound of an insistent bleeping. She glanced over in the direction of the sound. A flashing red light on Gerald White's monitor had alerted the attention of the surgical robot. She saw him switch the monitor off, and the bleeping instantly ceased. The screen went blank.

Bridgett caught the robot's attention and saw him shake his head.

'It is for the best,' the robot said respectfully and trundled off.

She knew the surgical robot was right. Gerald White was one of the lucky ones that hadn't regained consciousness, unlike David and herself. Now he was at peace.

*

Back at his workstation, Angus Macandrew's navigation computers were repeatedly advising him that *Argo* remained in an area of the galaxy that did not exist. But now the pressure was off, he was thinking more clearly, a little more analytically. He had a thought, and was rewarded with a tingling in his spine. The entity had always referred to the zone of the cosmos – not the zone of the galaxy.

273

The cosmos is everything that was, that is, and ever will be. So they could be anywhere. He commanded his computer's on board cameras to pan the entire sky that was visible from the ship.

His angel chuckled. 'I am impressed,' she said.

Encouraged by her comment, he waited the few seconds necessary for the operation to begin. The first view came on screen, and he recognised the chamber – *Argo's* boarding area. 'Okay,' he whispered to himself. 'That is part of the sky I will not be able to check.'

Each view of nature's palette was stunning. And each zone light years distant, so the areas in question were vast! And with each view, he commanded his computers inform him what zone of *The Milky Way Galaxy* it was in. All vistas did not match any area in the galaxy according to his computers. He edged forward in his chair. Now he felt he was getting somewhere. He had accepted at last, that the computers were correct, because they were not in *The Milky Way Galaxy*! The cameras continued to pan the sky.

The sky was getting brighter. Stars were beginning to fade in a wash of light. Then bingo! He felt a surge of excitement. His eyes widened. A great majestic spiral galaxy filled the screen.

Only when he'd accepted the fact that perhaps his computers were correct had he been able to make any progress. But what galaxy was it? At first glance it reminded him of M31, *The Andromeda Galaxy,* spinning and evolving like an awesome counterweight to *The Milky Way Galaxy* – two million light years distant from Earth. But its two small dwarf galaxies bound to it by gravity were missing, so the impressive pinwheel of stars could not be either of the two major galaxies in the local group. But then again, perhaps the satellite galaxies were obscured from his line of sight?

'You have done well, Angus. Your computers will soon be changed over to the relevant area of the cosmos you are in. All previous maps and information of *The Milky Way Galaxy* will be downloaded and stored, even though I can say with certainty that you will never have a need of that navigational information again. That is your home galaxy you have on screen.'

274

'That means that we are in one of the *Milky Way's* two satellite galaxies.'

'Correct. Your ship is parked in *The Large Magellanic Cloud*.'

Angus sucked in his breath. 'It is 180,000 light years distant from *The Milky Way Galaxy*!'

'That is correct,' his angel confirmed.

Angus exhaled. 'I must put our communication's officer out of his misery. There was no way he would be able to contact *Vela* and *Orion*. The officer had not had a thread of contact with Moonbase for months. Now he could stop trying.

He was gazing at his home galaxy, as it was 180,000 years ago, because that is how long it took for the light to reach where *Argo* was stationed. A time long before modern man walked planet Earth. Even before Cro-Magnon man – and before them, Neanderthal man. A time so long, long ago. A time when stone-age men were yet to leave their first footprints on the planet's surface.

Angus Macandrew continued to ponder as he gazed at the magnificent spiral galaxy, drifting in the vast ocean of space – rotating in stately elegance, once every ¼ of a billion years.

Perhaps someday a space faring race will return to the poor broken planet in shroud, where dinosaurs once roamed, and a species called humans lived out their lives.

275

Chapter Twenty Four

Fifteen months had passed since *Argo's* launch from the *Starway*. Angus Macandrew had set a course on advice from his angel. The ship was accelerating at 0.5G, in consideration of Bridgett and Nikki – the only ones alive from the original group of six. The other four had been given a short, respectful service before being set free of the ship. Nikki had remained comatose. Soon she would pass on without ever knowing about the aging nightmare that had befallen their small group, and for that Bridgett was grateful.

Cloning of each individual began as soon as they died, and after a full gestation period of nine months, were removed from the birthing tanks. Bridgett was delighted as each gorgeous baby was brought to her for frequent visits – sometimes by a surgical robot and sometimes by Amber and Lisa.

Gerald was the first born and was now three months old. Three weeks after Gerald's birth, Mary White had been born, and closely followed by Adrian O'Connor.

Amber's strong conviction that she would never see David alive again after her first visit did not eventuate. But he never regained consciousness, and slipped away a week after Adrian O'Connor died. Amber had told those assembled at his service how he loved to talk about astronomy, and how he dreamt of floating on a river of stars. Now he would – forever.

Remarkably, Nikki was still tenuously holding on to a thin thread of life.

Bridgett turned her head slowly in the direction of a murmur of voices growing in volume as they approached her bed. As they grew close her aged eyes recognised the Foundation Director, Floyd Burke, and *Argo's* commander, Wade Dryden. A surgical robot was escorting them. Probably the same robot that was caring for her and Mamma, she reasoned, but it was hard to tell, as all the surgical robots were identical in appearance.

Floyd Burke gazed down at Bridgett. He held her in high regard. She was a remarkable woman with a philanthropic outlook on life. Always caring of others and seldom complaining about the tragedies that had plagued her own short life.

'I have been informed that your mother is fading fast,' Floyd said gently. 'Everyone that knew her will miss her. Everyone loved her.'

'Thank you for your kind words,' she said in a frail voice, noting that he'd been talking about Mamma in the past tense. 'But the sober truth is,' she said in a hushed voice, 'when Mamma finally passes on, it will be a blessed release. For fifteen months she's existed behind a curtain of darkness. I am so glad she never awoke.'

Floyd and Wade could not argue with Bridgett's logic, and nodded their agreement.

'We wish to know if you are still of a mind to be suited up with a full tank of air and be set free of the ship with your mamma, when her time comes?' Wade asked.

'I certainly do,' she answered without hesitation. 'I know it's against everything you believe in, and I respect that.' She gazed up at them both. 'But I am just so weary, so tired. I need to let go of this existence.'

'Very well, Bridgett,' Wade answered, 'but you must allow us to administer a powerful sleeping capsule that will be timed to kick in five minutes before your air runs out. It will make for a peaceful end.'

Bridgett smiled, and for a moment both men caught a brief trace of the young woman they remembered before her youth was cruelly snatched away. 'Thank you. Thank you both. You are so kind, and of course I agree to the medication.'

Such an extraordinary woman, Wade thought to himself. He glanced over to the director and saw to his surprise, that Floyd was having difficulty holding it together. He had never seen that before, so he took over for him. 'Well that is settled then.' On impulse he covered Bridgett's hand with his own. 'We will carry out your wishes,' he said softly. He felt a deal of guilt that he, along with the director, had granted Bridgett and Nikki's request for passage on *Argo*. With hindsight, perhaps they should have refused their request and left them on Moonbase with the rest of the colonists.

277

As Wade and Floyd took their leave, the surgical robot began a scheduled check of Nikki's vital signs.

Blood pressure and body temperature was low, and her kidneys were beginning to shut down. The readouts showed that total organ shutdown was expected sometime in the next twenty-four hours.

Bridgett's personal computer, Beatrice, had been set up at the end of her bed a few hours after her admittance to the surgical ward fifteen months ago. At first, Beatrice had not recognised Bridgett or her voice commands, so reprogramming for voice recognition and Bridgett's radically altered appearance had been carried out.

'Beatrice.'

The computer screen came to life in a burst of coloured pixels. Seconds later Beatrice's face came into sharp focus – identical to Bridgett as a young girl.

'How can I help you, my dear?' The deep sensuous woman's voice still totally out of place on a little girl, and still a source of amusement to Bridgett.

Bridgett smiled. 'I wish to see the stars,' she said in a thin voice. 'Soon I will be joining them forever, Beatrice.'

'As you wish my, dear,' and added gently, 'when that time comes I will be very sad.'

'And I will miss you, Beatrice. You've been a true friend to me all these years.'

After half an hour she brought the starry spectacle to an end. The onscreen view just was not quite enough for her. She rose slowly and painfully from her bed and swung her legs over the side. Eight months earlier, Foundation engineers had manufactured exoskeleton legs to assist Bridgett's mobility. She struggled into the legs under the watchful eye of the surgical robot that knew better than to offer assistance unless requested. Once in place, a sensor instructed the contraction of each leg to secure them in place.

The exoskeleton legs were sensitive to each impulse her legs made and amplified them. It had been an ordeal to get used to them at first, but she'd resolutely stuck with the task. She rose from the bed with ease, and with each stride, the energising legs purred, and softly hissed air. She could hear the dim echo of each footfall, and with a minimum of effort she reached the view port, and contemplated the richness of stars.

She shook her head in fascination. The starry display took all the weariness inside and flooded her with wonder. 'My imagination is too limited to encompass your vast expanse and all your secrets,' she whispered to the eternal night sky.

*

Nikki passed away peacefully within the twenty-four hours predicted by the surgical robot. She lay at rest in an open, transparent casket and was dressed in a white, silken robe, which was fastened around her middle by a crimson sash. Friends had filed in to pay their last respects.

It was no secret that Bridgett would be set adrift with her mother, and most understood her need to do so. Except for those who would be present in the airlock, they bid her a teary farewell. Bridgett was wearing a crisp yellow jumpsuit that reminded her of the one she had worn as a young girl. She had smiled when the suit had been brought to her. Someone had thoughtfully embroidered her name on the suit, but now *Space Cadet* had been replaced with *Astronaut*. Above her name were sewn astronaut's wings.

Bridgett lifted a hand towards her friends as she lay on her bed. 'I could think of no better place to die, than out amongst the stars, and I will be with Mamma forever.' Bridgett paused a moment. 'And for the few hours left to me out amongst the stars, I will miss you all.' Her gaze settled a moment on Amber, Lisa and all of her friends including Spick and Span, the two little robots that she requested should be present.

Only the robots were dry eyed.

*

Wade and Floyd accompanied Bridgett in the airlock. All three were fully suited and had completed their two hour pre-breathe of pure oxygen, although in Bridgett's case it really was not necessary. Wade and Floyd had requested that she do so to enable them to spend a little more time with her. Bridgett stood next to Nikki whose clear casket was now sealed. They were coupled together by a flexible connection of robust cord.

The airlock silently opened to reveal the stars. Bridgett was given a final hug from each of the men. The beginning of the final few hours of her remarkable odyssey was at hand. They exchanged no further words. It was time. She nodded to both men.

Wade gave Bridgett a gentle push while Floyd did the same to Nikki's casket. They sailed out of the airlock into the ocean of stars and misty nebulas – to the edge of forever.

Cocooned in her warm suit, Bridgett was in rapture as she pondered the brightness of the stars. 'Oh, Mamma,' she cried out, her voice choking in her throat. 'It's so, so beautiful!'

The gentle whirring of her life-support was the only sound that broke the silence.

Unbidden, Jarrod's face came to her, and she felt the familiar hollow sensation of his loss course through her – the intensity of her unrequited love had never left her. She knew it had never occurred to Jarrod that she had deep feelings for him. He was in love with her dear friend, Lisa. As a consequence, for her, no man could ever take his place. She took solace from the fact that she had been privileged to know him – to be his friend. It was the best she could do.

Enough of this she silently scolded and refocused on the sky, ablaze with stars – bright jewels strewn with abandon across the darkness. But memories of Mamma, Papa and her friends crowded for her attention. She smiled. I am a woman and can multi-task. She let their names and images roll through her head, never taking her eyes off the stars vying for her attention.

She had no regrets and allowed herself a dry chuckle. There was so much she'd experienced – even the four dimensions of *spacetime*.

'I have seen wonders undreamed of by my ancestors,' she whispered to herself. 'Not only that, I am, 180,000 years old! – 180,000 light years from home!'

After three hours, just before her life support was due to fail, her sleeping pill kicked in. The edges of her vision darkened, her breathing slowed, and she began to slip away.

She was smiling.

*

Three years, shipboard time had passed since Bridgett and Nikki had been set adrift from *Argo*. After a long period of grieving by Wade and Mirim, Jarrod's clone was born. He was now a delightful two-year-old and adored by all. Lisa and Amber feared he would be spoilt, but were as guilty as everyone in lavishing attention on him. Like all the children with their enhancement, he was articulate beyond his years.

*

Navigation officer, Angus Macandrew had familiarised himself with a sector of *The Large Magellanic Cloud* of particular interest to his angel. *Argo* was locked onto a *Main Sequence* star – spectral type G2. A full spectroscopy study had showed that it was hauntingly similar to the Sun – therefore warranted further investigation. A technique of destructive interference cut out the glare of the star and allowed the on board telescope to detect three gas giant planets. It confirmed that the slight wobble of the star detected earlier was indeed due to a large planet or planets in orbit around it. There could be smaller rocky planets present that would be able to be detected as *Argo* drew closer. Perhaps one might be orbiting its star in its habitable zone?

Wade had just finished a hull integrity and air pressure check. Both were within normal parameters. 'I was under the impression that you required our expertise in warfare urgently?' Wade asked his angel.

'We do. Time is relative,' she countered patiently. 'Your perception of time is vastly different to ours, as the indigenous humans' were to you. You are needed to patrol vast distances and occasionally make planet-fall. There, you and your crew can satisfy your deep curiosity by exploring its environment, and more importantly, checking for a nascent presence of the

Rabidde – the rogue race that carry the seeds of chaos, which we unwittingly allowed safe passage through the *Starway*.'

'Well we are in no hurry to meet up with them, I assure you. But we will not break our pledge of military assistance when we do. In the meantime our sleep tanks are fully utilised and the rest of us have our day to day duties. Any spare time is taken up with a number of research projects that keep us fully occupied. You will be aware that we are used to long hauls through space.'

'Yes of course. You were born between the stars, and Earth's moon was the first solid body you ever walked on.'

Wade nodded. He remembered well, the footprints in the dust that he and Mirim had left on that silent, lonely world, and wondered how the colony had fared.

Chapter Twenty Five

Some of the children were assembled at the medical ward for appropriate memory updates. In the case of Adrian O'Connor, the surgical robot had been carefully programmed to edit, and when necessary, introduce false memories.

Although not due for updates, three and a half-year-olds Bridgett and Nikki were also present. Meanwhile Jarrod was with Wade on the bridge, having explained to him all the various functions of the controls and computers.

Amber and Lisa accompanied the children to make sure they didn't get up to mischief.

Dressed in matching yellow jumpsuits, Bridgett and Nikki sat disconsolately next to Amber, their little legs dangling off the edges of adult-size chairs. Neither had any notion that their relationship was one of mother and daughter. They had pleaded with the surgical robot for a memory update without success. Their last update was on their third birthday, and it had opened up a whole new experience to them. It allowed them to remember a place lost in the immensity of time. A world of blue nitrogen skies, verdant forests, high mountains frosted with snow and restless oceans. A world where one could breathe the sweet air, feel a gentle breeze caress their face and walk unencumbered by a pressure suit and life support system. A gentle world called Earth. When they got older they would learn what had befallen that gentle planet.

Two years earlier, three gas giants in tow of the Sun-like star had become visible in the ship's telescopes, with atmospheric bands clearly visible, as high velocity winds raced around the planets. None had rings like Saturn, the jewel of Sol's system, but each had many moons. The outermost of the giant planets had an entourage of eleven moons. Surprisingly the fifth moon out from its giant parent planet contained a significant atmosphere. It was rare for a moon to hold onto an atmosphere because their mass is not great enough, their gravitational field too weak to stop the air leaking away to space. This moon was only marginally larger than Earth's moon. It managed to hold on to its atmosphere because being so distant from the warmth of *Tanith*, the upper atmosphere was so cold, the molecules could not move quickly enough to reach escape velocity, and so was prevented from trickling into space.

And now the crew was jubilant. Three hours earlier, a rocky world, slightly larger than Earth was discovered approximately the same distance from its fusion furnace than Mars was from Sol. It was at the extreme limit of the habitable zone of its star and warranted further intense investigation.

The basic ingredients of living matter are hydrogen and carbon – if the temperature of a planet is too high the bonds of these elements will rupture. But if too cold, water won't be able to exist as a liquid. And at cooler temperatures, chemical reactions would take place too slowly.

Being of significant mass, the planet's atmosphere hadn't leaked away to space as most of Mars had, and its light was being analysed to see if oxygen and water were present, and all the other elements necessary for life to exist.

*

Simon hunched towards his computer screen. 'I have a preliminary report on the rocky planet coming in now, Wade.'

Jarrod was balanced on his father's knee and sensed the intense interest in the air. 'Great! Read it out please, Simon.'

'Right, I will give it to you verbatim. Water vapour is present in the atmosphere and it appears that the ultraviolet light from its star is breaking it down into oxygen and hydrogen. But this report believes this alone would not account for the high oxygen content – it is similar to what Earth's was. So we expect that there is vegetation on the surface which is absorbing visible light and releasing oxygen. And so it's not unexpected that a protective ozone layer has been detected in the atmosphere.'

A molecule of Ozone is made up of three oxygen atoms and has a scent like weak chlorine.

'In addition to water vapour in the atmosphere, carbon dioxide, methane and a variety of other gases help to retain the heat that the planet would otherwise radiate away to space. In short, the planet has a greenhouse effect, although a little less than Earth's. So these gases allow the warming of the planet. Without a greenhouse blanket, all areas on the planet would be below the freezing point of water. And without a greenhouse effect, all of Earth's oceans would have been frozen over – a little greenhouse is a good thing! As we expected the polar caps at each pole extend double to what Earth's did and are most probably frozen water ice. So if there was life of any consequence, it would be expected in the equatorial regions. Further reports are pending.'

Simon glanced over to Wade. 'An interesting analysis.'

'Overly long though.' Wade sighed. 'The consequences of the data didn't need to be explained to us.' Irritation coloured his voice. 'Be assured, Samuel would have written the report. Oh how he loves to lecture. And his slant on "life of any consequence", I did not agree with. Even unintelligent life is important.'

'Of course it is,' Simon agreed.

Wade narrowed his eyes, thinking. 'In an oxygen atmosphere, the presence of methane is a sign of life. Could be bacteria in bogs or burning vegetation.'

'Or a vastly more evolved species than bacteria,' Simon chuckled. 'Could be smelly bog creatures.'

Wade smiled. 'You could well be right, Simon.'

*

A surgical robot glided towards Bridgett and Nikki with an economy of movement, finally coming to a halt in front of the children, and hunkered down to focus its attention on them.

'You both looked so sad, so I requested to Control, on your behalf, that you wished to be granted a memory update. I am sorry to say my request was turned down.'

'Thank you for trying, Mr robot,' Bridgett said despondently. She brushed a lock of her long honey-coloured hair from her forehead, as she regarded the tall robot.

The surgical robot extended its manipulators and clasped Bridgett's tiny hands in his long, slender, titanium alloy digits, just like he had seen humans do. 'However,' he said in his characteristically smooth baritone voice, 'permission was granted to allow you both to scroll through your memories up to the present day, in a three dimensional display. Would you both like to do that?'

'Oh yes please,' Bridgett answered eagerly. 'I never knew that was possible.'

'Well you will be the first non Foundation humans to experience it.' He turned his attention to Nikki. 'And what about you little, girl?'

'Oh yes.' Nikki clapped her chubby hands in excitement.

'Very well then. Let me get permission from your minders then.'

Lisa and Amber gave their consent, relieved to see that the little girls' disappointment at not having a memory update had now vanished. The robot said he would return with the children in an hour's time.

The tall slender robot and the two girls made their way to a special viewing area where they were joined by another surgical robot. One robot ushered Bridgett into a small chamber while Nikki was guided into another identical chamber for their separate viewing.

The adult size chair sighed softly as Bridgett's weight settled into it, and she felt it adjust to the contours of her body. A metal helmet was carefully placed on her head by the robot and connected to a compact computer on a metal bench beside her. She clasped her chubby fingers together and hunched forward in expectation. The room dimmed, then dissolved. A spot of light pooled immediately in front of her. It swelled, intensified. And she stared in wide-eyed wonder, lost in the past as three-dimensional images of half forgotten memories re-awoke and played out before her in astonishing clarity.

She was dancing in a meadow, laughing with delight. Papa was close by. He was smiling, walking towards her. He stooped down and gathered her in his strong, muscular arms and twirled her image around and around. Her red polka-dot skirt flared out in the generated breeze.

As she watched the scene, her eyes suddenly filled with

tears. She had been told that she would never be reunited with her dear Papa again. The angels had claimed him in their home galaxy, far, far away.

Twilight surrendered to darkness. Papa was hunkered down beside her, his arm on her shoulder and was pointing to the *Orion* constellation amongst the twinkling myriad of stars. Her eyes were wide in wonder. The scene slowly faded.

Now she was standing on a chair in the kitchen of her home in Paris, helping Mamma make an apple pie. Her face was covered with flour. Mamma watched on, a smile playing at the corners of her mouth. She was about to roll out the pastry when the scene ended. And Mamma, she knew, had the same name as her dear friend Nicolette.

Sitting in her chair, gazing at the scenes being played out before her, Bridgett reflected how beautiful her mamma was, with her large brown eyes and chestnut hair spilling down to her shoulders. She had been promised that one day she would meet with Mamma again. She would just have to be patient.

Her face was a mirror of emotions as scene after scene continued to unfold. It was late afternoon in the garden of her Paris home. Something had alerted her young black Persian cat's attention to an area of the garden in need of maintenance. It darted off and disappeared in a tangle of bushes and undergrowth. Her eyes prickled with tears. She remembered it was the last time she ever saw her cat.

The scene changed. She was tucked up in bed on a cold winter's morning listening to a whisper of raindrops on the bedroom windows. The light rain ceased and the weak, butter-yellow sun broke through the leaden sky. Gazing out the bedroom window, she smiled at the magical scene. Drops of water sparkled like jewels on the winter-naked branches of a silver birch.

As promised, scene after scene rolled on for a full hour, but to Bridgett it was a very brief hour.

The surgical robot carefully removed the helmet from Bridgett's head and placed it on the metal bench beside her. Bridgett thanked him for his kindness.

Reunited with Nikki outside the chamber, they immediately

chatted away with great excitement about their experiences in the chambers.

They skipped along the hallway leading to the surgical ward, full of giggles, their eyes shining, escorted by the kind surgical robot. They burst through the ward's door as soon as it opened for them and raced towards Lisa and Amber, impatient to tell them about their adventure.

Amber and Lisa thanked the surgical robot. 'It was good of you to go to so much trouble,' Amber said. 'I hope they behaved themselves.'

The surgical robot gave a small gracious bow. His reward circuits tingled. 'I assure you, they were well-behaved little humans,' he said smoothly. 'If they had not been, I still would have coped. I am a robot. I have infinite patience.'

Chapter Twenty Six

Eight years shipboard time later.

Argo continued to fall towards the distant sun; its navigational systems locked on to the warming glow of the Main Sequence star the Foundation now called *Tanith*, named after the great sky goddess of ancient Carthage. Four years previous, two, tiny, tide-locked planets in close orbit around the star were discovered, but held little interest to the Foundation. The third planet was still the overriding interest in the *Tanith* system, and so the Foundation decided that it was deserving of a name. They called it *Olympia*, which in Greek means "heavenly" – all aboard hoped it lived up to its name. Seventy percent of the planet's surface was ice covered and background radiation was low – comparable to Earth's. It had one tiny potato-shaped moon, probably a captured planetoid.

Argo had cut its acceleration one year earlier and had remained in coasting mode for that time. Artificial gravity had been engaged and set at 1G to help the landing party get used to *Olympia's* gravity.

Now under advisement from his navigation officer, Simon had cut the artificial gravity and engaged *Argo* in a 1G-breaking mode, which it would remain for the next six months. Then the ship's deceleration would be fine tuned monthly in preparation of *Olympia* orbital insertion.

*

Twelve months, shipboard time later, the final delicate deceleration manoeuvre was completed. *Argo* was in a stable, low equatorial orbit, three hundred kilometres above *Olympia*. From orbit it was an achingly beautiful world. The dominant features were the polar ice fields extending over much of the planet but girdled by the equatorial region of predominantly green vegetation, a handful of snow capped mountains, blue lakes and two green oceans, complete with icebergs.

A dozen probes to the surface had sent back valuable information confirming that it was within the parameters for humans to survive its environment. But further digestion of the information would be carried out before the Foundation would risk a landing party.

It was little Mathew's dearest wish that he be included in that landing party.

'Good to see you, Mathew.' Wade remained seated behind his desk. Reaching over he shook the diminutive air-conditioning specialist's tiny hand, being careful not to squeeze too hard. He gestured for Mathew to be seated across from him and waited while the chair adjusted to his tiny frame. When it did, the chair telescoped upwards to prevent Mathew craning his head up to the tall commander.

Wade steepled his fingers. 'What is it you wanted to see me about, Mathew?'

Mathew leant forward in his chair. 'I know that plans are well advanced for a landing party to *Olympia*,' he stated in an even tenor voice. 'I wish to be included in that party.'

'I am sorry, Mathew. The party of one pilot and six personnel has already been chosen, and notified. And they are all excited about the upcoming mission. The landing craft only has room for seven personnel, and I could not pull one of them out of the mission at this late stage and replace him with you, Mathew.'

'Of course not, Commander. I would not expect you to, but there is a way that I could still be added to the team of seven.'

'Well if there is a way, and you can persuade me that you would add value to the squad, I'm prepared to consider it.'

'Thank you, Commander.' He nodded respectfully. 'Your consideration is all I ask. I could travel in the cargo bay and be harnessed safely in the terrain vehicle.' He fixed Wade with a determined gaze. 'I've noted in the specifications that the chair can fully recline, like the seats on the shuttle.'

Wade's eyes narrowed in interest. It was a compelling suggestion. 'And what value could you add to the landing party?'

Mathew leaned forward. 'Air pressure on *Olympia* is close to what Earth's used to be, so pressure suits will not be needed. But special environment suits will be worn?'

'That is correct, Mathew,' Wade confirmed. 'They have already been manufactured to the personal measurements of each individual. But if you can convince me that you would be an asset to the lading party, another suit could be manufactured for you.'

'If I can convince you of my worth, sir, I will not need an environment suit.' He noted Wade's eyebrows rise in question and hastened to explain his plan. 'The suits are to protect against Olympia's organisms or poisons our enhanced immune systems may not recognise as dangerous, or be able to cope with, even if they do.'

'All this is true, Mathew. And our angels tell us they have no influence on our immune systems or our biology. So it is up to us how we deal with any potential hazards.'

'But I remind you, Commander, that we were not used to Earth's diseases, but our immune systems coped well – better than the indigenous humans in fact.'

Wade smiled tolerantly. 'So you want to be a guinea pig so we can speed up our investigation of the planet?'

'Precisely, sir.' He sank back in his chair. 'If my biological processes are compatible with the planet, then the cumbersome environment suits will be unnecessary on further field trips. This will allow a greater freedom of movement to explore and gather samples for experiment.' To press home his case, he added. 'If it was necessary to flee any danger that presents itself, an absence of the bulky suit would be another advantage.'

Wade remained silent while he digested Mathew's reasons to be added to the landing party. It was a noble request. His air-conditioning expert was tiny in stature he mused, but huge on bravery. He cocked his hands behind his head and rocked back on his chair. 'Each and every habitat I'm sure, chooses the biological structure best suited to itself.' He leaned forward on his chair and clasped his hands together. 'The life forms on *Olympia* might be drastically different to ours. Their chemistry could be based on silicon instead of carbon…'

291

'Silicon based life would more likely evolve on planets where temperatures are too high for carbon-based species like ours,' Mathew countered. 'I would not expect it to have evolved on *Olympia*.'

'True,' Wade conceded. 'That was not a good example.' He had forgotten that Mathew's other specialty was planetary science. Now he understood why Mathew was so keen to join the landing party. With this specialty, he could be a real asset to the squad.

In his lecturing tone Mathew continued. 'Organic molecules based on carbon are the building blocks of life as we know it, but very few are used at the core of life. The main ones are the building blocks of proteins and the nucleotide bases, and they in turn are the building blocks of nucleic acid...'

Wade lifted a hand to stop Mathew's lecture. He chuckled. He could see that Mathew was trying to impress him with his knowledge, and press his case to be included in the landing party – and to his credit, he was very persuasive, but could he as the commander allow it? He straightened in his chair. 'Your request could cost you your life, Mathew.'

'I certainly realise that, but my curiosity overrides my fear.' He fixed the commander with a determined gaze. 'If I did succumb to a contagion it is highly likely that we could synthesis an antidote. This is not a sudden impulse request, sir. I've been thinking about this for some considerable time.' He leant forward in his chair to press home a point. '*Olympia* may be the closest to an Earth-like planet that we might come across for centuries.'

'I understand that, Mathew, but unprotected you may pick up a contagion with no personal effect. But you could spread it to the crew.'

'Any one of the landing party could carry a microbe back to the ship on their environment suit,' Mathew countered.

'The E-suits are a close-fitting garment, Mathew. And the material is so smooth – slippery in fact. This will make it very difficult for microbes to attach themselves to the suits.'

Mathew conceded the point with a nod. 'Very wise, but if the landing party come back clean from contamination, we will

292

have learnt nothing of the potential hazards of *Olympia's* microscopic life. With respect, sir, we really need to know as early as possible what the dangers are. Then we can explore the possibility of creating a base there – possibly even establishing a colony. And with our responsibility to our angels, we would constantly monitor for the presence of the Rabidde.'

'Experiment and observation will be the final arbiters of deciding whether *Olympia* is a suitable planet to establish a base or colony, Mathew.' Wade stroked his chin and narrowed his eyes in thought. All the points Mathew was making were compelling. He straightened in his chair. 'On returning to *Argo* the squad will be quarantined, and in your case, I suspect our disease control team would require you to be quarantined for a considerably longer duration than the rest of the squad.'

'That is understandable and would be perfectly acceptable, Commander.'

'Very well, Mathew. Let me get back to you. I will discuss it with the Foundation Director.'

'Thank you, sir. Out of interest, who will be leading the squad?'

'I will, Mathew.' He noted Mathew's eyes widen in surprise.

'With respect, sir. With all the responsibilities of command, I am surprised you would place yourself in such danger.'

It was the same argument Mirim had used, but more bluntly. She was far from happy about his decision. She had scorched him with a furious look when he had broached his intention of leading the landing party. But he felt he could not place any crew in a danger that he was not prepared to face himself – with the exception of Mathew of course. Without an environment suit, Mathew would be facing a far greater danger.

*

Radio emissions in *The Large Magellanic Cloud* could be a perfectly natural phenomenon. Electrons trapped in the powerful magnetic fields of planets can simply generate them. So could atmospheric phenomena, thunderstorms and resulting lightening flashes. Or they could be artificial.

Modulated radio transmissions are artificial and are a signal of intelligent life.

*

Mirim sat on the side of her bed with her head in her hands. Although she'd finally accepted Wade's decision to lead his team to *Olympia*, uneasiness enveloped her. The door chime broke into her dark thoughts. It would be Wade. She hurriedly composed herself and was relieved she had not been crying. She didn't want him worrying about her.

He entered the room and stared down at her for a brief moment, concern knitted his brows. Weariness and worry had brought pallor to her face. But she smiled up at him and he was relieved her dark mood appeared to have fled. Or was she doing a good job of hiding it? He continued to gaze into her infinitely deep, endlessly dark eyes. She pulled him down beside her. Their lips brushed lightly and withdrew slowly. She leaned her cheek against his.

'Be careful down there,' she said softly. 'Don't go catching some strange virus.'

'If they are like Earth's viruses, they will need a host organism. On their own they are incapable of doing anything,' he explained, 'and our environmental suits will offer us enough protection, so there's nothing to worry about.'

Mirim was far from convinced but remained silent – her face neutral of expression.

'Will Mathew be joining the landing party?'

'Yes. His skills could be very useful.'

'And you turned down his reckless request not to wear an environmental suit?'

'Well, no.' He saw a fleeting look of dismay on Mirim's face. It was not the answer she had expected. 'It is a risk he is willing to make, and it will speed up our exploration of the planet if it proves to be a benign environment.'

*

294

The shuttle crew was in their pressure suits and harnessed in their chairs in the couch position. Their environment suits were securely stowed to the walls beside them. Memories had been downloaded from the crew, and in the event of their demise they could at least live on in their clone.

In the cargo bay, a suited-up Mathew had the company of Titus. The robot was strapped securely to a wall to the left of Mathew, and all its functions had been closed down, so no dialogue could be exchanged. But the presence of the robot was comforting, Mathew admitted to himself.

Mathew's chair had been set for maximum shrinkage. Even so, it still had to be packed with thick, soft material to allow his tiny frame to be secured comfortably for the ride to the planet's surface, and now was in the fully reclined position. For a fleeting moment he wondered if he had been prudent for volunteering to join the mission that could be fraught with danger – especially as he alone would not have the protection of an environment suit. But he put his thoughts to one side, rationalising that it would negate much of his usefulness if he allowed the protection of a suit. He felt his pulse quicken, his excitement rising in anticipation of the mission ahead.

Mathew's earphones crackled. It was the pilot.

'Take off in five minutes, Mathew,' Brett said crisply. 'Are you prepared?'

'Copy, Brett. I'm all tucked in – can't wait.'

As time ticked away, the pilot, Brett Taylor, felt naturally produced opiates – endorphins pumping through his body, connecting receptor sites to his brain. He could feel the tension in the cabin. His finger trembled with excitement, as he punched a code into the central processing unit above his head and began his final systems check – hull integrity, fuel capacity, cabin pressure, engagement of seat restraints – all systems were within normal parameters. He caught a reflection of himself in the transparent cockpit screen. With helmet visor open, a lean hard face, painted in the eerie green glow of the instrument panel, stared back at him.

The lights in the launching chamber flickered from green to yellow to red as the air was pumped out of the chamber and

295

equalised with the cold vacuum of space. The transporter doors silently opened, revealing a star-field shining with steady unblinking lights.

Brett punched out the take-off code on his console and scanned the regiment of lights and instruments. Twenty seconds later pre-tensioned springs liberated the shuttle from *Argo*, catapulting it into the dark abyss. Another five seconds and the chemical motors fired, accelerating the craft rapidly away from the starship – the high G's forcing the crew hard back in their couches.

Brett concentrated on his central display, which instructed him to come twelve points to port. He complied and concentrated on the guidance indicators. The flight path had been preset, and now his screen informed him that his piloting of the craft had been surrendered to the on board computers. He relaxed with a sigh. With luck he would not be needed for some time. The inertial computers provided a continuous positioning read-out on the navigation screen. He gazed out the cockpit. He could make out the hazy border of *Olympia's* atmosphere and to the brightness below, as seventy percent of the planet was ice covered and reflected most of the light it received from *Tanith* back to space.

Meanwhile *Argo's* intricate sensor systems continued to probe and test for signs of activity in the atmosphere and the surface below.

It was thirty minutes later when the shuttle was heading for the terminator and into the planet's dark side that things turned bad. The craft was preparing for atmospheric insertion. The engines cut out; computer screens flickered and died as the craft plunged towards the planet below. Anguished cries around the cabin reverberated in Brett's helmet earphones.

Brett hunched forward and punched in the override program. Responding long seconds later his central control lit up, the engines re-fired. But the shuttle's incursion angle was too sharp. Uncorrected the craft would spectacularly burn up in the atmosphere. He programmed a firing of his attitude thrusters to lift the craft's nose. No response! Brett felt a chill run down his spine. Tapping in the fault analysis code and looking urgently at a screen above his central display, it printed out information, informing him attitude and guidance systems had inexplicably failed. 'Well I know that,' he hissed in frustration. He shut down the affected systems; his long fingers danced over his keyboard to reprogram those systems and confirm he was taking over those functions manually.

The shuttle lurched sickeningly as he concentrated on the guidance indicators. Snatching at the steering wheel in an automatic response, he immediately cursed himself silently for his stupidity. Reflex made him do it. The steering wheel was for use in the atmosphere only. He punched in the manoeuvring jets to bring them to full impulse and felt the craft respond – his instrumentation confirmed it. But the outer edge of the atmosphere was approaching fast – too fast! The shuttle's angle of approach was still too great. Brett frantically manipulated the controls. Attitude jets were firing in frantic sequences trying to maintain stability. Desperately he tried to shallow-out the shuttle's angle of entry when he felt it bite into *Olympia's* outer atmosphere.

Gravity shielding cut in to its descent allowable maximum – fifty percent. If shielding was higher when descending, it would take too long to land and fuel consumption would be high.

The craft bucked, groaned, and heated up. In seconds the leading edges of the wings along with the protective nose-cap and ceramic underbelly were glowing cherry-red, caused by friction from the atmosphere – it could spell doom!

Brett tapped out the code for flying the craft in the atmosphere under manual control. As soon as the command was displayed in green, he grasped the steering wheel with both hands and pulled the whole assembly towards him, straining to bring the craft's nose up. Although servo assisted, he was exerting tremendous energy. The horizon tilted crazily but instruments confirmed the shuttle was responding – but infinitely slowly. Prior to launch the shuttle's integrity fields had been set to maximum. Even so, the hull continued to shake and groan. Could the alien craft's construction hold up? he asked himself as they plunged towards *Olympia*.

Chapter Twenty Seven

A blazing trail of exhaust gases from the shuttle's chemical motors traced their descent to the planet below. Checking his display screen, Brett allowed himself a frugal grin. All commands were now displayed regimentally in glowing green.

Cutting the thrust of the motors, he did a series of braking burns, following up with intermittent blasts of the directional thrusters. Aeroelastic wings allowed wing warping, helping to reduce vibration and increasing manoeuvrability. Even so it was a lumpy ride, but Brett suspected it was his piloting skills of the alien craft, rather than a design fault.

His central display screen divided in two sections as scanning systems cut in to convert *Olympia's* topography below to on-screen computer graphics. Favourable landing sites flickered green until out of range. Brett would soon have to choose one.

The shuttle had dropped well below the hazy border of atmosphere, which was now a deep magenta. A further braking burn lasted a full minute. In a swirling current of air, the shuttle lurched to starboard. Brett corrected it with delicate firings of the attitude jets. The craft steadied and continued to fall to the planet's night side below.

Minutes later the shuttle overtook the terminator into bright daylight. Brett's visor transitionally dimmed as the silvery curve of a sea on the horizon reflected the fast rising sun into his helmet. He steadied the rate of descent to allow the shuttle time to cross the expanse of water. In minutes the craft had passed over the liquid sea to the edge of a great ocean of rock-hard ice that stretched all the way to *Olympia's* North Pole. Brett conferred to his NAV system and manipulated the controls to its recommendation. He would keep the edge of the massive ice flow to his right for another five minutes then turn the craft ten degrees to port.

As directed by the NAV system, Brett was slowing the craft. They were now over a forested area of land that girdled the planet. His central control suggested two favourable landing spots ahead. They were two volcanic plateaus. One was on the lower slopes of a majestic mountain, just below the snowline at the edge of a forest. The other possible landing spot was an oasis of solid volcanic rock surrounded by the same large forest. He took a deep breath and chose the former, so that they could take a cautious approach to the forest and all it could be hiding.

Slowing by way of braking thruster jets, Brett lowered the shuttle's nose, letting it cut smoothly through the thickening atmosphere. He banked the craft to port in a high-G turn to avoid overshooting the chosen landing spot – an area of magma that had spilled over the landscape eons ago, emitting gases into the atmosphere. Now it had long cooled to a barren, black volcanic rock. The craft continued to circle, losing altitude and passing directly over a gently steaming crater-lake at the mountain's summit.

Slower and slower till all forward motion ceased. Retro-rockets fired against the planet below in a controlled descent to its surface. Burning exhaust gases from the rockets scorched the planet's surface as three landing legs telescoped out. Volcanic dust rose vertically, quickly clearing in a light, but chilling southerly breeze, straight off the ice field. Touching down, the shuttle bounced minimally – cushioned by the hydraulic suspension of the robust landing legs.

Closing his eyes and breathing deeply, Brett punched the air in exaltation. 'Yes!' he exclaimed.

With the release of tension, spontaneous cheering and clapping radiated around the cabin. Brett adjusted the cabin pressure, increasing it so that it was marginally higher than *Olympia's*, preventing foreign contaminants making entry into the shuttle. Then he communicated with *Argo*.

Filled with restless energy, the crew struggled out of their heavy pressure suits, and carefully stowed them. With the exception of Mathew, and with extreme difficulty in .95G, they donned their lighter single-piece environment suits. Being extremely close fitting, there was a degree of cursing. Gloves and boots were sealed above the wrist and ankles with heavy-duty, impregnated elastic material. Artificial air supply and ventilation was by way of a backpack to prevent the wearer

299

breathing *Olympia's* air. They donned balaclavas made of a soft felt-like material that covered their neck and head with an opening for their face. Finally they put on their lightweight bubble helmets, clicking them in place to make an airtight seal.

Mathew had an earpiece fitted to his right ear to allow communication with the squad.

Back on *Argo*, Mirim was churning with anxiety, pacing her cabin. Her dark eyes lost their focus as she imagined in horror, grotesquely ugly, creatures gazing out from the protection of strange bushes, stalking their new prey. She was finding it difficult to wrench the fearsome vision from her mind. In an instant her world could be torn apart.

She could contain herself no longer. She needed to clear her head. Vacating her cabin, she hopped on the mobile path outside her door. Three minutes later she stepped off the path at the junction that led to the agriculture area of the ship. Striding down the stationary walkway, her footfalls echoed rhythmically off the corridor walls. Passing the laboratory that manufactured nourishing food from recycled organic compounds, she finally arrived at her favourite refuge – the ship's hydroponics farm. It always had a calming effect on her. No robots were operating in the immediate vicinity of the huge chamber – the quiet broken only by the distant whisper of circulating air being processed through the plants, and the gentle gurgle of nutrients at their base. She breathed in the richness of chlorophyll scented air. It reminded her of old Earth.

She paced the avenues of plants, their foliage predominately in various shades of peaceful green. It took thirty minutes to amble through all the chamber's pathways. She decided against checking out another garden chamber. Her mood had lifted marginally, and so she decided to make her way back to her quarters where she would await anxiously for news from the landing party.

On *Olympia* it was quiet – ominously quiet. It was early morning at the landing area of age-hardened volcanic rock. To the east beyond the liquid sea, the horizon rippled with *Tanith's* reflected light from the ice field.

In the forest below, there was no birdsong or sounds from

creatures that might be lurking in it. But an absence of sound did not necessarily mean an absence of living, breathing life.

The environment suits denied the landing party's olfactory senses experiencing the scent of the planet – except for Mathew.

Mathew cautiously tested the air and detected a pleasant trace of aromatic scent drifting up from the forest below, and he desperately hoped biological processes would prove to be compatible to old Earth's. His life would depend on it.

Wade led his team down the exit ramp, closely followed by the terrain vehicle with the tall, dark robot taking up the rear. For now, a disappointed Brett Taylor was chosen to remain to guard the shuttle. Heavy-duty particle acceleration weapons with pulse feeders and linear boosters were slung over the shoulders of three troopers. The rest of the party, excluding the robot, carried lightweight particle beam handguns holstered to energy packs at their hips.

The terrain vehicle's modification to the operator's seat had been removed so Guy Raven, the team's geologist could drive it. Under instruction from Wade, he carefully overtook the team to lead and offer it protection. Its balloon tyres and suspension was smoothing the ride over the lake of hardened magma. It was a tall machine and so offered an excellent vantage point to scan the alien landscape ahead. Meanwhile, an equally tall Titus continually scanned in every direction for sign of potential danger as he trundled over the ancient lava flow. Heavy-duty tracks and sprockets had been fitted to the robot to suit the expected conditions, and a special filter now covered his air intake that cooled his electronics. Protection of the squad was hard-wired into its circuits. He was meticulously careful not to point the manipulator that terminated in a wide-angle laser projector at the squad ahead.

It was mid-summer on *Olympia*. Even so, it was cool. A comfortable warmth was rare on *Tanith*. If *Olympia* had been huddled a little closer to its star as Earth was, the ice fields would not have advanced as much as they had. It was a puzzle they hoped to solve as to why the ice had not completely covered the planet. Or perhaps it once did and was now in retreat?

301

They set a steady pace and as they grew closer to the forest, the morning mist lay cool and damp around them. Mathew could feel its cold hands reaching for him, chilling him. The in-built heating of his denim-blue jump suit kicked in.

They were alien explorers on a strange land and had been briefed earlier to respect the indigenous life forms on it.

Wade's gaze slowly swept the edge of the forest ahead and picked out a sparse area of vegetation. He radioed Guy Raven in the terrain vehicle and instructed him to turn five degrees to the left and head for it. That would be their point of entry to the forest.

A few long minutes later, *Tanith's* early morning light dimmed as the forest cast long shadows over the landing party. The temperature dropped a few degrees. Environment suits compensated by increasing their built-in temperature control. Mathew's jumpsuit did the same. His balaclava was keeping most of his head warm but the temperature was bitingly cold on his exposed face.

The terrain vehicle cautiously entered the forest. Wade instructed his squad to draw their weapons and proceed with caution. He and the troopers were trained in weaponry, but it had not been a discipline for the scientists.

The trees were tall, their trunks impressively broad and encased in longitudinal corky bark. Many had bark stripped from them – probably some creature's food source. But the botanist, Liam Gaul was noting, if a creature was eating the bark, it was being careful not to ring-bark the tree. On Earth, if the bark was completely stripped around the circumference of the tree it would die. Perhaps the same could hold true on *Olympia*.

For the first three metres from the ground the trunks were bare, then were graced with springy branches all the way to the canopy high above. The branches were dressed in uniformly dark green, linear leaves that were coniferous in appearance and were responsible for the aromatic scent. Liam wondered how hard the wood was. On Earth, conifers were mostly softwood. Some trees had tangled yellow-leafed vines climbing up through the branches, to finally erupt in a riot of crimson flowers, a full hand-span wide in the canopy high above. If there were animals

302

living in the safety of the trees, they were very quiet. Perhaps they perceived the presence of the squad presented a danger? Or perhaps there was a dangerous predator prowling in the vicinity? On the forest floor there was a sparse tangle of fern-like plants with pinnatifid leaves, intermingling with squat shrubs with soft, trifoliate, pale green leaves and adorned with bright crimson berries.

Mathew picked three of the berries and although tempting, he stored them in a clear specimen bag. They would be analysed later. On this field trip he was warned to only consume the food he carried in squeeze tubes in a pouch at his side.

Threading its way between tall trees, and crushing undergrowth, the terrain vehicle was making it easy for the squad to follow. The scientists were hurriedly gathering leaves and twigs and sealing them in specimen bags as they went.

A short time into their exploratory mission, Wade called a halt. He waved the team to silence so they could listen for any sound in the forest. The environment suits dampened sound to a degree, so Wade slid a glance to Mathew who gave a negative shake of his head. Nothing stirred in the shadows. And if there was any avian life, it was strangely quiet.

'Right here's what I propose we do,' Wade said crisply. 'We will be able to cover a greater area if split into two groups.' He gazed at each individual to gauge their reaction. Their faces were neutral of expression. He continued on. 'Trooper, Nathaniel Durant, Botanist, Liam Gaul and Mathew Steele, planetary scientist; you will form the first group. Titus will accompany you.' He gazed down at little Mathew. 'You will lead the group, Mathew.'

Mathew's eyes widened. 'Yes, Sir.' He thought to himself that he was lucky to be included in the landing party, and now he was leading a group. Unbelievable! Unconsciously he straightened his shoulders and stood a little taller, and grinned inwardly with pride.

'Titus will carry six replacement air tanks and a collapsible bubble dome in case it is needed for resting or shelter.' Wade glanced at his watch that was sealed to the arm of his suit. 'Your tanks will need to be replaced in a little over two hours.' He gazed down at Mathew, the only squad member breathing *Olympia's* air. 'Any ill effects, Mathew?'

'None at all,' he answered brightly.

'Good. Head west and keep in radio contact, Mathew.'

'Will do, sir.'

Wade turned his eyes to the remaining individuals – Brad Clarke, trooper, and geologist, Guy Raven, who would be accompanying him. Wade's eye's twinkled and he gave a thin grin. 'And ... I will be the team leader.' They all chuckled and Wade was glad his levity had broken any tension the two teams might be experiencing. 'Mathew's team can continue pressing forward from our present position with Titus leading and clearing the way ahead.'

Mathew turned to Titus and instructed him to fetch the air tanks and resting bubble from the terrain vehicle.

When Titus returned with the gear in a soft, green bag slung over one shoulder, Mathew gave Wade's team a wave, and with weapons drawn, his squad set off into the depths of the woods.

As soon as the forest swallowed Mathew's team, Wade led his team off in an easterly direction, but after a kilometre on, he directed his squad to cut to the right and head west, the same direction as Mathew's team. He didn't want too great a separation from Mathew in case either squad needed the others' help. They could not get lost because built into their suits was a device registering a personal marker frequency unique to each squad member. In Mathew's case he wore his device like a watch on his wrist. If for any reason there was a catastrophic failure of the devices they had backup. With their mind they could set off an emergency beacon by way of microchip technology implanted in their brain.

Back on *Argo*, a restless Mirim was gazing through a sealed clear glass screen at suited-up engineers working in the zero gravity launching area. The large launch hatch was open to the vacuum of space. Thousands of beacons shining with a steady light, waited patiently to witness the launch of the first of four multi-task remote detection satellites into designed orbits. Each satellite had a solar array either side of the central module. Also attached to the main module were x-band antenna, remote command antenna, zenith s-band antenna, thrusters and support structure, communication module and radar with deployment mechanism.

An engineer threw a switch. The spring-loaded mechanism on the launch pad released and ejected the satellite smoothly into the dark sea of space. Precisely twenty-two and a half minutes later the second satellite would be released, and so on until all four satellites orbited the planet below, equidistant from each other in an equatorial orbit.

An anxious Mirim didn't wait around to witness the deployment of the remaining three satellites. She turned on her heel and continued on her way back to her quarters. Every minute away from Wade seemed like an hour. She wished she were with him to share the danger. Her anxiety increased. Her imagination was running wild again, picturing fearsome, grotesquely ugly aliens confronting the squad.

On *Olympia*, neither of the two squads had detected any sentient life let alone any of Mirim's imaginings. But that could change in an instant.

An hour into their exploration of forest, Mathew radioed his commander informing him that he had nothing of significance to report. Wade replied that he also had nothing to report.

Searching the forest floor for footprints, Mathew saw none. He knew it would be difficult though, because of the dense carpet of fallen, needle-like leaves. Any footfalls would compress then spring back denying any claim that a creature had passed that way.

Advancing deeper into the forest it got darker, so the squad tuned their eyesight to the infrared. With such a scarcity of light there was very little vegetation at ground level. Mathew was relieved; it did not sit well with him, trampling on, and possibly killing *Olympia's* plants. And he was feeling a little easier, that now they wouldn't be leaving a detectable trail for some beast to stalk them.

But his relief turned to concern as he had a chilling thought. Perhaps they already were being stalked? For that reason he instructed Titus to take up the rear.

The squad pressed on, gathering specimens as they went.

305

Ahead something stirred in the trees. Mathew waved his men to an abrupt halt. Their eyes lifted to the canopy above, but they could see nothing, and moved on cautiously.

Then ahead, something skirted up the broad trunk of a tree.

'Hold up,' Mathew hissed and raised a hand for silence.

The creature, perched on a low branch, gazed down at them. At first glimpse it resembled a tiny opossum with thick, grey fur.

The trooper activated his suit's television camera to record the event.

Moments later, twenty or so tiny furry bodies popped up on their hind legs from the forest floor. Their gaze was unwavering as they took in the strange group of humans and the giant robot.

'Hunker down slowly,' Mathew instructed his squad. 'Make yourselves as small as possible so that we appear less threatening to them,' he whispered. But there was nothing they could do about their menacing looking robot except to instruct him to be motionless. At least he was at the rear of the squad.

'I don't think the critters are man-eaters,' the trooper joked.

'Do not be so sure,' Mathew answered.

In relation to their body, the creatures' dark eyes were huge. Probably a good evolutionary design for dealing with the low light of the forest, Mathew reasoned. Each of the creatures had a pair of strong front teeth protruding from its mouth. They could be responsible for stripping the bark of the trees. On Earth, an animal's front teeth that were used for gnawing, grew as fast as they wore away. Their rich, grey fur appeared well groomed and shiny and would offer good insulation from the coolness of the forest. They possessed a relatively long prehensile tail – good for balance and assistance of movement in the trees. Their front legs were a little shorter than the hind legs. Mathew suspected the creatures would be more at home in the trees than the ground. Later they would find that each of the creature's feet had three toes and three retractable claws by way of an elastic ligament and a front digital pad and rear plantar pad.

The impasse stretched.

The little creatures seemed to have the patience of rocks.

Mathew's squad was motionless.

Then one of the creatures dropped down on all fours and cautiously took a few steps towards the squad. With no reaction from Mathew's team, it crept forward. With each step it would look up with its engaging dark eyes at the crouched humans for a reaction, then lower its eyes. Mathew wondered if it could be some kind of ritual.

And as it inched closer, Mathew could see it trembling. His heart went out to it. The band of creatures was only risking one of their kind, and this poor little fellow had drawn the short straw.

It stretched its neck forward – its frightened eyes uplifted to Mathew as it sniffed his gloved hand.

Mathew felt a strong urge to stroke the cute little creature but resolutely abstained.

The creature was about to move on and inspect the trooper when it froze. It sniffed the air. Emitting a short sharp squeak, it darted away, and scrambling up the nearest tree it disappeared – so did the rest of the critters.

Mathew narrowed his eyes in thought. Something had spooked the little creatures and he didn't think it was his team.

Twenty Eight

They looked at each other uneasily.

Mathew stiffened. Without the impediment of a helmet to dampen sound, his keen hearing caught the faint snap of a twig, a rustle of fallen leaves behind them. Turning slowly, and in one smooth movement, he drew his energy beam handgun. Nathaniel and Liam followed Mathew's lead.

Titus was a formidable barrier between the team and any creature that could be lurking in the vicinity of the noise. In keeping with their brief to respect all forms of life on *Olympia*, Mathew ordered his team including the robot, to set their weapons on stun and only use them if absolutely necessary.

A flicker of movement caught Mathew's eye. Could be just a shifting of shadows, he told himself. Then movement to his left!

The trooper and botanist spied two indistinct forms drifting to their right!

In clarity born of fear, Mathew realised there could be any number of predatory creatures stalking them – skulking in the shadows. They might be highly intelligent and could be encircling them.

'Keep an eye out behind us, Liam. They could be surrounding us.'

'Very prudent,' the angel inside Mathew's head agreed.

It was Titus who drew Mathew's attention to a creature's camouflaged head peering at them from behind a broad tree trunk.

Slinking quietly on soft padded feet, claws retracted, the animal emerged fully from the cover of the trees and froze, eyes unblinking, regarding the strange prey.

The creature was smiling!

Because of this, Titus reported his observation. 'Creature friendly. No danger.' His voice was a monotone.

But to Mathew, something in the eyes of the animal was cold and calculating, belying its smile. Feline in appearance and about the size of a tiger, the beast was splendidly muscled, its

308

thick coat of fur a light grey with dark green stripes – the colours of the forest.

With elegant grace, it padded a little closer. It was then that Mathew and his team noticed the smile of the beast was false. It was a dark shadowing of fur curving up from either side of its large jaws. Mathew wondered what its teeth would be like. He wouldn't have long to wait.

'It is a fabulous looking beast,' whispered the trooper in admiration. 'A splendidly designed killing machine.'

'Yes,' agreed Mathew wryly. 'A smiling assassin.'

*

Wade was getting concerned. Mathew's team was overdue to radio in. Probably absorbed with an interesting discovery, he reassured himself.

As his team ventured deeper in the forest, avian life was making its presence known in an increasing cacophony of sound. But up to now there'd been no actual sighting of the elusive screeching birds – presuming of course they were birds.

It was the trooper who broke the drought. Wade followed Brad Clarke's pointing finger.

Wade activated his camera to record the sighting on film.

It gazed quizzically down at the strange humans, fixing them with two large owl-like, intelligent eyes. It showed no fear. Well perhaps it was not so intelligent after all. Even the terrain vehicle hadn't disturbed it. The bird was perched on a low branch, clinging to it by way of dagger-like talons. Its dusky-brown feathers looked oily and were probably waterproof. A sharp vicious-looking beak suggested it was a bird of prey.

'Remarkable,' Wade whispered to Brad. 'The first sentient life our team discovers is Earthlike.'

As they moved on, the owl-like creature followed them with its eyes.

*

The trooper's radio bleeped for his attention. It was the

309

commander. He lifted his arm and spoke into his wrist radio.

'Not now, sir,' Nathaniel rasped as he gazed at the beast.

'Sorry. We have a situation. I will get back to you.'

The creature, an alpha male paced back and forth as if caged, its nostrils flared, sniffing the new scent that overlaid the heavy fragrance of the forest – the scent of man. It was keeping its eyes on the strange prey before him, puzzling. They should have turned and run by now. Perhaps they were stupid? The beast sensed the fear in Mathew and Liam. The robot's countenance was unfathomable. But the trooper's expression was hard, resolute and showed no sign of intimidation. The beast could sense it, and was confused by it.

But the feline creature was patient. Soon the prey must turn and flee. Then he would pounce on the youngest – the weakest – the sweetest. The rest of his pride encircling would overwhelm the rest.

Yes. On this day he would feast on a new kind of prey!

The minutes stretched.

Mathew tried to regulate his breathing. Inside his insulating gloves he felt his sweaty palms.

The beast ceased pacing. It had finally run out of patience. It was time. Sitting back on its splendidly muscled haunches, it let out a low growl of exasperation, deep from within its cavernous chest. Then hunching forward on powerful shoulders, it tossed his head and gave out an intimidating roar, revealing impressive dagger length, carnivore teeth.

'Be nice. Be nice,' Titis entreated in a conciliatory tone to the beast.

'Be quiet, Titus!' Mathew hissed.

'Titus offer food. Make friends.'

Mathew gave the robot a glare that could blister paint. 'We are the food! It wants to eat us! Now be quiet.' Bloody stupid robot, he added silently. He heard Nathaniel chuckle, reminding him that the trooper was genetically engineered never to feel fear. Well he had enough fear coiled tight inside for both them.

The beast crouched down, its empty belly resting on the forest floor.

Feeling the creature was showing more interest in him than

the others, Mathew felt his neck hair rise. And he wondered whether the animal's roar was a call to others of its kind to attack. Seconds later, his chilling speculation was answered.

Six splendid, smiling assassins emerged from the forest from all directions. Mathew's team was surrounded. With feline grace they paced back and forth, never taking their eyes off the humans and robot.

The botanist blinked back sweat that was running into his eyes, cursing his suit that was preventing him rubbing them.

'Permission to scare big cats?' Titus asked Mathew in a low whisper.

Mathew was about to scold the robot when he had second thoughts. Perhaps it was not a stupid request? Perhaps it could work?

'Permission granted. Scare – not kill,' he reminded the robot in a low murmur.

The robot's tracks burst into motion and headed in the direction of the beast that had been eyeballing Mathew, his manipulators waving in all directions. 'Shoo, shoo,' he bellowed in his most menacing voice.

The trooper chuckled and it annoyed Mathew.

The beast rose and circled round the robot, eyeing Titus warily and sniffing the robot's strange scent.

Mathew silently cursed. The situation had worsened. Now the animal was that much closer to him, and Titus was no longer between them!

Another assassin had circled around and had drawn the robot's attention. It appeared to be taunting the robot and was easily avoiding its flailing manipulators.

Very clever, Mathew's angel commented silently.

Please. No comments, Mathew replied with his mind.

The original beast now favoured Mathew with its full attention once more – crouching, bunching its muscles, and preparing to leap.

Mathew had no choice. The cats would have to be taken out. 'Stun as necessary,' he ordered.

The trooper raised his heavy-duty particle accelerator weapon and took aim.

311

With shaking hand, the botanist whose back was to Mathew raised his particle beam handgun. He aimed at the threatening beast nearest him.

Then all hell broke loose.

Laser bolts sizzled. Two beasts cut down in quick succession from the trooper's accurate aim.

But Liam had only managed to graze his chosen target mid-leap. He threw himself sideways to avoid the large paws and gaping jaws.

Mathew was taking careful aim at the cat preparing to leap on him. He was about to fire when the beast that Liam had narrowly avoided, bowled him head over heels. His beam weapon skittered away to his left, just out of reach.

The assassin that had unavoidably crashed into Mathew returned his attention back to Liam.

A winded Mathew quickly regained his composure and moved to his left to retrieve his beam weapon.

Too late! In one graceful leap the beast was upon him. Mouth opening wide it snared little Mathew, clamping down with its powerful jaws, but just enough to secure its prey. Its instinct was to allow it to live. No need to kill it until he was ready to eat. That way it would be fresh. It bounded away with Mathew and melted into the forest.

Meanwhile the remainder of the group was fully occupied, in no position to help their little leader.

The trooper's attention was focused on four of the circling assassins. They were attempting to take him and Liam from behind and drag them down. On Earth, lions had used the same ploy on prey.

Titus did not attempt to fire at the beasts in case he hit one of the humans. But he reached out and snared a tail, dragging the complaining beast towards him. Another manipulator was attempting to stroke the animal's head to calm it. 'Be nice. Be nice,' Titus said in a silken tone. His voice turned threatening. 'If kitty not nice, Titus will scorch with laser projector.'

With two of their kind taken out, it did not deter the beasts. But with Titus attending to one of the cats, the other three circling were no match for the humans. The trooper took them out one by one, before dealing with the beast that Titus was tormenting.

*

Mathew was still conscious and struggling to free himself from the mouth of the beast. But struggling only made the predator's jaws clamp a little tighter, so he ceased. Even though his head and shoulders were free, he could smell the animal's fetid breath from the rotting flesh of a previous kill caught between its teeth.

Mathew could see that the frequency beacon on his wrist had been broken, and in his shocked state he was unable to concentrate enough to activate the emergency beacon in his mind.

Broad tree trunks slid by as the animal made steady progress through the forest. Arriving at a small clearing, the beast set its prey down and secured it with a heavy paw. It would be a change from the usual flesh it feasted on.

Strange speckled light danced before the beast's eyes, then quickly abated. It felt a pressure in its head and a fast river of warmth course through the long length of his body.

Uneasiness came upon him. Something was wrong – something beyond his comprehension. He tensed, sniffed the air and felt the fur on his back rise.

Weaving through the labyrinths of the creature's brain, Mathew's angel was switching on previously unused areas of awareness and potential intelligence to allow communication with the beast.

A nightmare played out in the animal's energised brain showing what would happen if he feasted on Mathew. The strange creatures and robot surrounded him. Fountains of light erupted from their outstretched upper limbs.

The assassin witnessed its own painful death!

Then the nightmare fled the beast's memory.

It gazed down at Mathew in confusion. For a reason its mind would not reveal, it knew it must flee.

Mathew felt his angel return to him. He would thank her

later, but for now he shook in the after-wash of terror. When he calmed down he would activate his mind's location beacon so his team could track him.

Minutes later and still shaking, he heard a whisper of sound. A fresh surge of fear washed through him. He started to crawl towards a tree trunk for cover. Then relief, as first the trooper and then the botanist, closely followed by Titus emerged into the clearing.

They were astonished that unarmed, Mathew was still alive and the smiling assassin gone. Later they would find out how Mathew had managed to escape.

They rushed to his side.

'How did you trace me?' Mathew blurted out. 'My locator is busted and I have been unable to switch on my mind's beacon.'

Assisting Mathew to his feet the trooper answered, 'Your legs must have been dragging on the ground from time to time. We just followed the scuff marks.'

The trooper communicated to Wade that their situation had been resolved satisfactorily and updated him on the two species they had discovered. Mathew appeared none the worst for wear but would of course be given a thorough medical when he returned to *Argo*. They were instructed to rendezvous with Wade's team at a second clearing a few kilometres ahead – one of the landing areas that had been suggested earlier by the shuttle's computer.

After the trooper and botanist replaced their air tanks, the team pressed on without incident, although Mathew felt that something was watching them. He hoped it was just the cute furry critters.

*

The full landing party was cutting their way through a new area on their way back to the shuttle. The broad tree trunks were still sufficiently spaced to allow the terrain vehicle to manoeuvre through the forest. Mathew, seemingly none the worse for wear, was taking up the rear with the trooper directly behind Titus.

314

Pride had made him refuse offers earlier of riding atop the terrain vehicle, or being cradled in one of the robot's manipulators.

Mathew still felt eyes upon him. He glanced nervously around. A large family of critters was scampering behind them – single file. Mathew chuckled. One was walking upright on its hind legs with a distinct swagger. It was mimicking the gait of the trooper. Another was copying Mathew's quick tiny steps. Mathew drew the attention of the trooper to the comical little creatures.

The trooper gave out a deep belly-laugh. 'I go with my first assessment. I don't think they are man-eaters.'

Mathew gazed down. One was walking upright beside him. Large eyes returned Mathew's gaze. To his delight, it slipped a tiny paw into his hand. He wondered if it was the same critter that had nervously sniffed his gloved hand earlier. The little animals had probably witnessed, and were impressed with the way they had dealt with the assassins.

Hours later at nightfall, they reached the shuttle. The little critters crowded around the landing party that was taking a few moments to take in the diamond-studded sky. To the north, just above the horizon, the *Milky Way Galaxy*, 180,000 light years distant, was rising over the ocean of ice extending all the way to *Olympia's* North Pole.

Little Mathew turned and smiled down at the critters. To them he would be a giant. Unbidden, a line from an old Terminator movie came to mind. 'I'll be back,' he said in the deepest voice he could muster.

*

The room was buzzing with chatter and laughter from the children gathered for the start of their first study period of the day. Lisa let the cadences of their voices wash through her for a few moments.

'Settle down please.' Lisa's gaze rested fondly on each child, as the room grew silent. 'Your tutor for this period is busy inspecting and testing specimens from *Olympia*. I will be taking his place, so please be good.'

'Is all the landing team out of quarantine then?' Jarrod asked.

'All except Mathew. He will remain quarantined for a few more days.' Thoughts raced through her mind. Would Jarrod fall in love with her when he matures? She had been told all the romantic times they'd had in his first life would be edited out for psychological reasons. Only Jarrod would be able to choose whom he had a relationship with. It could be Bridgett.' She remembered how beautiful Bridgett had been before she had tragically aged.

Lisa's eyes had gone distant. She quickly refocused her attention back to the children.

'Are we still doing mathematics this period?' Bridgett asked excitedly in the French accent she had retained from downloaded memory.

Lisa was aware that it was one of the little girl's favourite subjects. And Bridgett was at a level where mathematics became an abstract discipline.

'Sorry, Bridgett, but if everyone is good, I will tell you a story.'

Bridgett giggled. 'We are always good.'

'But it's not bedtime,' Jarrod challenged.

'Nevertheless it is a very special story I've been given permission to tell you this period.'

'Will we see holographic images as you tell us the story?' Adrian O'Connor asked.

Lisa pointed to her head. 'It is all in here,' she said. 'But I will draw the picture with words. Now make yourselves comfortable because it is a very long story.'

The room grew silent once more.

'Once upon a time in a galaxy far, far away there was a planet called Earth where dinosaurs once trod and humans lived out their lives...'

*

Wade's cabin vid-phone chimed. He picked up. It was

316

Simon. His look was one of great urgency.

'Simon?'

'Commander, we have been testing the electromagnetic spectrum for evidence of artificial broadcasts.' He paused for a quick breath. 'Moments ago we picked up a high frequency radio pulse from *Olympia,* three quarters of a degree off the limb of the planet.'

'Orbital?'

'Yes, sir. The radio emission was clearly artificial and has now ceased. The vehicle's orbit has now taken it over *Olympia's* horizon into radio shadow, but we have recorded it.'

Wade felt his heart rate quicken. 'I will see you on the bridge shortly so you can play it back to me. Thank you, Simon.'

Simon acknowledged the commander and the screen faded.

Wade turned to Mirim who had witnessed the entire communication. 'Intelligent, technological life!' he said in a voice barely above a whisper.

'Yes,' she said, 'but we should not be completely surprised. Intelligence would grant an evolutionary advantage.'

In his mind, Wade's angel commented. 'This intelligent life may not be indigenous – it could be our enemy, the Rabbide.'